MADE IN THE SHADE

A HUMOROUS PARANORMAL WOMEN'S FICTION

DEBORAH WILDE

te da media
vancouver

Book Cover Design by ebooklaunch.com

Issued in print and electronic formats.

ISBN: 978-1-988681-53-5 (paperback)

ISBN: 978-1-988681-54-2 (epub)

1

BEING A FIXER IN THE MAGICAL COMMUNITY WAS supposed to be like an action film, explosions and high-octane thrills as I took jobs that pushed my moral boundaries and hardened my soul. Instead, it was like perpetually being the birthday kid's parent at a Chuck E. Cheese: I had become the unwitting shepherd to an endless flock of whiny disasters.

My first assignment was to "liberate" a ferret from a prolonged stay at a spiteful ex-husband's house who had agreed to joint pet custody with his equally unpleasant former wife. Fun fact: the Latin name for ferret translates to "stinky weasel thief." I spent a good half hour chasing the slippery bastard around a spacious penthouse whose design aesthetic was "Russian mobster fucks ESPN" or, as I dubbed it, "Borat Does the Sexy," finally catching the animal under a black leather bar whose gold countertop was mounted with television screens.

I shoved the ferret in its carrier, musing on how thoughtful it was of the husband to let his hook-ups catch the sports highlight reel during their ten minutes of doggy-style, and drove the pet to our client. The wife took one brief glance at her "beloved, irreplaceable companion animal, without whom life would be a desolation," handed the carrier to the help, and dashed off to her club. I was glad to be rid of all of them.

The next scintillating gig involved finding and returning a briefcase left behind during negotiations between two gangs. Our Ohrist client, Steele Night, who I suspected pulled his name off a *Zoolander* name generator, had attempted and failed to retrieve it, so I was dispatched to his rival Rasputin's HQ.

The place was strewn with bongs, titty magazines, and a blow-up doll propped in a sex swing, all under a layer of dust and questionably sticky surfaces.

"It's not here, but hey." Rasputin smirked, and ran a hand over the sex doll like he expected me to clutch my pearls. "Knock yourself out, if you want to check."

I planted my hands on my hips. "If you're bringing partners to this shithole, it's no wonder you need a blow-up doll, because nobody wants to fuck in an STI factory." I shook my head. "Have you no dignity?"

Or antibacterial wipes?

Rasputin flashed his fangs. Crud. I hadn't expected a vampire in the mix. "Get the nagging old broad out of here."

Some dude with an upside-down cross tattooed on his forehead flicked his fingers and my blood turned to ice—literally.

My teeth chattered, every movement a sluggish haul, but I deployed my magic, grabbed Rasputin's shadow like it had weight and substance, and squeezed, a darkness oozing through my fingers. Normally a vamp's shadow was freezing cold, but compared to the rest of me, this was quite pleasant.

The vamp was rooted in place, which evened my chances of getting out alive.

I dipped my hand through the darkness behind the sex swing and summoned my shadow scythe. Except nothing happened. No weapon, no nothing, and I couldn't understand why. The scythe manifested in the presence of dybbuks, and both they and the undead fit into the "aberrations from the natural order of death" category. Even more confusing, my magic tingled up through my feet expectantly.

We lived in a world with over sixteen million online results for how to use a bar of soap, but I had to suss out my powers through tingle interpretation. Having no time for such antics, I went with good old Plan B: threats.

"Dr-drop the m-magic," I said. "And perhaps I won't kill you for insulting me."

At least my shadow still held onto Rasputin's because that was enough to convince him to call off the man who was icing my blood.

The Ohrist magic left my body in a rush. I bent double, loudly gulping down air as a cover to pull out my new Zippo. Originally, I'd used a lighter taken from the victim of a vampire to avenge his death, but it was too macabre to hang onto, so I'd bought a fancy gold one that was also windproof. No pesky gust would stand between me and my mission of vanquishing evil.

I teased Rasputin's shadow with the flame.

There was a collective intake of breath from the lackeys and a squeaked "Boss!"

"Let go of me," Rasputin snarled.

"Admit you got your terminology wrong," I said. "I'm not a nagging old broad, I'm a badass broad. This handy lighter and your shadow are all I require to take you from trash to ash and porn lord to dust." I smiled brightly. "Wanna see? Or are you going to apologize?"

"Sorry," the bloodsucker grunted. His expression was strained, his body fully paralyzed. His lack of movement while in my grasp placed him on the younger, weaker end of the Vamp-O-Meter.

"Say it like you mean it." My magic tingled more insistently, sending prickles along my back. At this point, I would have accepted charades to understand what it wanted from me.

"I'm sorry."

"Was that so hard? Now, tell your friends to back up." I waved the lighter.

For a second, I swore the flame looked like a scythe, but it was gone in an instant. Yes, thank you, I did have scythe abilities, but since they were utterly failing to materialize right now, this taunting reminder was unfair. Was it too much to ask my magic to communicate via a quick message on the wall in ghostly letters?

Rasputin cut his eyes to his crew. "Do as the nice lady says."

"Pussy," one of the humans coughed.

I unwound my shadow from Rasputin and cracked my knuckles in the direction of his insubordinate underling. "Want me to deal with him next?"

"Nah." The vampire rolled out his shoulders, hauteur once again returning now that he had freedom of movement. "He's mine. But you, you're quite the wild card, lady. Wasn't expecting someone like you to pack that much of a punch."

Approving murmurs went up from the minions. Great. All I had to do to ingratiate myself with these weirdos was threaten them with bodily harm, though I had no problem using that to my advantage.

"Thanks, but don't think that's going to distract me." I put on my best mom voice. "Now, did you really check for the briefcase? Because if I start looking and find it immediately, I am going to be very unhappy."

The gang dropped their eyes to the floor.

It was just as I thought. They hadn't even bothered searching. Once we'd remedied that and I had the briefcase, I gave them all a stern talking-to, saying that no one would respect them if they didn't respect themselves, and left them organizing a clean-up. Vamp or human, boys with mommy issues were comically easy to deal with.

I returned the briefcase to Steele and told him to get a day job because if he needed a nanny to make sure he didn't forget his things, then he clearly wasn't cut out to be a criminal mastermind.

Shockingly, the younger white man did not take this suggestion to heart. He made several less than complimentary remarks about my age and gender, despite me being the first of his many hires to actually get his briefcase back, and then stormed out in grand fashion. Even so, having embraced my magic and triumphed over dangers much worse than a pissy wannabe, I was disinclined to apologize for being a middle-aged woman expressing opinions born of experience.

Now I was up at the ass crack of dawn on this rainy "Junuary" Wednesday (a Vancouver specialty of solid rain and cold in June) to chauffeur a spoiled Gen Z to his family's private jet. Apparently, Taroosh "Topher" Sharma always pitched a fit about going back to his Chemical Engineering degree at Caltech and the latest tantrum had been impressive. Two antiques had been gravely injured after his father had forbidden Topher from hanging out at the beach house in Los Angeles, insisting his son devote July and August to an academic research project before starting his senior undergrad year. Boo fucking hoo.

I'd been assured that the jobs wouldn't all be of this ignoble caliber, but Topher was known to bribe other drivers to help him play hooky, so a trusted professional had been engaged. Mine was not to question why, mine was to do or die trying.

As my employer, Tatiana Cassin, had impressed upon me, failure was not an option. Should I blemish her impeccable reputation, I'd be on my own without her protection for my loved ones and with no help to solve my parents' decades-old murder. A murder that may well have been intended to be my end, too.

Bleary-eyed, I drove from my duplex off Main Street in East Vancouver to the University of British Columbia, yawning far too often under the hypnotic rhythm of the wipers. There was little traffic on the road, and I made it across town in half an hour to the University Endowment Lands, which housed both the enormous campus and a lot of expensive homes.

The Sharma house was a mid-century modern stunner with clean minimalist lines and an eye-catching asymmetry. Unlike many expensive homes in Vancouver that were hidden away behind tall hedges, the ones in this area tended to floor-to-ceiling windows designed to capture the best light at all times of day, leaving them lax on privacy.

As the gate to the driveway was open, I pulled up to the front door, and took a sip of my lukewarm double espresso before popping the trunk with a sigh. It was a two-hour drive to the Chilliwack Airport where daddy's private plane was stationed, and Topher Sharma screamed douche canoe from the tips of his platinum-frosted over-gelled hair to his sunglasses worn before the sun had fully risen and his excessively tight V-neck, exposing a small triangle of brown skin under a partially zipped hoodie.

I was tempted to ask him if he could make his pecs dance but when I got within ten feet, I tasted the cologne that he'd gone water rafting in and thought better of it. At least he hadn't been late—as I'd been warned he was prone to be.

Topher grunted good morning, graciously allowed me to load his suitcase into the trunk, and only showed signs of life when I offered to put his leather satchel in with his luggage. He slung the strap over his head as if worried I'd wrestle him for it and got into the car. Given his wealth, I'd expected his suitcase to be embossed with his initials or some luxury brand name logo, but he only had a single banged-up hard plastic case on wheels. The 1 percent, they're just like us!

The only upside of this assignment was that Tatiana had procured a fully tricked-out luxury SUV by means I chose not to question. It was like steering a silver cloud that warmed my butt and massaged my back at an almost spiritual level.

The silence in the car lasted about three minutes before Topher switched on the radio, tuning in to a hip-hop station without asking me if I minded. Basic car etiquette 101: the driver controls the music.

My hands tightened on the wheel.

And where was my bribe? Not that I'd take it, but according to Tatiana, this kid tossed them out like beads at a Mardi Gras parade. Was I not worthy of one? Frowning, I chalked it up to my Big Mom Energy.

Topher's leg bounced light-speed fast, and he didn't stop fiddling with the satchel's clasp. While he wasn't constantly sniffing—which was the extent of my knowledge on cocaine side-effects—his shirt was soaking through with sweat, so maybe methamphetamines?

We left the manicured streets and swung onto one of the wider avenues leading off campus, the forest pressing in on either side. The gray sky bathed the trees in a cold light, pine needles spiking out from branches like witches' fingers.

"Los Angeles, huh?" I'd merely intended to make conversation but given the way Topher jumped and swung his wide-eyed gaze away from the window, you'd have thought I'd forcefully dragged him back into his physical body from the spirit realm. Was this all an elaborate act to guilt the parent figure of the vehicle, also known as me, into taking pity on him and not driving him to the airport? Snorting, I turned off the music. Amateur hour. Nonetheless, I chatted on like the professional I was. "I hear the Getty Museum is outstanding. Have you ever been?"

He pulled the oversized hood of his sweatshirt up, throwing his face into shadow. "No."

Crushed by his stellar conversation skills, I finished my now-cold beverage and settled in for one hundred and twenty minutes of my life that I would never get back. In my head, I made a new to-do list consisting of one item: get Twitchy safely bundled onto the plane as soon as possible, at which point he'd become the flight staff's problem.

The sour stench of sweat overwhelmed the car. I didn't want to embarrass him, but I wanted to be trapped in a small space with bad smells even less.

7

"Do you need water or medical attention?" I said.

"Picked a bad time to quit smoking," he muttered. Smoking what, though? He pulled a package of Life Savers out of his pocket and tossed a green one in his mouth—the most disgusting flavor and another strike against him. He offered me the last candy, an orange one. "Want it?"

I subtracted one point off his douchiness and accepted. "Thanks."

Nodding absently, he dropped the empty packaging in the cup holder. I ground my candy to orange-flavored dust. Why yes, I'd love to clean up after you.

The rain sluiced down under a dark sky and my wipers worked double time in a brisk staccato. I slowed down on account of the weather, so when a speeding car came up behind me, I flicked on my signal and moved into the right-hand lane to allow the driver to blast ahead and roar around the curve.

I shook my head at his reckless driving, then checked on my passenger, still slumped in the seat, staring out the window.

At least my butt was toasty warm.

Suddenly, there was a deafening bang and a blinding flash of light that made me see spots. I couldn't even tell what side of the car it was on or where we were on the road, just that we were going sixty miles per hour and fishtailing. I yelped and jerked the wheel against the onslaught of g-forces, fighting to avoid a spin.

I was really starting to regret signing up for book club and not upper body toning or Pilates.

With one last herculean burst of effort, my weak noodle arms wrenched the SUV back into our lane. My eyes still wept out a stream of tears from the bright light and my ears rang a bit, but we were okay. We'd made it. I did a small fist-pump. Years of defensive driving in Vancouver had paid off.

Topher had lost his sunglasses in the scuffle and his eyes were wide with shock. "What was that?"

I shook my head. "I don't know. Maybe a transformer blew? Sometimes that—"

But whatever small talk I was going to make Topher would never hear, because that was when a second blast sent us careening on the wet road.

As the car hydroplaned, I went into emergency mode. Get to safety. Don't lock the brakes. Can't fucking see.

Topher breathed rapidly, terrified like a little kid before opening night of their second grade drama production.

"Hang on." Furiously pumping the brakes, I steered away from the telephone pole dead-ahead, but the car had taken on its own skidding momentum.

Topher threw his arm up over his face.

My hands on the wheel felt oddly disconnected, stuck in an unfamiliar sluggishness.

Time sagged, and I let out a breath, feeling like I was sinking into a sea of molasses, already a ghost. The world sharpened into a crystal-hard spike of pointlessness. There was no to-do list, no problem solving, and no multitasking that could save us now.

We bumped onto the shoulder of the road and smashed into the pole.

My neck snapped forward, my head hit the air bag, and I blacked out.

When I came to, everything was blurry and I wasn't sure how long I lay slumped over the wheel, confused. I latched on to a pinging sound, aligning my breathing with it, until I could carefully raise my head.

The smudgy trees beyond the front window bobbed up and down, and I swallowed, hard. What had that been? A bang, a flash, a wet road. The air smelled normal and the power lines above were clear, nothing broken. Had it been magic? A blindspot, maybe? But no, those were much more contained and much, much less explosive.

I groaned, head aching from all this thinking, then gasped, remembering my passenger. As I turned to check on Topher, a shaft of pain rumbled along the side of my neck, and I hissed through a clenched jaw.

My gaze landed first on the crumpled hood, then on the open passenger door that was the source of both the binging sound and the cold air blowing in. The empty seat belt banged against the doorframe.

The young man was gone, replaced by a meaty red lump and crimson smear on the passenger seat like an offering to a cruel god.

This was some kind of sick joke.

"Topher?" I said tremulously. I poked at the object, realizing quickly that it was not only heart-shaped, it was an actual, wet heart.

"This isn't funny," I snapped, grinding a layer of enamel off my teeth. "Cut the gross tricks and show yourself."

There was no answer. Just the heart and... one of his sunglasses lenses, discarded on the floor mat.

My fingers drifted up to touch my burning right cheek from the air bag injury, coming away from the rashy scratched skin damp with blood. A quick check in the rearview mirror showed it wasn't all mine.

Bile surged up my esophagus and I fumbled with my seat belt and the door handle, falling to my knees at the side of the empty road and vomiting coffee until I dry heaved. My retching and the pinging of the door-open alarm were the only sounds.

The road stretched out as solid as ever, but my beliefs that everything would be okay were as mangled as the hood. I'd driven past a gruesome pile up before, glass and bumpers strewn on the ground, with somber officers keeping drivers from slowing down to gawk at the covered bodies on gurneys. Death happened in crashes, but not like this. Not with a person's heart savagely torn out, their corpse gone.

This wasn't speed or drinking or wet roads.

It was murder.

I froze, listening for the distant roar of an oncoming car, but it was early morning during summer semester on a university highway and there was no traffic.

I was alone. A dead man's heart quietly bled into the passenger seat. And somewhere out there in the forest lurked something that might want to do the same thing to me.

2

My shoulder blades prickling, I huddled in the seat, forcing myself to look at the body part. Something horrible had occurred, but I could deal with it. It was only a heart. *Yeah, Feldman, and you know who leaves hearts as gifts? Serial killers.*

After wiping my mouth with a crumpled tissue from my coat pocket, I found my phone by the emergency brake, and dialed Tatiana with a trembling hand. My eyes darted between the rearview and side mirrors. No one was going to sneak up on me.

"I need—"

"Miriam? Why on earth are you phoning?" Tatiana said. There were a couple of quick ka-tunk noises from her side of the phone, almost like gunfire, and I flinched.

"Did Topher do a runner again?" Her whiskey-soaked, cigarette-raspy New Yorker accent turned "runner" into "runnah."

I pushed a soaked strand of hair out of my eyes, my brain stumbling over how to explain that technically I hadn't lost her *entire* client, but we could now fit him in a cooler with room for a six-pack and sandwiches.

Another ka-tunk.

She gave an impatient sigh. "Hang on, I'll call him."

I squeaked out a "No!" but it was too late. She'd put me on hold. I gnawed on a cuticle for several tense minutes, the rush of wind in the trees an eerie dirge accusing, "Yooooooouuuu yoooooouuuuu."

I'd driven dozens of kids over the years on field trips, aware of the trust that parents placed in me to get their children to the destination in one piece. But I'd failed with Topher. No, I hadn't even conceived that keeping him safe would involve more than good driving skills. Should I have? Was death the ever-present baseline in my new job?

"I'm sorry," I whispered, but the tree branches rattled, nature unfeeling to my apology.

It hurt to think and to breathe, and the pain wrapping me in barbed wire did an admirable job of consuming all my energy.

I started the car to check if it was still drivable, but a grinding noise and bitter smell through the vents kiboshed that idea so I turned it off, leaving the door partially ajar to clear the air.

When Tatiana returned, her voice was steel. "Topher is still waiting. I thought I made my expectations clear about your professionalism, Miriam, especially during this probation period."

"Are you seriously giving me shit when I almost—" The first part of her statement penetrated my angry haze. I glanced at the organ and my stomach heaved. "If Topher's alive, who was I just driving?"

There was a long silence. "What do you mean, alive? Is someone else in the car with you?"

"Does a ripped-out heart constitute personhood?" I said in a shaky voice. "Because it's on my passenger seat and the rest of him has gone AWOL."

"A heart on the seat? You don't say." She sounded as unflappable as if I'd called to let her know that I'd forgotten to pick up milk.

"I *do* say, and this is not part of my normal routine!" I screeched, every part of my body sore, my heart hammering, and my clothes gradually dampening in the creepy-ass mist-rain blowing into the car. "Normal is two passengers qualifying a driver for the carpool lane. Not drawing googly eyes on an excised muscle and hoping it fools the traffic cameras."

"Oy vey, bubeleh," Tatiana said, "Take a breath. You're sounding pitchy."

There were a couple more of those ka-tunks.

My eye twitched. "What are you doing?"

"Stretching canvas," she said calmly.

My multitask-loving-self found that oddly reassuring, and my shoulders unhunched. "I need to go to a hospital, but the car is toast. Send someone to get me."

Then we'd have to identify this poor man and give his family the bad news. Was he even magic? How was I supposed to handle this? I rested my head back against the seat. I'd figure it out. The family deserved closure.

"The car doesn't matter," Tatiana said.

Had my brain not been a jumble of half-coherent thoughts, I would have asked about the insurance implications of crashing an SUV that wasn't mine, but it was easier to simply nod at her statement.

"This was an attack, Miriam. Now, put on your hazard lights and walk me through it."

"Okay." It calmed me down to have quantifiable tasks, even small ones. Under her guided questioning, I haltingly told her the entire story, my brain foggy.

The first vehicle I'd seen since the crash drove past, sending a tiny metal object skidding closer to my partially ajar car door. Leaning over with a wince, the freezing rain running down the back of my neck, I picked up a metal ring.

The car had stopped up ahead and a woman got out.

"Oh shit," I hissed. Exactly when I didn't need the milk of human kindness to show up, there it was in the form of a concerned female driver, popping open a Marimekko umbrella and walking over.

"Are you all right? Can I call you a tow truck?" Her hand flew to her mouth. "Oh my gosh, you're bleeding."

Tatiana was calling my name from the phone, the job was toast, I had a dead man's heart in the passenger seat and now some good Samaritan was going to completely destroy any chance I had at salvaging things. It was too much. I zombie-lurched at the upstanding citizen, arms windmilling. "Noooooo!"

The woman froze, one hand in her coat pocket. For a moment I thought I was, on top of all these other indignities, also going to get shot, but no, it was her phone.

I pasted a smile on and prayed I looked mildly convincing. "It's not my blood."

She took a step back.

"I mean, it is my blood, but it's a superficial wound." I waved my own cell at her. "My mom is on the phone and she's already called the police and paramedics."

After assuring the woman that I had a tow truck on the way, and that I was really okay waiting by myself, she wished me well and peeled out in her car.

I sagged with relief. One problem neutralized. Now for the next on the list. "Tatiana? You still there?"

"Yes. I had to grab my hammer. Who was that?"

"Nothing to worry about," I said, cursing as I kicked a small steel canister with my foot. I stopped, then bent down for a closer look. This wasn't just road trash.

Pushing the deflated air bag aside, I collapsed back onto the driver's seat, because even that short journey left me feeling like someone was trying to split me open with an ice pick. "Someone used a flashbang on me."

"Why?" She hammered her canvas a couple of times.

"I'm the ex-librarian. You're the magic fixer. Does this sound book-related to you?" At the distinctly chilly silence pouring through the phone, I took a breath and moderated my tone. "Has this happened to your people before?"

"No, that unique distinction is all yours. Nor do I know who this imposter was," Tatiana said, accompanied by more hammering. "Since this was a semi-regular assignment, anyone could have learned about it. Is the man's luggage still in the trunk?"

So much motion. Couldn't I simply lay here and moan? I popped the latch and heaved myself out of the seat once more to check.

"Yes," I said, "but the satchel he had with him is gone." I fished a mint out of my purse and sucked on it, the artificial peppermint clearing away the taste of sour saliva.

"How about the body?" Tatiana said.

"There's just the heart."

"You're positive of that?"

Well, now I sure as hell wasn't.

"Go check," she said. "I have to grab some shims."

Was she speaking English? I really had to get to a hospital.

I motioned at a car slowing down to keep going, flashing the driver a thumbs up.

However, traffic had picked up in the opposite direction heading into the university, and the last thing I needed was to be caught next to a corpse. Like most people in the world who were powerless Sapiens, my ex-husband, Detective Eli Chu, had no idea that magic existed. I intended to change that so that his eyes were open to the dangers hidden in this city, but I'd been hoping to ease him into the revelation, and I doubted this qualified.

My heart in my throat, I went around the car, my wet shoes squelching on the gravel shoulder, frantically searching from the car to the tree line. I found the missing sunglasses under the car, but no real sign of a struggle. Whatever happened, happened quickly.

I drummed my fingers on the car roof. The man had been on the short side for a dude, only an inch or so taller than my five-foot-five, but it still took strength to haul a corpse away. Also, where was all the blood? His heart had been ripped out and the rain hadn't washed it away, because there would have been some trace of it left on the gravel.

The amount of blood in the car was negligible, all things considered, and how did the killer manage to slice open my passenger's chest so fast? Obviously they'd used magic, but even so, I didn't think I'd blacked out for long, and this was a very specific way to kill someone. Tear the ribcage open to get at the heart, instantly cauterize the blood to contain any spill, and do it all in record time.

I frowned. There was one Ohrist who checked all the boxes and did so on a regular basis because this was how he killed dybbuks.

"Laurent," I said faintly, my hand pressed over my mouth.

Laurent Amar, like all Ohrists, had the ability to draw upon light and life energy. Their powers covered a wide spectrum such as firing hard balls of light or manipulating organic matter, though generally each Ohrist had only one talent. Laurent was a wolf shifter, but he was the only Ohrist also trained to sense and kill dybbuks, wicked parasitic spirits who leeched onto and then took over magic-users.

Once a dybbuk fully possessed a host and that person was essentially dead, leaving the dybbuk in charge of the body, Laurent could scent them out, and by ripping out the heart, release the malevolent spirit with comparatively little blood loss. I bit my bottom lip. Was he involved in this?

Fake Topher's murder fit a dybbuk killing, except I hadn't seen anything weird about the man's shadow. My Banim Shovavim magic made me sensitive to a dybbuk's presence, though in this weather, everything was bathed in a flat gray light that didn't cast any noticeable shadows. I crouched down by the bottom of the blood-flecked doorframe, my frown deepening. Even if I'd missed the dybbuk's presence because I couldn't see the deceased's shadow, I also hadn't gotten the edginess that I usually did when I was up close with an abomination that had to be destroyed.

I wouldn't have overlooked both indications.

And why would Laurent bother to cause a car accident? If he was after the dybbuk, he would have told me and I'd have handed the man over.

The wind gusted my coat open and I pulled the flaps tighter with one hand. Laurent had been pretty angry about me working for Tatiana, to the extent he'd been texting me regularly over the past couple of weeks with his unsolicited opinion that I'd be better off hiding my magic again and quitting working for his aunt.

Did he think that I'd have protected her client at the expense of allowing a dybbuk to roam free? No. I stood up, rubbing my lower back. Whatever his feelings, he wouldn't have chanced me getting seriously injured. Weeellll... not deliberately, but what if he'd gotten too caught up in a situation to think rationally, or his self-destructive streak had kicked in and he hadn't been able to think logically until it was too late?

I was so caught up in my thoughts that I missed what Tatiana said when she returned to the call. "You want me to do what?" I said.

"Get rid of the heart."

"Why?"

"It's the one thing tying you to that man. I'm the only one who knows you picked him up. Let's keep it that way."

"We have to identify him." I cradled the phone between my ear and my shoulder so I could button up my jacket.

"How do you propose I do that?"

"I don't know, but we have to tell his family."

"We most certainly do not. No good deed goes unpunished."

"But—"

"That's an order, Miriam."

I gnashed my teeth and shook my fists like a Scooby Doo villain. "Do you expect me to flush it down a toilet? Go full Sweeny Todd and make pies?"

"Deal with it in a manner that leaves no trace," she said brusquely. "Creative problem solving is essential to your job."

Is that what we were calling destroying evidence? Was hiding murder "risk management"?

"My mind is willing but my body is unable." I could barely see straight, and my headache was so bad that my entire face throbbed, so how was I supposed to pull off making a heart disappear?

"Nonsense," she said. "It's one simple task while I send someone to deal with the car and get you a ride home. I'll handle any other nosy parkers alerting the police or emergency services."

"You mean concerned human beings."

"Potato, potahto."

I rolled my eyes. "Fine."

"Good. There's a blanket in the trunk." I was about to thank her for the tip because I really was freezing, when she added, "Throw it over the seat to hide any blood." She disconnected without saying goodbye.

Once I'd finished miming choking her out, I huddled into the front seat with the heater cranked, my teeth chattering. Cautiously, I probed my forehead with a finger and hissed. I'd gone my entire life without getting a concussion and week one on the new job, here it was. I certainly hoped it wasn't setting the standard for things to come, because what was I supposed to do, keep coming up with weekly excuses in emergency rooms like "I tripped"?

I should have negotiated an employment contract with every contingency, though to be fair, it's not like there were legal templates to provide guidance when working for magic fixers.

After two minutes, I slammed the heater off and cracked the window because the heat intensified the smell of blood. The hot copper tang brought memories of my parents' murder roaring up front and center, mixing with this grisly crime scene.

I jammed the heel of my palms into my eyes, but that made my dizziness worse.

My parents' killer had never been caught and I'd lived the last thirty or so years denying all aspects of my powers hoping whoever it was wouldn't come back to finish the job. And while this was the perfect moment to question the life choices that had landed me here, I had only one thought in my head: was Fake Topher the only one in the car who was supposed to die?

Had I been spared because of motive or because of opportunity? Would the murderer come back for me? My shoulders hunched into my ears, I checked all the mirrors, but there was no sign of anyone sneaking up on me. Still, it took me a good thirty seconds and the world's saddest carrot of a future hospital visit before I unlocked the door to carry out Tatiana's command.

Rubbing my hands together, I pulled an Indiana Jones, swiping the heart and leaving the blanket draped over the stained seat. The heart was lighter than I expected, but tougher too. There was a poetic metaphor in there, but flowery images were of little use to me at this moment.

Since it was possible this was the first and last time my boss would ever trust me with such a deluxe vehicle, I committed the feel of the contoured leather seat cradling my ass to memory, then, double-checking that the hazard lights were still on and the doors locked, cupped the fist-sized organ in my hands and trudged into the forest.

I didn't even have the comfort of my magic shade, Delilah, for protection, since the overcast light didn't provide the correct conditions to cast a hard shadow that I could animate.

Squatting down under a leafy tree that kept most of the rain off me, I dug a shallow hole in the rich, dark mulch and placed the heart in the wet ground. The flame from my lighter smudged one tiny corner of the organ, sent up a disgusting sweet-charred smell, and... that was that. Three more attempts failed as spectacularly. Fan-freaking-tastic. I couldn't even bury the damn thing, because a dog or a coyote would scent it out and dig it up.

Besides, it was wrong to inter him here like some nameless schmuck. "I wish that I'd bothered to talk to you. Maybe nothing would have changed, and if this was set in motion when you impersonated Topher Sharma, well, you still deserved better than a senseless murder and some stranger trying to ditch your bits." I brushed some dirt off his remains. "You had shit taste in Life Savers and your cologne could be smelled from outer space, but you made a difference to someone out there, and I'm sorry for their loss."

As eulogies went, it was pretty pathetic, but I was extrapolating from an internal organ and a short car ride. Sighing, I picked up the heart. What was security like on crematoriums these days?

An eerie yowl made the hairs on the back of my neck stand up.

Speaking of coyotes... I turned my head to the gap in the trees and swallowed.

The fiend was black as pitch, its eyes cruel yellow slits reflecting the seething resentment of its cry. One of us was going down.

The small black shape leapt through the air, intent on the heart, but I whipped the muscle out of reach. This animal was one indignity too far for the deceased to bear.

Before I could stand up, the predator swiped viciously at me with a razor-sharp claw.

Pulling away with a wince, I sucked my wounded finger into my mouth.

Cats were *such* assholes.

"You can't have this." I deployed my cloaking magic. Take that. Even werewolves couldn't sniff me out or track my heartbeat under here.

The house cat sat down, its head tilted and its eyes locked on the lump in my hand. It flicked its tail imperiously.

"You are truly evil."

The cat blinked at me, nonplussed, like invisible beings talking at it was a fairly mundane annoyance.

"How about showing a little respect?" I said. "This was a person, and now you want to eat his heart? Your stomach isn't big enough to finish it and then what would I do with the leftovers? Pack them in my purse? Now, if you had some friends to help out, we might have something to discuss."

The animal considered my request, then broke into a run, knocking into my legs.

The bottom dropped out of the world...

... and we tumbled backward through the shadows.

3

I LANDED ON MY ASS IN A DIMLY LIT CAVE THAT
reeked of fabric softener. This wasn't a stunning sea cave with a
charming grotto of turquoise water; there weren't luminous
crystal geodes or Paleolithic paintings. There was, however, an
excess of grayish-black rock that pressed in from all sides.

Someone cleared their throat. Shifting slightly to avoid
getting frisky with a stalagmite, I squinted at their scuffed brown
men's shoes, up along their brown pants that were belted high
on their waist, and to the brown plaid shirt bearing a name tag
that said "Pyotr" in clumsy printing.

Of average height for a dude, but whip-thin, the wearer of the
unfortunate outfit had bug-like eyes that drooped over his gaunt
cheeks and downturned thick lips, years of sorrow carved into
his face. And when I say carved, that was factually accurate
because he was a gargoyle. I'd only met one other gargoyle,
Harry, and he was a helpful sort, so I opted for positive thinking
that all of his kind were the same way.

There were no windows, no doors, no indication of how I'd
gotten here, and more importantly, how I was going to get out.
After years of hiding my magic and living a safe, sensible life that
had left me in my forties feeling like a sidekick in my own story,

I'd shaken things up. Sure, today I'd jumped into the deep end, but I was damned if I'd get stuck in some limbo now.

I had to give Fake Topher a decent send-off.

Jamming the heart into my coat pocket to keep the dead guy safe, I wiped the blood off my cheeks as best I could. You only got one chance to make a first impression, even if unable to stand up because pain had made you its little bitch. "Hello?"

The cat shook itself off, spattering me with water, then twined around the gargoyle's leg before jumping nimbly back into the shadows and disappearing.

"A minute." His voice was a bassy rumble, and he pronounced "minute" like "meen-it" in his Russian-accented English. He smacked a tiny black-and-white television whose screen featured mostly static snow and the garbled sound of cars revving.

I used the time to roll onto all fours and then push to my feet, swaying like a tree about to fall.

One of his folded leathery wings knocked against the rickety TV table, and for a single moment the picture of a street drag race snapped into perfect clarity.

Pyotr's eyes lit up, his mouth falling open with a soft sigh.

The image disintegrated into a fuzzy blob and the gargoyle's shoulders slumped.

My phone had no signal to call for help, if such a thing were even possible. The heart was a literal dead weight against my hip, and I had never craved a shower so badly. "I don't suppose you have an urn?"

The gargoyle's expression grew more morose. "That's a special requisition. Lots of forms. In triplicate."

"So that's a no." I showed him the heart in my pocket. "Any thoughts on a fitting resting place?"

Pyotr hit the television again. "Do you know how *Fast and Furious* ends?"

"Um, which one?"

"There's more than one?" He lost his slumped posture, his

face lighting up. Then his glance landed on his crappy TV that couldn't even channel one movie properly, and his lip trembled.

I stepped back, because if gargoyles could cry, I didn't want to be in the splash zone. But his misery narrowed into a look of pure venom for the defenseless TV. He swore in Russian and snapped the power off the old set so hard that the knob fell off in his hand. "I hate this job."

"Sorry to hear that." I massaged my neck. "For the record," I said, "mine isn't all that great either."

"Really?" He brightened. "Tell me. How bad?"

I wasn't about to bare my soul for a stone creature with a bad case of schadenfreude, but establishing rapport was an important communications tool. "I'm still in my probation period and I picked up some imposter instead of the real client. Then some other asshole ran me off the road into a telephone pole, and when I woke up, the guy was gone and his ripped-out heart was on my seat, and now I have to get rid of it without a trace while still giving him some dignity."

My head weighed in on all this talking by tightening the throbbing vice around my temples.

The gargoyle gestured at the TV. "I wish I had your problems."

I took a deep breath and silently counted to ten. The sooner I got through this, the sooner I got to go to the emergency room. "Where am I and how do I get out of here?"

"You're in Kefitzat Haderech." He frowned, his eyes narrowing. "Why you not know this? You're too old for first visit."

"First of all, I'm in my prime, and second, I've never heard of this place before."

"Maybe you'd get better job if you were smarter," he said under his breath.

"Yeah, well at least I can watch the endings of the *Fast and Furious* movies." I jutted out my chin. "Every single one of them."

"Be like that. See if you get sock." The gargoyle crossed his arms and jerked his head to the left of the cave, where a light came on illuminating an enormous pile of mismatched socks balanced atop a long, flat rock. Tiny pink socks, stretched-out dingy sport socks, fancy knee-highs in various colors with and without ribbons, striped, fleecy, and far too many black trouser socks. The pile was at least twenty feet high.

Single socks floated down from a chute in the rock-hewn ceiling. Had I unfairly blamed my washing machine all these years when some criminal sock abduction ring was at fault? What kind of sicko reveled in all our wasted time and energy searching for missing singles? I pictured milk cartons with sad photos and all the poor feet who longed to be clad in them again.

The weight of this knowledge was too much to bear. I curled my lip. "I will not be a party to this. Good day, sir."

The gargoyle pressed a finger to my forehead. "Are you not right in head?"

Now that you mention it... I didn't generally speak like an affronted Victorian gentleman. Hospital, stat.

"Keep your creepy memento," I said, wearily. "I just want to go home."

Pyotr sighed and stood up, his joints creaking. "Is basic facts. Kefitzat Haderech, Hebrew for 'shortening of way,' is shadow shortcut between destinations used by Banim Shovavim." He drew an invisible line from the television to the chair to illustrate his point.

My mouth fell open. "I can shadow jump?" Think of the money I could save on gas. Or airline tickets. Could I jump to Paris for dessert and Shanghai for dumplings?

Banim Shovavim magic kicked in at puberty, and I'd only had mine for about a year before my parents had been murdered and I'd shut down that part of myself. Shadow shortcuts fell into the many gaps in my magic knowledge.

"How far can I go?" I said, the rush of this new information kicking in a much-needed jolt of adrenaline. "And how fast will I travel?"

"Wherever you want and pretty fast. The space between

destinations shrinks here so it's never more than a few minutes travel."

I could put Fake Topher to rest and get myself to a hospital in two choruses of "I Will Survive." I pumped the air with my fist.

Pyotr held up a hand. "Provided you have sock. Which you do not, because rude."

"What's the deal with the sock?"

"Have you ever lost one for months only to have it reappear out of nowhere?" he said.

"Yeah."

The gargoyle nodded sagely. "Magic ability to travel through shadows. Like you."

So, the reason I only had one of Sadie's favorite Hello Kitty socks was because, what, its mate was traversing shadow realms? Like me? I planted my hand on my hip. Please, how gullible did he think I was? "Didn't my Banim Shovavim powers bring me here?"

"Your magic let you in, but sock is what gets you from A to B." He fit the knob back on the television set.

I pointed at the shadows. "Then I'll go back the way I came. Like the cat."

"Does not work that way. Come in through shadows, go out through door."

There was no door. Perhaps seeing one required a sock. Or perhaps he was fucking with me. Well, good luck with that. I had a dead man's heart in my pocket. My fuckability had reached its limit.

No, wait. Phrasing...

Whatever. I slammed my cloaking over me, engulfing me in a black mesh of invisibility, and lunged for the closest sock, but the gargoyle knocked me aside, shaking me free of my magic. Only one other individual had ever seen past the cloaking, and he was a powerful vampire.

The gargoyle tutted a finger at me. "Cannot cheat. I lose poor job with terrible reception if you cheat."

Sweaty and nauseous, I unbuttoned my coat. I was a woman of simple wants: deal with the heart and soak in a hot bath, followed by a couple of glasses of wine over dinner with my kid. My stomach lurched at the prospect of booze, so perhaps not that part... today.

"How about a trade?" I said. "The ending of the first *Fast and Furious* for a sock and somewhere nice I can bury this heart so it never resurfaces."

He screwed up his face, thinking hard, then nodded with a noise like marbles were rolling around in his brain. "Is deal."

"Big car race. Vin Diesel is a hero. Bad guys defeated." I held out my hand.

"Wait. What happened to Mitsubishi Eclipse? Does it show up again?"

I shook my head, regretting it immediately as the ground lurched sickeningly. "You wouldn't believe me if I told you."

Not like I'd seen the rest of the franchise, but it wasn't as if he could call me on it.

Pyotr patted his chest. "Try me."

"All right. Highlights. The car time travels so Vin can save his mom in the third movie, then in the fifth, it becomes a boat to battle a great white shark terrorizing a small beach town. But the most amazing thing it did?"

Pyotr leaned forward.

"It drove up the Empire State Building in New York so the heroine could fight off a giant ape." I nodded, and casually added, "Then in the thirteenth movie, it was declared a national treasure and fitted with an artificial intelligence system called Kit to help fight space crime. And given a sidekick called Shrek."

The gargoyle sat up straight and I worried that I'd pushed it too far, but he gave a low bow. "Thank you. Choose wisely."

I reached for a rainbow-colored toesie sock, glancing at his expression, which had become perfectly blank. Was this not a good choice? I mean, I had stepped into a magical new world or whatever this was, and this could very well be a test à la myth and legend since Pyotr was definitely a gatekeeper.

A neon-yellow ankle sock caught my eye, but I hesitated. Was my choice indicative of something, or was it purely practical? What if I had to unravel the sock to find my way out like Theseus marking his passage through the Minotaur's labyrinth?

I snatched up the longest one I could find, a green and white-striped thigh-high sock.

Pyotr blinked.

In approval? Horror? Had I made a literally grave error? I went for another option but he lightly slapped my hand away.

"Choice is made," he intoned. "Take heart to Door to Hell."

That was a rather extreme solution to my problem, wasn't it? Much like using a fire hose on a match. I snapped my fingers. "I'd love to, but I'm not wearing flame-resistant shoes. Is there perchance a Garburator to Purgatory?"

Pyotr stared at me with a slack jaw, his brows drawn together. "Door to Hell is crater in Turkmenistan Desert that's been on fire for decades. Burn anything."

That would fulfill Tatiana's decree, but it was such an ignoble end. Then again, the heart was now cold, congealed, and really had no opinions on the matter one way or the other.

"In that case," I said, "what do I do?"

"Fix destination in your head and Kefitzat Haderech will take you there. Don't lose sock. Don't stop moving forward."

"Why? Will something happen?"

A rectangular neon sign appeared, and the gargoyle clammed up. The sign emitted a low buzzing noise and the final letter in the message sputtered in and out. *He lies. Do not take the sock out of this room.*

Trust a faulty magic sign or a put-upon gargoyle? The decisions I had to make when deeply in need of medical attention, I tell you. I went with my gut instinct and pressed the fabric against my chest. "I shall become one with the sock."

"Don't make it weird," Pyotr said. He turned to the sign. "Is first visit."

The neon letters changed to a face with its eyebrows raised, then the sign stuttered like a movie projector going out of whack, jerky images superimposed of angels and a shrewish woman with a calculating gleam.

"When Lilith was first cast out of Eden," said a sonorous male voice coming from the sign, like the David Attenborough of the shadow world, "God sent three angels, Senoi, Sansenoi, and Sammaneglof, to kill her children as punishment for her disobedience."

I prodded Pyotr's shoulder. "I know this already. Can I go?"

He pointed at the sign.

"When Lilith and Adam came together the second time," the narrator continued, "after he'd been tossed out of the Garden as well and Lilith was now branded a demon, she hid their new offspring, the Banim Shovavim, her 'wayward or rebellious children.'"

Cue close-up of a horde of the ugliest babies ever. I wrinkled my nose. I had been an adorable baby and so had my—admittedly non-magical—daughter.

"Typical. Only brand the woman." I wagged a finger. "Lilith didn't impregnate herself."

"The angels couldn't find Lilith's progeny to kill them," the disembodied voice said over an image of the three angels on a hilltop. "But fearing their magic, the angels convened to set conditions on these demonic children's powers. If the darkness within a Banim Shovavim overwhelms their humanity—if they lose their way—they'll be doomed to roam the Kefitzat Haderech forever and be consumed by darkness."

My mouth fell open. "Are you serious?"

There came a series of graphic visuals depicting how, unlike Ohrists' magic that could randomly set off a blindspot with the tiniest magic action, Banim Shovavim would not experience a hot bright devouring, the agony lasting seconds. Our insides would be eternally eaten away, and we'd remain just sane enough to be aware of our torment. The final image was of someone screaming in agony, their eyes rolled back to show the whites.

I stood there, dumbstruck. Because of a patriarchal bullshit judgment of Lilith, all her children were potentially doomed? "How many Banim Shovavim end up like this?"

The neon sign remained frozen on that final image, but Pyotr sucked in a breath through his teeth.

"That many?" I said.

"I say nothing," he muttered, giving a contrite look at the sign, like a lowly employee at a big box store not wanting to catch shit from the floor manager.

Did any moral or ethical decision merely buy me time until the inevitable? I frantically waved the sock. "I want out!"

The neon letters changed to a pouty face, but a narrow green door appeared in the rock face.

Fixing the image of the burning crater in my head, I bolted out of the room.

The scent of fabric softener was replaced by the cold metallic bite right before a rainstorm. A path wove through more cave, pulsing gently with a dim light that let me see about ten feet ahead, but mostly there was darkness.

So much darkness.

It wasn't merely an absence of light, it was the lonely void into which we were born and to which we would return. I shivered. The same darkness that I'd always felt within me. Twisting the sock in my hands, I walked as fast as my poor head allowed, ducking slightly to avoid the low ceiling. One good bash and I'd be done for.

I stretched out my fingers and toes as I continued along the path to this Door to Hell, feeling how my magic marked me: a dark smudge inside the curve of my elbow, a knobby dark ladder up my spine, a bendy stripe when I flexed my heel. I smiled, feeling the shape of it for the first time, but my gut still twisted. Darkness was the source of my magic, both within me and echoed here in the Kefitzat Haderech. It had a literal manifestation with my power, but were there other implications?

Dybbuks killed their host, existing to then cause suffering to others. I didn't feel bad about destroying them, but was my easy acceptance of vampire deaths some moral failing? My best friend, Jude, an Ohrist, had argued in favor of their intelligence and sentience, and I was firmly opposed to the death sentence for humans, so why did I judge bloodsuckers differently?

I'd always prided myself on having a strong sense of morals. Maybe I wasn't the poster child for following the Ten Commandments, but who didn't covet now and then? I didn't steal, and adultery and murder (excluding dybbuks and the undead) were a solid no. Thus, if you took the four specifically religious commandments out of it, I was still four for six on the rest. Okay, now that I did the math that was only 66 percent, but an uncontestable passing grade nonetheless.

I was rudely interrupted from my existential musings by a giant rock slamming into the path before me.

"Fuuuck!" I swayed backwards, hopping up and down. I hadn't had time to completely dodge it and my toes had bashed into its side. On top of all the other injuries I was suffering from, one more only made it harder to convince myself to keep going. I simply wanted to find this hell door, throw the heart into it, and go to the hospital.

Oops! It was the same sign, with the same sputtering last letter and buzzing noise.

"Ladies and gentlemen, the Kefitzat Haderech," I said, holding my side and taking deep breaths to stave off the nausea. "It's here all week. Try the shrimp." I paused. "On a scale of Mother Teresa to Hitler, how am I doing according to the conditions that the angels put on Banim Shovavim?"

The sign disappeared.

I gritted my teeth, squared my shoulders, and shuffled

forward, peering into the gloom for any other errant bone breakers.

Intellectually, I knew that *all* magic talents could be used for atrocities depending on the user's intent, but passing through the heart of darkness now, I circled back to the idea of mazel. If my powers were rooted in darkness, especially the darkness living within me, then was accepting magic back into my life the same as turning down a bad path? You wouldn't think I'd run into that many prophecies about me, but I had, and every one of them had mentioned darkness, screams, and me starting something. Something big.

I clutched my sock tighter, resisting the urge to whisper, "the horror." I'd been taught that Jews had mazel (destiny) but we also had free will. Did that not apply to those of us descended from Lilith?

The sign appeared again. *Why was the baby Banim Shovavim born with sunglasses on?*

I waited for the punchline, but none appeared and the sign winked out of existence. "First rule of joke telling," I said to the nothingness in front of me, "set up, pay off. Definitely don't quit your day job to pursue a career in comedy."

The path branched into two. I waved the sock at it and was rewarded with a slight tug to the right, but before I could head in that direction, a clammy hand came down on my shoulders and I jumped with a shriek.

"Please, I need help," a tremulous female voice said.

I gasped and stumbled backward.

She was close to my age with dark hair, but that's where our similarities ended because her skin was translucent, stretched over a vast darkness.

"What can I do for you?" I said, watching her for any sign of attack.

She fixed her two haunted eye sockets on me, and I brandished the sock as if it was a shield.

"Kill me."

4

AM I STILL ALIVE? WAS NOT A QUESTION I'D EVER
grappled with before. What if everything after the car accident
was a weird end-of-life hallucination and I was a corpse, left only
with this cold dead heart—which suddenly took on a much more
sinister cast? Or worse, what if I'd killed Fake Topher, and I now
suffered from some "Tell-Tale Heart" madness, my guilt manifested in that disturbing short film?

I pressed two fingers to my wrist, exhaling hard at my racing
pulse. Upon closer look, even this woman had a heart, a dark
throbbing mass visible inside her chest cavity.

Did I love the fact that this was the second heart that I'd seen
before lunchtime? No, but hers was still beating, so she was
alive, if a tad more see-through than most.

The light was too gloomy to examine her shadow, though I
checked as best as I could for any sign she was either enthralled,
in which case I had a chance to save her, or dybbuk-possessed
and her wish would be answered. But probe as I might, I found
nothing.

From the moment she'd appeared, there'd been only one
logical explanation, but I desperately sought any other answer.
Maybe Pyotr had tricked me and this entire place was a trap for

Banim Shovavim? He hadn't seemed the type, but then again, I hadn't expected my passenger to be reduced to a bloody heart either.

"Do you have a sock?" I said. That was it. She'd dropped it and this consequence was part of the Kefitzat Haderech's sick sense of humor.

The woman thrust out the remnant of a newborn baby's sock, the white lace yellowed and tattered, with a tear in the heel.

I swallowed, my eyes skittering off the void inside this woman that was barely contained by her thin layer of skin. For all its silly socks, depressed gargoyles, and snarky signs, the Kefitzat Haderech wasn't simply shadow travel. It really was a scale balancing a Banim Shovavim's humanity against the darkness inside us. The socks weren't indicative of the darkness within, they revealed how much humanity we had left. Looking at this woman, there was no other conclusion I could draw.

"Where were you trying to go?" I said.

"Friedrichshain in East Berlin."

"East Berlin hasn't existed since 1989," I said slowly.

The neon lit up. *Keep moving!*

"Come with me." I grabbed the woman's sleeve, but when I tugged, she had no weight. It was like pulling a helium balloon. I dropped her arm like I'd been scalded, but she stepped closer, forcing me up against the cave wall.

The void inside the woman rippled, much like a pebble tossed in a deep pond, and a shudder wracked her body from head to toe. "Help me. I beg you." Her voice cracked.

The neon sign glowed brighter, providing just enough light for me to cast a hard shadow.

I eyed the sign warily. Was I supposed to reason with a magic sentience presiding over me like judge, jury, and executioner—or, I clutched the pocket with the heart—was it already too late?

"The angels were right," she said. "I lost my way."

This wasn't my future, my insides being eaten away and destined to wander here forever. It couldn't be.

Was this woman my path to redemption?

She wasn't a dybbuk and she wasn't a vampire, but if she belonged to the "aberrations from the natural order of death" category, then there was a slim hope.

"There may be a way..." My shadow flowed up my left arm into a scythe, which was promising. I slammed it down into her shadow like I did with enthralleds, hoping to release that void from inside her.

The scythe bounced off the ground with a recoil kick that left me shaking my wrist out, but that was about it.

The woman clutched my hand and I cringed. It was like having a used Band-Aid brush against your skin in a public washroom. "You have to kill me," she said. "Please."

The neon sign kept its impassive expression.

"What's the catch?" I jabbed the scythe at it. "Is mercy killing a sin here? Will I lose my humanity in one fell swoop and be damned like she is?"

Is that what you think? The words pulsed outwards from the sign with an almost tangible weight.

I slammed the wall and swore, having bashed my palm against a pointy chunk of rock.

My mind was tangled up in doubt and second guesses, the hands on my moral compass bent into unrecognizability. I closed my eyes and took a deep breath. Even if this woman was some kind of serial killer, she'd been tortured and wandering in the dark for decades. Wasn't that payment enough for whatever had landed her here?

The merciful choice was to accede to her wish, but did mercy count in the scheme of right and wrong? She had a human heartbeat, so I'd still be taking her life, which was a sin.

Even if it wasn't, I'd never taken a human life.

I opened my eyes to find the woman watching me with a fevered desperation, twisting her fingers. Within the void under her skin, her heart beat rapidly, her chest rising and falling in the shallow movements of one hyperventilating.

I couldn't kill her. There'd been too much death today. "I'm sorry," I whispered.

The woman sagged, sobbing.

The sign made a tutting noise and the path behind me curled into a thick dark fog, reforming itself into a skeletal face with razor-sharp teeth.

I screamed and sprinted toward a blue door that appeared in the rock face maybe fifty meters on, pushing through the pain of my injuries. Please let that be the Door to He—I squashed that mid-thought. There's no place like home.

A hot breath raised the hairs on my neck.

Teeth snagged my shirt, tearing through fabric and scratching my skin, and blood welled up, hot and tingling, as I pressed beyond the burn in my lungs to go faster. There wasn't enough light to animate Delilah here to fight back.

The path dropped out entirely from under my heels, and I flailed for a horrible second before I flung myself forward, landing on solid ground at the blue door. There was no knob.

The face loomed over me, its teeth bearing down with a terrifying speed.

I screamed and lobbed Fake Topher's heart at the skeleton specter like a grenade. A fraction of a second later, I realized what I'd done and fumbled to snatch the heart back, but it was too late. The heart flew through a nostril and disappeared into the darkness.

"Rest in peace!" I cried.

The skeleton face froze in shock.

Uncertain of where I'd end up without the heart, but praying it was an upgrade, I flung myself against the door and bashed it open, skidding on my side across wet dirt, back in Pacific Spirit Park on the University Endowment Lands, with a damp mist sprinkling on my face.

The dizziness had subsided but stabbing pain rolled from my

temples down to my teeth. I sat up, hugging my knees to my chest. It didn't matter if I avoided the Kefitzat Haderech, when my humanity was found lacking I'd end up there, because the darkness that fueled my magic bound me to it.

This wasn't the first time I cursed out my parents for not having educated me better in all things magic and it wouldn't be the last. If I had continued using my powers after their murder, especially during my selfish teen years, would I already be haunting that darkness in eternal torment like that poor woman?

Ohrists played Russian Roulette with blindspots every time they used their magic, forcing them to consciously weigh out if using their powers for something was worth the risk. It was a constant reminder that magic came with a price. I'd always assumed the Banim Shovavim were free from that, since our magic was passed down to us by Lilith and Adam, but, as I'd been shown by the Kefitzat Haderech, that wasn't the case.

I pressed my hands against the heavy dullness in my chest, tilting my face to the sky. It was the worst of all Vancouver weather, gray, drizzly, and bleak, but birds still twittered and the sun would come out once more. Though, not for that woman. She'd forever only know darkness and torment, but sitting here with a concussion wouldn't change that. I gingerly stood up, brushed the mud off my coat, and searched the woods for a familiar landmark to get me back to the car.

Tree, trees, fallen log, tree... oh look, there was something I recognized: a pair of brilliant emerald eyes too astute for the wolf's face they inhabited. The creature padded silently closer as though drawn by an invisible connection to me. I snorted. Oh, I knew that furry killing machine all too well.

Laurent Amar, my erstwhile team member, was truly majestic in his wolf form, his fur white as snow, and his body a hard line of muscle that screamed "top of the food chain."

Not that he was all that different in his human form.

I crossed my arms and stood my ground. "If you think I'm

going to cower or hide, guess again. I'm hungry, wet, broken, and I have to pee. Fuck with me, Huff 'n' Puff. I dare you."

He gave me a wolfish grin, his tongue lolling out, and the tenor of his stalking changed, no longer an intimidating prowl, just his run-of-the-mill arrogant loping. At over six feet long and two hundred pounds, that was still a ton of arrogance.

"Yes?" I arched an eyebrow.

The animal reared up onto his hind legs, resting his front paws on my shoulders and I clenched my pelvic floor muscles as hard as I could, because his jaws could snap my neck with no effort whatsoever. He smelled like an ancient forest, rich and earthy with a hint of mustiness.

Maybe it was the concussion talking, but there was something incredible about being close enough to see the wolf actually had eyelashes and how his forepaws on my skin felt cooler than the heat pouring off his body. I trailed my finger against the tips of the wiry fur on his side.

He flicked his tail at me, his heavy claws flexing gently against my shoulder and making me squirm, before he nosed at the lump on my forehead.

I smoothed my bangs over the injury and he growled softly. Cursing Tatiana for calling in this particular cavalry, I pushed him, but he didn't budge. "Make yourself useful and take me to the hospital."

He dropped down onto all fours and caught my coat sleeve none-too-gently.

"You're going to rip my jacket," I said testily. "And I don't get paid well enough to have a massive outfit budget once I've covered my mortgage and fed a teenaged vacuum cleaner."

He graciously allowed me to tug free, then butted me in the small of my back with his long, blunt muzzle to get me moving. He kept the pace slow, guiding me on a circuitous route that was a gentle slope uphill, while deftly avoiding anyone masochistic enough to be hiking the trails in the rain.

I was snapping twigs all over the place, but the wolf trotted along like his paws didn't touch the ground. Grr. I pulled out my phone to check we were headed back to the crashed car. I'd survived the accident, my passenger's murder, and the Kefitzat Haderech. I wasn't incompetent, and the fact that the shifter kept darting glances back like I was a pup who needed minding made my blood boil.

"I'm only following you because I have to go this way," I said.

The wolf ignored me until we reached the tree line. Beyond it was the university highway, but I didn't see the damaged SUV that Tatiana had loaned me.

I planted my hands on my hips. "Now what?"

He sat down with another flick of his tail.

"You want me to wait here. Whatever. Go."

The wolf narrowed his eyes.

I narrowed mine right back. "Where am I going to go in this condition? You're my ride to the hospital. Shift and make yourself useful."

He nudged me back a couple of steps—to be an asshole and show that he could—then he trotted into the trees.

I played Tetris to take my mind off what I'd seen in the KH and how I was being judged but staring at the screen worsened my nausea and dizziness. Unfortunately closing my eyes was also out of the question. My cloaking worked, but honestly, I was too drained to bother, and besides, the only thing I felt like hiding from was the sarcasm Laurent was bound to throw my way.

Staying mostly dry under the leaf cover, I weighed my recent actions. Dispatching dybbuks and vamps had to count as benefitting the greater good, because human welfare had to come first. But what about my other behavior since I'd started working for Tatiana? I'd stolen a ferret for someone with questionable caregiver skills and told some guy he was too incompetent to pursue his criminal dreams.

Then I'd lost the heart.

Was one's humanity destroyed in the face of a single terrible act or did one tiny transgression after another add up to the same fate?

Laurent returned fairly quickly, towering over me with a scowl that was a welcome relief from my thoughts and a large black umbrella gripped in one hand. His shaggy chocolate curls were dark licks plastered to his scalp, and rain spattered his worn brown leather jacket. He did another head-to-toe sweep of me, his expression impassive.

"Enjoying your new gig?" His French-accented English imbued his droll sarcasm with an extra-special haughtiness.

I clenched my fists because even conveying his disdain, he sounded sexy. Damn Frenchmen.

"Did Tatiana send you to shift and eat the evidence?" I said, sweetly. "No need. I dealt with it."

Laurent grasped my elbow and pulled me under the umbrella. "I don't eat humans. Without salt."

He already knew about the death? I stiffened, but forced myself to immediately relax so as not to arouse his suspicions.

His phone beeped and he pulled it out to check the screen.

Laurent was adamant about killing people only after they'd been possessed by a dybbuk and their soul was gone. If he'd become feral, he'd have attacked me in wolf form and he certainly wouldn't be responding to a text with his grumpy face on. He went to great lengths to help people and nothing in my experience painted him as some psychopath able to hide the fact that he'd just murdered some innocent human.

Fake Topher wasn't entirely innocent though, was he?

Given everything that had happened today, could I trust my judgment? I searched his face for reassurance that the man I believed him to be was still present.

Yes, Laurent killed dybbuk-possessed hosts on a regular basis, but there was something very personal about that war he waged. He wouldn't care about what some criminal toddler was up to.

Even if Laurent's powers matched up with the facts of this

killing, other Ohrists magically manipulated organic material and could have pulled it off. Or one could have worked with a vampire with that kind of strength and speed. The murder had occurred in the early morning under an overcast sky, so there was no sunlight to harm a bloodsucker.

The faint scent of cedar that always clung to him washed over me and a knot in my chest loosened. Without question, Laurent was still Laurent, the person who'd repeatedly had my back and helped me deal with some tough emotions.

Also, there was a good chance that if driven to murder, he wouldn't bother to deny it.

"Where were you?" Putting his phone away, he brushed a paw-shaped clump of mud off of my shoulder. "I show up to find a smashed-up car, blood, and no sign of you." His voice was tight. "I found your scent in the woods but it disappeared."

"You know my scent?" I surreptitiously sniffed myself, having started the day with a hot flash that left me soggy. I'd wiped myself down with a damp cloth, but a quick swipe probably didn't make me fresh as a daisy to werewolf smelling.

"I got it off your purse in the trunk," he said.

"My bag!" I looked around. "Wait, where's the SUV?"

"It was towed and sent to an Ohrist for detailing. I have your purse, don't worry."

"Oh. Well, sorry, if I scared you." I wasn't ready or willing to share my experience in the Kefitzat Haderech until I'd processed it further.

"You wasted my whole morning. I'm not being paid for this. Tatiana called in a favor."

"Then allow me to send you on your way." I stomped off across the wet grass, the rain worsening my bedraggled state. Mad and embarrassed and exhausted as I was, his snarkiness rubbed me raw.

There was a reality in which I sailed off, leaving the shifter in the dust feeling pricked by my triumphant exit. Too bad the KH hadn't taken me there.

5

LAURENT CAUGHT UP WITH ME IN A HANDFUL OF long-limbed strides, his hand under my elbow and the umbrella once more over my head. "Tatiana wants to see you."

My heart sank, but I had to face her at some point. "Hospital first. Where's the loaner vehicle?"

"What loaner?"

"Are you kidding me? I can't go with you." I shook my head, immediately regretting it as the world swung sideways.

Laurent's grip on me tightened, his voice a wolfy growl. "Why not?"

"I have a concussion," I said. "As important as Tatiana thinks she is, my well-being's got to take priority."

His hold eased. "And here I thought that lump was cosmetic."

"You got me. I was going for a boob job, but the plastic surgeon assured me this was just as attention-getting and fit my budget better."

His gaze dropped to my chest, and even though I was once more bundled up against the shitty weather, I crossed my arms with a tight smile.

"Not quite as attention getting," he said, not the least bit abashed.

"Allow me to clarify." I massaged a knot in my shoulder with stiff fingers, vowing that if an ER nurse gave me one of those heated blankets, I wouldn't even complain about how long it took to see me. "I refuse to ride on your motorcycle because I'm not confident I can do so without throwing up."

"Sad as it is to deprive myself of that particular joy, I have a truck." Laurent jerked a finger to a blue pickup parked on the other side of the street.

He kept me dry and steady as we jaywalked over to his vehicle, the shifter beeping a fob at it to unlock the doors.

I climbed up onto the seat next to my purse and fastened my seatbelt. Sitting down beat orgasms at this moment, though I suspected that was more a commentary on my lack of a sex life than my injury. "When did you get this?"

"Bought it a few weeks ago and picked it up first thing this morning from a nearby dealership." He shut my door.

I ran a hand over the dashboard. There was no dust other than the mud I'd tracked onto the floor mat, the interior was pristine, and the new car smell was strong, giving credence to his explanation. His proximity would also explain why he'd been sent to assist me.

Outside the truck, Laurent swore loudly in French, wrestling to close the now inside-out umbrella.

I smirked and he glared at me, but when a gust of wind smacked his hair into his eyes, he merely shook his head with a rueful smile.

He finally wrangled the umbrella closed and tossed it into the cargo bed with a clatter.

Jellybean-fat raindrops splattered against the windshield, and I leaned away from the driver's door as Laurent climbed in, running a hand through his hair to shake it out.

"Careful," I said, holding my hands up so I didn't get wet.

He grunted and gently grasped my chin, turning my face into the light.

"What are you doing?"

Laurent nudged my legs aside to pull up the edge of the floor mat, his shoulder and arm pressed against my thigh, his biceps shifting under his jacket, and his hair flopping forward. I curled my fingers into my palms against the temptation to see if the damp curls were as soft as they looked.

There was a soft hiss and a hidden panel popped open, revealing a built-in storage unit. Laurent sat up holding a tiny tube of antibiotic cream and some gauze.

"You picked up your truck today and already have a First Aid kit squirreled away? Aren't you the Boy Scout?"

"Came with the truck." He carefully wiped air bag powder off of my scraped-up face.

As a single mom, I wasn't used to people taking care of me anymore, especially not a younger man whose lush bottom lip was made to be sucked on and whose long lashes dusted his olive skin like a shadowed crescent moon when he looked down at me like this.

My poor brain must have been coshed worse than I thought to be going down this road. I dropped my eyes down to the flex of his denim-clad thigh. Folding the gauze square, he shifted, his quads tensing, leaving me staring at his groin. I jerked my head up so fast that I cracked my nose on his knuckles.

"What's wrong with you?" he said.

I motioned at the gauze. "I can do this myself."

Our gazes clashed, then he tossed the gauze and cream in my lap. "Have at it."

I felt oddly disappointed as I pressed a drop of ointment to my fingertip and worked it into my skin. "Are you still pissed off that I'm working for your aunt or did something else crawl up your ass and die?"

Tatiana wasn't his aunt by blood; Laurent's grandparents were her best friends. She'd known him since he was born and she'd been a large part of his life, but that didn't mean his interactions with her were easy. From what I'd seen, they were anything but.

"This is your third assignment," he said, "and you ended up with a dead man's heart for company. What's on next week's agenda? The apocalypse?"

"No. We negotiated that for my one-month anniversary." I squirted another drop of cream on my finger. "Wait. How did you know it was my third assignment?"

His jaw tightened and he looked out his window.

I felt lighter than I had all day. The weirdo cared about me.

"Are you keeping tabs?" I rubbed cream on my other cheek. "Aw, Huff 'n' Puff, you missed me."

"Like the Jabberwocky missed the vorpal blade."

I screwed the cap back on the tube, stuffing the used gauze in my coat pocket. "Snicker snack."

He turned an annoyed scowl my way. "I offered you a job where you could have made a difference."

I tossed the ointment into the kit, closing the panel lid and smoothing down the mat with my foot. "Working with you without Tatiana's protection would have been a death sentence."

He flicked a finger against the pocket that the heart had been in. "You've got a bit of gristle there."

I glanced down, but there was only some dried blood. Aaand that now counted as a win in my world. "Granted, your concerns about me working for Tatiana were fair, all things considered." I paused. "You don't think that the SUV was targeted because it belonged to Tatiana, do you? That this murder was a message to her?"

She had acted rather blithely about the whole thing, but I'd only ever seen her take things in stride. I made a note to ask her.

"No." Laurent started the engine, a lively violin concerto streaming through the speakers.

I cranked the heat, eagerly anticipating having feeling in my toes again, but he flipped the switch to the air conditioning and rolled down all the windows with a press of a button.

Shivering, I hunched deeper into my jacket. "Most people

freeze others out with body language, not actual sub-zero temperatures. This is a new experience for me."

"You have a concussion, and between the heat and the ride, you might fall asleep." He sounded so annoyed about being concerned about me that a perverse warmth spread through my chest, defying the frigid wind turning the rest of me into a Popsicle.

"That's nice of you."

"Yeah, well, I don't need Tatiana bitching at me if you're out of commission for too long."

I scratched my nose with my middle finger.

He smacked the wheel. "Whether it was or it wasn't a message, you could have been killed. I saw the car. You're lucky you walked away from the crash. Hell, you're lucky you blacked out. The murderer might have assumed the accident did their job for them."

"I know," I said softly.

"Do you? Because for all your talk about protecting your loved ones, I question whether you have any self-preservation instincts. Working for Tatiana, probably not."

"Your opinion was noted the first three times you texted me on the matter," I snapped. "Besides, you're the last person allowed to lecture me on that topic." I crossed my arms. "After all we went through together finding Jude and everything I handled, why don't you have any faith in my ability to take care of myself?"

I looked out the window, blaming the sharp sting of tears on the wind blowing directly in my face.

Laurent pulled a U-turn and headed back into town. "If you were useless, we wouldn't be having this talk."

"I never said 'useless,'" I muttered.

"You're smart and as a Banim Shovavim, you've got powerful and rare magic." He punctuated his words with sharp jabs, leaving only one hand on the wheel, and driving perilously close to the car ahead of us.

47

I grabbed the oh-shit handle, my entire body stiffening, and my foot slamming on imaginary brakes.

He placed a hand on my tense shoulder, slowing the vehicle down. "Your powers don't just make you valuable," he said, "they make you a threat. Now you're working for Tatiana, and the wrong kinds of people are going to notice you."

I twisted around to look at him, shrugging his hand off. "I'm not hiding my magic again."

Laurent shot me a sideways glance but remained silent. Fine by me. I rolled my window up a bit and watched the city speed by.

"There's this couple that disappeared the other day," he said. "They were celebrating their anniversary with champagne. Only a couple of glasses each, but it was enough. They walked away from jobs, friends, family, everything. Their families suspect they were possessed and now I get to hunt them down and dispatch them. If you'd caught them while they were enthralled, they'd still be around to celebrate next year."

"How? Should I have gone door to door checking Ohrists? Is saving these people important? Yes. Do you have a viable way for me to find them in the first place?"

He didn't answer.

"Yeah. That's what I thought. No plan, no promises, just a lot of feel-good what-ifs and false hope."

"And if I did have a way," he said, "would you stop working for Tatiana?"

When I didn't answer he made a quiet scoffing sound. "That's what I thought."

"Would you pay me enough to support my kid, like she does? Help me find who killed my parents all those years ago? Keep Zev off my back?"

He flipped the bird to a car that was cutting him off and then switched lanes. "What if I could? Would you quit?"

Taking all the reasons I signed up with Tatiana off the table, would I work with Laurent channeling my magic solely into saving the enthralled, rather than catering to the whims of the rich and shady, and ending up in dangerous situations like today?

I had a concussion, every part of my body hurt, and yet my brush with death had intensified my lust for life. "I want more out of life than being a caretaker." I shrugged. "I still am with Sadie, and I love being her mom, but I'm also not going to apologize for wanting some adventure in my life. I suppressed my magic and hid away in dry libraries for too long. No more."

The image of that poor woman in the Kefitzat Haderech flashed before my eyes and my hand tightened on my seatbelt. I would find Fake Topher's killer and redeem myself for yeeting his heart into the abyss. Bring closure to his loved ones.

Topping up my karma points with the KH was a happy side benefit.

I bit my lip. Did it count as doing good if it was in my best interests to do so? Did I have to be a virtuous person for its own sake versus to avoid being punished? Was even feeling good about an anonymous good deed considered selfish?

"Amazing," Laurent said. "Even with a concussion, I can hear you thinking." He sighed. "Go ahead. Speak."

I clasped my hands together primly and spoke with an exaggerated gooeyness. "Thank you for your permission. How did I ever stumble through life without your guidance?"

His lips quirked up. "Beats me."

"When you figure it out—"

"I'll be sure to let you know."

"I was going to say, 'Keep it to yourself.'" I smiled sweetly and he laughed. "Anyway, someone offed this guy exactly how you kill a dybbuk, except there wasn't one. I'd have sensed something." I stuffed my poor ice cubed hands into my armpits.

He pulled a pair of gloves out of his pocket and tossed them at me.

I put them on with a moan: kid leather with a thick fur lining. "Aren't you cold?"

"If I was, would you give them back, Mitzi?"

I pursed my lips, but ended up grinning. "No, but I'd feel bad for half a minute."

White wolf fur burst out over his hands. "Save your guilt. I keep them for going out in public when I can't partially shift."

"Show-off," I said. "Okay, so other than you, who could have pulled this off?"

"A Banim Shovavim," he said. "The only other ones who can kill a dybbuk."

I made a noise like a buzzer. "Thanks for playing, but we don't need to rip out the host's heart. I doubt I even can, so that's hardly the best way to throw suspicion on my kind. Now, if it wasn't a Banim Shovavim..."

"Then someone is hoping I'll take the fall." His tone was grim.

I turned the idea around in my mind, sighing at how well it fit—except for one important fact. "Why would anyone frame you when you have full permission to kill dybbuks? How would anyone other than you know the victim wasn't possessed if you say that he was? You're the only one who can scent them."

"You've never seen one of their corpses once rigor mortis sets in. They get red streaks similar to blood poisoning." His hands tightened on the wheel, the fur spreading up along his wrists before he made it vanish altogether. "A lot of people don't see any difference between me killing the dybbuk-possessed and killing a person. If the Lonestars decide I've crossed that line and gone feral..." He pressed his lips into a thin line, then shook his head. "It's best if I know who actually did it before they get involved."

I stared out the window, closing my eyes against the wind that was rather winter-like for June. If the corpse wasn't found, Laurent might be able to claim the deceased had been possessed, but if it was and there weren't red streaks, he'd be the prime suspect for sure.

I'd spent decades avoiding all Lonestars, and until I could

definitively prove what their role in my parents' murder almost thirty years ago was, I wasn't inclined to trust any of these magic cops. I certainly wasn't about to insist that Laurent put his faith in them.

"It's still not the only possibility," I said. "The heart could be indicative of a message. If not to Tatiana, then perhaps to the victim's family. The only thing we know for sure is that whoever did it worked quickly and was able to remove a heart with very little blood loss."

"All signs pointing to my magic, which is publicly known." His words were rushed, his accent heavier in his distress.

"Calm down," I said. "It just means magic, period. The one power you have that other Ohrists absolutely do not is scenting out dybbuks. As for the rest of it, can you definitively say that no other Ohrist has the magic to pull off this crime?"

"No, but…" Laurent braked at a red light, drumming his fingers on the steering wheel, then sharply swung his head my way. For all that he was a wolf shifter, being caught in the focus of those twin emerald lasers was like having captured the attention of a deadly jungle cat. "Did you suspect me?"

"No."

He scoffed bitterly, but when the light turned green, he slowly pulled forward so my post-crash anxiety didn't flare up again. "Lie. Your heart sped up."

"I firmly dismissed you as a possible suspect due to your charming demeanor," I said. "If you planned to hurt me, you'd make sure your face was the last thing I saw."

Laurent shifted his fingers to claws and flexed them at me. "Snicker snack."

He gave a rusty laugh and my heart twisted. It was exactly how he'd sounded when I first met him, though he'd laughed more freely over our handful of days working together.

Laurent had assisted me recently when a date had gone horribly wrong, but other than that and his annoying texts after that night, work had consumed me once I'd given notice at my law firm. I'd had to sit in on interviews for my replacement, then I'd been ensconced with Tatiana and the first two jobs. He and I hadn't interacted much and I'd missed this irritating human.

We bounced over a pothole that jarred my teeth together.

"Someone deliberately made it look like a dybbuk killing," he said. "They're trying to frame me."

I nodded. "I'll help you."

"Absolutely not."

"Did you or did you not just say that I was smart and powerful? I believe you also used the term 'valuable.'" I curled my toes giddily. Laurent was not one to freely give out praise. If he truly was being framed, he'd need a stealthy partner like me digging up info behind the scenes.

"Words I'm already regretting," he said.

"Is your inability to accept help some pride thing?"

"Don't be ridiculous."

"Then do you not trust me to help you?"

"That's not it," he said begrudgingly, and sighed. "Look, the more people poking around, the harder we'll kick the hornet's nest. I'll deal with it myself."

"I can't walk away. That kid didn't deserve to die. I was the last one to see him alive—"

"All the more reason to be grateful for your narrow escape and lay low."

"Even though I can't make things right for that young man," I said, "I can at least get him justice. Put my librarian and Banim Shovavim skills to use and find the murderer."

"No. It was one thing for you to tag along while we found Jude—"

"Tag along?!"

"But this is murder. You have no experience tracking down killers."

"Like you do?"

He shot me a pointed stare.

"Okay, yes. Dybbuks. But non-possessed killers?"

"It's no different," he said. "Stay out of this and let me find the responsible party."

As his friend, I wanted to respect his stupid wishes, but I couldn't. The image of my passenger wide-eyed and looking like a scared kid was burned into my brain. I owed him, and I was investigating this come hell, high water, or Laurent Amar.

Laurent pulled up to a Tudor Revival mansion with rustic doors, gables, and a brown-and-cream decorative façade in the heart of Shaughnessy, a historically WASPy, old-money residential neighborhood on Vancouver's west side.

"What happened to 'hospital first?'" I fanned the collar of my shirt, riding out a dizzy spell. Couldn't he see I required medical attention, not a lecture from my boss?

"I was told to bring you directly to the belly of the beast. She has a healer waiting for you," he added.

That sounded way better than sitting around in the ER. I unbuckled my seatbelt. "This seems like an odd choice of abode for Tatiana." I furrowed my brows. "I expected something more, well, less."

My boss wasn't merely a fixer for the magic community, she was a globally renowned painter with a career that had spanned decades. This place didn't scream "creative spirit" so much as "have another crumpet."

"Her late husband Sam had his heart set on buying here as a fuck-you, since his parents had been denied a home in this neighborhood despite their wealth because they were Jews. It's not her style but she stays in his memory."

"That's sweet, I guess." I would have moved into something more to my liking, but I'd never lost a partner I'd been married to for decades, either.

Some girl who looked about sixteen, in black high tops and an oversized sweater with giant pink poppies, threw open the front door and waved.

"Merde!" Laurent slammed his hand on the wheel.

"Is your aunt subcontracting to children now?" I said. "Because I will unionize that shit." I raised a fist.

Laurent yanked his keys out of the ignition. "That tricky bitch."

I smacked him. "Don't talk about the girl that way."

"I meant Tatiana." He got out of the car, foregoing the umbrella, and hopped puddles over to the newcomer.

Her face lit up and she leapt off the front stoop to run at Laurent, jumping on him.

He didn't stagger back a single step, however, he did heave a full-body sigh and make a point of wiping off the lip smack she pressed to his cheek.

The girl simply laughed, open and joyful, catching her hood before it slid off her dark hair.

By this point, I'd joined them, having grabbed the umbrella. "Hello."

"Hi. I'm Juliette." She pronounced her "j" like a "zh," her French-accented English more pronounced than Laurent's, though up close she wasn't quite as young as I'd imagined.

"Miri." We walked to the door. "Are you Laurent's... sister?"

"She's the bane of my existence," Laurent said. "Who was supposed to be back in Paris where she belongs."

"What Lolo means to say is that I am his favorite niece. I'm also your healer." She seemed to catalog my injuries in a swift glance. "I understand you've had quite a traumatic morning."

"You could say that." I shook out the umbrella and, closing it, rested it on the porch. "Forgive my rudeness, but aren't you a bit young to be a healer? Even with Ohrist magic?"

"I was in second year med school until I left to take a gap year, so I have a foundation in both magical and practical treatments." Juliette gave a very Gallic shrug and motioned for me to step into the foyer. "Being smarter than everyone else is terribly exhausting and my poor twenty-year-old self required a break."

I slipped off my wet shoes, wishing my socks weren't still damp, and stifled a snort at her melodramatic tone. Sadie would love her. Decision made: they could never meet. "Did your parents buy that excuse?"

She grinned, shaking her head. "Pas de tout."

"Is Tatiana around?" I said.

"She's working in her studio and will be out in a while," Juliette replied.

The inside of the mansion was more in line with what I'd envisioned. Walls must have been removed to open the space up and allow for maximum light and flow, showcasing massive colorful canvases hung on ivory walls.

Over the mantel was a painting of Jackie Onassis caught peeking out a window of the White House and signed with Tatiana's bold scrawl. Everything from the pleated folds of the curtain bunched in Jackie's hand to the intricate detail of the ornamental mouldings under the sill was painstakingly photorealistic, starkly contrasting with the plastic sheen to the woman's skin and fake stiffness of her individual strands of dark hair.

On either side of the painting were smaller framed prints of rough sketches of other famous women who were married to celebrated men, such as Eva Peron and Zelda Fitzgerald, along with smears of color used in the palettes of the paintings made from the drawings. A note in slanted block printing said *Dollhouse Collection*.

Every shade of green was represented in the lush plant life in the living room, some bearing tiny white blossoms, others waxy leaves, and one memorable plant with heavy purple spiky flowers. I closed my eyes and inhaled, imagining I was in the Italian countryside, then reluctantly turned back to the argument raging on behind me as it switched from a burst of French back to English.

"For someone so smart, you're making pretty dumb life choices. You should go home instead of being tangled up in Tatiana's business," Laurent said.

Juliette poked his chest. "How would you know what I'm tangled up in? You never come to visit me and you ignored my dad when he was here."

"Do I need to cross another ocean to get away from all of you?" he said.

"You can avoid us all you want, but it won't change anything."

This was above my pay grade.

I stepped backward, my shoulders tense, which only made my poor head throb harder. "Is there somewhere I could sit down?"

Juliette pointed down the hallway. "First room on the left. Let me finish getting it ready for you." She gave her uncle a smile with too many teeth and left.

"Not one word," he said.

A concussion, murder, and family drama. The last thing I wanted to do was continue fighting with Laurent.

"Thanks for the ride," I said. "I'll call Jude to get me once I'm done, since she's coming over for dinner anyway."

"Do I have your promise to keep out of this business?"

"Oh, the pain," I said, gripping my head. I hurried into the room that Juliette had indicated and locked the door.

"Yeah. He has that effect on people." Juliette lit a vanilla-scented candle and blew out the match. "Shall we begin?"

I lay down on a heated massage table that had been covered with a fuzzy blanket, the warmth seeping into my stiff back. "Ooh," I moaned.

While Juliette worked on my concussion, her magic infusing into my head like the whisper of silk, I darted glances at the locked door every few minutes while I silently ran through arguments until I had a reasonable case laid out for why I intended to investigate this, but Laurent didn't knock.

"Quit thinking about him," Juliette murmured.

"I'm not."

She chuckled. "My uncle inspires a particular tension in people and right now, it's got you wrapped like a fly in a spiderweb."

"Humph." I did my best to relax, but there was no way he'd accepted my decision.

I scowled up at the ceiling. Huff 'n' Puff would probably go behind my back and bounce me off this case. I bunched the blanket in my clenched fists. Let him try.

"Miriam." Juliette sighed. "My magic won't be as effective or efficient if you cannot relax."

I mimed pulling the thoughts out of my head and blowing them away.

The healing session lasted a while, and under Juliette's gentle ministrations, the heat of the table, and the scent of vanilla, my entire body unwound. I must have dozed off, because I started awake at the sound of the door opening.

Juliette was gone.

Tatiana stepped inside with her customary oversized red glasses and silver pixie cut and I tried not to gasp at her appearance. The spry eighty-year-old wore a red sweater that I swear had begun life as a shag rug before being pressed into fashion service, a black mini skirt, and chunky black-and-white runners.

"Nu?" She barked out the Yiddish question. "You all fixed?"

I ran a finger across my forehead. The lump was gone and my head was clear and pain-free. "Yes. Juliette does good work. Thanks for letting me see her."

"Well, my parents didn't flee communist Russia so that my employee could sit in a waiting room pissing in the wind with a concussion."

I frowned. "That's not really a direct correla—"

Tatiana raised an eyebrow and I shut my mouth. She insisted

on driving me home, since I'd totally forgotten about phoning Jude, and my boss wished to discuss something with me.

Putting on my damp shoes was almost as bad as the dread in my gut at whatever she was going to say. Was she mad about what had happened? Had Laurent already dissuaded her from having me work this case?

Tatiana tottered out to the sidewalk, while I followed behind her with my arms out, ready to catch her if she fell. She turned in a slow circle, trying to spot her vehicle. "Where did I leave you?"

At least it had stopped raining.

After several trips back and forth along the rows of parked cars, she slapped her forehead. "I'm on the next block. Did you deal with the you-know-what?"

Reluctantly, I followed her over to a big old gold Buick from the 1970s. Dorothy could have dropped it on the wicked witch and saved herself a house. "Yes. No one will ever find it."

"Good." Tatiana unlocked the doors, settled herself behind the wheel, then took a good minute to find the slot for the key.

I nervously buckled my seatbelt.

She moved our bench seat forward and back several times before returning it to the exact same spot it had been in, accidentally turned the wipers on, and managed to pop the trunk—making me go close it—all before she'd pulled out.

"I could call my friend," I offered. "It's no trouble, really."

Tatiana narrowed her bright blue eyes at me and I gave a weak laugh.

"I'm an excellent driver." She pulled out without checking over her shoulder for oncoming cars.

The VW camper van behind us screeched to a halt, the driver leaning on the horn.

Tatiana stuck her hand out the window and shot the guy the finger.

I dug my nails into the side of the seat and spent the next few minutes giving myself a pep talk that I was in a vehicle only slightly smaller than Noah's Ark and if we hit anything, we'd probably run right over it.

"What happened with Topher?" There was no avoiding that I'd screwed up, albeit accidentally, and not actually picked up her client. I checked my face with my phone's camera but not only were the abrasions gone, my skin had a dewy youthfulness that no amount of face cream ever achieved. "Did he get a ride out to the airport?"

"When you didn't show, he made up some excuse about catching cold from standing in the rain and postponed his departure a few days. The deal's off; the Sharmas will make other arrangements elsewhere. In the meantime, neither of us can be implicated in this scenario."

The Sharmas still didn't know what had happened, including the fact that Fake Topher existed. Had existed. I plucked at a loose thread on the hem of my shirt.

Decades of habits like making safe choices, and staying under the radar of the Lonestars, or anyone tied to my parents' deaths, were hard to break. Burying this under the rug was the safest option for me. I could walk away, and no matter what happened, there would be no proof of my ever having met the victim.

It might have been safe but it wouldn't be right. I'd shared Life Savers with the dead man, and there was probably some proverb somewhere about candy bonding making you the one to lay their spirit to rest.

"Is there any way the killing was some kind of message for you?" I said.

"To what end?" She shook her head. "Besides, people who come after me don't tend to be subtle about it."

I twisted a curl around my finger. Given the manner of death, Laurent's theory that he'd been framed was the most plausible right now. Was the victim an innocent pawn or had he been chosen specifically for some reason?

"Take a couple days off," Tatiana said, slowing down through a green light.

I flinched, hitting an imaginary gas pedal with my foot. "I want to speak to the real Topher and get to the bottom of what happened."

"Leave it alone."

"What?" I frowned. "No."

"This is a fakakta situation. Also, we haven't been hired to get involved. Contrary to what they'd have you believe at temple, mitzvahs don't get you a villa in the French Riviera."

I gaped at her. "You have a villa?"

"Do you think I bed down in some ramshackle Airbnb with the rest of the shmucks?" She took her hands off the wheel to punctuate her words, almost taking out my eye with her large topaz cocktail ring, and sent the car drifting to the left.

I'd be lucky to afford a campsite in Cannes, never mind something with a roof and walls. It was a sad day when shmuck was an aspirational goal. I grabbed the wheel and jerked us back into the center of our lane. "Then get us hired."

"You're very agitated, Miriam." She took her eyes off the road to root around in her bag—while making a right turn. "I've got some Ativan in here."

"Face front!" I grabbed the purse away, thankful for a street empty of pedestrians, kids on bikes, or other tempting targets for Tatiana. "I'm not agitated. You're a menace."

My boss grinned impishly. "Guilty as charged. Tell me why you care so much about this?"

I took a few calming breaths, formulating the best strategy. "Someone used their knowledge of your clientele against you. This wasn't random."

"That's true," she said, "but the Topher imposter is dead, and no one other than you, me, Laurent, and the murderer knows that the victim was actually in the car. None of us are going to let that slip. My trustworthiness is intact, but if we go poking around, our involvement will be known and my reputation questioned. So, we are going to let this lie."

"What about the fact that I was in that car and I could have been killed? For all I know, someone still might come after—stop sign! Stop sign!"

Tatiana slammed the brakes on halfway through the thankfully empty intersection, her arm flinging out to keep me from going through the window.

"Pull over." I reached for the seat belt release. "I'm walking the rest of the way."

"Unclench your ovaries, bubeleh. You're almost home."

I remained in the car, waiting another block before I spoke. "I want justice for the victim."

"Eh. I'm still not convinced this is a good use of my resources."

How nice to live in a reality where you didn't have to worry about justice, only convenience.

I didn't want to play this card, but if it got me on the case…

"Laurent thinks he's being framed, okay? He doesn't want me to get involved, but if he goes charging into this on his own without backup, who knows what will happen?"

Technically, this was a very real concern. However, regarding any other motivations I had? Let's just say I didn't entirely trust her. She'd never asked if I could travel through the Kefitzat Haderech and I wasn't about to enlighten her. Who knew what she'd do with that information—or worse, have me do?

"Lolo was smart enough to figure that out, huh?" Tatiana mused.

I did a double take. "Do *you* think he's being framed?"

The duplex that Eli and I had bought after our divorce ten years ago, each taking half in order to give our daughter some stability, came into view. My ex had mowed both our lawns last weekend and recently applied a new coat of stain to the front stairs. It wasn't a mansion, but with its wide porch, arched windows on the second floor, and large cherry tree in the front yard, it had its own inviting charm. I'd never been so happy to be home.

We drove past it.

"That was my place," I said, gesturing over my shoulder.

"I'm aware."

Tatiana drove around the block several times until she found a spot large enough to accommodate this behemoth. Half a block seemed a bit excessive, but once she started backing in, hitting the curb no matter how she turned the wheel, all the extra room made a lot more sense.

She parked in a diagonal, half up on the grass, but still hadn't answered my question about Laurent being framed. Did she think he'd done it? Was that why she'd made me get rid of the heart in the first place?

"About Laurent," I said.

Tatiana pulled a slim manila envelope out of her purse. "I looked into that other matter that you asked about."

Tamping down my disappointment and confusion that the subject of investigating the murder appeared to be closed, I scanned the first page, labelled "Fred McMurtry." He'd been the Lonestar in charge of Northern British Columbia when my parents were killed.

The elderly artist grabbed a lipstick out of her purse, pulling down the car's visor to reveal a mirror. "Are you sure the Lonestars set the fire?" She painted bright red over her lips then made a couple of kissing noises, her mouth puckered, swiping her finger to wipe away a smudge. "The assassins could as easily have burned down your family home to hide evidence of the crime."

"We lived in a rural area, and whoever set it timed the call to the Sapien firehouse for our place to become engulfed, but not spread to the woods or any other home." I flipped to the next page of the dossier. "They must have been intimately acquainted with the roads in that area and known precisely how long it took to respond to calls. Also, prime directive of keeping magic hidden, remember? It was the Lonestars, but I'm not out for revenge. I simply want to find out who gave them the heads-up in the first place."

That was who I'd take my vengeance on.

I tapped a paragraph that Tatiana had underlined. "Are you positive?"

She squinted at the paper. "Yes. McMurtry got a diagnosis of terminal liver cancer right before all this happened and then shortly after the murders he disappeared for three weeks. When he came back, he was fine."

"I'd say so, considering he's lived another thirty years. Could he have gone to an Ohrist healer?"

"Not for terminal cancer."

"Thank you." I pressed the envelope against my chest, deciding to make one last appeal. "And regarding Topher, we don't have to admit that the fake client was in the car or anything about Laurent. Tell the Sharmas that someone pretending to be Topher was waiting for me outside their home. I got suspicious, sent him away, and called you. Don't even mention the murder at this point, simply that we'd like to figure out who this person was out of concern for the family's well-being. Fake Topher seemed a little odd and I'd like to reach out and maybe get help for the troubled guy."

Tatiana smirked. "How devious, Miriam. I didn't think you had it in you."

My chest grew tight, as if a tiny bit of my humanity had been sucked out. I felt like Westley in *The Princess Bride*, strapped to the Machine and whimpering every time another year was taken off my life, while that asshole neon sign loomed over me, encouraging me to be honest about my feelings.

"It's not deviousness," I said. "Why make the Sharmas feel unsafe when we don't know if this was a harmless prank gone wrong or not?"

She made a non-committal sound and released the emergency brake with a clunk. "I'll speak to the family and convince them it's in their best interests to hire us."

"I appreciate it."

"Don't get excited yet. You're not doing anything unless they meet my fee. I won't have it put about that my people do pro bono work."

"Oh, the horror." I grinned at her.

"Go away, before I regret my generosity." She waited until I was out of the car before calling me back to the open passenger window.

I bent down. "Yes?"

"Laurent may be a wolf," she said, "but he's like a dog with a bone when he puts his mind to something."

I tilted my head, mentally weighing the evidence of whether he was in league with Tatiana. "And?"

"If my nephew decided he doesn't want you involved, there's only one thing I can say."

"What?"

She waggled her fingers at me before putting the beast back into gear and beginning the process of backing out once more. "Have fun."

"HE KEEPS WHIPPING IT OUT TO SHOW IT OFF." MY best friend Jude Rachefsky pulled three white plates out of my red maple shaker kitchen cupboard. She was dressed in her usual black jeans and a faded black shirt with a smear of clay on one arm. "I should have made him a three-foot dick to stand around on instead. Bless his heart."

"Careful, there. Your Georgia is showing." Most of the time her Savannah-born-and-raised accent was just a hint of molasses flavoring her voice, but every now and again, she busted out some priceless saying that only a true Southern woman could pull off.

Jude winked at me.

"Poor Emmett." I set bamboo mats out on the table, motioning for Jude to put the plates next to the stove. "In his defense, he was a pretty miserable golem without his leg. He's probably over the moon to be bipedal again."

"Oh no, he's just as miserable. Maybe more, only mobile." She held up the robust Merlot we'd already made good inroads on with a questioning look, and at my nod topped up both our wine glasses. "He sits there on my couch drinking and watching *Golden Girls* reruns."

I took my glass but moved a bit too quickly into her personal space and she flinched.

"Whoops." Her laughter was slightly forced, but I smiled, going along with her bravado. Jude had never been one to dwell on the bad times; however, the PTSD of her abduction and dybbuk enthrallment three weeks ago was still fresh, and you didn't easily bounce back from something like that. Luckily, her shadow had grown back, her magic was at full power, and she'd found a good therapist who specialized in magic traumas.

"If Emmett starts spouting stories about when he was a girl in Sicily," I joked, "we'll do an intervention."

She slumped over the butcher block countertop and said darkly, "Or I'll unmake him."

"As if." Lifting the lid off the Bolognese sauce, I was hit with the scent of earthy tomatoes. I dipped a spoon in for a quick taste. "More salt?"

Jude had offered to order take-out for us all, but this simple act of cooking something familiar grounded me in a desperately needed normalcy.

My friend blew on the spoon before trying the sauce. "A smidge more." She ground in some kosher salt, while I dumped pasta in the pot of boiling water. "I'll rework Emmett into an ugly teapot and candlesticks if he keeps pissing me off."

"Sure you will, which was why you didn't even wait until your fractured fingers had healed before making him his new leg. Face it, Dr. Frankenstein, you created him and now you're responsible for him." I set the timer on the stove. "That's how it works."

Any Ohrist with animator magic could fashion a golem and make the clay limbs move, but Jude's ability went deeper than that. She'd been able to give Emmett sentience. And divination magic, but that was a whole other can of worms.

"Bah." Jude grabbed the colander and placed it in the sink. "You're a great mother," she said. "How do you feel about adoption?"

"I think that even the Sapien perception filter couldn't keep Sadie from noticing a clay man with a filthy mouth bunking with us."

The motion sensor in our backyard turned on and I peered out the window. "Speak of the devil, she's home."

My daughter tramped up the back stairs with all the grace of a waterlogged elephant.

"I'd never have guessed," Jude said wryly.

I closed the vintage white curtains with the cherry print with a frown. I'd always maintained they added a touch of whimsy to the room, but a pop of cherry was no match for the tsunami of beige that permeated my home. Maybe I should paint the house, liven the place up a bit.

Sadie threw the door open, one hand flying to her forehead, and the breeze ruffling the hem of her yellow sundress. "Feed me, Mother, for I am about to expire of famine." Her stomach rumbled.

I'd been asked more than once when Sadie was growing up if I was her nanny due to her Chinese heritage, which was stupid, because put us side by side and there was no doubt this kid was mine. People could be remarkably short-sighted. "You are so your father's child, O melodramatic one."

"Like she only gets that from Eli." Jude tossed Sadie a bun from the bread basket beside the plates.

Sadie caught it and bit into it with a grin. "Thanks, Aunt Jude," she said, spraying crumbs everywhere.

I was grateful that Juliette had done such a great job with my injuries and I didn't have to come up with a story for my daughter because I hated lying to her and Eli about this part of my life. My ex already thought I was crazy to quit my job as a law firm librarian to archive and manage decades worth of documents while Tatiana wrote her memoirs.

If he knew the truth about my work for her, our hard-won friendship since our marriage had blown up would be decimated. I was the responsible, grounded, *risk-averse* parent, while Eli pursued his dream of being a homicide detective, with all the crazy hours and dark dives into the human psyche that entailed. He'd always been clear about keeping Sadie and me away from all that, and if he learned how much I'd deviated from my assigned role as the safe, predictable parent, he wouldn't take it well.

Hopefully, for my peace of mind, he'd never find out, although I did still need to break past his perception filters to show him that magic existed for his own safety. However, that was best attempted when he was relaxed and in a good mood.

The timer went off, and I grabbed the pot and dumped the pasta into the colander. A cloud of steam fogged up the window, making me blink against the blast of heat.

Sadie wriggled out of her backpack, which landed on a chair with a thud.

"Come here, kid." Her honorary aunt held out her arms and Sadie hugged her.

My daughter scraped Jude's chin with her fingernail. "You've got clay schmutz."

Jude shrugged and planted a kiss to the top of Sadie's head. "What else is new?"

As a potter with a successful line of dishware and teapots, Jude always had bits of clay in her hair and under her fingers and dust streaked across her black clothing. It had been hard enough for her to return to her studio since she'd been abducted from there, but today she'd spoken excitedly about a new line of dishes that she'd come up with inspired by the ceramic designs of Bordallo Pinheiro, the Portuguese artist. Part of me had worried that she'd never want to create again after what had happened, so this was huge.

Jude didn't use her Ohrist animator magic for her art, and thankfully, was not inclined to make another golem.

Emmett was one of a kind and it was best he stayed that way.

"Guess what you two get to do tonight?" Sadie said. "Other than drink?"

Jude scrunched up her red curls with her hand. "The child is judging us, Mir."

"Her sister judged us," I joked, rinsing the pot out with cold water. "And look what happened to her. Shipped off to a gulag with only a goat and her wits."

"Yes, yes," my daughter said impatiently. "I live in terror. But seriously. It's not like you guys are doing anything important, right?"

"For your information, smarty pants," I said, plucking the driest answer out of my brain, "Jude and I intend to discuss a proposed foreign stimulus package."

"Yeah." Jude smirked. "A French one. I think it has merit."

I flung my hair out of my face with my arm, grateful the flush on my cheeks could be attributed to the steam from the pasta. Welp, I'd walked into that one.

"What did you have in mind?" I threw the pasta back in the pot and ladled enough sauce over it to color it, before dishing it out with more sauce on top.

"I'm going to show you my three-hundred-page yearbook in painstaking detail," Sadie said. "There will be a quiz."

I groaned. "Is this payback for making you take gym this year?"

"Got it in one. Also because if you'd given me a sibling like I asked for, I could have shown them." Sadie unzipped her backpack.

"But you wouldn't agree to feed and change it, so that's on you," I said. "We're about to eat, so wash your hands and take your locker contents into the living room."

Jude followed Sadie out of the kitchen, grilling her on her last day of tenth grade and her upcoming job as a junior counsellor at a theater camp for younger kids.

I'd kept my mind on dinner, but when I grabbed the fridge handle to get the Parmesan, I came eye-to-eye with the heart-shaped magnet on the corner of the photo of Sadie mugging with her cousin Nessa and shivered, the feel of dried blood and that rubbery heart sending me racing to the sink to wash my hands.

Fake Topher had expected to steal a ride and do what? If he'd known about the assignment, then he'd been aware I was going straight to the airfield. Do not pass go, do not collect $200. Had he planned to take Topher's place and fly to Los Angeles?

And what was in that satchel? The deceased had been extremely protective of it, and it was gone along with the body. Did the motive for this murder lie with whatever was inside it?

I longed to call Laurent so the two of us could strategize and spitball theories together, but he was so adamant about doing this on his own that I decided to wait until I had something concrete to share. He'd still argue, but if I was already knee-deep in the investigation, hopefully it would be more of a grumble than a thundering "Thou shalt not."

Not that his protests would stop me.

"Mom?"

"Ack!" I pressed my hand to my chest, water droplets flying.

Sadie got me a glass. "I'm cutting you off. Drink some water."

"I'm not drunk," I said, but had some water anyway.

Dinner was an easygoing meal, and while I did my best to stay in the moment, I compiled questions in my head, antsy to dive into this case.

Jude knew the truth about my job, and if nothing else, Sadie had to learn about vampires. Not having magic, she was safe from any dybbuks trying to use her as a host, but bloodsuckers only turned Sapiens, since Lonestars had decreed Ohrists off-limits. Perhaps Banim Shovavim were fair game, but it seemed the vamps stuck to Sapiens. I didn't know if Sadie would be terrified or fascinated and wasn't sure which would be worse.

I kept up my end of the conversation and was even feigning enthusiasm after dinner for all the strangers she pointed out in her yearbook, when her phone rang.

She paused her story about her weird math teacher, glanced

at the screen, and then turned the phone face down before jumping back into the tale.

Jude shot me a questioning look over Sadie's bent head and I shrugged.

The phone rang again and I recognized the ringtone. It was Carly Rae Jepsen's "Call Me Maybe."

"You can answer that," I said.

"I'll call them back." Sadie tapped a photo. "Now this is Ms. Spenser. The one who got caught smoking weed with the grade twelves on the senior camping trip."

Jude mimed snapping her fingers in disappointment and I hid my grin. Our nosiness would have to wait. If the child had a crush, she was playing her cards close to her chest.

My best friend left around eleven when I couldn't stop yawning, and Sadie took off to phone whomever had called earlier. My bed had never felt as comfy as it did that night, and I only barely remembered settling in under the covers before I was out.

I woke up Thursday morning to a text from Tatiana with the all-clear to speak to Topher, and flung off the covers, a spring in my step.

Cranking a little Donna Summer, I applied my favorite Dragon Lady Red lipstick and three coats of mascara, my hips wiggling, and threw on a black one-piece jumpsuit that I'd bought for work. Normally, I'd wear it with a conservative blazer, since it clung to my curves in a way that was super sexy but not business appropriate. Those days were over. No more lawyers' demands, no more researching case law that put me to sleep, and no days that bled into each other without end.

I had a murder to solve and karma points to build up. In the grand scheme of things, my actions had to matter more than my motivation.

I settled in at my kitchen table with a latte and a scone to do some digging, starting with the real Topher Sharma. There had to be some reason that the deceased had chosen to impersonate him, but Topher didn't have much in the way of a social media presence beyond an Instagram account with photos of him surfing in tropical locations and partying it up with the rich and beautiful.

However, it answered the question of how Fake Topher had intended to fool the staff on the airplane, because the man I'd chauffeured yesterday resembled the real client, from his frosted platinum hair to his similar build and South Asian heritage. If the imposter had kept his oversized hood up, he would have pulled off his ruse.

I jotted down notes in an unused hardcover notebook with a green paisley print that I'd gotten as swag at one of my law librarian conferences. Yes, those were exactly as exciting as they sounded. The only noteworthy time had been when we'd been booked into the same hotel as a mob wedding. I'd never heard so many F-bombs or had so many scary people express their willingness to kick ass with a single glare. And that was just the women.

Further searches on Topher brought up a number of family photos. The Sharmas were good looking and obviously comfortable with being photographed.

Taking a sip of now-cold latte, I made a face, pushing the mug away to scroll through news articles about the engineering firm that Mr. and Mrs. Sharma had established and catapulted into a successful global player.

Neither of them fit my clichéd image of engineers. Both in their early fifties, Krish Sharma looked like the former rugby player he'd been, with a nose that had been broken at least once, while his wife Ellis was a cool, dignified blonde. However, they held master's degrees in mechanical and electric engineering respectively.

I chewed on the pen tip. There had to be something more to this than the fact that the imposter looked like Topher and the Sharmas had a plane. How had the victim learned about them in the first place? I kept digging.

The final member of the family was the daughter, Asha. Two

years younger than Topher, putting her at twenty-one, she had carved out her own niche as a competitive swimmer.

The family had a good reputation in business circles, but of course, there was no mention of their magic, so I had no clue what type of Ohrists they were. Nor did I know if the dead man was a Sapien or an Ohrist. I wrote that down, drawing a circle around it to look into later once he'd been identified.

He was unlikely to have been Banim Shovavim, though I'd check. Sapiens made up most of the world's population, and while Ohrists were a much smaller percentage, they comprised about 99 percent of every human with magic. My kind were incredibly rare nowadays.

The research hadn't unearthed anything. Hopefully my interview with the Sharmas would.

After putting my dishes in the dishwasher, I left Sadie a note that I was off to work. I doubted I'd hear from her, however. One of her friends was having an end-of-the-year pool party and Sadie was going over early to help set up.

As I locked up, Eli came up our shared front walk yawning. His suit was rumpled, and his police badge sat askew. He blinked at me, rubbing a hand over his bald head. "Hey, Mir."

My heart did a little squeeze, remembering all the times he'd rolled in from working some homicide case with that same fatigued look, wanting only to decompress on the sofa holding me in his arms. We'd been divorced ten years now, and while I wasn't that person for Eli anymore, no one else was. That made me sad, because he lived with so much darkness of his own that he needed someone to be his sunshine.

I patted his bicep, which was bulkier than when we'd been together. "Rough night?"

"Yeah. We got a tip about a body out at UBC in the woods yesterday. The VPD put out a press release."

"Oh yeah?" I croaked, shoving my clammy hands in my jumpsuit pockets.

They'd found my passenger's corpse because Vancouver

74

didn't have that much violent crime. Why would the killer leave the body to be found? Did they have no other choice? And why, of every detective in town, did the case have to go to my ex? All the optimism I'd been coasting on fled, even though I assured myself that there was no way Eli could tie me to this murder.

He shook his head. "I really hope this was a gang hit."

"How come?"

"Obviously, I can't get into specifics," he said, "but if this wasn't targeted, it could be bad news, because the crime scene was just the body dump. That means it was premeditated, at least to some extent."

Not to mention, from the cops' perspective, a body missing its heart that had been left in the woods could be indicative of a serial killer.

"Any leads?" I was so focused on keeping my expression neutral that I didn't realize I was nervously bouncing my leg. I stopped, standing there stiffly. "Has he been identified?

Eli yawned again, luckily too exhausted to pick up on my odd behavior. "Yeah. Raj Jalota. We're not releasing his name until tomorrow while we search for a next of kin, so keep that under your hat."

Jalota was a South Asian surname. I'd been holding on to a slim hope that the victim wasn't Fake Topher, but those strings broke, hope floating away like a balloon.

The cops had a body and a name. They wouldn't find a murder weapon because given the short time frame, the killer had used magic, and I doubted they'd find the perpetrator. This made it even more imperative for me to get Raj justice.

As determined as I was, I was relieved that I wouldn't have to be the one to break the news to his family.

"What about CCTV footage?" I'd been so shaken up between the accident and having to deal with the heart, that I hadn't checked for cameras and I was drawing a blank now about their placement.

"There's no CCTV in the woods," Eli said, "and coverage is

only on campus itself, not the roads in and out. The only tip we do have was that there was an accident yesterday on the Fourth Avenue route. Someone called in an abandoned car that had rammed a telephone pole."

That must have happened when I was in the Kefitzat Haderech. Curse people for trying to be nice! I swear, how many do-gooders did I have to fend off for one accident? I squeezed my keys hard enough to leave grooves on my fingers. "You think it's connected?"

He shrugged, the movement pulling his gray suit tight around his well-defined shoulders. "No idea. Could be a stolen vehicle taken for a joyride. We've got the make, color, and a partial plate number, so we're trying to track it down."

Tatiana was going to freak the fuck out. On the upside, I wouldn't have to worry about the Kefitzat Haderech torturing me when my humanity failed, because my boss would kill me today.

I let out a shaky breath.

Eli pressed a hand to my forehead. "You okay, babe? You're pale."

I'd had a plan, damn it. Eli was neither relaxed nor in a good mood, but he was on this case now and he had to have his eyes opened. The trouble was, I'd already attempted several times to show him my magic and failed.

Maybe I had to tenderize him first by planting the idea in his head before the big reveal. A soft sell like realtors used to open a potential buyer up to the possibilities of a property.

"Do you ever get the feeling that there's more out there than we realize?" I said.

"Like aliens? Have you been watching those History Channel marathons again? Because once again, that little green man you saw was the Lees' chihuahua under those creepy motion sensor lights they had."

I jabbed a finger at him. "Anyone could have made that mistake after drinking that rotgut sangria you'd made."

"And yet you had four glasses."

"I didn't want to bruise your ego over your shitty mixology skills. Giving me one of those alien dolls from *Toy Story* with a dog collar on it afterwards was uncalled for. Besides, that's not what I'm talking about." I rubbed my chin. "Remember when your grandmother died and your mom was convinced that her spirit was still in the house so you went over there and had the same feeling?"

"Sure," Eli said. "We were grieving and it was comforting to think that she was still with us."

"Ah, but what if she was really still with you?"

"There's no such thing as ghosts, Mir."

"Yeah, no." I waved my hands as if banishing them. "Not ghosts but... miracles. Things that seem to happen as if by magic." I leaned into those last two words.

"Like Jesus's face on a piece of toast?" Eli yawned. "Is there a point to all this?"

"Magic is real."

"I know."

I blinked at him. "You do?"

"Sure, because there's no way the tacos at that place by the station with the skeezy owner could taste that good without it."

My shoulders slumped. "Ha. Yup."

He shot me a puzzled look, then clapped my shoulder. "By the way, could you keep Sadie next week? I know she's supposed to come to me on Sunday, but this new case is going to be a lot. You guys can finish your *Buffy* marathon, right? Awesome, thanks." He was already partway up the walk before I answered.

"I can't."

Eli stopped and turned around, his mouth hanging open. "What?"

"I can't. You know this new job doesn't come with regular hours like my old one did."

He chuckled. "I'm working a murder case. You're documenting letters and shit for some artist's memoirs."

Actually, I was working the same murder case as you, but that wasn't the point.

I crossed my arms. "A librarian job has worth and value."

"I didn't say otherwise."

"Really? 'Documenting letters and shit'?" I made the air quotes.

"I meant that it's easier for you to rearrange your schedule than it is for me. I'm sure your boss can be flexible."

"That's not the point. We have a co-parenting agreement. I haven't minded all the times you've had to change things around because of work, but I'm saying no now, and regardless of the reason, my life and my time is as valuable as yours."

My words ended on a tiny rush of breath, because they'd tumbled out of me. It was hard to say who was more surprised after my speech, me, or Eli, who openly gaped at me, wide-eyed.

"Obviously your time matters," he said stiffly. "I'm sorry if you got a different impression. I'll figure something out."

He went into his place without a look back, while I pressed my lips together to keep from calling out and saying that of course I'd do it. I'd been honest when I told Laurent that I didn't want to be a caretaker anymore. This wasn't a one-time request with Eli, and if I didn't stand my ground now, I'd keep scheduling my life around his.

I accidentally hit the alarm on my key fob instead of unlocking the car, the shrill siren drilling into my brain. Scrambling to shut it off, I sank into the driver's seat. Eli would always occupy part of my heart, but would the reverse still be true in three months? In six? Hell, would it even be true once the dust settled on this murder case?

Fitting the key into the ignition, I sighed, the world outside my window a little bleaker and the complicated past that Eli and I had so carefully stitched closed bursting its first seam.

8

THE SUN BLAZED IN A CLOUDLESS SKY, BUT DESPITE how hot and stuffy it was in the car on the drive back to the Sharma house, I kept the windows rolled up and the air conditioning off because my skin was dotted with goosebumps.

Surprisingly, when I phoned Tatiana, she wasn't concerned about the police having the license plate of the car since it wasn't stolen and there was no way to trace it back to her. I didn't ask how she'd managed that. Plausible deniability and all.

"One good thing that came out of the police press report," she said, "is that the Sharmas are very concerned that their son was the intended target and I negotiated a higher fee." Between Tatiana's pronunciation of certain words—Shawma, highah—and her vocabulary choices, she sounded like a high-class Wiseguy.

"French villa, you will be mine," I said.

Tatiana snorted. "It might be better that Detective Chu is the lead on it. You claim you two have a good relationship, so perhaps he can be dissuaded from bringing you into this, should he find out about your involvement."

Good might be overstating it right now, and she didn't know how by-the-book Eli was. "It's not as if I killed Fake Topher," I said, respecting Eli's wishes that I keep Raj's name a secret for now. "Even if there was footage, which there isn't, it would clearly show me unconscious in the car when he was killed."

"Aside from the optics of you not mentioning to your ex that you were with the victim, it's not just CCTV footage you need to be concerned with. If they catch this killer, that person can conclusively put you in the vehicle and at that point, it's their version of events against yours." There was a loaded silence on her end. "I'm beginning to have second thoughts"—thawghts— "about the wisdom of bringing you onboard. These complications outweigh your usefulness."

Icy tendrils snaked through me and the world turned to a blurry haze. A sharp honk brought me back to my senses and I jerked the car safely back into my lane. "Eli won't find out."

"How can you be so sure?"

I wasn't, but negative thinking didn't help anything. As it was, my mouth was dry and there was a heavy feeling in my stomach. "You can't be tied to the car, there's no CCTV video placing me in it, and the tow truck driver and detailer were both Ohrists, loyal to you. No one has any idea that kid was in the car. Eli can't connect me to this."

"We'll see," she said, and hung up.

After a couple of trips up and down the stretch of road where the crash had happened, I found the pole that I'd hit, thanks to a thick black scrape at hood height, and pulled over. After verifying that there really weren't any CCTV cameras, I looked around for any crime scene tape or possible incriminating evidence, but other than that mark, there wasn't anything. I got back in the car, gripping the wheel and taking calming breaths.

Nothing in my plan had changed. I would still find the killer, not just to build up immunity from the Kefitzat Haderech, but to get Raj Jalota justice.

I threw the car into gear, my resolve rock-solid.

Once I parked in front of the Sharma house and rang the bell a verrah proper butler showed me into a formal living room decorated in shades of sage and white.

"The family is in another meeting. They'll be with you short-ly," he said. His stick-up-the-butt gait was impressive. I bet he practiced.

I sat on thick cream sofa cushions resting on a narrow burnished wood frame with attached side tables. It was a magnif-icent piece and I ran my hand over the gleaming wood, deeply envious. The furniture complimented the mid-century modern exterior, but was surprisingly comfortable.

I waited for ten minutes, planning out my dream living room, until I heard voices and laughter.

"Forget Provence," a familiar voice said. "The area around Toulouse is magnifique. I'll hook you up with family friends who have a villa there."

I peered into the large marble foyer and rolled my eyes. Laurent was slathering on the French charm so hard I'm amazed he didn't throw in a few chef's kisses and an ooh là là.

Given Krish Sharma's hearty shoulder slap and enthusiastic "That would be great," Huff 'n' Puff was killing it.

Except now I was distracted wondering if Laurent meant Tatiana or if the Amars had multiple friends with French villas? I gasped. Did *they* have a French villa that Laurent hadn't bothered to mention? I planted my hands on my hips. These people could start ponying up with the invitations anytime now, because the best offer I'd ever gotten from friends was to go camping in a six-person tent when there were only three of us.

"Ellis," Krish said over his shoulder. He was dressed in busi-ness casual slacks and a light sweater, like he'd worn in most of his photos. "What do you say? Would a villa be up to your standards?"

His wife glided into view, a goddess in jeans and a white, tailored man's shirt. I'd never been able to pull off that look and after seeing Ellis, I wasn't going to bother trying. I smoothed down my jumpsuit. I looked just as good. So I wasn't Grace Kelly. Patrician blondes were highly overrated.

Ellis laughed huskily, drawing Laurent's eye. "You know how low-maintenance I am, Krish."

Her husband chuckled good-naturedly, and I pressed my palms against my thighs so I didn't clench my fists.

Both kids were present as well. The actual Topher Sharma was about the same height as the fake one, making him shorter than his sister. He slunk behind his parents, scrolling through his phone with a bored expression, while Asha sat down on the stairs, her arms wrapped around her knees, and a distant expression on her face. Her hair was wet and the faint scent of chlorine floated off her.

Laurent still hadn't looked my way. Jerk. He knew I was here thanks to his wolf super smelling. And how dare he make dark jeans and a button-down short-sleeved shirt appear tailor-made?

Ah well, this was for the best. Since I was officially on the case, and the only one outside of the homicide unit with the victim's name, he could get over his issues and start breaking down information with me. There was no point in us covering the same territory.

"We need to talk," I said quietly while still in the living room, knowing he heard me. I stepped into the hallway to join everyone. "Hello. I'm Miriam Feldman. I believe Tatiana said I'd be stopping by to speak to Topher?"

Laurent finally deigned to glance at me. Something predatory flashed in his green eyes, and I had the wildest urge to run and see if he'd catch me. I wrenched my gaze away, a professional smile on my face.

"I'm so grateful that your suspicions were raised about that man," Ellis said, coming forward to greet me. "When Tatiana told us what had happened, we were extremely upset. Then to learn he was killed so soon after leaving our home?" She put a protective arm around her son, who shrugged it off like a prat. "If Taroosh was the intended victim…"

"God forbid," his sister said sarcastically.

"Asha," her mom said sharply.

Krish patted his daughter's shoulder.

She rolled her eyes and headed upstairs.

"Nothing would have happened." Topher deigned to look up from his phone. "Dead guy was obviously looking for a way to get out of the country or he wouldn't have wanted on our plane. Whoever offed him had some personal vendetta."

"Ms. Feldman can clear up one detail for us," Laurent said. "How closely did the victim resemble Topher?"

"Yes," Ellis said. "Tell us that this was all a ridiculous mistake." Her anxious air was at odds with Krish's frown, but my heart sank. They were so going to shoot the messenger.

I clasped my hands behind my back so I wouldn't punch Laurent for creating a divide between the Sharmas and myself before I'd had a chance to interview their kid.

"Very," I said. "His hair, his body type, the way he was dressed, his South Asian heritage, he would have fooled anyone only casually acquainted with your son."

"Damn it, Topher." Krish pounded a fist onto the bannister. "Did you hire some lookalike to take your place on the plane?"

"I didn't, though good idea, Dad. Maybe I'll try it next time." Cocky little shit.

"For once in your life, could you live up to the family name instead of dragging it through the mud?" Krish stepped forward, but Ellis placed a hand on his arm, and after a moment, he retreated.

"How well did your staff know your son?" I said. "Would they have spotted an imposter once he got on the plane?"

Ellis shook her head. "We've always hired private planes, but we recently bought our own. The staff was new."

How convenient.

Laurent crossed his arms, briefly assessing Topher, before addressing me. "I've got this in hand. No need to subject the Sharmas to more people questioning them."

"They did agree to Tatiana's representative looking into the facts," I said pleasantly. "And as I have no desire to distress them further, I'll be brief." I turned to the parents. "Where would be the best place for Topher and me to speak privately?"

Laurent's gaze clashed with mine for a brief second but I stood my ground, and he gave the family a warm smile. "I'll get back to you about the villa details, once I've wrapped up another urgent situation." He shot me a pointed look and I sighed, trying not to feel guilty about that poor dybbuk-possessed couple who'd merely wanted to celebrate their anniversary. "But we'll chat soon."

Krish thanked him for his help and assured Laurent if he had any further questions to call.

"Always a pleasure, Ms. Feldman," Laurent purred.

Ellis gave him this melty look, which I couldn't exactly blame her for, because Laurent could read a shopping list and it would sound like a love letter. It wasn't his shifter magic that made him dangerous.

I gave him a finger wave. "Au revoir." Until we meet again.

As Laurent passed me, his voice dropped to a murmur. "Butt out, Mitzi."

While Topher told his parents that he'd talk to me out on the patio, I spoke to Laurent through gritted teeth, though I kept a smile on my face.

"Pull your head out of your ass."

He didn't acknowledge me, leaving without another look back.

I shook my head at the front door closing. Laurent was so bad at accepting help that he was cutting off his nose to spite his face. No, that wasn't fair. Part of it was concern for me getting hurt, but my choices were exactly that. Mine to make. The other part of it, sadly, was that he was such an outsider that there weren't many people in his corner. It was as if anything other than the most superficial concern for his well-being made him uncomfortable.

"Miriam, if you'd like to come this way?" Ellis escorted Topher and I to the patio, offering to bring us coffee.

The two of us sat down at a teak bistro set on the back porch in a patch of sunlight. I shifted my chair so the sun wasn't blinding me, because I'd left my sunglasses at home, and studied Topher.

His leg jiggled, vibrating the table.

"This conversation is confidential," I said. "The cops are involved now, so if you know anything about this, tell me, and Tatiana and I will fix it." Not that I had any idea how, but we'd find a solution—and one that kept me out of the whole thing.

He didn't lose any of his sullenness under my calm stare. "I'll tell you what I told the French guy. I don't know who that dude was or how he found out you were supposed to drive me to the airport."

I really wanted to spring Raj's name on him and see how he reacted, but I'd promised Eli. I crossed my legs and tilted my head. "And you're really not worried that you were the actual target?"

"Nah." Topher met my eyes a little too deliberately, which Eli said was often the case with liars.

"Why not?" I said.

His lack of concern that someone pretending to be him had been murdered was setting off alarm bells. I didn't have any detective training, but I'd been with Eli through his police academy studies and first years on the force, and I'd picked up a few things. Plus, I was a sucker for a good mystery book or British crime show. Either Topher was convinced of his own invulnerability, like many young people, or he was feeling guilty about something and covering.

Topher scratched his neck. "Like I said before. If he went to all that trouble to hitch a ride on our plane, he probably had assholes after him. I don't care who he was or that he looked like me. The sooner my parents agree I'm safe, the sooner I go back to Los Angeles. I want to get out of here because they're driving me crazy."

I'd wager that last part was the first honest thing he'd said.

"I thought you didn't want to start your research program or go back to school."

He gave me a cheeky smile. "I don't."

"Have you told them that?" A withered bloom from one of the hanging baskets out here blew onto the table and I brushed it off.

"There's no point." He kicked a pebble into the side of the house. "They're determined that I take over the family business and the hell with what I want."

"Which is what?" Besides partying at their beach house and living off their dime?

"I dunno yet." He got this far-off look, then shook it off. "But I'm young and I have a lot of time ahead of me to figure that out. It's my life and I want control over it."

I nodded. It's funny, but I'd never had any of the growing pains that Topher did in trying to establish himself as an adult out from under his parents' thumbs. And while Topher might not be going about things in the best way, he knew the path set out for him by his parents wouldn't make him happy.

"I do think you should talk to them, but I hear you," I said.

He gave me a grateful glance that was almost startled. "Thanks."

No point wasting the rapport we'd established. "How do you think the victim found you?"

The sliding door opened behind us as I spoke and Ellis stepped out with a tray.

"It's obvious," she said.

I clenched my fists under the table because I didn't want *her* answer. "I'd actually like to hear from Topher."

He shrugged. "Nah. Mom knows a lot."

Ellis set the tray on the table and poured the rich steaming brew into a mug. "It's our fault. Krish and I have made no secret of our success. We're heavily involved with philanthropic endeavors and we've raised our children to be part of them as well. Some con artist who resembled my son saw one of the many media articles about our family and decided to impersonate Taroosh to get out of the country."

Nice and neat with a bow tied on it.

"Like I said in the first place." Topher checked his phone.

Ellis could leave at any time, because this echo chamber was pointless.

I added milk to my coffee from a small ceramic jug. "This is one of Judith Rachefsky's pieces, right?"

"It is." Ellis fixed her son's coffee for him. Topher stiffened imperceptibly, but she didn't even notice. "Are you a collector as well?" she asked.

"She's my best friend. I get really good gifts." I sat back, my hands folded on my stomach. "I happen to know that she's working on a new line and could put in a good word with the artist for a pre-order."

Ellis's smile widened, the corners of her eyes crinkling. With that one little statement, I'd turned into a person of trust. Heh. Huff 'n' Puff could take his villa and shove it where the sun don't shine. "You must have all kinds of wonderful pieces," she said.

"Yup. I'm pretty lucky. Ellis, I want you to know that I'm a mother, too, and I appreciate how scary this must be for you. I give you my word that I'll find out who was behind this."

She pushed Topher's cup toward him. "Thank you. I'll let you two get back to it."

Finally.

She took the tray and headed for the sliding door.

Topher pushed his coffee away.

I stirred my drink. "What kind of magic does your mom have?"

"I've got low-level light magic like Topher," Ellis said.

So much for letting us get back to it. She'd taken helicopter parenting to a new extreme, but I'd faced more than my share of these people back when I volunteered at Sadie's elementary school. Bring it.

9

I ASKED MY NEXT QUESTION MAKING EYE CONTACT with Topher and hoping Ellis would get the hint and actually go inside. "What about your dad and Asha?"

He quickly typed something on his cell. "Dad can optimize his physiology or some shit. Something about better oxygen flow and muscle performance."

"That's right," Ellis said, once more approaching the table. "It makes him one of the faster rugby players."

Wasn't that cheating? Ah well, I wasn't here to debate the ethics of performance enhancers. "Does Asha do the same thing?"

"Nah. She's got shifter abilities." Topher rolled his eyes. "Practiced for years but finally pulled off a whale tail and gills."

I blinked. "You mean she becomes a mermaid? That's astounding."

Ellis snapped off dead flowers from the closest hanging basket, arranging them on the tray like delicate fairy corpses. "It's a party trick. She can't use it to help her win swim meets."

"Or do something cool like turn into a raptor or a lion." Topher jiggled his leg again. "She couldn't even manage a full shift with all her training. Anything else?"

"One more question, and humor me here. Can you think of anyone who would want to hurt you?"

Topher laughed and thumped his chest. "I'm rich and good looking. Haters gonna hate."

Ellis beamed at him fondly, before breaking off a stem with a loud snap.

I swallowed the rest of my now-bitter java so I wasn't tempted to throw it at them in frustration.

Krish and Asha didn't have much to add when I spoke to them later. The parents always left for work early and Asha was at the pool. When I asked them who would want to hurt Topher, Asha snorted and said, "He's a dick. Who doesn't?"

Krish kept mum.

Topher was certainly entitled, and sure, kind of a dick, but he was also chafing under the micromanaging. Ellis railroaded over him when I asked a question and Topher caved because it was easier. Krish was inclined to think the worst of him, and Topher's reaction was to be sarcastic. There weren't any clear lines of communication between him and his parents and at his age, he was no longer inclined to try. While there was a ton of dysfunction in this family, my gut instinct was that Topher hadn't killed Raj—though he was hiding something.

The fact that Raj Jalota had impersonated Topher on the exact day he was due to get a ride to his dad's private plane with a new staff who didn't know him, and at a time when no one else in the family was at home, was too much of a stretch to be coincidence. Someone had given Jalota this information, and I'd put my money on it being Topher.

Krish's theory about Topher hiring a lookalike had merit, so when I got home, I scrolled through Raj's social media to find any connection to Sharma Junior, again making notes in my green paisley print notebook.

The dead man was a puzzle. On social media, he came across as a proud nerd and university student. This kid didn't frequent clubs or surf and travel like Topher did. He posted memes of physics puns, diagrams of D&D campaigns with little figures drawn on them, and photos of his fancy polyhedral dice. Where he'd crossed paths with Topher—or someone who saw his resemblance to Topher, if I was keeping an open mind about this —was a mystery.

He'd made a number of jokey posts about how working at a temp agency left him feeling like he was doing a "mic drop, bitches. I'm out." on a regular basis. I zoomed in on a rare selfie, which he'd captioned "cubicle drone chic" with him dressed in pressed chinos and a sedate button-down shirt—with nary a frosted hair in sight—to get a better look at the sign behind him.

"Aries Employment." The company, which according to its website was currently hiring, had a well-established internet presence with a lot of reviews from workers and companies that had used them, so it was unlikely to be exclusively Ohrist.

The chances of this being the connection between Raj and Topher were slim, but someone there might know why Raj wanted to get out of the country. If, perhaps, he'd stolen something from one of their clients while on a temp job.

I scarfed down a banana, dumping the peel in my countertop composter, and called Laurent, intending to lord the fact that I had the victim's name over him, but it went to voicemail.

Since I was in phone call mode, might as well cross another one off my list. I pulled out the dossier that Tatiana had compiled on Fred McMurtry, the Lonestar in charge when my parents had been killed, and read over Tatiana's findings more carefully. Fred had remained on the job for two more days after the murders, at which point he'd disappeared. His bank account and credit cards hadn't been touched. It was as if he'd woken up one morning and simply walked away from his life for three weeks.

He'd remained a Lonestar for another fifteen years before retiring. I calculated his current age: seventy-five.

Tatiana had included his contact number, so I called it, though I hesitated punching in the final digit.

Learning the truth about why my parents had been killed could lead to some unpleasant facts about what they'd been up to. I wasn't naïve enough to believe that they were innocent victims of Banim Shovavim hatred, because one or the other of my parents had gone on too many sudden trips when I was young, our lives fluctuating between, well, not feast exactly, but well-fed and famine. They'd ensured that I had a happy childhood, but looking back, there were a lot of hushed conversations between them about the fatigue from this financial instability, and how they could achieve a more solid future for us all.

My fingers slid over the screen, my pulse fluttering in my throat. Was I ready to go from not knowing the specifics to seeing them in a light that would taint my memories? This was ancient history and I could still walk away with my illusions of who they'd been—slightly shady but good people—intact.

I fluffed up a cushion on my stain-resistant beige couch, once more wishing I'd bought the orange velvet one I'd drooled over but hadn't because I thought it was too flamboyant.

I'd brought enough danger into my life and my daughter's life by reclaiming my magic. I'd pissed off a master vamp and aligned myself with Tatiana, the Loki of the hip replacement set. Whoever had gone after my parents had left me alone all this time, so why stir up more trouble?

My finger hovered over the "end" button, but, taking a deep breath, I hit the final number.

Aaannd voicemail. I left a message as Miranda Edelman, the fake name that I'd chosen for this encounter. If McMurtry called back, my own voicemail didn't include my name in the greeting, so the deception would stand.

Since Laurent couldn't have made the connection to Aries Employment, I made an appointment with the firm for later today, intent on using Raj as a reference for how I'd heard about the place. While I updated my resume, I put together my cover story about wanting short contracts that I could slot in around my unusual work hours.

After a quick check-in with Tatiana to let her know that the temp agency might contact her and that Topher was hiding something, I rummaged through my fridge for lunch, which was, in my opinion, the worst meal of the day. Sandwiches bored me unless some fancy restaurant made them and I hated washing lettuce, though anyone who got to the bottom of those pre-washed big boxes of lettuce before the leaves went moldy was a better person than me. If I didn't have leftovers, I ended up scarfing down a bowl of cereal like today, excited to get out there and hunt down leads.

Throwing a conservative blazer over my jumpsuit, I dug out my leather briefcase, stuffed a few copies of my resume in it, and touched up my makeup. Corporate disguise or no, I wasn't wrestling myself back into tummy control garments. Those days were over, baby.

Aries Employment was located at the top of a winding marble staircase on the second floor of a domed building that had been featured in a ton of television series filmed here in Vancouver. I opened the door and came face to face with Eli's partner, Detective Rose Tanaka.

My ex was chatting with a man that I recognized from the website as the owner of the agency, Don Egerts.

I froze in the doorway.

"Hi, Miri." Like Eli, Rose wore a dark suit, her black hair pulled back in a neat bun, and her polished badge clipped to her belt. "What brings you here?"

I scrambled for an answer, because my cover story of short-term contracts would imply that I was having financial difficulties in my current job, and Eli could not be given that impression.

"Good to see you, Rose." I looked around as if confused. "But I think I got the wrong office. I was looking for two twenty-one?"

The men joined us.

"The criminal law firm?" Don said. "Other end of the hall."

Eli's eyes narrowed.

"Great. Thanks." I spun around, but Eli draped an arm over my shoulder.

"Hey Rose," he said, steering me out the door. "Give me a second with Mir."

"No problem."

Once in the hallway, Eli dropped his voice. "Criminal law firm? Are you in trouble?"

I shrugged out from under his arm. "It's work business."

"Why does an artist's memoirs require the services of a criminal lawyer?"

Tempting as it was to joke about Tatiana being a part-time serial killer, complete with a clown costume, the faster I got rid of Eli, the faster I could speak to Don Egerts.

"Not that it's any of your business, but Tatiana sent me to get some documents pertaining to a libel case she had with a gallery owner a few years back."

There really had been a gallery owner, but the "libel case" had been a magic duel that left Tatiana's minion dead and the gallery a smoldering pile of rubble. That fact had been annoying when Laurent had texted it to me as yet another reason why I should quit, but it came in handy now as creative inspiration.

"Now, if you'll excuse me," I said frostily. "I won't take up more of your time."

He rubbed a hand over the back of his neck. "I'm sorry. I've taken advantage of your generosity over the years. I got used to you always being available."

His apology was genuine, but it landed with a hollow thud at the realization of how little time I'd carved out for myself while Sadie was growing up.

"I forgive you. And when the day comes that I seek a new job," I said, "I've found an employment agency."

Eli glanced back at the firm's door. "Don't use this guy."

"Why not? Too many one-star reviews?"

"Nothing like that. He seems all aboveboard but in addition to the regular monitored security system on the office, Egerts has a biometric lock on his personal office door."

"Like a retinal scan?"

"More cutting edge."

"Do tell." I leaned in.

Eli chuckled. "Oh no. That's your 'hungry for new facts' face."

I poked him. "Consider it part of your apology and explain in detail." Years of teasing about my love of random facts was finally playing into my favor. Eli had no clue that this information was important to me for more than just trivia.

"Most alarms use motion sensors," he said, "which can be defeated, but this one identifies and authenticates the individual from their unique electrocardiogram signature. I don't think it's even available to the general public yet."

"So this Egerts is the only one who can get past his door. Fascinating. What if someone got into the office a different way? Like through a window?"

"Wouldn't matter. Even if someone found an alternate entrance, the monitor would scan the heartbeat, compare it to Don's, and sound the alarm."

I glanced back at the sign next to the door. "That's hardcore for an employment agency."

Eli scratched his jaw. "He's up to something. My guess is money laundering, but it's not my area and not my problem. I'll get the white collar crimes unit to look into it."

Sadie texted, asking permission to sleep over with a few other girls after Hannah's pool party.

"The child?" Eli said.

"How'd you know?" I messaged back that it was okay if Tracy gave permission.

"You either give a half-smile like you're doing now, or you snort."

I smacked him. "I do not, you freak."

He placed his hand on his heart. "Swear to God."

"You're an atheist." I got a thumbs-up emoji from my daughter.

"Still, don't ever take up poker."

"I could have married an accountant," I said. "Way fewer creeper skills."

"Yeah. Wow." He tapped his detective's badge. "You really screwed the pooch on that one."

"Right?" Less than a minute later, I got another text from the mom, saying it was fine.

Rose poked her head out. "You guys done?"

"Yeah, I guess I'll get to the law firm."

"We good?" Eli said.

Totally—except for the guilt I felt at lying about this case.

"All good." I returned Rose's wave and strode down the hallway.

As soon as their footsteps faded away, I cloaked myself and returned to the employment agency, waiting until another client exited to sail through the door unnoticed.

Bless my ex for all that intel. This extreme alarm system on Don's office door confirmed he was an Ohrist.

Don had rocketed to the top of my suspect list. He'd kept something in his office that he didn't want anyone of magic abilities getting their hands on. Had Raj managed somehow to bypass the system, stolen this item, and fled? I had to get inside that office to find out.

Remaining cloaked, I peeked through the glass of the different offices until I found Don's. The door was closed, but that was perfect for my needs. I examined the lock, which was connected to the heartbeat sensor, but didn't learn anything new.

If I could have sent Delilah through the crack under the door to look through his things, I would have, but when animated, she was a living shadow. When I looked at her closely, I could just make out the faint tremor of my heartbeat rippling her surface.

She'd set off the alarm.

I was down but not out. Smiling, I headed downstairs back to the lobby. Wasn't it fortunate that I knew a golem who'd be perfect for the job?

10

IF YOU HAVEN'T SEEN A RED CLAY GOLEM CLAD IN A gold lamé catsuit, sitting spread-eagle on a leather couch watching *Golden Girls*, have you really lived?

The answer was a vehement yes, and if I could have scrubbed the image from my retinas, I'd have been on it in a flash.

I stood in front of the television. "Well?"

Emmett pushed me out of the way with a black cane topped with a silver dragon that he'd received back when one of his legs had been broken off. "Breaking and entering sounds like a lot of work."

"Is it work or is it a fun adventure?"

He banged the cane twice against the ground. "I need a drink!"

There was a growl from the kitchen and my best friend charged out, murder in her eyes.

I shoved her back into the room. "Breathe."

Standing in Jude's kitchen was like being inside a kaleidoscope but in a good way, with its cheerful yellow walls and her colorful ceramic art decorating an antique distressed bookcase. Even better, it smelled like cookies.

"I'll give you a million dollars to give me one night off from

Downton Abbey out there," she said, grabbing an oven mitt. "Not only has he stretched out the top of my favorite Halloween costume, if I hear that *Golden Girls* theme song one more time, I'm going to snap." She poked her left eye. "Look. I've developed a twitch." She checked the tray of snickerdoodles inside the oven, before adding another couple minutes to the timer. "You think Laurent wants him?"

I laughed. "Ask him and record his response. Let me see if I can get Emmett off your hands for a couple hours at least." I walked back into the living room, taking a seat under the abstract tapestry hanging on Jude's wall. "Emmett. Turn off the show and talk to me."

"But this is a good one. Dorothy snarks at Blanche."

"That's every episode." I grabbed the remote and shut off the flat screen television. "You can't sit on the sofa all day. You said it yourself. Golems need to be useful." I nudged his side. "You're the only one who can break in to this office."

"Because I'm smart?"

"Uh..."

He frowned. "Stealthy?"

"Yes?"

He crossed his arms.

"Because you don't have a heartbeat," I said. He threw his hands up with a huff. "Come on. How many others can claim that skill?"

"Every single vampire," the golem said.

"If you want to be technical about it, sure, but they still can't get in."

"Why not?" His hand drifted to the remote, so I grabbed it and stuffed it under my ass.

"Bloodsuckers can go into any public space, like the reception area of a company or even a workspace shared by many employees, but not a private office. Same rules apply as a house. Even though they don't have heartbeats, they can't enter that office uninvited." I'd educated myself on the whys and wherefores of all things undead in the past couple of weeks. "You are literally the only one in the world that can break in and look around Don's office. That makes you special."

"That makes me valuable," he said with a sly look. "Ten thousand dollars."

"A hundred bucks and I won't let Jude unmake you." I nodded my chin at my best friend now holding a meat cleaver with a deranged grin.

"No deal. All that and you take me on as your partner," he said.

I wanted this loose cannon working with me on the regular about as much as a hole in the head, but since it was unlikely I'd ever have any more jobs for him, I was willing to negotiate this point. "I'll farm out assignments to you if I can, like a subcontractor, but you need to fix your appearance and become a lot more inconspicuous."

"No problem." Digging under the cushions, he unearthed Jude's Cher wig and slapped it on his shiny bald head.

Jude brandished the cleaver, but I grabbed her arm. "We'll work on the disguise."

I brought Emmett home with me, since Sadie wouldn't be there and Eli was still at work. I even let him ride in the passenger seat, though I made him put on an enormous floppy hat and giant sunglasses so if he attracted attention, it wouldn't be because he was a supernatural being with unnatural red clay skin, merely a bohemian woman with manly shoulders.

"Why is your house the color of rotten cottage cheese?" He half-heartedly opened the door to the coat closet in the front hall, then brightened and pulled out Sadie's purple velvet trench coat. "I want this."

"My house is beige, not rotten," I said, wrestling him for the hanger, "and that's not yours."

"No shit. That's why I want it. Other people's stuff is more interesting." This golem needed a steady diet of *Sesame Street* life lessons stat.

With a grunt, I got the coat away from Emmett and he wandered into my kitchen.

"Maybe not your stuff though," he said, with a sniff.

"I'd forgotten what a delight you are."

He shrugged, uncapping a bottle of sambuca from my liquor cabinet. "That's on you."

Delilah rose up and smacked him.

Emmett startled, almost dropping the bottle. "I'd forgotten how mean you are."

"That's on you. Now stay here while I find you some better clothes. And don't drink." I ran upstairs into Sadie's room, rummaging through her dresser for the old pair of her dad's sweats that she had. Eli and Emmett were about the same height, both around five-foot-ten. I held up the black track pants and top and snickered. The two weren't built all that differently either.

"Oooh," I heard the golem say from far too nearby. "Now this is interesting."

There was a buzzing noise.

"Argh!" I ran into my bedroom to find Emmett using my vibrator on his shoulder. I tackled him, sending my toy flying across the room. It hit the wall then spun merrily on my floor. I smacked Emmett over and over again, the golem covering his head with his hands. "Don't. Touch. Someone. Else's. Vibrator."

Emmett gave a full body shudder and somehow managed to go pale. "Vibrator?"

I picked the toy up, turning it off and tossing it back in my bedside drawer with a mental note to boil it. Or burn it. "What did you think it was?"

"The box says personal massager." He slapped his shoulder. "Ew. Ew. Ew. Vag cooties!"

I sat down on my bed, looking up at my ceiling as if I'd find a heavy dose of patience hiding there. "That's not a thing."

"Oh, yeah?" He grabbed the sweats that I'd dropped during the tackle. "What about pubic lice?"

"Are you implying I have them?" I smacked him.

He rubbed his shoulder. "No, but that's a thing," he said sulkily.

"Well, I guess, okay... how do you know about pubic lice and not that a personal massager is a euphemism for a sex toy?"

"I have the soul of a porn mag kingpin and the life experience of a vestal virgin. I'm a conundrum."

"Put the sweats on."

I kept him quiet for the rest of the evening by letting him spend time with his four favorite women: Dorothy, Rose, Blanche, and Sophia. The first couple of times I sang along to the theme song, by the fifth I'd removed myself to a different room, after the eighth listen, I, too, had developed a twitch. It was almost as bad as when a twenty-month-old Sadie had insisted on watching "The Lonely Goatherd" on repeat for a week straight.

Sure, if I listened to the parenting experts, she should have been exposed to only twenty minutes of screen time, three times a week maximum, but she'd turned out fine. I looked at the small framed photo of her laden down in every single scarf she owned—about fifteen of them—and mugging at the camera. Mostly fine.

Right before we headed out, my phone rang with a blocked number, which I didn't bother to answer since it was probably a telemarketer.

We timed our arrival to ten minutes before Aries Employment closed for the night. Emmett, now in black sweats and a black baseball cap with his feet stuffed into a pair of Sadie's size ten runners, skulked outside, armed with a walkie talkie that I'd found from a long-ago trip to Disneyland.

With my cloaking in place, it was a piece of cake to learn the alarm code for the main office. I stood very still until the last employee had locked up, punched in the code, and called Emmett on the walkie. I stayed invisible while I ran back down to the lobby to open the front door for him, and then we were in.

I'd made the golem up with a bottle's worth of cheap

drugstore foundation so that any red skin on his face was now a pasty white person color and he wore gloves on his hands. If he was glimpsed on the hallway security cameras under his cap, he'd look human enough to pass.

Luckily, there were no cameras in the agency itself, so I dropped my magic.

Since Egerts's personal office door had that biometric scanner on it, I wasn't sure if opening it even without a heartbeat would trigger the alarm, so I ordered Emmett to punch the glass panel next to it, but it didn't crack.

"It's that unbreakable shit," I said. "Keep at it."

While he smashed away, I checked for security guards out on the second floor, because Emmett was being loud. I breathed a sigh of relief once the glass shattered and he ducked through into the office.

Locking the agency door, I sat down next to the hole he'd made and peered inside.

Whatever Raj had in the satchel couldn't have been that large. Don's shelves held a number of industry awards and the filing cabinets contained contracts and miscellaneous paperwork.

"Hand me the laptop." I went through some common password combinations, getting lucky with "Aries1," while Emmett scoured the office for anything out of the ordinary and any sign of a safe.

Don's browser history was full of hentai porn and the thought of going through his documents made me shudder, but I couldn't take the laptop with me. He might or might not file a police report over broken glass, but throw in a stolen laptop and he'd at least want the insurance replacement. I scanned through everything fast as I could, but they were boring spreadsheets and client documents.

"There's no safe," Emmett said.

"Check the desk drawers for a false bottom." The laptop was a bust.

"False bottom for the win." Emmett held up a small black notebook.

"Toss it over." I slid the laptop through the hole in the glass for Emmett to put back on the desk, and flipped through the first couple of pages in the notebook, finding initials written next to dates and some kind of code.

Was this the reason for Don's alarm? I revised my theory. Perhaps Raj hadn't stolen from Don, but had worked with him to rip someone else off? My gut was telling me this notebook was the reason for the heartbeat alarm. Now to decode it. "We've got a lead."

"Oh good. Saves me the trouble," Laurent said, entering.

"Ah!" I pressed my hand to my heart. I was so getting him a bell. I eyed the agency door, wondering if he'd show me how to pick a lock sometime. "Did you follow me?"

Laurent wore all black, with a baseball cap covering his curls, the brim pulled low, and sunglasses covering most of his face. "First I followed the investigating detectives. Libel case, huh?"

I startled. "You spied on my private conversation?"

"You mean the one with your ex-husband who's the lead detective on this murder case? Then yes."

"If you hadn't been so boneheaded about working with me, you'd have known that. I didn't even see you."

"Oh, Mitzi." He sighed contemptuously. "When are you going to realize you are so outmatched?"

"Stalker."

"I prefer to think of it as working smart, not hard. I'm not some amateur."

I held up the notebook. "Well, I'm an amateur with the victim's name and a notebook written in code. How you doing, Sherlock?"

"You weren't the only one I've been stalking," Laurent said. "Topher went to the Bear's Den looking for Harry."

The Bear's Den was this awesome Ohrist speakeasy hidden in

the basement of a parking garage. Harry was its gargoyle bartender.

"Why Harry?" I said.

"He's known as a neutral party. If you want to get a message to someone and you're worried about delivering it yourself, Harry'll do it."

"Don't shoot the messenger, huh?"

"You better hope that's the case, because Tatiana is usually the first person hired for this kind of work, and as her minion, you'll be that messenger." He smiled tightly at me. "Now are you having second thoughts about your new job?"

I counted to ten in my head. "Would Harry tell us what the message was and who it was for?" I said. "If we asked nicely, or paid him or whatever?"

"I cashed in a favor and he gave me the name. Someone called Celeste. Now who's Sherlock?"

The plot thickened. Could Celeste be the owner of whatever Raj had in the satchel? Whoever she was, Topher was either scared enough of her to use an intermediary, or didn't know how to directly contact her himself. She was now on my list to track down as well.

"Do you know who Celeste is?" I said. "No? Maybe she's in this notebook. You know, the one *I* found?"

"Must you two always bicker?" Emmett stuck his head out of the hole he'd made and wrinkled his nose at Laurent's appearance. "Figures I was stuck with the Dollar Store burglar disguise, but I thought you'd dress more badass, dude."

Laurent strode toward the golem, his expression hard. "I just had to kill a dybbuk and there's another one still on the loose. I'm not in the mood."

I chewed on a knuckle. Who had Laurent killed, the man or the woman? Laurent didn't look injured, but some scars were invisible. He treated ridding the world of dybbuks like a holy crusade, but was it a calling or a burden? If I could save enthralleds and prevent him from going through this process, would I be taking away his purpose or being merciful?

I clenched the notebook. No, I had enough to deal with. People knew the dangers of lowering their inhibitions during the Danger Zone, and it wasn't on me to save everyone with poor decision making skills.

In my head, I heard the ratchet of the lever and the water starting to flow over the squeaky water wheel as Count Rugen started the Machine.

"Get out here." Laurent beckoned to Emmett, who remained inside the office. "Time to leave."

Emmett took one look at Laurent's expression and backed up, thudding against the exterior window. "You can't come in or you'll set off the alarm."

"While the longer you don't come out..." Laurent made a slashing motion with his hand.

Emmett audibly swallowed. "I want to go home now, partner."

"Good idea." Laurent turned back to me and imperiously held out his hand for the notebook.

My black invisibility mesh swam up to my waist, and with my cloaked lower half, I no longer cast a normal shadow. I looked like I had a dismembered torso, which was disturbing.

"If you want it," I said, "ask me to work with you. Nicely."

Laurent opened his mouth to answer, but stilled and inhaled. "Vamps. Two."

Emmett eeped and ducked under the desk.

"They've come to finish the job from yesterday," I croaked, my heart thundering in my ears. Shoving the notebook in the small purse slung across my chest, I sprinted toward the back of the main room. "We have to get out of here."

"If I don't shut them down," Laurent said, "they'll come after you again and you won't walk away."

I flung open the only door at the back, but it led to a break room.

"Fuuuck!" Visions of Raj's bloody meaty heart danced in my head. Eyes wide, I hammered on the windows, but they didn't open and the drop was too far even if they did. "There's no other way out."

We were sitting ducks.

Laurent swore under his breath. "Cloak yourself and the golem and go," he growled. "Now."

I was trembling, overwhelmed by the phantom stench of the murder, but I couldn't leave Laurent to fight my battles for me. Especially when he hadn't shifted and victory against two vampires was far from assured. I flicked my fingers to call my shadow scythe up, but without the presence of a dybbuk or whatever aberration that woman in the KH qualified as, it didn't work. I shook my head. "I won't leave—"

He turned the coldest gaze I'd ever seen on me. "You're a liability."

Knowing intellectually that he was deliberately trying to drive me away didn't stop a half-sob, half-gasp from escaping my lips.

A body thudded against the employment agency door.

Fur burst out over the back of Laurent's hands, his fingers shifting to claws. He stormed toward the front of the office, planting himself between me and anything that came through the door.

This wasn't the same man who'd regarded my magic with awe and told me that if I figured it out, I'd be unstoppable. If I stayed, he'd be angry and distracted, and truthfully, I was so terrified of ending up like Raj that my few "fight" instincts had been curb stomped by "get the fuck out of here now."

I stumbled into motion, running over to Don's office, my cloaking rising to shoulder height, but the golem was hiding. "Emmett, hurry, let's go."

He shot out from under the desk and popped his head through the hole in the wall, right as a female vamp with crazy eyes and impressive biceps broke down the employment agency's door. With a "Nope," the golem retreated once more.

Hot on her heels came a wiry bloodsucker, bouncing on his toes like he couldn't wait for the fight to begin.

"Where's the satchel?" The female vamp jerked her chin at me.

"I knew it was important!" I crowed.

Glaring, Laurent moved, blocking her view of me. "Are you Celeste?"

The wiry vamp laughed, which withered under the female's "shut it" glower.

She stared into Laurent's eyes. "What do you know about her?"

"You call that a compulsion?" Laurent tsked the female, who lunged for him. He deflected her with a forearm strike, ducking into a low roundhouse kick that knocked her feet out from under her, but the bloodsucker was up in seconds, both fiends blocking the shifter in against a cubicle.

He reached behind him, grabbed onto the top of the cubicle with his claws, and flipped himself backwards over it, sticking his landing with such flawless grace he'd have brought tears to the eyes of Russian Olympic judges.

I gestured frantically at Emmett, who shook his head at me, refusing to leave Egerts's office. I was taking a second to decide whether to haul the golem out, alarm be damned, when the female pole vaulted the cubicle chasing Laurent while the wiry one went for me.

What was in the satchel? I ran an obstacle course through the main room, weaving through desks, my magic falling off me like a loose pair of pants. Pens, mugs, even a computer monitor, I lobbed anything I could at my pursuer, but the gap between us dwindled down to nothing.

The bloodsucker cornered me by the supply room, where we played Ring Around the Photocopier, while I fumbled for the lighter in my purse, screaming silently at myself to hold it together. With a quick feint left, I dove the other way, intending to grab the vamp's shadow, but he saw through my ruse and caught one of my legs.

The wiry vamp dragged me along the carpet back to Egerts's office, his shadow out of my reach, and my kicks to his person barely registering.

My shirt rode up underneath me, my skin burning with rug rash.

Outside the hole to the office, he dropped my leg. "I'll give you one chance to tell me where the satchel is, then I start ripping off limbs."

A body flew at him, tackling him to the ground.

Laurent had lost his baseball cap and glasses, and one of his shoulders was bleeding, but that didn't stop him from slicing the wiry vamp across the collarbone with his claws.

Chest heaving, I scrambled to my feet and flicked the lighter. My magic once again tingled up from my shadow and through my body, but I didn't have time for cryptic clues. The faster I dispatched this one, the faster Laurent and I could team up on the female and get answers.

Again and again, Laurent slashed at the vamp. Blood spurted, but he didn't stop.

I grabbed the vamp's shadow and squeezed, cold darkness oozing through my fingers, but I wasn't the only one who'd arrived at this particular party.

"Bad pup," the female vampire said. She lifted Laurent up by the back of his neck and slammed him against the door of the office next to Don's.

A demented light came into Laurent's eyes and, laughing maniacally, he headbutted her in the face. He could ratchet down his glee a solid 45 percent and still be described as rapturous.

"Why do you want the satchel?" I said to my captive.

The male bloodsucker bolted up into sitting position and reached out to grab me. I jumped back. He appeared to be the weaker of the two undead, but while his feet were stuck to the ground, he could still move his body under my magic hold.

That meant the female was extremely deadly—and currently on Laurent like a condom, the two of them rolling on the floor in a tangle of limbs. She pinned Laurent between her thighs, his wolf claws trapped under him, and licked his neck, her fangs grazing his skin.

Really, Mr. Notoriously Guarded with His Personal Space? Tear out her throat already.

Snarling, Laurent bucked her off. I sniffed. That was something, at least.

The wiry vamp glanced at them and leered. "Someone's having fun."

I thrust his shadow into the lighter's flame, coldly satisfied when he dissolved into a pile of ashes.

"Whoa." Emmett had stuck his head out of the broken glass. Sweat and foundation dripped off him in streaks, exposing his red clay.

Sensing an easier prey, the female sprang to her feet.

Laurent barreled into her, but she threw him across the room, and he crashed with an audible thud and a grunt, drywall chunks hitting the ground.

I grabbed at the vampire's shadow, but she jumped up the wall out of my reach, like a spider waiting for a fly. There was no way to get Emmett without her attacking me, and Laurent was still down.

It was hardly a surprise that she hadn't answered my question about the satchel.

Taking a steadying breath, I sent my animated shadow, Delilah, up after the vamp, an expectant tingle running through our connection. Was this why the scythe didn't work in the presence of vampires? Delilah wanted to fight the vamp on her own? My shadow glanced down at me and once more, I felt the weight of her expectation, as well as my own uncertainty.

The vamp slammed Delilah against the wall hard enough to rattle my teeth. Pain lanced through *my* skull and black spots danced through my vision. Delilah didn't feel anything, but all her injuries were inflicted on me, thanks to our psychic bond. Before I could shake off my dizziness, the fiend grabbed Delilah by the throat, dropped gracefully to the ground, and squeezed.

The breath was knocked from my lungs, my throat burning under her crushing hold. I couldn't even recall my magic and free myself from this asphyxiation.

The vampire's eyes widened, her mouth opening in a soft gasp, and a thin line of blood burbled out of a newly-made gash across her neck, like lipstick on a smile.

She slowly crumpled, but Laurent impaled her on his claws halfway down to the carpet, savagely tearing into her chest.

His eyes were lit with a crazed glint and his hair was matted to his scalp in bloody curls. Locking his eyes onto mine, he teased her heart out of her.

"Fuuuck," Emmett whispered from behind me.

The vampire dissolved into a shower of ash. Not taking his focus from us, Laurent flicked his claws to disperse the dust. His chest rose and fell in ragged harsh gasps, and while his face was human, a feral animal blinked out at me from behind his eyes.

"They knew you were in the car. They knew about the satchel." His voice was glacier-cold. "They came here for you because you stumble around leaving tracks any idiot can follow. What did I tell you about hornet's nests?"

"If they knew about the car and the satchel," I said, "they would have come for me regardless. This has nothing to do with my stealthy investigation."

"And everything to do with working for Tatiana." Each predatory step of Laurent's felt like a nail pounded into my coffin.

Emmett and I backed up.

"Which we've been over a billion times," I said. "She's my protection."

Laurent's mouth curled even more into a sneer.

The golem and I ducked behind a large potted rubber tree. Yeah, that argument was a tad weak. Tatiana had assured me that the head vamp wouldn't be a threat to me while I worked for her.

But if our attackers weren't Zev's to command? I hadn't considered that.

"I did kill one of them," I pointed out.

Laurent punched a door.

Emmett gulped. "Nice knowing you."

Laurent lived his life like a burning star, daring the universe to make him go supernova. Yet I was supposed to stay inside some prescribed box?

I jutted my chin out. "I'm not backing down. I feel a sense of obligation to the victim."

"And that matters more than—" Laurent systematically shredded a rubber tree leaf into oblivion. He didn't seem to realize he'd partially shifted again.

I opened my mouth to say something and push his animal side to the background, but I was scared that his human half *was* in control and any friendship we'd previously had was gone for reasons I couldn't comprehend. "Matters more than what?"

Laurent was so close that he filled my vision, his anger palpable. "You have everything to live for. You have a kid. Stop acting like any of this is more important."

I sucked in a breath. "Don't *ever* say I don't have my priorities straight when it comes to my daughter." He opened his mouth, but I shook my head, dark magic swirling around my feet. "If you know what's good for you, you'll keep quiet."

I grabbed Emmett's hand, stepped into the shadows, and got us out of there before I did something I'd regret.

11

———

THE SHADOWS GAVE WAY AND EMMETT AND I LANDED at Pyotr's feet in the cave. The gargoyle was dressed in the same brown plaid I'd last seen him in, except this time, he held a clunky box that was connected to the television set by a long cord.

The screen was angled away from us, but I recognized the robotic blips and beeps.

"Is amazing," Pyotr gushed, his Russian accent turning "is" into "eez." He rose up from his chair in excitement. "They have this thing called video game." He pronounced the "v" like a "w." "You know this?"

Gaming systems had come a long way since Pong, but he was all lit up like a little kid on their birthday and I didn't have the heart to crush him, even if I was choked with rage over Laurent's comments. "Yeah. Pretty fun."

Emmett sniffed. "Why does it smell like unicorn shit in here? And how about you turn up the lights? This is getting pervy real fast."

I stood up, straightening my clothes. "That's fabric softener, and we're in the Kefitzat Haderech. It's a shortcut for people with Banim Shovavim magic. Highly top secret. Speak of this to anyone and you'll be giving yourself your own rectal exam, got it?"

Emmett nodded, edging away from me toward the spotlit pile of socks, his fingers twitching.

I slapped his hand. "Touch one and you'll wish I was the one torturing you."

"Save your bitchiness for the wolf," he grumbled.

"Sorry." I exhaled slowly.

Pyotr regarded the golem with his dark marble-like eyes. "You brought a pet?" He awkwardly patted Emmett's head then turned back to his game with a scoff. "Hairless. Hate those."

"I'm not—" Emmett winced as I elbowed him.

"I'm choosing a sock," I said.

The neon sign popped up. *Want to hear a joke?*

"Not particularly," I said, as Emmett said, "Yes" enthusiastically.

Why was the baby Banim Shovavim born with sunglasses on?

"This again?" I crossed my arms.

"I got it." Emmett waved his hand around. "Because their future was so bright, they had to wear shades."

The sign changed into a face emoji mirroring the incredulous look on my face.

"What?" Emmett tugged at the collar of his sweatshirt. "Jude was playing this all-'80s station and I heard that song like three times."

"Uh-huh." I searched the socks for another thigh-high, but there weren't any that long. The pile had dwindled, its pickings slim. My best option was decorated with a deformed witch and a ghost that looked like a cracked egg. It was barely knee-high.

The woman stuck roaming the KH highway had clutched a tattered baby's sock. I shook my head. Screw all of this. I hadn't done anything wrong. Laurent was the one who was way out of line. I'd walked out of that car alive; Raj hadn't. So yeah, I was deeply invested in this, but how dare Laurent imply that anything meant more to me than Sadie?

I grabbed the cheaply made ghost sock. "I didn't do anything to lose points. Seeking justice is a good thing."

"Points for what?" Emmett said.

Pyotr ignored me to start a new game of Pong.

The neon sign buzzed. *Didn't you?*

I wrapped the sock around my knuckles like a boxer's wrap, weighing my recent choices. I took care of my loved ones and I'd taken care of my golem team member, but Laurent was my team member, too. Hadn't I pushed him to declare us partners in the first place? Then I'd left him there to handle his fucked-up mindset on his own. No wonder he was so resistant to asking for help, if it was so half-assed.

On the other hand...

"Laurent followed me there. He could have cloaked with me and we'd have found a different time and place to make a stand. One that wouldn't have pushed him into that state. His sanity is a frayed rope that he can take better care of, because I'm not his mother. Nor are his legion of issues mine to bear." I flung my hair off my shoulder with a "so there."

"Dude." Emmett shook his head.

I scrubbed a hand over my face, immediately wishing I hadn't because it was the one with the sock and I'd gotten a nose full of fabric softener, which really did smell like unicorn shit.

A second, more sinister meaning to Laurent's words crashed over me. Had he lost a child and that's where his anger about me not valuing my daughter properly came from? My lungs couldn't inflate and my head spun.

Pyotr's game ended and he poked Emmett's shoulder. "Ugly." Emmett smacked his hand away and the gargoyle laughed. "Little baby. No fangs or claws."

Emmett turned, well, redder, apparently still sore about that moniker. I'd told a three-year-old that Emmett was a baby—unlike her big-girl self—and she'd run with it.

"Enough," I snapped. "We're going."

"I'm not a baby!" Emmett walloped Pyotr with a fist,

knocking him backwards. Then the golem gasped and stared at his hand like he couldn't believe he'd done that.

That made two of us.

Pyotr roared, and pulled himself out of his slouched position, towering over both of us. His wings snapped out behind him, the tips deadly sharp points.

I grabbed Emmett's wrist before the gargoyle obliterated him, and ran to the narrow green door, hammering on it. "Let us out."

Pyotr kicked the table out of his way, while the sign face silently snickered.

My money's on the gargoyle.

Focused on our destination, I threw myself against the door as it opened, spilling through and yanking Emmett with me.

With the gargoyle thundering behind us, there was no time to take it slow. We flat out sprinted through the near-darkness, tripping over bumps and potholes, whatever the KH saw fit to throw our way.

A silver door shimmered into existence up ahead.

Emmett and I crashed through it, shoving our bodies against it to slam the door against Pyotr's arm, until he snatched his limb away and we could close it.

The door vanished, leaving us sprawled against Jude's wall, breathing heavily.

We were alive with no vamps, no gargoyle, and no KH, just a very astonished Jude, her mug of tea hitting the fluffy carpet.

Emmett checked that we were safe, then beelined for the remote control, huddling into a ball on Jude's sofa.

I yearned to collapse in the cream leather chair and drag the fuzzy blanket over me, but if I lay down, I wasn't getting up.

"He's all yours," I said, and left.

By the time I'd retrieved my car from where I'd parked it near Aries Employment and gotten home, I was exhausted, but I had to speak to Laurent. I called three times, but he didn't answer.

I spent the night stress dreaming, bursting awake in fits and starts. I finally fell into a peaceful slumber only to wake up with a jolt on Friday morning at Sadie's frantic call of "Mooooom!"

"What?" For a second, I thought I'd gone blind, but my sheet had gotten twisted up over my face. Tossing it aside, I raced out of bed and flew down the stairs, envisioning my child bleeding out with an axe through her skull. My mom superpower: imagining the worst in the blink of an eye.

"Okay, listen." She tucked a strand of her long black hair behind her ear, the shorts and T-shirt she'd worn yesterday now substantially more rumpled, but there wasn't a scratch on her.

I pulled her into a tight hug, resting my cheek against her silky black hair and breathing in her coconut shampoo.

"You okay?" she said.

I squeezed her one more time, then headed for the kitchen. "I'm fine and you're not dying, so I want coffee first."

"Let me get it." She tossed her backpack on the ground, then glanced at me and picked it up again. "I'll put my bathing suit in the wash."

I watched suspiciously as she opened the closet door hiding our washer and dryer and put her stuff in without it having gone moldy. "I'm not giving you money."

"I don't want money." Her bright smile faltered at my eyebrow raise. "Come get your coffee."

"Spill, Sadie." Yawning, I sat down at the table.

"You know your nightgown is inside out?" she said.

I shot her a pointed look.

My daughter emptied the old espresso grinds into the counter composter and filled our stovetop Moka pot. "It's nothing bad. I just want to have a friend over today."

"Is this friend a killer clown wearing another human's face? Because you're being weird."

"No," she said huffily.

My mouth fell open and I smacked the table jubilantly. "It's a boy. Or girl. But a crush? I'm right, aren't I?"

"Forget it," she mumbled.

I sang "Sunrise, Sunset" from *Fiddler on the Roof*, asking where had my little girl gone.

"This is exactly why I didn't want to say anything. You'll totally embarrass me in front of him." She flicked on the burner, her body tense.

My child was about to melt down, her anxiety kicking in.

"I won't," I said gently. "I swear. I was teasing you."

She gripped the counter, her head bowed, taking slow, even breaths.

I eyed my phone, wanting to call Laurent and hear his voice to know how he was doing, but my kid needed me right now.

"Okay," I said, waiting until we both had our lattes to grill her further. "Is he good at school? Do you guys have stuff in common? Is he funny?"

She dumped sugar into her mug. "I dunno. Yeah."

"To which question?"

"Oh my God, Mom. Just yeah."

I dropped the subject, enjoying Sadie's bribe of breakfast—she was highly skilled in the scrambled egg arts—while she chattered away about the pool party.

After a quick shower, I got dressed and readied myself to face the day. The past was the past and I had to make good choices moving forward, like being polite to some hormone-ridden teenager who was coming over to spend time with my hormone-ridden teenager.

Fingers crossed that he'd be dybbuk-possessed and I could use my shadow scythe on him.

Laurent still wasn't picking up his phone and his voicemail message oozed French arrogance. "Why are you bothering me? I'm certain I have no desire to speak to you. If you think otherwise, leave a message and try your luck."

"It's Miri. I... I'm sorry for yesterday. Can we talk? Call me." I shoved the phone in the pocket of my capris. If he didn't call by tonight, I'd swing by his place.

Sadie paced the front hall, also cleaned up and now wearing a cute blue sundress. According to the frustrated screams I'd heard coming from her bedroom earlier, it was the thirteenth outfit she'd tried on.

My phone rang and, thinking it was Laurent, I answered it, looking at the number as I raised it to my ear. Blocked, ugh, probably a telemarketer.

"Hello?" I said skeptically.

"Where is the satchel?" The speaker used a voice distortion app.

My eyebrows shot up. "What satchel?" I lied, hurrying into the kitchen and out of Sadie's earshot. "Is this Celeste?"

There was a pause. "We know you have it. Return it at midnight tomorrow or face more of my associates." They named a drop-off spot and hung up.

I dropped heavily into a chair. There was way too much interest in this satchel, making whatever was inside it either extremely valuable, extremely dangerous, or both. This phone call had clarified one thing: the vampires last night had no connection to the murderer. They worked for this mystery caller and if this person had killed Raj, they'd already have the satchel in their possession.

Tomorrow night, I would go to the meeting and discover what everyone was after.

There was a knock at the front door, so I temporarily shelved any burgeoning ideas on how to accomplish this goal and went to be a supportive mom. I entered the foyer to find Sadie counting to ten under her breath.

She hissed at me to behave and flung the door open with a casual "Hey."

Good call. Play it cool. Tamping down a smirk, I checked this kid out, extremely curious as to what kind of real live boy made my girl's heart beat faster, since she'd only ever had crushes on fictional characters.

Caleb Bailey was a well-mannered if somewhat gangly young

man wearing a T-shirt with a picture of the TARDIS on it. He shook my hand as Sadie introduced us.

"This is my mom. Miriam, Caleb."

"Very nice to meet you," I said. "So did you and Sadie have classes together?"

"No, I took junior theatre tech, and I was on the backstage crew for the play that Chu here was in." The two of them turned to each other and fired finger guns with "pew pew" noises, then burst into laughter.

That's sweet. Sadie had an in-joke. With an almost-senior when she'd just finished grade ten. I checked his shadow for any crimson flecks but was sadly disappointed. It was fine. Dating a girl a year younger wasn't a killable offence. Not that they were necessarily dating, since he called her by her last name. Ooh, maybe he'd friendzoned her.

Except that made me want to kill him as well, because he should be so lucky as to date my daughter, but I kept my crazy-pants ramblings to myself, my smile on my face, and told them they were free to hang out in the living room and to help them-selves to any snacks.

"Thanks, Mom. This way." When Sadie led him off, she was blushing and he had this small besotted grin on his face. If they weren't dating already, it was headed that way fast.

My baby was going to have a boyfriend. Could I wrap her in barbed wire? Rent a tower to lock her in until I was ready for this? Who was I kidding? I'd never be ready. I puttered around the kitchen cleaning up until I'd resigned myself to this new reality, checking my phone every couple of minutes to make sure that I was still getting a signal and hadn't missed Laurent's call.

While I waited for him to reply, I paged through the black notebook that Emmett had stolen from Don's office. I found the initials RJ next to some dates, but couldn't make heads nor tails of the code, even after several attempts at basic cyphers, which I wrote down in my green paisley notebook. Topher's initials didn't appear anywhere.

Stymied, I wrote down possibilities of what could have been in the satchel: magic amulet, cash, drugs, cursed necklace, some other supernatural object that it wouldn't occur to me in a million years to come up with.

There was a knock at the front door.

Frustrated, I threw my pen down. "I'll get it."

Eli stood there in his police blues. I hadn't seen him in that uniform in years, not since he'd made detective. "Hey, Mir, can I get that book I lent you back?"

I raised an eyebrow. "Sure. Remind me which one it was again?"

Eli cocked his head, hearing the television go on. "The one in the living room."

I snorted.

He winked and strolled past me to where the kids were, grabbing the closest book on the bookshelf. "Oh hi," he said, in a surprised voice and held out his hand. "I'm Detective Eli Chu. Sadie's father."

Caleb eyed the badge clipped to Eli's belt and swallowed. "Hi. I'm Caleb."

At least Eli hadn't brought his gun.

The kid redeemed himself with what appeared to be a firm handshake under pressure while Sadie shot me a "help" look.

"They worked on the play together," I said.

"Fun," Eli said. "So you're a fellow thespian?" He said the last word with a weird Shakespearean accent.

Sadie glared at her dad so hard, I'm amazed he didn't burst into flames.

"Caleb did theatre tech for the play that your daughter was so great in," I said.

"Uh-huh. Tech. So you're thinking of going into…?"

"Computer sciences," Caleb said.

Eli gave a forced laugh. "That dot com bubble is long gone, but I guess there's always IT."

I covered my wince with my hand. The poor boy was seventeen. He didn't have to have his life mapped out.

Our daughter turned beet red, not so much embarrassed but as if the mercury had hit the top of the thermometer and was about to blow.

I tugged on Eli's sleeve. "You should be getting to work."

"Oh yeah. I just came to get my book back." Eli held it up, doing a double take because it was bell hooks's *Feminism is for Everybody*, then held up a fist. "Gotta be a good ally. Am I right?"

I kept my sigh in through sheer force of will.

"Well, I'll leave you to it," Eli said. "Don't do anything I wouldn't do."

I hustled him out of there before there was a body count. "You're a shit," I said, once we got on the front porch.

He held out the book but I shook my head.

"Do you *not* want to be a good ally?" I said. "How do I break this news to our daughter?"

He tucked the book under his arm. "Fine."

"Are you even going to work or was that just for that poor boy's benefit?"

"Totally put on for the mouth breather. I'm going to the gym after this, but I saw him coming up the walk and couldn't resist. She couldn't find a nice Chinese boy? I bet he drinks boba and thinks that makes him woke."

"Right. And computer science? At least the last one was going into medicine."

Eli frowned. "Isn't this her first boy—oh. You mean my mother when she met you."

I smiled tightly. "Don't I just? This is our daughter's first crush, Eli. Leave her alone."

"I was teasing, but, just in case, what's the kid's full name? I'll run him through the system."

I crossed my arms, leaning against the door frame. "You can't do that."

"Can't I?"

I hesitated a little too long before replying in the negative.

Eli laughed and went inside his own place.

Laurent still hadn't called back. Heading into the kitchen, I fired off a text, in case he hadn't gotten the voicemail. *Updates. Please call.*

I added a second text. *Or text.*

Then a third. *Whatever's easiest.*

Text number four. *Or stand under my window and howl. That works.*

I banged the cell against my forehead.

"Mom, is it okay if we go out?"

Thank God. Saved from myself. I slid my phone in my pocket, then gathered up both notebooks and put them in a drawer. "You've barely been home."

"I know, but a bunch of kids are going to hang out all day, they know Caleb, and I really want to go." She bounced on her toes, making puppy dog eyes. "I only have a week before I'll be working all summer. Please."

"Which kids?"

She named her usual crew, including her cousin Nessa, and some boys I didn't know.

"Where are you going?"

"The beach and then to grab something to eat and a movie."

"Early show or you come home." She opened her mouth to protest but I cut her off. "I'm serious." After that vamp attack, I wanted my daughter safely inside before dark. "If the movie gets out after sundown, you phone me to come get you. Understood?"

She shot me a weird look. "Yeah, okay. I'll tell Caleb to walk me home if it's early enough."

There was another knock on the door.

"If that's Dad again, I'm going to kill him." She marched out of the room, returning a moment later. "There's some woman here to see you."

Thinking it was Tatiana, I headed to the front door. "Hey, good timing. Oh. Hello."

"Come on doooowwwn!" An unfamiliar curvy woman, maybe thirty tops, in a white flowy skirt and a *The Price is Right* T-shirt stood on the front stoop.

I looked around in case there was someone on the sidewalk to explain this behavior, but we were alone. "I'm more of a *Jeopardy!* chick, but thanks?"

"I'm kidding. There's no game show." She held up her wrist, revealing a tattoo of a six-pointed gold star that glowed with the authority of its office, and winked. "Yippee ki-yay, shady lady."

My worst nightmare had come true. The Lonestars had found me.

12

"WHAT DO YOU WANT?" I WAS PROUD OF MY STEADY
voice. Had I missed a security camera at Aries Employment and
Egerts had identified me and called in the theft?

"Don't be nervous." The woman waved her hands around my
solar plexus, her cartoon-large blue eyes at odds with the chili
pepper-red hair that was shaved on the sides. "I can tell because
your emotional aura is mud and that energy point is all bunged
up. Want me to cleanse it?"

"That's more of a fourth date move." Sweat ran down the
back of my neck. "It's just a hot flash." I had to get rid of her so I
could go over to Jude's and get some more brains on this code,
because if Laurent didn't want to speak to me yet, I had to
respect that. "I've got to work, so—"

"I know." She performed a pirouette, her skirt spinning out.
"With Tatiana. Far out."

Was this hippy flake for real? "Listen, Woodstock—"

She clapped her hands together. "Ooh. I love that little
bird."

I patted myself down for an errant sock sticking to me,
because if I wasn't still in the Kefitzat Haderech, then what the
fuck was happening? *This* was one of the Lonestars whom I'd

spent almost thirty years living in fear of? "Riiight. Why are you here?"

She pulled a sad face. "The Sharmas called us." In other words, save us both any stories. Though I could cross my burglary last night off the list of reasons for her appearance. That was something.

I should have prepared myself to meet the Lonestars because magic crimes were their territory, but in my defense, I'd been a little busy. Plus, once the Sapien police had found the body, it hadn't occurred to me that the Lonestars would also investigate.

There was no cause for concern. All the Sharmas could have told her was that I'd met the dead man, nothing more. Still, my tank top stuck to my back.

"Anyhoo," the Lonestar said, "come back to HQ for a little chat. I make a wicked cup of rooibos and we still have some shortbread."

No way. I had to buy myself some time to work through every question I could be asked about my magic and my entire past, but she stuck to me like a wisp of dandelion fluff. If need be I could cloak myself and escape. Get Sadie and go... where? Shoot, why hadn't I researched countries without extradition treaties?

I took a step back, gauging whether I could lock my front door before she cleansed me or blew out a chakra or whatever. "You know all about me and I don't even know your name."

"I'm Ryann Esposito." She gave a low curtsy. This flower child persona had to be some act to throw people off balance before she went in for the kill.

I wiped my now-drenched neck with my arm.

"Peppermint oil," Ryann said. "My aunt swears by it for hot flashes."

"I'll keep that in mind."

Sadie and Caleb joined us. She shoved her feet into flip-flops as Caleb told me it was nice meeting me. I guess he could live. My daughter gave me a quick peck on the cheek, and the two of them headed out, their hands almost but not quite brushing.

"Early show, Sades," I called out.

She waved without turning around.

"Cute kid," Ryann said.

Lonestar interest in my child worked wonders to cool me right down.

"Her father is a Sapien cop," I said.

If only the Lonestar had shown up half an hour earlier. Eli's car was gone now, so he was at the gym.

She nodded. "Neat."

Well, so much for that threat.

But then Ryann spread her hands in front of her, like a dealer laying out cards. "Look," she said quietly, "you're Banim Shovavim. I'm an Ohrist. You have no reason to trust me after how we've mistreated your people."

Of all the things I'd expected, it certainly hadn't been that. Still, I'd seen enough good-cop-bad-cop routines on TV and in real life to know better. "That would be the understatement of the century," I said. Ryann wasn't only an Ohrist; she was a Lonestar.

She nodded. "The thing is, we've got a murder on our hands and you were the last one to see the victim. You might know something, no matter how seemingly irrelevant, that turns out to be important. Don't you want justice served?"

There was a frustration in her expression that I recognized from Eli when a case was getting away from him and a person his gut told him had valuable information wouldn't talk. Had I unfairly judged all Lonestars because of McMurtry's actions after my parents' deaths?

"It really is good shortbread," she said, looking down at her feet. "I don't have much time for baking these days, but I did make it myself and I'm proud of it."

I sighed. "Where's HQ?"

"The Park."

I stared at her blankly. "What park?"

Ryann grasped her skirt in her hands, waving it back and

forth like she was dancing to a song in her head. *The* Park." She frowned at me. "Stanley Park?"

I put my hands on my hips. "Because you have a sudden urge to see the dolphin show? Or wait, I know. We're going to ride the mini train and discuss this incredibly serious topic. Okay, I'll talk, officer, but only if you buy me some popcorn. It's kind of a family tradition." I leaned against the door. "Like I said, I have to get to work so we can set up an appointment and—"

She jammed in her foot to keep me from closing it. "This won't take long, but I do need you to come with me."

"That feels like a threat." I nudged her foot but she put her weight on it, staying put.

"That's not how I intended it."

My phone rang. Laurent?

The Lonestar wasn't budging, but I had to answer that call. Delilah rose up to shove her out of the way, but before her knuckles connected, Ryann darted forward and tapped me in four different places quicksilver fast. A blaze of searing energy pinballed from my head to my heart to my kidneys, traveling down to my left foot with the mother of all electric shocks.

I crumpled in a heap. My animated shadow deflated like a cheap bouncy castle and I curled into the fetal position, the floor cold under my cheek and my entire body stinging like I'd been slapped by jellyfish. Fun fact: the collective noun for a group of jellyfish was a smack. Appropriate, right? I would have laughed, but nothing in me could move.

"I'm really sorry," Ryann said. "But you did attack first."

"Shortbread," I wheezed, "sounds good."

"Awesome." She extended a hand to help me up and I flinched. "Silly." She grabbed me under my armpits and hauled me to my feet. "Where's your car?"

The Lonestar had to help me get my purse and keys because I was still shaky. I checked my phone before I threw it in my bag, but the missed call wasn't from Laurent. It was from my ex-sister-in-law. Fabulous. I just got chakra-slapped for her?

That said, visiting Lonestar HQ was more appealing than phoning Genevieve back. "Let's go."

Ryann assisted me into the driver's seat with a pat on the head before twirling around the car to the other side.

My limbs still felt like wet noodles and my bones like mush, so I took a moment to hunch over the wheel, trying not to whimper through the agonizing pins and needles prickling that raged through my extremities. When I'd finally caught my breath, I flapped a hand at her outfit. "This is all some schtick, right?"

A steely look suffused with intelligence flashed across her face before she blinked at me with an innocent smile, clicking her seat belt in. "What are you talking about?"

I finally regained motor control and turned on the engine. "Don't you have your own car? I could follow you."

"I'm part of a car share co-op. Better for the environment." She'd plucked a dandelion before getting in and now propped it behind her ear.

"Shocking plot twist," I muttered. My shadow was an itchy presence against my back, but unleashing Delilah in close quarters would be round two of "paralyze the nice Feldman lady." Best to save my magic for a surprise attack.

A news clip played on the radio of the VPD press conference, releasing Raj's name, his status as a university student and that he had no next of kin. When they moved on to asking for tips from the public, I snapped the station off.

"Poor kid," I said. "No family to fight for him."

"That's why we're here." Ryann spent the rest of the drive humming some weird little atonal melody until I took the exit lane off West Georgia Street into Stanley Park, and she fell silent.

Much like the reality of Blood Alley—a two-block cobble-stoned stretch of restaurants in touristy Gastown—hadn't prepared me for the hidden version controlled by the vampires, I couldn't imagine what I was in for now.

Stanley Park was one of the top attractions for both locals

and visitors. Larger than Central Park in New York, it jutted off the West End downtown, with a ten-kilometer seawall running its circumference that was popular with cyclists, joggers, and stroller-pushing power walkers. This time of year, the bike rental places around the park would be sold out, with groups of the many foreign students who came to study here riding the seawall in identical helmets. They'd have a hilarious time weaving through the crowds, some wobbling on tandem bikes.

Being so big, Stanley Park had something for everyone. There was an aquarium that Sadie and I had spent hours at when she was little, mostly watching the floating otters hold paws and visiting the starfish in the shallow touch pools. The open-air theater had begun its summer season with two musical productions. There was a tea house, three beaches, an outdoor pool, huge totem poles that were a popular photo-op spot, and the mini train.

Sadie's favorite thing as a little kid had been to put on waterproof clothing from head to toe and then be turned loose on one of the many trails in the woods while it rained, jumping in as many puddles as she possibly could before wearing herself out.

We cleared a roundabout with roads leading to different areas of the park and Ryann pointed at a little stone bridge over to the right. "Just through there."

Revealing hidden magic spaces was like staring at one of those 3D stereograms and getting the picture to show itself. I pretty much sucked at it, though I'd recently discovered that if I used my magic cloaking, I could see them no problem. Since I wasn't about to try that while driving—or have Ryann interpret it as a threat and take me down again—I said that I'd leave it to her to get us through.

We drove under the bridge but instead of coming out next to Lord Stanley's statue and the first main parking lot by the horse and trolley stand, with part of downtown visible across the harbor, there was a white flash and we shot out under towering cedars, spruce, and Douglas firs in a pristine forest.

My mouth fell open and I pulled the car over to the side of the narrow dirt road, under a dogwood tree bearing its last few white blossoms. "Holy shit."

It was as if we'd travelled back in time. I rolled down the window, listening to the raucous bird calls and inhaling the scent of rich earth, cedar, and old growth forest. It smelled like Laurent, and heat crept into my cheeks because I still didn't know how he was doing.

"Is the Park only for Lonestars?" I said, once more driving down the road.

Ryann trailed her fingers in waves out the window. "Of course not. Everyone's welcome, though I'd stay away at night, especially on full moons."

The ground rumbled and the sky to my right belched a corrosive reddish-orange cloud that stank of sulphur. I calculated where in the real park it correlated to and my heart sank. The tiny island was currently home to a naval base, which was no big deal. The fact that it was called Deadman's Island, was a former burial ground, smallpox site, and all-around haunted place, with a sky straight out of Dante's *Inferno* in this version, was somewhat more disconcerting.

A tortured scream was cut short with a terrifying suddenness and I hurriedly rolled up my window. "Do I want to know?"

Ryann glanced quickly that way, her lips pressed together in a thin line as she shook her head. "Pray you never find out."

Majestic trees lined the road, hiding what lay beyond in the heart of the park, but I caught a flash of a deer's tawny brown fur with white spots, and later on, a fox darted across the road.

"Is it all forest in this version?" I said.

"Pretty much. Beaver Lake and Lost Lagoon both exist here as well. Some of the shifters really dig all the birds and fish there, and of course it's practical."

An eagle soared overhead, lazily circling twice.

I adjusted the sun visor. "Practical as in good for the forest ecosystem or practical in the *Godfather* sense of 'sleeping with the fishes'?"

"Right?" That wasn't actually an answer, you manically happy scary person. Ryann threw me a thumbs-up, which I weakly returned. "Aha," she said. "Turn here on the left."

The trees pressed in more closely on this bumpy road, and their leafy canopy grew thicker, the light instantly turning gloomy. Points for setting the mood.

She directed me to park in a small dirt lot next to a couple of Range Rovers. We walked into the woods and I came to a stop with a soft gasp.

Lonestar HQ was a treehouse complex built on brown metal struts shaped like trunks that branched off to support the various buildings. The natural wooden shingles and foliage peeking out of every space under and around the buildings made it this magical hideaway. Angled solar panels on the roof drew sunlight and the windows were tinted to reflect the sky.

Even the front entrance was enchanting. An archway had been carved into a huge hollow tree, concealing the lower stairs up to the wooden carved doors. The insides of the tree were covered in a spongy deep green moss, while colorful tiny red and purple flowers grew along the railings.

I took the stairs slowly, craning my neck to take everything in. It was straight out of a fairy tale—which people always said like it was a good thing, conveniently forgetting the trauma of these fables. You didn't sleep for a hundred years or eat a poisoned apple from your stepmother without some serious PTSD. They always included the prince's kiss and left out the therapy and medication these poor women needed.

Ryann chuckled. "I never get tired of that look on people's faces." My look of astonishment or my fear? Best not to ask. "Look." She pointed up and I leaned over the railing for a better view.

On the roof, above a small round window fit for a hobbit, was a copper weathervane with a single star adorning its top.

"Nice branding," I said.

Ryann told me a bit about the building's history. She spoke so enthusiastically about it, her face lit up over the tiniest details, that I couldn't help but warm to her. Somewhat.

The inside of HQ smelled like pine needles thanks to the Douglas fir growing up through the lobby. Glossy framed portraits lined one wall, with Ryann's at the end of it. Employee of the month?

I shot her an assessing look as we passed the reception desk. There were plaques mounted behind it, each with a single name and date range at the top, followed by a list of other names in alphabetical order. The latest plaque, with no closing date, featured Ryann's name at the top.

Yikes. She wasn't just employee of the month. She was the head honcho of all Vancouver Lonestars and she'd taken an interest in me.

But everyone greeted her cheerfully, and more than once she popped her head into someone's office to ask how their kids' soccer league was doing or compliment them on catching a perp. No one was in uniform and they didn't use any rank designations when they spoke to Ryann. Some even praised her shortbread, though another ribbed her about cooking every free second and she laughed. Of all the police offices I'd been in with Eli, this was probably the most at home I'd ever felt in one.

I slowed down, trying to make all my previous assumptions fit with this new evidence, but Ryann motioned me onto a curved covered walkway with rooms running off it. If I got into a closed room with her, I might never get out, but I couldn't cloak because that would look like I had something to hide.

"I don't really know much about the Sharma situation, so why don't you ask me your questions here?" I planted myself on the walkway.

"Nothing to set the teacups down on in the hallway." Ryann gave me a vague smile, then politely asked some guy in a Hawaiian shirt to bring tea and shortbread to Room C.

He scowled and I braced myself, ready for everything I'd witnessed to be exposed for the charade that it was, but he immediately chuckled. "I hid the shortbread, hoping no one would notice."

"Miriam is here to help us with the Jalota murder," Ryann said.

"That trumps my cookie cravings. Thanks for coming in and doing your civic duty." He shook his head. "You'd be amazed at how many people don't want to step up. Okay, I'll bring everything to the interview room."

I trailed after Ryann. Maybe after we discussed Raj, I could bring up McMurtry? No. Even if her interest in me was benign, he was a former Lonestar. I was on my own for that.

Some of my tension drained away. Perhaps our chat wouldn't be too bad.

The interrogation room smelled like pine, though the lack of windows and the two-way mirror cut down on the charm factor —as did the stern silver fox in jeans, motorcycle boots, and a fitted long-sleeve shirt waiting for us. Whether he was a literal fox remained to be seen.

Ryann motioned for me to take a seat and then joined her colleague on the other side of the table. "Oliver Anderson, meet Miriam Feldman."

He nodded at me with no sign of recognition. I wanted to scoff, but held it in. Oliver Anderson and I knew each other already, thank you very much. My day was complete.

13

I'D COME ACROSS OLIVER ON A DATING PROFILE LAST year. He was handsome and I'd liked the quote he used: "After darkness comes the light." Looking it up, I'd found it attributed to Cornelius Nepos, an ancient Roman historian, and was curious if Oliver had an interest in past civilizations. He ticked a lot of boxes, from his age (then forty-eight) to his statement that he was seeking a mature woman, so I'd indicated I'd be open to contact, since the seven years was a difference that I could live with.

Nada. When I checked his profile again a couple of weeks later, he'd amended it to put a maximum age of thirty-three for this mature woman of his. He was a dick and that had nothing to do with being a Lonestar.

I nodded at Oliver, and the questioning began. I answered everything to the letter, not offering up additional information, a trick taught to me by the lawyers I'd worked for. Yes, I'd seen Raj outside the Sharmas' house and gotten suspicious. No, I didn't know who he was or what he was after. No, I didn't know he was an Ohrist. No, I didn't know who would want to kill the victim.

No, I didn't see the murderer.

I helped myself to another piece of shortbread. The tea was

bitter, but Ryann was right about the cookies. They were buttery, melt-in-my-mouth deliciousness. Much as I hated to admit it, they were better than mine.

Oliver braced his hands on the desk. "To review, your assertion is that you left Raj after telling him to move on from the Sharma house."

"Yes."

He smiled slyly, flipped open the laptop on the table, turned the screen around to face me, and hit a key. "Technology is incredible these days. You can hide a surveillance camera anywhere and they have an impressive range."

The grainy video footage came from a house across the street and captured me pulling up, with Raj waiting there. I took his suitcase, he kept his satchel, and then the most damning part—he got into the car and off we drove.

Oliver hit another key and the video stopped. He smirked, like this was all tied up. "Anything to say for yourself?"

Once again this man was dismissing me, and honestly, I was getting a little tired of that power dynamic. If things went sideways in this interview, I'd cloak myself, get the hell out, and regroup with Tatiana for the next move. Her protection was, after all, why I'd aligned myself with her.

And how did that work out with the vampire attacker at Aries Employment?

I pushed that thought aside and toyed with my old engagement ring that I now wore on my right hand. "Raj was in the car, but I didn't kill him."

Oliver walked in slow circles around the table. "Someone like you would say that."

Ryann shook her head. "Oliver," she said in a mildly chiding tone. "Let's keep this civil, please."

I nodded at her in thanks. "I don't have magic capable of ripping out his heart."

"Banim Shovavim can kill dybbuks though," Ryann said. "So cool."

Oliver gave her a sharp look and she shrugged unapologetically, taking a dainty bite of shortbread cookie, her white teeth flashing.

They were aware of that, too, huh? I waited for my fear to immobilize me, but instead a curious sense of calm descended. Lonestars had fucked with my life once before, but I wasn't a kid now, and I wasn't going to go down without a fight.

Besides, Ryann wasn't threatening me and she was keeping her colleague leashed.

"If you're concerned that as a woman past her *mature* years, I'm too senile to know my own magic," I said, "I'd be happy to get you drunk during the Danger Zone and have a reason to demonstrate my power."

He frowned, then gave the tiniest double take, a hint of red flushing his cheeks. "Are you threatening me?"

"Nope. I'm offering proof. You know, that important thing you don't have? Being in a car with someone isn't a crime and if I was an Ohrist, you'd probably be treating me as a witness or a possible victim rather than a suspect."

"The car you were driving—" Ryann began.

"Wasn't mine," I said.

"Yeah." Oliver sat on the edge of the table. "We checked it out. However, it had already been detailed. Why hurry and get it professionally cleaned if you didn't have something to hide? That doesn't look too good for your claims of innocence."

"That wasn't me," I said, hotly.

"That's not what we heard," he said.

Had Tatiana thrown me under the bus? Getting rid of the heart had been her idea, as had the detailing. Her claim that she didn't want either of us tied to Raj made sense at the time, given we didn't know about the doorbell footage placing me in the car. There was nothing illegal about driving someone—especially if that person was pulling a fast one on us with a stolen identity.

However, if her first reaction was to distance ourselves from this job, instead of calling in the Lonestars, was there more to this than I knew? Was Tatiana in on the murder? She'd sounded truly annoyed that Topher had been left waiting, but a good actor could fake that no problem.

Or was she protecting Laurent at all costs?

I fiddled with the zipper on my purse. If she was involved in this, or something illegal connected to this job, why agree to let me work with the Sharmas? I shook my head. I'd drive myself crazy with theories; I needed facts. Answers.

Ryann licked cookie crumbs off her finger. "What about Laurent Amar?"

"What about him? He didn't kill Raj either," I said. Laurent's history with the Lonestars was only marginally better than mine. They clearly had no respect for the vital public service he provided, but would they go so far as to pin this murder on him? "What's his motive?"

"That's what we're investigating since the execution aligns with his style of killing." Oliver tapped his chest, the tip of his gold Lonestar tattoo peeking out of his sleeve. "The ripped-out heart." The cops hadn't released that detail which meant Lonestars had informants on the force. "How do we know he didn't finally go feral? Murdering people over and over again has to fuck you up."

The memory of the other night hit me hard and fast, goosebumps dotting my skin at the recollection. Laurent's claws had sunk deep into the female vamp's chest, his blown-out pupils fogged with the same bloodlust that made his nostrils flare as he teased out her heart. But he hadn't spared a glance for the way her legs scuffed wildly against the industrial carpet at the employment agency. No, his gaze remained locked on mine, as if daring me to turn away from this performance.

I swallowed, grasping at the one thing I could, with all certainty, dispute. "He doesn't murder people. He takes out the dybbuk-possessed."

Oliver shook his head sadly. "There were no red streaks on

Jalota's corpse denoting possession, but if Amar can no longer tell the difference...?"

"And the possessed still look like their hosts." Ryann gave me a sympathetic smile. "Did you team up with Laurent again? We know you were working with him recently."

I almost preferred Bad Cop's outright hostility, because Ryann's smiles were beginning to grate.

"You're proposing that Laurent supposedly went feral and took this guy out, and I helped him by getting into a car crash that could have been fatal, why?" I said.

"That's what we have yet to determine," Oliver said. "You were the only one who knew Jalota was in the car prior to his murder, and we're *proposing* that if you didn't help Amar, then you murdered the man yourself."

"I told you I don't have that magic."

"We'll be verifying that, don't worry," Oliver said. He'd leaned into my personal space, so I "accidentally" jabbed him in the side when I took another sip of bitter cold tea.

"Whoops," I said. "I'm all hormonal imbalance and pointy elbows today."

Ryann nodded sadly. "It's because of your blocked energy. You really should cleanse."

Oh, I would. With a bottle of wine, as soon as this was over.

"What about the Sharmas?" I said. "This happened on their dime and the deceased resembled their son. What if they found out about Raj planning to hitch a ride on their plane, determined he was a threat, and decided to neutralize him?"

"It's possible," Ryann said. "But I was with the family when they first saw the footage and they were all genuinely shocked."

"Then Raj was working with someone else who turned on him," I said. "And they're looking to scapegoat Laurent."

Or me, because someone out there was convinced that I had the satchel.

Ryann reached for another cookie, then sighed, shook her head, and dropped her hand back into her lap. "You believe that

Raj Jalota, who resembled your client Topher Sharma, teamed up with someone with the same magic ability as Laurent, and then was double-crossed? That's far-fetched."

"Since Raj wasn't possessed," I said, "whoever killed him didn't need Laurent's ability to scent dybbuks. They'd just have to be a wolf shifter. Or any Ohrist who could manipulate a body well enough to crack open the ribcage and pull out a heart. I bet I could throw a stone and find three of those."

"That's true." Ryann pursed her lips. "But you're the connecting factor. You knew Jalota was in the car and you've worked with Laurent before. If you're hiding the fact that he's gone feral, you need to tell us. You aren't helping him if that's the case."

"Forget it." Oliver slashed a hand through the air. "She's a BS. She won't help us."

Under the table, I dug my nails into my thighs. "BS" was a slur for my kind and even though I wasn't surprised to hear it from Oliver, I thought given all the camaraderie amongst the Lonestars that even he'd be above that.

"I will do everything I can to help ensure the actual murderer is caught," I said evenly.

"More lies," Oliver said in a bored voice.

He was worse than a dog with a bone. I pressed my lips together to stifle my snort. The situation was no laughing matter, but I couldn't help the visual of this giant dick with his mini boner going on this witch hunt.

"The only thing I lied about was Raj being in the car," I said, "and as I explained, I don't have the ability to rip out his heart."

"But had you reported the murder immediately," Ryann said, "we could have located the corpse first. Even if you're cleared of any involvement in the murder, we can bring you in for jeopardizing Ohrists' ability to stay hidden." She poured me more tea and gently slid my cup closer.

Had I screwed up? I was still feeling my way through rejoining the magic community, and I didn't have the proper procedures memorized like the rest of them. Didn't that buy me a grace period? Would it, if I was Ohrist?

I shot her an accusatory glare. "Let me guess, you didn't intend that as a threat?"

"I'm honor bound to explain your situation to you."

"Well, then let me explain something right back," I said. "I suffered a concussion in that car accident. Tatiana had me treated by her personal healer and I wasn't in any kind of mindset to be thinking clearly about procedure. Plus, for all I knew Raj had left me the heart in lieu of a tip and taken off. I'm under Tatiana's protection so whatever you think of me as a Banim Shovavim, you better have hard proof if you're going to charge me with violating your prime directive."

"Right. The fixer." Oliver snorted. "Well, Tatiana will finally learn the limits of her power if we do find proof."

I pressed my thumb into a piece of shortbread, the cookie snapping into crumbs. My limbs felt like elastic bands stretched to the breaking point. "You Lonestars may have a lot of leeway, but you're not a South American dictatorship. Even you can't make people disappear when they have valid reasons for their actions."

"Everyone knows where they are," Oliver said.

I glanced at Ryann for clarification. Were these people in some kind of cold jail cell? She looked away, her lips pressed into a thin line. It was the same expression she'd had in the car—that tortured scream and the Lonestar's admonishments about Deadman's Island echoed in my ears, and I almost knocked over my tea, grabbing it at the last second with trembling hands.

Not a cell, but a much worse prison.

The room filled with an ominous brittle silence and a frozen fury lashed across my skin like a frigid winter wind over the lacy tide.

"Let's all take a breath." Ryann took a couple of calming inhales and exhales, waving her hands like a conductor in a symphony.

"I've told you everything I know," I said. "If there's something else you want from me, then spit it out or let me go."

"What was in the satchel?" Ryann tilted her head. "From the footage, Jalota seemed insistent on keeping it, and yet it wasn't found with the body. It could provide us with a motive."

This satchel was this season's hot-ticket item.

Had it been Ryann and me, I'd have told her everything, including about Celeste. I might even have asked her to help track down my mystery caller before our meeting. But I could totally see Oliver forcing Ryann to railroad us, burying any evidence that didn't fit his theory of Laurent or me as the guilty party. He'd been such an asshole that I wasn't about to help him out.

"Find the murderer and ask them," I said.

Ryann pulled a card out of her pocket and slid it across the table. "How about you go away and think on it and if you feel differently, call us?"

"Because if you don't," Oliver said with a smile, "we'll find out the truth anyway, and it'll be that much worse for you, BS."

I stood and gathered my things. Even if I handed them the killer on a silver platter, it wouldn't matter. As much as Ryann was trying to get me to believe otherwise, there were still plenty of Lonestars who'd be happy to see me rot away because of who I was, not what I'd done.

But even so, they wanted the satchel badly enough to let me walk out of here in the hopes that I might find it for them. That bag was the key to this murder, thus I had to find it first.

"You people have your priorities seriously screwed up," I said. "You're spending all this energy on me and Laurent, when an actual murderer is out there and could strike again." I gestured to the door. "I'm leaving."

They didn't try and stop me. Why bother? They knew where to find me.

14

I DROVE HOME WITH A TIGHT JAW, OBSESSIVELY pondering what would keep the Lonestars from imprisoning me on Deadman's Island if I was charged with violating their prime directive. Throwing them in the Kefitzat Haderech would work. If that skeleton face showed up, I'd pitch them through its nostril. I wrenched the wheel hard on a left turn, the tires squealing around the corner, but my anger wasn't for those two alone.

Had Laurent agreed to work together from the get-go, we might have had something more conclusive to present to the Lonestars, but noooo, he'd decided that he had to go it alone, and look how that had ended up.

Did he come back from the brink last night?

Had he been a dad?

I ground my teeth, driving three more blocks before my resolve broke, and, swearing, I pulled over to the curb to check my phone. The texts had yet to be read, unless Laurent had seen the notification pop up and not opened the app. I flung the cell down on the seat. He was probably fine and just annoyed that he'd had to put himself out on my behalf without being paid. He absolutely wasn't running through the Park in wolf form, the last traces of his humanity banished.

Slamming the car back into drive, I pulled aggressively into traffic, throwing a middle finger at the driver behind me who hadn't done the right thing and let me merge.

By the time I got home, I'd worked myself into a state of cold clarity with a solid to-do list. First, I would track down Celeste, second, I would decode the notebook, and third...

I glanced at my phone's screen one last time before shoving it in my purse. There was no third. I was still totally committed to obtaining justice for Raj. More so, now that I knew he didn't have any family.

Head high, I sailed into the house.

I called the Bear's Den and asked the hostess who answered if Harry was around?

She answered yes and told me to hang on.

"Oi, Harry speaking," he said, in his English accent.

"Hi, Harry, it's Miri. Laurent's friend?" I massaged my instep. I'd grabbed the first pair of shoes I'd found to go to Lonestar HQ and, discombobulated from Ryann's attack, had forgotten the cute espadrilles pinched my feet.

"Sure, luv," the gargoyle said. "I remember you. What's up?"

"I heard you deliver messages and I was wondering if you'd get one to Celeste asking for a meeting as soon as possible?"

There was a long pause. "Bit dodgy, that. I heard you were persona non grata with the vamps."

I pressed my thumb into a sore spot harder than I'd intended and flinched. Celeste was a vampire? Why did Topher want to meet her? Did he fancy a walk on the dark side or was she the link to Raj? If so, did Topher believe she'd killed Raj—or worse, had meant to kill *him*?

Conversely, if she wasn't the murderer, being a vampire herself increased the chances that she'd sent our undead attackers last night and was my mystery caller. I shook my head.

As every good mystery book and British crime drama had taught me: no jumping to conclusions.

"Technically, I was discouraged from ever returning to Blood Alley," I said, massaging my other foot. "Mr. BatKian never said anything about not speaking to vampires. Thus, I'm suggesting a nice neutral territory. Of Celeste's choosing."

I'd either rule her out of the pool of suspects or dig deeper into her.

Through the phone came the sound of ice cubes in a cocktail shaker. "You're positive about this?"

"I am."

Harry said he'd see what he could do and signed off.

Home ten minutes and I'd already made good progress. I grabbed the notebook that we'd liberated from Egerts's office, but while I was searching for a pen to start codebreaking, my phone rang.

I snatched it up. "Hello?"

"Howdy," a man said. He complemented his good ol' boy jovialness with a couple of shallow puffs and an exhale. It wasn't the deep drag of a cigarette, probably a cigar. "Is this Miranda Edelman?"

My disappointment that it wasn't Laurent turned into anticipation, because only one person had that fake name.

"It is. Is this Fred McMurtry?"

"Sure is," he drawled.

"The Lonestar in charge of northern B.C. about thirty years ago?"

"You want my blood type, sweetheart?" Fred said, in an amused voice. "This is him."

"Thanks for getting back to me so quickly. The reason I'm calling is that I'm hoping you knew my uncle Jake." Jake Edelman had been my dad's best friend and the man who'd hidden me after the murders. More importantly for this call, he'd been an Ohrist.

"Of course." Puff. Puff. "Good man. I was sorry to hear of his passing a couple years ago. What can I do for you?" Having invoked small town rule #1—thou shalt connect thyself to a known entity—I was no longer a suspicious outsider.

"I inherited some of my uncle's things, but they were in storage until recently, and while I was going through them, I found a bunch of photos in an envelope addressed to a Noah Blum." I flipped open the green paisley book with all my notes, my pen poised. "The thing is, I tried to track him down online, but the only person who lived near Uncle Jake with that name died years ago in a fire, according to an old article from your local paper."

I'd changed my surname from Blum to Feldman when I'd gone to live with my mom's Sapien cousin Goldie Feldman after the tragedy.

"That's right." McMurtry clucked his tongue. "A real shame."

My hand tightened on the phone. "I'm sure. The article mentioned that a child had survived. Since you're a fixture of the Ohrist community, would you know who that was and how to contact them? They might like these photos of their parents."

There was a long slow pull on the cigar. "Can't help you," he said. "The Blums weren't Ohrist and I don't know what became of the daughter."

I tapped the pen against the notebook. He didn't sound suspicious or annoyed, just matter-of-fact. A knot in my chest loosened, because McMurtry, at least, wasn't keeping tabs on me. I jotted that fact down. "You mean they were Sapien?"

"Worse," he said.

"What's worse?"

"BS."

"No. Uncle Jake would never be friends with a BS." It was true, he and Dad hadn't been friends, they'd been brothers in every way but blood. Mom always joked that she hadn't realized she was marrying a twin.

"Believe it. Far be it for me to speak ill of the dead, but it was better for all concerned when that friendship"—I could feel his air quotes—"ended."

I shot the phone double middle fingers. "My God. You think you know a person," I said primly. "Well, BS do have a history of unfortunate accidents."

My stomach churned saying this drivel, but I had to lead him to the night in question.

Before I could quiz him further, McMurtry said, "I could try and find the daughter if you like. Get those photos off your hands. Where did you say you were calling from?"

Something fine and soft brushed the side of my neck.

I yanked the phone away but there was nothing there. "That's okay," I said. "I'll just trash them. I don't want to take up more of your time, but thanks for speaking with me."

The silence on the other side was loaded, like McMurtry was debating what to say next, but he simply wished me a good day and hung up.

Reclaiming my magic hadn't come with a perky new butt, a better metabolism, or less leg hair, but one thing it had done? Made me about a thousand times more paranoid, and given my baseline before that, that was saying something. Compared to me, conspiracy theorists took candy from government agents in unmarked panel vans.

I ran upstairs to my bedroom, yanked a large metal briefcase out from under the bed, and spun the dial—04-01-40—April Fool's Day of my fortieth year, aka the last time I'd had sex. It was a depressingly easy code to remember.

Once opened, the briefcase unfolded with a snap of the wrist to become a bulletproof shield. I transformed it now, scattering the contents on the ground.

The analytical part of my brain decreed that McMurtry was thousands of miles away and there was no way he could get to me, but the side of my neck tingled where something had touched it.

It had taken me a week's worth of research down crazier and

crazier rabbit holes to find the Ohrist store that I'd used to cobble this contraband kit together. The online merchant had the goods to fit my needs, plus expedited shipping and glowing reviews from @MyNeckIsSacrosanct and @Draculasuckedmypussydry who swore by the "Bite This" vampire kit.

Okay, I wasn't too sure about the trustworthiness of that last reviewer, since they suffered under the misapprehension that the kit was to entice rather than dispel vampires, but their private YouTube channel had some great tips for organizing a supernatural neighborhood watch.

Thanks to my Banim Shovavim magic, I could grab hold of a vamp's shadow like it had heft and weight, pinning the bloodsucker in place. Should I shove their shadow into a flame, the vamp went up in ash, as that wiry attacker had learned. Useful, sure, but if I was facing more than one of them, telling the others to "take a number, Fangs, I'll be with you in a minute," wouldn't cut it.

Hence, this puppy. I grabbed the mini flamethrower which was guaranteed to take out a cadre of vamps at once or your money back, no questions asked. One could argue that if it didn't work, getting your money back would be the least of your problems, but I liked a store with a strong return policy.

I fingered the ignition, but fun as it would be to go all Ripley from *Alien* on any undead daring to show their faces, my fire insurance didn't cover these gadgets as anything other than arson. I'd checked. Reluctantly, I put the weapon back and stuffed my gold lighter in my pocket. The flamethrower would have to be an outdoor toy.

Truthfully, I wasn't that worried about vampires because they couldn't get into my home unless I invited them, so whatever had reached out to brush my neck wasn't a bloodsucker.

I flicked the lighter a couple of times. Ohrists couldn't transport and McMurtry was a wolf shifter, so he couldn't have reached through the phone. Had a third party been eavesdropping? I grabbed the solid silver handcuffs, grateful that I'd impulse-bought them because they were 40 percent off. McMurtry wouldn't be able to shift while wearing them.

The final weapon I decided upon, a bead of sweat trickling into my eye, was a metal sphere roughly the size and weight of a squash ball. I'd paid $300 for a "one-of-a-kind" demon-buster with a hair trigger—which if I looked at it wrong would ensure a closed casket. That, or I'd bought a total dud that resembled an OG Ben Wa ball without a string for easy removal.

I edged along the hallway wall, the cuffs weighing down my capri pocket, the shield held out in front of me, and the sphere cradled against my chest. I could have cloaked myself, but that was no guarantee of invisibility, after all; a powerful vampire had seen through it, and whatever had brushed my neck might have the same ability. Besides, I was kind of excited to try out my new toys and vanquishing evil had to buy me a few karma points.

Avoiding the squeaky floorboard outside Sadie's bedroom, I cocked my head. All was silent and still, but the air was charged like a blast wave cresting closer. I crept toward the stairs, tensing as if that wave was about to whump into me, when someone grabbed my biceps.

From behind.

When I was standing flush against the wall.

Swallowing, I slid my eyes sideways. Knobby fingers covered in age spots and a dusting of hair on random knuckles gripped my upper arms.

I butted my head backward. I'd totally have broken someone's nose had there been a face there. Instead, I cracked my skull on the wall.

A man chuckled, allowing me to tear free. My mouth fell open as Fred McMurtry stepped into my hallway. And sure, portly, cigar-chomping seniors in cowboy shirts coming out of my wall weren't an everyday occurrence, but had that been the only issue, I'd have called the day a win.

Shadow strings led from Fred's shade to the Lonestar's wrists, ankles, and top of his head, piloting him like he was a marionette. It wasn't a dybbuk because other than this unusual love of puppetry, there was nothing odd about the shadow. It wasn't a sickly gray flecked with crimson, indicative of a magic host who had been fully possessed, nor was there the fainter sense of an abomination that I sensed in people who were in stage one enthrallment.

The final nail in the argument against it being a dybbuk was that I couldn't manifest my magic into a shadow scythe. So what was it? Vampires had their own bodies and this wasn't an Ohrist's regular shadow, which brought me to a demon. But if that was true, what was it doing? It didn't seem like it was feeding off the man, just moving him around.

"I was going to phone back," McMurtry said, the cigar clamped in the corner of his mouth, "but my battery died. Darned technology."

I slammed the metal sphere at the shadow's foot. It hit the floor with a sharp crack and detonated in a blinding flash of light that engulfed the dark puppeteer.

"Good heavens, girlie." McMurtry rubbed his eyes. "What'd you do that for?"

The only change to the shadow was that it now glimmered silver before its radiance died out like a fading sunset. So much for a demon buster. I was so invoking the return policy on this.

"What are you?" I moved closer to the stairs—and the waist-high bookcase nestled there with a mirror hung above it.

McMurtry followed me. "Just your friendly neighborhood Lonestar."

"And you brought a friend."

"What?"

I motioned at his shadow.

McMurtry looked at his reflection in the mirror, which only showed him, not the shadow that stood behind him, pulling the strings. "You been hittin' the cooking sherry?"

Did he really not know about that thing? That was impossible... wasn't it?

"If you are what you claim," I said, "how did you get here? Ohrists don't transport."

He stopped and blinked, his brows knitting together and his tanned face breaking into leathery creases. "I—stop changing the subject." He puffed twice on his cigar, the end glowing red. "Why did you phone me? Who are you really?"

The shadow worked the strings and the man lunged, closing the last few steps between us.

I slammed my invisibility cloaking down, ducking underneath him and back into the corridor.

Fred laughed, a mean sound, while the shadow jerked on the string attached to his head to move it in time with his laughter. "The missing BS. Isn't that interesting? What did you want, darlin'?"

First and foremost, for you to stop calling me by diminutives, you misogynistic asshole. I assessed my weapon options. I could animate Delilah, but without a more thorough assessment of Fred's shadow's abilities, I'd save her until I had the upper hand.

Darting behind a pacing McMurtry, I made a scooping motion to grab his weird shadow, but couldn't catch hold of it, so I ran at the man and slammed the bulletproof shield into the side of his head.

He crumpled to the ground, the shadow falling limply on top of him like a puddle of silk. The cigar fell out of his mouth, but I caught it—with a grimace, because I'd grabbed the damp, nasty end.

After tossing the cigar in the toilet, I checked the Lonestar's pulse, which was faint but steady. I cuffed him with the silver handcuffs so he wouldn't shift, then raced into my bedroom, snatching up a few items that I'd left behind. Kneeling in front of my quarry, I secured his ankles with zip ties before binding him in a sturdy rope like a calf at a rodeo. I wrinkled my nose, because this was more like a bondage victim being secured by a blind and inexperienced dominatrix.

I rummaged through the junk drawer in my kitchen for duct

tape, but all we had was an old roll of Scotch tape that was no longer sticky, so I stole a polka dotted roll of Sadie's washi tape and was using an absurd amount to seal McMurtry's mouth shut when there was a knock on the front door. I froze, waiting for the person to go away, but they knocked again.

"Miri?" Eli called out. "You home?"

Shit. I patted the still unconscious man on the head. "Stay here."

Flinging my hair out of my face, I hopped down the stairs, pasted on a smile and opened the door.

Eli held up a measuring cup. He was in a suit and tie, his police badge on his belt. "Can I borrow some milk? I'm making post-workout smoothies."

"Did you really go to the gym or have you come to scare Caleb again with some lame excuse? Because the kids aren't here."

He flexed his biceps. "Worked them good. Want to feel?"

"Nope." I took the measuring cup from him. "Wait here."

Eli did not do as commanded and followed me inside, his footsteps barely audible under the thundering of my heart.

"How did it go with the criminal lawyer?" he said.

"The what?" I darted a glance up the stairwell, but McMurtry wasn't visible from this angle.

"The libel case documents. Did you get what you needed?"

There wasn't a trace of sarcasm or disdain in his voice. I appreciated his genuine interest, but couldn't he have expressed it, say, two hours from now?

"Yeah. Lots to sort through." I grabbed Eli's elbow and hauled him into the kitchen, motioning at the fridge. While he poured some milk into the cup, I leaned against the counter, drumming my fingers and listening for any sound from upstairs.

THUMP! THUMP!

Eli paused with the carton halfway back into the fridge. "What's that?"

"Pigeons." I lied like a teenager to her parents, hating myself for it, but now was not the time to come clean to Eli about magic. I was reasonably certain that my amiable ex would be replaced by hard-assed Detective Chu upon finding a man hogtied on the upper landing.

He stared flatly at me as the next thump rattled the ceiling.

"Oh." And like a teenager, I was easily busted. I pointed upwards. "You mean that? Jude. She's helping me rearrange my bedroom furniture."

Eli shut the fridge door, his suit jacket falling away to show his gun.

We'd never role-played cop and bad guy when we were married, and I had no desire to go there now. I swallowed. "How's the murder case going? Any leads? What happened with the car accident?"

He rubbed his bald head, carrying the measuring cup to the front door. "The person reported the partial license plate number incorrectly and there are too many cars like that to track them all down. We've got feelers out with all the autobody repair shops in metro Vancouver, but so far no hits. I suspect it's a dead end."

"Aww. Too bad."

He furrowed his brows because that didn't sound as sympathetic as I'd meant it to. "The rest of it is proceeding slowly." He opened the front door. "We've ruled out any gang connection, but that's about it."

"Do you know how the victim was killed?"

"Not yet, though we know which injury was responsible for the death." D-uh. Ripped out heart. "But not how it was caused. You know how it goes, we have to sort through the minutiae of the victim's life and find a thread to pull on."

There was another thump and I glanced over Eli's shoulder to the top of the stairs to where McMurtry had maneuvered himself. My eyes widened. "Better get back to Jude," I said, and shoved him out the door, slamming it shut in his face.

I rested my head against the wood. That wasn't nice of me. I whipped the door open a fraction of an inch and cheerily called out, "Have a good day!" as my ex headed into his side of the duplex.

"Yeah, go back to your partner in crime." He shook his head, chuckling.

The second the door closed, I ran up the stairs and shoved McMurtry back with a grunt.

He snarled at me, making weird facial expressions to work the tape off.

The shadow floated a few feet away, loosely holding the strings but not doing anything.

"What exactly is your deal?" I demanded. When it didn't answer, I plunged my hand into its center. It passed harmlessly through and my shoulders lowered a fraction from my ears. I'd half-expected to be able to connect, like others could with Delilah, but this wasn't some bastardized Banim Shovavim.

I grabbed the metal case-turned-shield again and knelt down next to the Lonestar, keeping an eye on his shadow. "I'm going to remove the tape. Make a sound and I'll bash you upside the head again. Nod if you agree."

He nodded and I ripped the tape off. "You're in a boatload of trouble, girlie."

I smacked him lightly on the cheek with my hand. "Call me any version of your patronizing little nicknames and the next time I won't use my hand. What's going on with your shadow? What is that thing?"

He squirmed, attempting to look over his shoulder. "What the heck are you going on about?"

I explained about the shadow puppet master, Fred's face draining of all color. "Is this tied to your disappearance thirty years ago?" I said. "Those three weeks you went missing?"

"I went fly fishing. Caught a ten pound rainbow trout." His chest puffed out, his panicked expression wiped clean, but there was a robotic quality to his voice, like someone reciting a memorized answer.

The shadow hadn't moved but I sensed it watching me. Waiting to make its move.

"Tell me about the fire you set in my family home," I said.

"It was faulty wiring." More robotic rote memorization.

"No, it wasn't." My hands flexed on the rope binding him. "You set the fire. Who told you about the murders?"

Fred stared at me blankly.

"What did they give you? Was it a cure for your cancer? Is that why you were healthy when you got back? Was it—" I swung my head sharply to the shadow.

It flew straight at me, hissing, enveloping Fred and me in a freezing blackness.

Ice coated my skin and the zip ties and rope holding Fred snapped, slithering against my body as they fell away. Immediately after came a loud CRACK and the clang of handcuffs hitting the ground.

The Lonestar grunted and pushed me down the stairs.

15

I LAY SPRAWLED ON THE FOYER FLOOR, BLINKING dazedly at my right arm, because I didn't remember being flexible enough to bend it backward like that. Feeling pretty smug about my middle-aged level of limberness, I made the mistake of breathing and an excruciating pain lanced through my ribs.

The world swam in a nauseating blur around me, made worse when I moved my shoulder and was hit with a torturous grinding sting.

Fred marched down the stairs, his shadow controlling him from behind. He morphed his hands to claws—his actual power versus that strange wall-stepping ability that must have come from the puppeteer—a cruel smile spreading over his face.

I squirmed backwards, but pain and dizziness left me gasping for breath.

Fred's body bowed. His spine rippled, fur bursting along the ridge.

The shadow yanked on the string connected to Fred's head and he threw it back with a howl.

My injuries left me unable to muster Delilah up for more than a second so I grabbed the lighter out of my pocket in desperation.

The shadow floated closer...

Ignoring my brain screaming at me to run away, which was a no-go in my condition, I ignored Fred's shifting and waited for his shadow to get into arm's reach. I flicked the lighter and shoved it into the puppet master. It wouldn't turn Fred to ash, since he wasn't an aberration from death, but maybe it would harm whatever manipulated him.

The flame once more morphed into the form of a scythe, my magic pulsing insistently under my skin.

The shadow recoiled.

I jerked the flame at it again.

Fred's legs buckled out from under him and he swayed, barely catching himself on the bannister. His shadow stuttered like a frame stuck in a movie projector, causing Fred to flicker between creepy wolf-human partial shifts: a muzzle protruding under bulging human eyes, a paw attached to an arm with the elbow grinding in different directions.

McMurtry's shade stuttered a final time and then froze. The man fell forward.

I threw my good hand up, bracing for impact, but he disappeared before we collided.

Whether the shadow had reacted to the fire or to my powers, they were gone and that's all that mattered.

A rush of adrenaline raced through my veins, and I broke into great big belly laughs that hurt, but I couldn't stop. Curled into the fetal position, I fumbled in my pocket with my uninjured arm for my phone, which mercifully hadn't been broken in my fall. Four tries later, my eyes watering from the pain radiating through my arm and chest, I'd punched in my passcode, sticking out my tongue at the phone because it didn't even spell anything funny. Getting my contacts open was a whole other ordeal involving dropping the phone twice and a number of time-outs to rest and not vomit.

Sweaty and breathless, I finally dialed Jude. When the call

kicked in after many rings, I said, "Wouldn't it be awesome if my password was 'boobie'?" and blacked out.

I came to on top of my duvet cover with its lush blue and purple swirls. "Thanks for coming to my rescue."

"To keep you from changing your password to 'boobie'?" Laurent said in a droll voice. "You're welcome."

I scrambled up, my stomach sinking into my toes, but other than a little stiffness when I rolled my injured shoulder, I was fine. If a little confused. "You're not Jude."

"Nothing gets past you." He flipped a page in Don's notebook, his presence filling the wingback chair in the corner of my room. A hint of stubble dusted his jaw, his legs extended carelessly in his faded jeans and a chocolate curl falling over one eye.

Laurent's contact was listed right after my best friend's. Fuck. "I've never given you my address."

"And yet here I am."

Whether his presence was an accident or a subconscious act on my part, he was here. That counted for something in my book, but unless we hashed out our last conversation, our friendship would remain broken.

I was still unsettled from Fred's visit, but there was no handy pile of laundry to fold until I regained my equilibrium. I smoothed the duvet cover, sorting through the residual anger and dread churning in my gut to find a neutral way in to our discussion. "Laurent—"

"You owe Juliette a bottle of nice wine for her services and her silence. You had a concussion, two fractured ribs, and your scapula was broken. I suggest one of those stupid sweet ones. She likes those."

One concussion in a week was unfortunate, two reeked of carelessness. I gingerly moved my head from side to side, but there was no throbbing and no nausea. Juliette was getting an entire gift basket.

"I appreciate everything you both did," I said, "but we need to talk."

"Why is the rest of your house..." He paused. "Not more like you?" He waved a hand at the mural of colorful wildflowers that one of Jude's artist friends had painted on one wall. "Like this?"

He saw me as wildflowers? I pressed my hands to my flushed cheeks. "It's a work in progress." Enough distraction. "Look, about last night—"

"I was out of line," he said in a clipped voice.

"But—"

He flipped another page in the notebook.

That was it? He didn't want to discuss it so we wouldn't? Fine. Have it your way, mister, but you'd be giving me that notebook back.

I lunged forward to snatch it away but he held it out of reach. "That's not yours," I said.

"Not yours either if you want to get technical about it."

"*You* were the one who didn't want to work with me, *you* were the one who followed me, and *you* were the one who went all—"

He raised an eyebrow, his expression carved from granite.

I slouched back and he returned his attention to the notebook. A hot tight whirlwind spiraled up inside me. If he believed he could make those comments and then cow me into submission because he didn't want to explain himself, he had another think coming.

"Did you have a child? Is that why you said what you did?"

Laurent fumbled the book. "*That's* what you thought? The only explanation was some overly dramatic backstory that you could romanticize?"

"Get over yourself. It'll be a cold day in hell before I romanticize you." I swung my feet onto the floor. "Then why did you say it? And don't ignore me again. You owe me—"

"I? Owe you?"

"Stop interrupting, you giant asshole! Yes. You owe me the respect of answering me honestly."

Laurent's mouth fell open and he blinked quickly a couple of times. Then he schooled his expression. "Are we comparing failings? Bien." He crossed his legs, leaning back against the chair with one arm draped on top. "Care to tell me why I broke in to find you passed out at the bottom of the stairs with pieces of broken rope on the ground? Were the vamps not exciting enough for you?"

I whipped a blue silk pillow at him, but he only registered the hit to catch it one-handed and toss the pillow onto the tufted cream bench at the foot of the bed that complemented the curtains and the headboard edged in silver.

"The Lonestar who covered up my parents' murders came out of my wall puppeted by a shadow," I said. "I hog-tied him and interrogated him, but he didn't have answers, and I guess the shadow didn't like some of my questions, because it drowned me in this freezing darkness allowing the Lonestar to pop his ropes and push me down the stairs before both of them peaced out. That enough honesty for you?"

Laurent stared at me for a long moment, then he licked his index finger, flipped another page in the notebook, and kept reading.

I tore the book out of his hands and tossed it aside. "Why did you say that I have everything to live for because I have a kid? That I didn't know what was important to me? Because that was a seriously dick move."

He stood up and headed out of my bedroom.

I scrambled in front of him. "Oh, no you don't." He tried to slide around me, but I shoved him back. "I. Want. An. Answer." Again and again I pushed him, until the back of his knees hit my mattress.

He grabbed my wrists, his eyes wild. "Because all I see is death! People don't realize how good they have it! Every day, something terrible happens that you and everyone else don't have to see, but I do. And for all your shadow magic, you keep acting like you live in the light, but you don't. Not anymore."

Laurent could sense dybbuks, those wicked spirits made of

rage and violence. Could he tell how far into the darkness I'd already fallen?

"I'm not evil," I whispered.

Laurent's brows came together and, shaking his head, he released me. "That's not what I meant. I was talking about the things you'll have to do working for Tatiana." He sat down on my bed. "When you walk down the sidewalk, you get lost in your head. You leave just enough awareness to watch for people or cars, but I see it." He tapped the space between his brows. "The deeper that 'V,' the longer it takes you to cast off the whirring of your brain."

"So what?" I perched myself on the edge of my mattress, my chin notched up defensively. "Everyone zones out now and then when walking."

"I don't. Nav doesn't. Those everyday actions of ease and relaxation that others take for granted are luxuries denied to us." He slowly bunched my blanket up in his hand. "It sets you more and more apart until..."

I leaned forward to catch the rest of that thought, but he shook his head.

"It's okay to let your guard down," I said.

"Not in the world of darkness." A sad smile flitted across his face. "You belong in the light, Miriam," he said gravely.

If there had been even a trace of sarcasm, I'd have given him a piece of my mind, but his seriousness unmoored me. I'd felt invisible and overlooked for years, and it was in large part the respect that Laurent had shown me after I'd used my magic again that had led me to envision a different future for myself. I was forty-two years old, smart, capable, and mostly confident, but jumping back into a world of magic that I'd rejected for so long was as scary as it was exhilarating.

Earning some seal of approval from Laurent had mattered. Not because he was a man, but because I'd recognized a kindred spirit. He too, was smart, capable, handled shit other people didn't want to deal with, and was dismissed by far too many. The thought that all those dybbuks with human faces that he'd killed stopped him from seeing any beauty and hope in the world broke my heart.

"Laurent," I said gently. "I live in both worlds." If I didn't cling to the light with both my heart and my actions, I'd be lost to darkness and doomed to roam the Kefitzat Haderech in eternal torment. It was the only way to save myself, but more than that, it was the only way to live. "You do too," I continued, "but you won't let yourself believe it."

The usual glint of challenge in his eyes when he looked at me faded like a dying firefly. Laurent took a very deep, very controlled breath. "Whatever you say."

I caught my shirt as it slipped off one shoulder, the cotton bunched in my fist, something tangible to grasp against the sudden melancholy left in the wake of his regard.

Outside, neighborhood kids yelled over the muted buzz of a lawn mower.

I followed him into the kitchen, wringing my hands and wondering how to make him see the truth.

Laurent's boots lay on their sides halfway in the room, as if they'd been hurriedly kicked off. He toed his boots upright and shoved his feet into them.

"Wait," I said. "Don't go."

His emerald eyes sparked. "Why not? You did."

I nodded. It wasn't fun to have that thrown back at me, but he was trusting me enough to finally share his emotional head-space, so I'd suck it up and acknowledge that. "I'm sorry that I left you last night. I was angry and I needed space but I should have stayed."

"To patch me up? To save me from myself?" His lip curled.

His contempt lodged under my skin like a splinter and with a bitter laugh, I snapped. "I'm magic, not a miracle worker."

I wished I could take the words back as soon as I said them but throwing myself against his emotional walls was exhausting.

He grabbed his motorcycle helmet and walked out the back door.

"Don't leave," I said.

Laurent stopped on my back porch, his helmet propped on his hip. "There's no reason to stay. We're not friends. We're not colleagues. You paid me to do a job for you once and I did it. You don't want to take my advice so stop getting in my way and stop calling me when you need help."

His words landed like blows in my hollow chest.

"I *thought* I was calling Jude!" I threw my hands up. "Forget it. Thanks for clearing up our non-friend status. Next time the Lonestars blackmail me with a one-way ticket to Deadman's Island to give you up, I'll roll with it instead of trying to protect your self-destructive ass." I slammed the door but he leaned his shoulder into it, a wave of cool evening air washing over me.

"They what?" he said in a dangerous growl that sent shivers up my spine.

I took a step backward, more in surprise than fear.

Laurent prowled back into my kitchen. "Deadman's Island?"

"Nope. As we are neither friends nor colleagues, take your overprotective bullshit and fuck right off." I made a shooing motion.

He raked his fingers through his curls. "I'm unused to..." His brows drew together and he spoke slowly, much like a little kid having to explain themselves for the first time. "Monsters always win."

I crossed my arms. "Is this about me not saving the enthralled?"

"No! Can I...?" Laurent gestured at the door and I nodded. He closed it far more gently than I expected given the tense line of his shoulders, but he stood there uncertainly, tapping his helmet against his thigh.

I pointed at a chair. "Sit. I'll make you some chamomile. Calm you down."

He narrowed his eyes. "Chamomile tastes like ass."

I stepped closer so we were almost nose to nose. Even without inhaling, I smelled the faint trace of cedar that always followed him. "If you don't want to end up on the other side of my back door, you'll drink what I make you and say thank you."

He blinked, startled, then awkwardly brushed past me to sit down in the chair. "Put in lots of honey," he grumbled.

"Yeah, you like things sweet. I remember," I muttered.

His cranky frown would usually have warmed the hollow spot inside me, but now I concentrated on filling the kettle instead of braining him with it. Our friendship wasn't wishful thinking on my part. Only an idiot would be deluded into imagining a friendship where none existed with Mr. Hates Everybody. Sorry, Monsieur Hates Everybody.

Laurent waited for me to turn off the water before he spoke. "Where do you see yourself in thirty years?"

I shrugged. "Playing with my grandkids?"

"I don't even envision where I'll be tonight, because eventually the monsters always win and those of us fighting them always die. Maybe that's today. I've made my peace with it. Have you?"

"No." I flicked on the gas burner, which hissed into action. "Nor will I. Tatiana has had a long life. I expect to have the same."

"Tatiana is a master delegator who's always looked out for number one. She never fought vampires and she never put herself on the line for something as optimistic as justice. The things you want? Playing with grandchildren, watching your daughter grow up, living a long life?" He tapped his fist gently on the table, his gaze soft and distant. "You deserve to have them, but if a bloodsucker tears out your throat, or a Lonestar sends you to Deadman's Island, can you honestly tell me that your recent choices are worth sacrificing all that?" He shook his head. "If I had what you had, I'd walk away from this lifestyle without a look back."

"Bullshit." I slammed the two mugs that I'd pulled out of the cupboard onto the counter.

"Don't ascribe some nobility to me," he snapped.

"Oh, I'm not. You're a selfish bastard, which is exactly why you wouldn't walk away. You love what you do." I held up a hand at his protest. "You hate it in equal measure. I get that. But you wouldn't be content living a small quiet life, and after years of doing that, I won't put myself back in that box. Sometimes playing it safe is just another way to die."

"At least that death won't be violent."

"Laurent, you're so fixated on death, you keep forgetting about quality of life." I threw tea bags into one of Jude's teapots, adding the boiling water to let them steep. I rode out the silence for a few minutes. "I know I have a lot to live for, but isn't my happiness, my identity as something other than Sadie's mom, or Eli's ex, or whatever, as important? Especially given..." I swallowed.

"Given?"

I lifted the lid of the teapot and peered inside, launching into the tale of the Kefitzat Haderech. "I don't know how good my odds of escaping this fate are."

"That's why you were investigating this." He rubbed a finger over his lip, a contemplative expression on his face. "Every good deed preserves your humanity."

"Sure, that's one part of it." I poured us both steaming mugs of golden yellow tea. Truth be told, I hated chamomile too, and this box had probably been gathering dust for three years. But if I had to muscle this shit down to retain my moral superiority, I would. "But ever since I let my magic back in, I've been slammed with one wake-up call after another. I want to be happy. So no, I won't return to a quiet life and I won't resign myself to the monsters or being tortured for eternity in the darkness, because I'll curl up in a paralyzed ball. I want to live the fuck out of life, however long I have."

Laurent cradled his hands around the mug, steam swirling up

around his face. "I shouldn't have made that crack about us not being friends. I don't have many of them."

"Shocking, what with your winning personality." I placed a hot pink ceramic honey pot with a pink and black bumblebee on the lid on the table, warmth spooling through my chest at his admission.

"*And—*" he said, with a glare.

I mimed zipping my lips and throwing away the key.

Frowning, he poked the bumblebee, as if something that existed as pure whimsy was outside his range of understanding. "Naveen is an asshole."

"No argument from me." The one time I'd met Laurent's best friend, he'd made his prejudices about Banim Shovavim loud and clear.

"But you are..."

"A riotous garden of wildflowers."

Laurent poked the bee one more time. "An optimist. Who I mistook for being naïve. I'm sorry." He held out his hand, palm up. "Forgiven?"

I made him squirm a moment before I placed my hand in his. "Forgiven."

He folded his fingers over mine. "But you have to promise something."

"That I won't do anything dangerous?" I tugged but he didn't let go.

"That if you're getting close to the wire, overextending yourself, you tell me. Your overdeveloped sense of responsibility makes you the biggest danger to yourself. Don't take shit on for me, or anyone, that you don't need to, okay?"

I squeezed his hand, certain that if I let go, I'd float away on all the bubbles dancing inside me. Laurent didn't expect me to be infallible or on constant alert, aware of everything that could go wrong, and making lists six plays out to counter them. I'd never realized how nice it was to hear that said aloud.

"I promise. So..." I took a sip of tea. "Does this mean we're working together on this case? You know, like I suggested in the first place, which would have saved us all a great deal of trouble."

"Don't get sanctimonious, Mitzi. It's not a good look." He dumped an obscene amount of honey into his cup. "What have you learned?"

"You first."

"I don't know anything."

"As if. You were all bright-eyed and bushy-tailed at the Sharmas'." It felt like five hundred years ago, not yesterday morning. "There's no way you didn't keep investigating."

He sucked honey off his teaspoon. "Wolves are supposed to have bushy tails, but I didn't shift."

I suppressed a smile. "It's an expression, Laurent."

"A stupid one," he muttered, and heaved a sigh. "Jalota and Topher were in Little League together as kids. I tracked down some of Raj's friends and showed them Topher's photo. One of them was with Raj when he ran into Topher a few months back. Raj did not have anything good to say about his former teammate."

"That's the link. Well done. So Raj and Topher run into each other as adults, then Raj impersonates him en route to the Sharma family plane and ends up dead. Topher is absolutely neck deep in this, but I still don't think he's a killer." I filled Laurent in about Topher chafing under his parents micromanaging him and pushing him into the family business. "It might be why Topher wants to cavort with a vampire. A fuck you."

"What vampire?"

"Celeste. Harry let that slip when I asked him to set up a meeting with her. It's even more important now that we have proof Topher lied about not knowing Raj."

"Smart thinking."

After I retrieved Don's notebook from my bedroom, I unearthed a package of dark chocolate digestive cookies and put a few on a plate. "Did the Lonestars bring you in for questioning?"

"They tried." He snarfed two treats down in rapid succession. "I told them that if I'd gone feral, they'd be the first ones to know. Then I told them to come back when they had actual evidence and until then to fuck right off. I take it you had a slightly different experience?"

"They have surveillance footage of Raj driving off with me. In light of that, I apparently wasn't just guilty of covering up that you'd gone feral, but I also have the satchel. They want to know what's in it."

"It's a straightforward motive if Raj was killed for whatever was in that bag," Laurent said. "You free at midnight tomorrow?"

I grabbed a second cookie. "Whoa, I was going to ask you the same thing. You got that call, too?"

"Yes." Laurent munched on his third cookie. Damn him and his metabolism. "Who could place Raj in the car other than you?"

"Topher probably. I'm betting Celeste could as well, but whether as the murderer or our mystery caller remains to be seen. Possibly Don Egerts? Depending on what that code yields." I wiped the crumbs off the table into my hand and then brushed them into the sink.

Laurent reached for Don's notebook and a pen that was on the table, flipping through the pages with a frown. "Even if Celeste killed Raj, why would the Lonestars get involved? Sapien police aren't going to collar a vamp murderer and Lonestars let Zev BatKian deal with rogues. One word from him and they'd drop the case."

I wiped down the counter. "Always?"

"Pretty much. I heard that Raj was an Ohrist, so it's even more likely that a vamp killer would get off scot free. Unless a vampire murdered Jalota for no reason whatsoever, BatKian would support any perceived betrayal as justified and that would be the end of the matter." Laurent scribbled on a napkin, playing around with cyphers.

"Do you think Tatiana had me get rid of the heart because she's worried you killed Raj?" I said.

"I'd like to think she knows me better, but…" He gave a wry half-smile and kept working on the code.

"Or rather—" I hurried to amend my statement. "Tatiana thinks you're being framed and wants to protect you?" I rinsed out the rag, wringing it out and hanging it over the kitchen faucet to dry. "Someone is murdered on a job she's been hired to do and she doesn't call the Lonestars in? Was she protecting you or protecting herself because she's involved?"

Laurent crossed off the current key he was using, starting from scratch with a different cypher. "Tatiana wouldn't have risked your life if she wanted Raj dead."

"You think?" I looked at him hopefully and he nodded.

"I do. Whatever her feelings about my involvement, the only thing she's guilty of here is protecting her own interests. The heart was the one item tying you both to the murder at the time, so she had to dispose of it. Without that surveillance footage, the Lonestars couldn't have disputed your story that you got suspicious of Raj and made him leave."

"Yeah," I said bitterly, "but they do have the footage so it's a whole other can of worms."

"It still doesn't prove you—" His eyes darkened. "Mitzi," he said softly, "did the Lonestars accuse you of threatening their prime directive because you didn't call it in?"

I bit my lip, my gaze dropping to the table, before nodding.

"Merde." It came out as barely more than a whisper.

"It's fine." I busied myself gathering up mugs. "We'll find the satchel, maybe even the killer, and make them retract this ridiculous threat." Unless getting the Banim Shovavim out of the picture was more important to them than solving this murder.

One of the mugs slipped from my grip, the handle breaking off when it fell into the sink. Even concussed, I'd remembered that magic had to remain hidden, which was why I hadn't called Eli. And between my decades of fear that if the Lonestars found me I'd end up like my parents, and Tatiana operating in some weird gray area, I hadn't alerted the magic police either.

"I'm fucked," I said under my breath, and slammed the broken mug into the trash.

"No, you're not." Laurent stood behind me, not touching me, but close enough that the heat of his body soaked into my skin.

I turned around. There was barely an inch between us, and I wrapped my arms around myself to keep from reaching for him. "Don't lie. You said it yourself. I'm out of my depth."

"Well, yes," he said, with a haughty shrug. "But I'm working with you now."

A weak laugh burst out of me, but the wolf had my back, even hamming things up to make me laugh. When was the last time someone did that for me? The late afternoon shadows lost their sharp edges, smoothing out to reflect a world that felt a little less dire, and a lot more hopeful. "That you are."

16

"BUST OUT THE PROPER BOOZE AND LET'S ORDER SOME food," Laurent said, "because I'm starving. Wolves need to eat. A lot. Then we'll come up with a plan."

He deemed the Merlot I had barely acceptable, grumbled when I insisted on ordering Chinese food, and then added four extra dishes to the order, all of which he polished off. I almost lost a hand trying to get some spicy prawns and snap peas.

By mutual unspoken agreement, we didn't discuss anything work-oriented while eating. He asked about some photos of Sadie and me, and shared stories about Juliette when she was younger. They'd obviously been close, and I didn't understand why he wouldn't want her around, other than the working for Tatiana part, but I didn't pry. There was some trauma in his past and if he ever wanted to share it with me, I'd listen, but it wasn't my place to push him.

Laurent told me how he'd found the couple that had celebrated their anniversary with champagne. They were indeed possessed, and he'd only managed to dispatch the woman.

"Even though the dybbuk was in control of the host, the man still had all his memories of the two of them. His grief was like a live wire." Laurent gripped his chopsticks so hard that he snapped one, then slid the paper off a fresh pair. "I have to find him."

"You will." I didn't know what else to say. "Might as well get back to cracking the code."

"Sure."

Unable to eat another bite and wishing I could pop the button on my capris, I doodled little stick figures in my green paisley notebook: one for Raj and another for Topher with a line connecting them.

Laurent watched me. "Did you ever try writing with your right hand all those years you hid your magic?"

I shook my head. "No one would have been able to read it. Though don't ever force me to use leftie scissors. I despise them." I paused, back for a moment at my parents' kitchen table, the pencil feeling awkward and slippery in my five-year-old self's grip. "When I was first learning to print, my grandfather kept taking the pencil out of my left hand and putting it in my right one."

"Because all Banim Shovavim are lefties and he didn't want you identified?"

"Funnily enough, it wasn't so much that, since enough Sapiens and Ohrists are left-handed. He had his litany of cultural prejudices associated with the evils of being left-handed. Sinistra in Latin, gauche in French. Se'mol in Hebrew for left-side derived from Samael, the Angel of Death."

Laurent methodically went through each take-out container, eating any leftover scraps. "Charming. How come he didn't win that fight?"

"My mom quoted a bunch of famous lefties at him like Da Vinci, Mozart, and Marie Curie, and said her daughter would use whatever hand she wanted." I grinned and held up my left fist, the pen still in it. "Lefties for the win."

"Tatiana is left-handed," he said.

I raised my eyebrows at him. "And?"

He swallowed the last bite of spicy pork. "And whatever else I think about my aunt, she's a fascinating woman."

"Nice save."

He wiped his mouth off with a napkin, but I caught his small smile.

I clicked my pen and wrote "Facts."

"Another list?"

"Knock lists at your peril, buddy. The act of writing things down reduces the burden on the brain of remembering everything, freeing up mental space to become more effective in carrying the items out. It also reduces task anxiety and breeds creativity."

"I never use them and I have no anxiety."

"No, you're totally zen." I jotted down bullet points. "Here's what we know. Raj is dead, his satchel is missing, and someone thinks one of us has it. We have to find the killer, how Topher and Celeste are involved, and whatever was in that bag."

"There's either something valuable in it or something incriminating." He pointed at my notebook. "Write that down."

"Like I didn't already come to that conclusion ages ago."

"Apparently not, since it's not on your list."

I clicked the pen at him in a menacing fashion, and chuckling, he held up his hands.

"Let's start with the satchel," I said. "Our mystery caller hired vamps to come after us. How hard is it to do that?" I stacked the dirty dishes in the sink, surprised when Laurent cleared the rest of the dinner things.

"If you have connections or enough money? Not very." He shrugged. "BatKian doesn't necessarily approve, but he doesn't expressly forbid them providing muscle for Ohrists, either."

"Would Zev know who hired them?" I squirted dish soap onto a sponge and gave the take-out containers a quick wash.

"Doubtful, but even if he did, he wouldn't say." Laurent cracked his neck, then resumed working on the code.

"Since the satchel was in the car when Raj was killed, I vote that our mystery caller and the killer are two different individuals." Once clean, I placed the containers in the recycling bin on my back porch.

"Agreed, and I bet Celeste is one of them."

"Me too. That gives us two avenues to pursue: the caller slash vamps and Raj slash the satchel." I unwrapped a pod and placed it in the dishwasher. "Jalota specifically assumed Topher's identity, someone he'd previously known, and he intercepted a car ride meant to take Topher to a plane that would get him out of the country. Hence, Raj couldn't do so under his own name. What or who was he running from and why not use an alias?" I hit the start button.

"It's not that easy for the average person to get a fake passport, especially one that would stand up to all the security protocols these days," Laurent said.

"In impersonating Topher, he'd still have needed a passport with that name on it. Unless Raj stole Topher's real passport." I grabbed my green notebook, back in notetaking mode.

The scritch of our pens blended with the dishwasher's hum to make a soothing white noise.

"Or Topher handed it over willingly," Laurent said. "Raj could easily have known about the Sharmas' plane and paid Topher to help a teammate out of a bad situation."

"Celeste the vampire would qualify as a bad situation."

"True." Laurent pointed at me with his pen. "Less likely, but still on the list, is Egerts. He's connected to the deceased through his temp agency and up to something with this code." Laurent rearranged some letters, then shook his head. "I'll try one more cypher, then we pay Don a visit."

I cracked my knuckles. "Dibs on bad cop."

"Easy, killer." His brow furrowed in adorable concentration while he worked.

I started at a knock on my front door, my stomach aching. Had the Lonestars come back?

"Expecting someone?" Laurent said.

"No." I padded into the foyer, bracing for the worst.

It was Eli, in his Vancouver Canucks T-shirt and board shorts, his après work outfit. "Is Sadie home yet?"

"She's at a movie."

"In the dark with that boy?" He scrolled on his phone. "Did you see her Instagram? I don't like any of this."

I put a hand over the screen. "Stop being so overprotective and let her enjoy it."

"How," he said sardonically, holding up the phone with a selfie of two familiar teens posing behind a huge carton of popcorn, "am I not letting her enjoy it?"

"Eli, you came over in your cop uniform to scare Caleb. Not cool."

"Heh. Yeah." He waved his cell at me impatiently. "And what? This doesn't bother you at all?"

"No. I'm terrified my baby is going to get her heart broken, but I'm also not going to act crazy. Good or bad, I want her to be able to share this with me."

"And if she doesn't?" He pushed past me, heading for the kitchen.

"Eli, wait."

He came to an abrupt stop, eyeing Laurent. "Who are you?" He was bristling. I sighed. Eli and bristling never led to anywhere good. Out of a misguided sense of protection, or, truthfully, heavy amounts of guilt, he was super suspicious of anyone he suspected wanted to date me, though it didn't make it right. I'd called him on it before and he'd stopped, so I was a little surprised that history was repeating itself.

"Eli, my ex-husband." I stressed the "ex" part as a reminder for him to back off, and closed the green notebook with all my notes. "This is Laurent. Tatiana's nephew."

Laurent shot me an annoyed look before nodding at Eli and then returning his attention to the code.

Eli grabbed a chair and straddled it backward. "So, what do you do?"

"How about that Instagram?" I said, tugging on him.

"I'm in security," Laurent said.

"I'm in law enforcement," Eli replied.

I crossed my arms. This wasn't about me at all. Eli, a cop, had super alpha tendencies, and Laurent, well, enough said. Ugh. That made it even worse. Stupid boys. I poked Eli in the shoulder. Hard. "If you're going to interrogate my guests, you can leave."

Laurent shrugged. "I don't care. I'm helping Miriam with some paperwork for my aunt."

"Oh yeah?" Eli craned his neck to see what Laurent was doing, but the shifter shut Don's notebook, sliding it over top of the napkin he'd been writing on. "Doing what?"

"Family secrets." Laurent folded his hands on top of the notebook and regarded Eli calmly. "So, you like hockey?"

Good one, Huff 'n' Puff. Create rapport.

Eli glanced down at his Canucks shirt. "Yeah. You a fan?"

"No. I prefer real sports, like football." Laurent's face fell. "Sorry. You people call it soccer," he said slowly and patronizingly.

It was impressive exactly how condescending it sounded when expressed with a French accent. Also, I wasn't aware that the top of Eli's head could turn that particular shade of red.

"That's where you're wrong, my good man," Eli said.

I mimed shooting myself in the head. There were about three steps from Eli's "my good man" to him running Laurent through the system looking for even a single outstanding parking ticket to hold against him.

"We people call it the 'game'"—Eli used air quotes to denote its dubious sporting status—"where a bunch of pussies get healed by a magic sponge."

Laurent clenched his jaw and I muscled in between the two of them. "All sports suck," I said, "matter settled. Now, Eli—"

The front door crashed open.

"Vey iz mir," Tatiana groused. "Somebody come help a lady already."

Laurent groaned and I smacked myself in the forehead.

Eli, Laurent, and Tatiana in an enclosed space? Might as well grab the flamethrower and get this party started. Or go scorched earth and find that country without an extradition treaty. Could this get any worse? Never mind, universe. Don't listen to me.

"That's Tatiana," I said to Eli. I swept up both notebooks and the napkin that Laurent had been writing on and shoved them in a drawer.

The artist sashayed into the kitchen, followed by two assistants staggering under the weight of banker's boxes, and came to a dead stop next to Eli. "Aren't you a goy and a half?" she said, briefly squeezing his bicep.

Eli's mouth fell open. On the downside, the elderly woman in a skinny bright green suit with oversized red glasses fondling him wouldn't make him any happier about my new job, but on the upside, he'd forgotten about Laurent.

Normally, I'd have told Tatiana to leave him alone, but Eli had acted like my house was his house. If he was so determined to stay, then he could deal with my guest's inappropriate attention himself. Maybe next time, he wouldn't barge in.

Tatiana barked at her assistants to put the boxes on my counter, then jabbed a bony finger at Eli. "Nu? What's wrong with you? You think you were going to find someone better than Miriam?"

I hopped up on the kitchen counter. The years of therapy after our divorce had guided me through all the stages of grief and anger and saved my friendship with Eli, and yet as his friend, I was enjoying this immensely.

"I... uh..." Eli looked to me for help, clearly out of his depth, but I simply smiled. Watching him sputter was deliciously satisfying.

"Eli prefers men," I said.

Tatiana sniffed. "Well, your gaydar's broken, bubeleh."

"Is that a job requirement?" I said.

She shrugged. "You never know." She peered at me over the top of her glasses. "You do have mannish shoulders. I can see how he got confused."

Laurent snorted and I ran a hand across my throat.

"I wasn't confused," Eli ground out. "I'm bisexual."

"Reaaaalllly?" Tatiana eyed him slowly from head to toe.

"All right," I said mildly. "That's enough."

"Please." She made a dismissive motion. "We're all mish-pachah here."

"Welcome to the family." Laurent smirked.

"Be that as it may, this family has boundaries," I said firmly.

"We're family?" Her baby-faced female assistant said, no doubt also dreaming of villas in France.

Tatiana looked at her like she'd grown a second head. "Yeah, and two of my cousins killed each other for asking stupid questions. Go back to the studio, Marjorie, and take boychik here with you."

Her male assistant didn't appreciate the Yiddish term of endearment for a young boy. "My name is Raymond," he sulked.

"And if I get home and you haven't finished packing up the canvases for the Prague show like I asked hours ago, your name will be Unemployed." She shooed them off and they slunk out of the house.

"Miri?" Eli jerked his head to the hallway. "A word?" He stalked out.

"Gey gezunterheit," Tatiana trilled.

I followed Eli to the front door.

"I don't like either of those two," he said. "And I don't want Sadie around them."

"Don't you dare pull that shit," I said. "How many of your twenty-minute relationships has Sadie met over the years? And now you're giving me grief about people I'm working with? I'm going to cut you some slack because you're clearly freaking out that your baby girl is out with a boy, but check your attitude from here on in."

His jaw tensed, then he jammed his hands in his pockets with a sigh. "Yeah, that was a total dick move. I'm sorry. I'll go home and glare at her selfies with that boy by myself."

"You do that." I locked the door behind him so no one else crashed the party.

Tatiana had made herself comfortable at my kitchen table. "Now that the big macher's gone, we can get down to business."

I lifted the lid off one of the boxes, coughing at a plume of dust. "What business?"

"Archiving and cataloging documents for my memoirs, of course," she said.

"That's just a cover story."

Tatiana pulled off her glasses, tapping the arm against her lip. "It was, but I got to thinking about how I've lived such a fascinating life as an artist. I have an obligation to share my story with the world. Anyway, you can start tonight. These are some of my press clippings over the years."

"But Laurent and I have leads to follow up."

"I can visit Don myself and we'll still meet up later," Laurent said.

"You're not going anywhere." Tatiana blew on the lenses, cleaning the fog off with a napkin. "Do you know how much trouble the two of you stirred up?" She smacked the table. "I told you this was a fakakta situation, but you made those puppy dog eyes at me, and I'm such a soft touch, I went against my better instincts."

"You're doing it for the money," I said, rifling through news clippings. "And if you'd called the Lonestars in from the beginning, we could have saved ourselves a lot of grief. Oh, and thanks for throwing me under the bus and saying that detailing the car was my idea."

"I didn't say bupkis to the Lonestars. They know better than to bother me unless they have to. They spoke to my guy."

"That's great that they can't touch you, but I'm the weak link they'll toss on Deadman's Island if they decide that I exposed Ohrists by not calling in the murder."

Would eternal torment in the Kefitzat Haderech be better or worse than Deadman's Island?

I yanked a yellowed clipping out of the box and winced at the paper cut I received. "Even you can't protect me from the consequences of violating their prime directive, no matter that it was your decision that landed me in this situation."

Laurent ran his thumb under his chin and then flicked it outward.

"What's that?" I gaped at him. "Did you just Frenchy French contemptuous me?"

"I told you not to work for her."

I shot him the finger.

Tatiana smacked Laurent. "Sha! Both of you."

We fell silent like sullen kids.

"Magic societies don't play by the same rules as Sapien ones," Tatiana said. "There are certain unspoken agreements where if all parties remain off the Sapien radar, they are free to continue with their activities." Laurent rolled his eyes and his aunt wagged a finger at him. "That goes for you, too. You think Sapiens would let you run around killing dybbuks?"

"More dubious morality. What pillars you all are." I rummaged quickly through another box, but it was more of the same. "How does this apply to this case?"

"Vamps are only allowed to turn Sapiens, but they don't do it all that often," Tatiana said, pushing the glasses up her nose and making her bright blue eyes look huge. "Their bigger concern is having enough food. Blood Alley being an Ohrist tourist destination helps with that, but they also require blood donors. In the same way that we collectively pay for Lonestars and Laurent's services, Ohrists are encouraged to donate. However, vampires who can afford it have private donors."

"You mean blood slaves," I said flatly.

"They're paid," Tatiana said.

The dishwasher moved into the next section of its cycle with a thunk.

"A little filthy lucre for any evil, huh?" I rooted through a box. There was no rhyme or reason to how these press clippings had been stored. And was that a shopping list? Oy vey. "Why don't more of them embrace synthetic blood like Zev?"

The head vamp in this city had been a rabbi back in his human life and still took the Jewish prohibition against drinking blood seriously.

"Taste," Laurent said. "So I've been told."

"Don Egerts ran the private end of things," Tatiana said, sounding like her patience was running thin. "And one of you stole his client list."

Laurent leaned back in his chair with a deadly smile. "Who's spreading rumors like that?"

She fixed her nephew with a cold gaze. "Don't insult my intelligence, Lolo."

"I wasn't," he mumbled, suddenly interested in fashioning a napkin into a paper airplane.

I widened my eyes, my lips pressed together so I didn't laugh at Laurent being nipped like a puppy.

He fired the paper airplane at me.

"Egerts called me in a panic this morning because his office was trashed and his donor list stolen," Tatiana said. "The same list that one Raj Jalota is on. If anyone else finds out it's missing, it will be taken as a sign of weakness and an opportunity for others to move in. There will be chaos until it's settled, and trust me, you don't want that havoc." She held out her hand. "Give me the notebook and leave this alone."

Laurent and I exchanged looks and he shrugged. I retrieved Don's property, but didn't relinquish it yet. "He can have the book back if he gives us the name of the vampire that Jalota *donated* to."

Tatiana stood up and snatched the notebook away in a cloud

of irritation and Chanel No. 5. "Stubborn, both of you." She gave a firm tug on the bottom of her suit jacket. "It's Celeste BatSila."

"Small world," I said.

"Why aren't either of you surprised?" Tatiana dropped the notebook into her enormous purse. "You two will be the death of me."

"Anything else we should know about Celeste?" Laurent said.

"Yes," Tatiana snapped. "She's Zev's granddaughter many generations down the line."

A news clipping fell from my hand. I'd asked Harry to arrange a meeting with Zev's granddaughter? Oh, fuck. I buried my head in my hands.

"Now what?" Tatiana prodded me with a bony finger.

"Nothing," I said weakly. "Why doesn't she have the same surname?"

Laurent propped his hands behind his head. "Let me guess. She was an Ohrist, so Zev convinced someone in a different family to turn her and take the blame if the Lonestars found out."

I made a "yikes" face. Vamps were prohibited from turning anyone with magic, so someone had totally said fuck the police on that one.

"Such a genius. That kind of cleverness gets you a nice slab in the morgue." Tatiana patted one of the banker boxes. "Let the Lonestars deal with this murder and stick to archiving my press."

I caved under her glower. "Fine."

"Whatever," Laurent grumbled.

"I'll hold you to it." She air kissed both our cheeks, and when she was halfway out the kitchen, called back carelessly over her shoulder. "How'd you get past Egerts's security system?"

Maybe it was rash to give away my secret weapon and put Emmett on her radar, but being forthright with Tatiana after the kerfuffle at the employment agency seemed like a smart move.

"Golem," I said. "No heartbeat."

Tatiana's footsteps slowed, almost stopping, and she gave this amused snort, quiet enough that I almost didn't catch it.

Almost. I gave a cocky grin.

"We were lying about dropping the investigation, right?" Laurent said, once the door had closed behind his aunt.

"No shit." I sorted a batch of clippings into a chronological pile. "I still have to find something to refute the Lonestar's assertion that I violated their prime directive, which I can't do if I stop investigating. I also don't trust them not to bury the evidence. Raj will get justice, but we'll table any meeting with Celeste for now and see what happens with our mystery caller."

"Unless our caller was Celeste. Voice distortion, remember?"

I rubbed a hand over the back of my neck. "Can we deal with that problem if we come to it?"

"We can. We'll work the Celeste angle from Topher's end, since he asked to meet with her. You'll call Harry and cancel the rendezvous?"

"Yes." I fit the lid back on one of the boxes. "Would he know how to ward things from coming through my walls? Or, do you?"

Laurent pinched the bridge of his nose. "Please call him immediately."

"Obviously." I shot him a pointed look. "It's not like I want to put my kid in danger."

"I know," he said, abashed. He stretched, his shirt riding up to expose a strip of his olive skin and rock-solid abs.

I gnawed the inside of my cheek wondering what it would be like to lick my way across his hipbone, then tore my eyes away, meeting Sadie's horrified stare through the back door window.

Play it cool. It's not like my tongue had been hanging out.

My daughter opened the door. "Mom? Who's this?"

I blushed so hard, you could have fried an egg on my cheeks. I'd always been super paranoid about Sadie hearing Eli and me have sex. Being sex positive was one thing, but the thought of my daughter hearing me—with anyone—made me cringe. While all I'd done was look at Laurent's belly, I felt like my lustful desires had been branded onto my forehead, flashing in neon for all and sundry.

"He's no one."

Laurent threw me an affronted look. Oops, so much for our friendship.

"I mean," I said, hastily recovering, "obviously he's someone. Laurent. He's a nephew." There was a long pause before I clued in that my description was not helpful on its own. "He's the nephew of the person I work for. Sorry," I said, wiping my forehead in a fit of inspiration. "Hot flash."

He smiled at Sadie. "Nice to meet you."

My daughter looked about three seconds away from pouring bleach in her eyes. I sighed. It had been a good run, but it was time to leave town, cast off my identity, and start somewhere new. Well, this time I was going somewhere more exotic than a Vancouver equivalent. If fleeing your life didn't come with a beach and a personal cabana boy, it wasn't worth the energy.

17

LAURENT LEFT SOON AFTER AND I DEFLECTED further questioning by conducting a little questioning of my own. "So, I hear you're posting Instagram photos with Caleb. The day went well?"

She blushed harder than I had, muttered that she was going to change her profile name so her stupid father couldn't find it, and then danced her way into the living room, falling onto the sofa with a dreamy smile. "Caleb's so sweet. He paid for my movie and we shared popcorn. His older brother is into cosplaying and goes to cons and stuff so Caleb totally gets it." She hugged a cushion to her chest. "He likes my weirdness."

I shoved her feet over and sat down beside her. "Then I approve."

Sadie sat up. "Laurent's not bad looking for an old guy."

"I'm not... that's..." I swatted the top of her head. "He's younger than me so thanks for making me feel ancient."

She held up a fist. "Turn that patriarchal stereotype on its head." Then she laughed.

Until I found my footing in this job, I didn't have time to date, but I'd like to at some point. Not that Laurent was dating material, but I'd bet he knew his way around a woman's body without detailed instructions. It was in the way he homed in on something with absolute focus, and how when he lost control, he abandoned himself to his wild side. I spent my life multi-tasking and making endless decisions and I yearned to be with someone who took charge in the bedroom. If I found an alpha in the streets who was generous in the sheets?

Sadie waved a hand in front of my face. "Yo."

I blinked my R-rated musings away. "If I did start dating, not Laurent, but in general, would you be okay with that?"

I'd actually gone on a few dates with a very nice man, Ben, intending to tell Sadie about him, but he'd turned out to be dybbuk-possessed, and the conversation had become moot.

She scuffed her foot along the throw rug. "You don't need my permission."

"I know, but it's been you and me for a long time."

"True. It'd be weird."

"And you're not great at sharing," I teased.

"Hey, that's on you. Only child. If I hadn't had cousins, I'd never have learned that skill set at all. But I'd be okay with you dating, provided I totally interrogated them and liked them. Otherwise..." She made a slashing motion across her neck.

"Duly noted."

Sadie tapped her finger against her lip. "Hey, Mom?"

"Yeah?" I straightened out the rumpled throw rug.

"If Caleb wants to hang out, can we do it here, even if it's my week to be with Dad? He really embarrassed me and made Caleb feel bad."

I braced my elbows on my thighs. "You can, but isn't that going to get really awkward? Wouldn't it be better to talk to your father?"

"He'll just get defensive and say he was kidding."

I frowned. She wasn't wrong. Eli was pretty good on the self-awareness scale in our relationship, but we'd had a lot of therapy, plus he still had some old-fashioned ideas about the hierarchy of parents versus kids. He wouldn't take any perceived criticism from his daughter well, no matter how fair, and I'd run interference for them more than once in the past.

"Hon," I said gently, "if you're old enough to have a boyfriend, then you're old enough to talk to your dad about this."

She flopped back with a strangled sound of frustration. "Why can't he have acted like a normal person in the first place? Why do I have to be the adult here?"

"If you want to be treated as a grown-up then you have to step up and initiate the hard conversations sometimes," I said. "This obviously pushed his overprotective buttons. Not to defend his behavior, just saying. In some ways, it was a lot easier to parent when you were little."

"Fine," she grumbled. "But if he still won't listen, will you help me talk to him?"

"Yes." I kissed her cheek. "Well, it's been a long day and I'm beat. 'Night, sweetheart."

"Goodnight."

I brushed my teeth and thought about families. Mine was complicated enough even without magic. I could only imagine how much messier it got in magic circles, like the Lonestars or vampires. My brushing slowed. Zev had gotten someone else to turn Celeste but I had no doubt if she was Raj's murderer, both BatKian and the Lonestars would look the other way. That sucked for Eli, because even if I showed him the existence of magic, he couldn't exactly drag a vampire through the legal system.

It was embarrassing to phone Harry and ask him to forget about arranging the meeting, but I couldn't risk angering Zev. Luckily, the gargoyle hadn't gotten through to Celeste yet so I wouldn't be pissing her off. And Harry even said he had a guy who could ward up my place, so the call wasn't a total bust.

Saturday morning, I woke up with a back that was as stiff as a board. I dragged out my yoga mat and props that I'd bought for a 30-day yoga challenge, of which I'd lasted twelve. I'd learned some good stretches though and I cycled through them until I'd loosened up enough to stand up without making weird faces.

I faced eating breakfast by myself, since my child was still dead asleep, but after staring bleary-eyed at a half-empty fridge with nothing appealing popping out at me, I settled for spoonfuls of peanut butter eaten directly from the jar and chased down with a latte. Afterwards, I toted Tatiana's boxes of press clippings upstairs, then pried off the first lid.

My office had generously been billed as a third bedroom when I bought the duplex. It was more of a glorified walk-in closet, but it held a desk and got natural light. I hadn't used it a ton since I didn't often bring work home, but if I was really cataloging and archiving for Tatiana, then a coat of paint and some filing cabinets wouldn't be out of line.

I'd gone through the first box, clipping the different piles together and making all kinds of notes for ways they could be archived for this particular project, when my phone rang with an unfamiliar number.

"Hello?" I said warily, wondering if the mystery caller was bailing on our drop-off tonight.

"Hola, Miriam, it's Ryann Esposito. How are you?"

I was better five seconds ago. "Peachy. How can I help you?"

"One sec. Mandy, set up the projector in Room A." There was a quick conversation with a woman about audiovisual equipment. "I'm back. Did you think about where the satchel might be?"

"Good news. I'm working on it and will hopefully have something for you tomorrow." I tried to staple a two-page article together that had come loose of its original binding, but the stapler was empty.

"Awesome!" She injected a more sorrowful note to her words. "It's a shame that your ex isn't plugged in to the magic community. He probably wouldn't be getting all the heat he is for not having a viable suspect yet."

Eli hadn't mentioned having pressure at work because of this case. I rummaged in my drawer for more staples. "I wish I could help him, but prime directive and all that."

"Yeah. Too bad though. Ah well!" Manic pixie dream girl was back. Or rather, that act of hers. "I'm glad I checked in and we'll speak tomorrow."

"All righty then." Frowning, I hung up. Why were they monitoring Eli's progress? Another threat, letting me know they could get to anyone close to me or was Ryann trying to tell me that she'd allow Eli to know about magic?

I filled the stapler and clipped the newsprint together.

If I could persuade him to close the case without magic becoming public, would her threat of bringing me in for violating the prime directive be off the table? That would be great, except if I'd been able to break through his natural Sapien perception filter which kept him from seeing magic, I'd have done it already.

I was recording details of the various clippings in a spreadsheet when my phone rang. My head still in documentation mode, I answered without checking who it was. "Hello?"

"Hello, Miriam. I called the other day, but I guess you were too busy to return it."

I made a stabbing motion at the phone, envisioning my sister-in-law's disapproving frown. "Yeah, sorry. Work has been nuts."

"That's right! Eli told me you had an exciting new job. An artist. If I had spare time, I'd paint, too." Genevieve chuckled. "Of course, you're not doing the creative stuff, but how brave of you to leave the law firm and the safety of extended health care."

Wow. Two, possibly three insults to me in there, and even a freebie lobbed at Tatiana.

"Quit your dentistry practice and I'm sure you'd be cranking out masterpieces." I had one question's worth of small talk in me. What would get me off the phone faster? Asking about her husband or children? "How's David?"

When her husband had turned forty-eight last year, he'd sold his lucrative software business and opened a running clinic to support his dream of doing marathons around the world.

"Amazing." Her voice was filled with warmth. "He's not stressed like he used to be. He's out there following his heart."

"So brave." I drew a hangman's scaffold. "What can I help you with?"

"We want to take Nessa to the cabin for her birthday in a few weeks and were hoping to bring Sadie. She said she could come over after work on Friday and drive up with us but it's your weekend with her."

"Not a problem. Thanks for inviting her."

"Of course. She's family."

I'd never been to the cabin, even when Eli and I were married. "Well, I've got a lot of work, so I better go."

"I'll get Sadie the details. Good luck with your new job. So brave! Bye."

"Bye."

Genevieve's passive-aggression was a slow constant leak. Like radiation at Chernobyl. After that call, I couldn't deal with organizing any more press clippings so I returned to the online forums where I'd found my weapons merchant, but my searches on whatever McMurtry's shadow was or how to break the perception filter came up blank.

Around 11:30PM, I popped my head in Sadie's room to find her chatting with Caleb online.

"Tatiana needs me. Artist hours." The lie sounded lame but Sadie either bought it or didn't care.

"Look at you being awake after ten," Sadie said. "Rebel."

"Yup, I'm breaking every rule. Keep your headphones off and don't answer the door. Set the alarm after I leave."

"Will do."

"You'll be okay this late?"

"With an alarm and my cop father next door? I'm guessing yes."

McMurtry wouldn't knock though. I motioned for her to get up. "Maybe you should stay at your dad's."

"Mom, seriously. Go do what you need to."

I gave her strict instructions that if she heard anything weird or got nervous to head next door immediately. Until I found a way to ward my place against Fred and that freaky shadow show, I'd live with a knot in my stomach.

The satchel drop-off was set for Vanier Park, a tranquil space with a large field and ponds that in the summer hosted the Bard on the Beach Shakespeare festival and was popular year-round for flying kites.

I arrived at ten minutes to midnight, having parked a few blocks off and walked in cloaked, in case the grounds were being watched.

Laurent had purchased a satchel similar enough to the one I'd described that would pass in the dark for the real thing and left it at the designated spot: a large rusted artwork in the shape of a stylized archway. He was supposed to have shifted and be hiding in the shadows under one of the weeping willow trees.

When I spotted him, I whispered his name to alert him to my presence.

The white wolf lifted his head, but since he couldn't see me, he went back to scanning for the mystery caller.

I hugged myself, the wind off Burrard Inlet snaking under my coat, and crossed my legs, deeply regretting the two espressos I'd fired back before driving here. I was a woman on the edge with a bladder the size of a walnut, thanks to my natural childbirth. My birth plan had had one item on it: all the drugs. What a bust. I got nothing. No epidural, no fun laughing gas, just an overly cheerful nurse who chanted encouragement like this birth was a multilevel marketing gig and she wouldn't get her commission unless I hit my target.

I stood next to the wolf, Kegeling with all my might, when a dark shape darted into the empty park. Still cloaked, I leaped on the person with a flying tackle as they strode past me with the satchel slung over their shoulder.

When we collided, I became visible and they elbowed me in the gut, knocking me, winded, onto the ground, and sprinted off. They were stupidly fast, so I let Laurent intercept the person, then casually sauntered over to where our mystery caller had been thrown down.

I yanked their hood off. "Krish?"

He swung the satchel at me and I grabbed the other end in a tug-of-war for possession. Krish yanked the bag free but Laurent snagged the back of the man's pants in his teeth and laid him low.

I retrieved the satchel, dumping out the old books we'd stuffed it with. "This is not the satchel you are looking for," I intoned. Krish didn't find me funny, but the wolf huffed. "What's inside it?"

Krish clamped his lips together until Laurent pressed his heavy muzzle against the man's neck. "You'd know since you still have it. You killed Raj. I saw the footage."

"You saw a man get into a car. I didn't kill him," I said. "But I want to know who did. You already told me you sent the vamps last night. How did you hire them for this job?"

Krish wasn't inclined to answer until the wolf pressed a huge paw on the man's chest, his claws outstretched. "The guy I bought the plane from had a connection. I didn't ask for details."

"What about Celeste BatSila?"

Krish shook his head. "Who?"

All right. She wasn't involved in this. "If we had the satchel, we wouldn't have bothered showing up tonight." I jerked a thumb at the wolf. "Tell me what you're looking for or I'll have my friend rip out your throat."

Krish swallowed, his Adam's apple bobbing. "The ring."

"Be more specific."

He'd gone slightly green. "Could you get him off of me?" Laurent growled and Krish yelped. "Okay! I'll talk!"

Once the guy got going, he really spilled his guts. Last Sunday, Krish and Ellis were going for their usual dinner at their club. They always invited the kids, never expecting them to come, but Topher said he would, since he was leaving soon. Ellis was delighted but Krish got suspicious since Topher never willingly went anywhere with them.

That night, he checked the safe in his office. The emergency cash was gone, as was a ring that had been passed down through his family.

"Topher had to be behind it because he had the safe's combination," Krish said. "What my son didn't know was that I'd installed another camera recently. The angle wasn't great, but when I watched the footage later, I was positive that Topher had robbed us and gone to dinner as some kind of smug asshole move. Only after the murder did I realize that it was the dead man on camera."

"Hold on." My head spun with all this new information. "Topher gave Raj the combination to your safe in order to steal a ring. But prior to the murder, still believing that Topher worked alone, had you intended to let your son get away with the crime?"

Laurent moved off Krish and sat down next to me. I angled my pinkie finger to brush his fur with a feather-light touch. It wasn't as soft as it looked, but I liked the fact that his outer coat had coarse guard hair protecting the softer undercoat. It was a rare privilege and a gift for him to allow anyone close enough to feel the hidden softness beneath.

"Are you kidding?" Krish sat up, shaking his head. "I hired a bodyguard to surprise him on the plane and retrieve the ring."

"Another vampire?"

"No. Human. He had to be able to go out in daylight. This man's entire job was to keep Topher from being... Topher. Get him to work, make him go to classes. Stick to him like glue until my son grew up and got a sense of responsibility."

My judgy parent opinion was that could take years. "Except Topher switched places with the victim."

Krish's eyes gleamed appreciatively at his son's cleverness. "A twist I didn't see coming."

"A twist that ended in a man's death," I said. My words hit Krish like a blow, but I tamped down my guilt.

"Yes." His shoulders slumped.

"Was the ring valuable?" Time to wrap this up and find a bathroom. "Is that why Topher stole it?"

"Not as a piece of jewelry," Krish said, proudly, "but it has a history that makes it priceless to some collectors. It's called Ghost Minder."

The wolf's eyes went dark and a scary growl tore out of his throat.

Krish yelped and threw his hands up over his face, whereas my bladder froze up.

Could have been worse. However, I was missing something big. I prodded Sharma with my foot. "Fill me in."

"Ghost Minder controls dybbuks. It was created by a BS." Krish didn't seem to realize that's what I was.

A gasp exploded out of me like I'd been punched. The Lonestars were gunning for Laurent because of the manner in which Raj had been killed and me because of the corpse being found by the cops. Throw in a ring with Banim Shovavim magic that controlled dybbuks and it'd for sure be a one-way ticket to Deadman's Island for both of us.

The Lonestars would assume we'd killed Raj for the ring because the two people in town who could sense dybbuks wished to be the two who could control them, in order to wreak more havoc and enrich ourselves.

Finding the satchel vaulted to the top of my to-do list in giant red blinking letters and an air raid siren.

I grabbed Krish's shoulder. "Who did you tell about this?"

"No one! Are you crazy?" He shoved my hands off him. "When I heard about the man showing up at our house and then saw the footage of my son's lookalike getting in the car that Topher should have been in, I knew the dead man was the thief and my son had helped him. I had to get the damn ring before anyone else found out it was missing. If Topher got tied to that man, then he'd be in a whole lot of trouble even we couldn't get him out from."

Laurent had verified the alibis of Krish, Ellis, and Asha, and all of them had been where they'd claimed that morning, so Krish hadn't killed Raj and he wasn't working with Celeste BatSila.

Was she involved in this crime at all or was Raj just her blood donor, with Topher intending to replace him for the thrill and the cash?

Or was there a more sinister motive?

"Do you think Topher killed Raj to get the ring back? Keep Ghost Minder's power for himself?" I said. When Tatiana had called him, he'd claimed to be waiting for me, but we only had his word for that.

"I never told the kids what the ring does. Topher was aware it was valuable though, and we had him on a tight leash financially. But murder?" Krish buried his head in his hands. "I don't know. How was the man killed?"

"His heart was ripped out," I said.

Krish flinched, turning a wide-eyed look on Laurent, before quickly dropping his gaze to his feet.

The wolf tensed and swung his head away, his flanks heaving.

I curled my fingers under so I couldn't pat him consolingly and gathered up the books.

Krish helped me place them back in the satchel. "I don't think he's powerful enough. His light magic isn't good for much beyond a few flashes. He certainly couldn't sear skin open or laser through bones."

There had been that flashbang before I crashed—though it hadn't been caused by magic. I slung the satchel on my shoulder and helped Krish up. "What's Topher been up to the past few days? Who has he seen?"

"No one." Krish brushed dirt off his pants. "Ellis has been so worried that she's got him locked down until this all blows over."

Topher had snuck out once already to go find Harry, but if his mother was keeping an eye on him, then his opportunities to get around were slim.

"What do I tell Ellis?" Krish wrung his hands together. "What if Topher *is* involved? How did we go so wrong with our son?"

Now I was supposed to play personal counselor to this guy? He got one piece of free advice, then I charged by the word. "You didn't listen to him about what he wants out of life."

He handed me the last book to put in the bag. "That kid has no idea what he wants. We're doing what's best for him."

That's what most parents believed, but it didn't automatically make our actions right. Look at how upset Sadie was with Eli, a dad who overall gave her a lot more respect and support than I'd seen the Sharmas give Topher in our brief interactions.

I readjusted the position of the satchel on my shoulder, white-knuckling the strap. "You hired a bodyguard to babysit your kid rather than talk to him about your suspicions around the theft. All of this could have been avoided if you'd acted like the adult you are and had a single conversation."

Two splotches of red appeared on Krish's cheeks, but the wolf growled and the man kept his mouth shut.

Good, because I wasn't finished. "If Topher had felt like he had one parent actively in his corner, respecting his wishes and listening to him, all of this could have been avoided. Raj would still be alive."

And the Lonestars wouldn't be after me or Laurent. I flicked a strand of hair out of my eyes, my breathing harsh.

"Oh, come on," Krish challenged. "There's not much I can do when the kid hides everything from me. It's not my fault. And don't act so high and mighty like you're some kind of perfect parent when you'd probably feel just as lost in my shoes."

"Of course I'm not perfect," I said. "But my daughter knows I'm in her corner and if there's something she's not bringing up, I ask. She's old enough that if she wants space, I'll give it to her, but she trusts that if she wants to talk, I'm going to be there. You asked for my advice, and that's it: talk to him. Then, listen." I shrugged. "Or don't."

18

I DIDN'T STOP KRISH WHEN HE STORMED OFF. I HAD TO pee so badly that stinging tears filled my eyes. I could make it home in ten minutes at this time of night. Hang in there, bladder.

"You okay?" I said to Laurent, trying not to dance in place.

He nudged his nose into my hand, then raced off into the darkness.

I hobbled to my car with my knees pinched, my entire body clenched for the ride home. Desperate, I fiddled with the radio to find music to distract me. "Islands in the Stream." Pass. TLC's "Waterfalls." Bzz. Thanks for playing. "Under Pressure." I slammed the radio off, shaking a fist to the sky. "Damn you to hell!"

I banged on the front door in our secret knock code, my legs crossed. There was a series of beeps from inside and the deadbolt was thrown open. I pushed past Sadie, popping open the button of my jeans as I stumbled into the powder room on the main floor, convinced I wasn't going to make it.

"That's sad," she said from the other side of the bathroom door.

"Thirteen hours of labor," I grunted as I locked the door and sat down. "You broke my bladder."

"The first of many achievements." She padded up the stairs.

I waited for the sweet relief, my pants at my ankles, but nothing happened. I'd clenched up so hard that I couldn't unfreeze my bladder. Half-sobbing, I turned on the tap, making accompanying whooshing water noises to get my muscles to loosen up.

The next five minutes were a tense descent into google searches on "burst bladder" and "dying of sepsis." I was on my third round of "Let Me Pee," my creative twist on The Beatles' classic, when I heard a faint tinkle in the bowl, encouraging the flow by whispering sweet nothings at it. By the time I'd voided my bladder, tears streamed freely down my face, and I was engulfed in a rush of euphoria.

I stopped by Sadie's bedroom on the way to mine, pausing in the darkened doorway to smile at the kid splayed out limp, already out like a light. Sadie's superpower: falling asleep immediately anywhere. She could pull attitude like a champ, and there had been some scary and heartbreaking incidents around her anxiety, but all in all, Eli and I had lucked out big time with this kid.

Totally spent, I flung off my clothes, scrounged up some pj's, and crawled into bed, wrapping myself up like a burrito.

Krish, the mystery caller, was off the murder suspect list.

Don Egerts was only connected as the blood donor pimp.

Therefore the only suspects left were Celeste BatSila and Topher. My gut still said Topher didn't have it in him to take a life, but Ghost Minder was valuable both in the fiscal sense and the power one. And power was something that Topher lacked.

What if he'd planned to cut Raj out and had teamed up with Celeste to make it happen?

The mysterious Celeste. I rolled onto my back, the world enveloped in its middle-of-the-night hush like a blanket. Everything was so still, I could almost believe I was the only one alive.

The first fact about Celeste was interesting, but not particularly useful: the estrie who had founded her line was called Sila. These female demons didn't share our concept of gender, and to them all their children were daughters. Hence why any vampire in their line took the Hebrew word "bat" meaning "daughter of" plus the estrie's name as their new vampire surname.

Second, Topher wanted to meet with her.

Finally, there was the fact that complicated everything: Celeste was Zev's granddaughter, and harassing her would be suicide.

If Topher was guilty, then I couldn't let it slide. I'd have to report him to the Lonestars, even though it would devastate Krish and Ellis. Sighing, I pulled the covers up to my nose. I didn't want to be responsible for another parent's pain, and I'd been bitchier than necessary with Krish earlier, but if Topher hadn't believed his only option was to steal the ring and smuggle it out with Raj, then that poor guy would be alive.

And yeah, I wouldn't have Deadman's Island hanging over me like an executioner's blade, so Krish could suck it up and deal with my anger.

I tapped my phone against my hip. No matter how I turned it over, I had only one option. I called Harry before I lost my nerve. I didn't blame him for replying to my new request like I was the flakiest person in history, but this was the smartest way forward. When the call was over, I braced myself and phoned my partner.

"Can't sleep?" Laurent's voice was low and sleep-roughened, and his lack of a greeting in answering imbued the call with a sense of intimacy.

Unlike our last call, this one wasn't a misdial. I curled my toes under, bouncing my heels against the mattress. I hadn't brought my phone into bed for a late-night conversation with a man in years, and even though this wasn't *that* kind of conversation and Laurent was going to lose his shit when I told him what I'd requested of Harry, a giddy thrill still rushed through me.

I turned off my lamp, plunging the room into darkness. "The puzzle is taking form."

Ooh, speaking of, I had a new jigsaw puzzle waiting for me to unbox and dive into. It was this psychedelic collage of pinball parts that I expected to be awesomely challenging. When I was done, I'd document it with a photo, and then take it apart with childlike glee. I'd inevitably have a moment of loss, like I'd kicked over a sandcastle I'd worked so hard on, but I'd box it up and donate it to a charity store. There were always more puzzles to look forward to. The joy for me was in completing it, not hanging on to it after.

"Mitzi?"

I shook off my thoughts. "I'm here."

"Did you make a new to-do list?" Ice tinkled in a glass.

"We talked about this. Never mock my lists." Was he stretched out on his sofa, an arm propped behind his head, and jazz swirling through his converted hotel? My home was my anchor, the place where I could always take a deep breath, and while Sadie and I both enjoyed our downtime, we also enjoyed having friends over. This wasn't some fortress of solitude.

Laurent's home was this beautiful gem renovated with his own two hands and a lot of love, but wasn't it lonely rattling around in there? A lone wolf strategy worked as a survival mechanism, but long-term, it had to be exhausting constantly battling the world by yourself, keeping vigilant about who you let inside your walls.

"Did you fall asleep on me?" he chuckled.

"Just thinking."

"Horrors," he said dryly.

"I wish people weren't so quick to believe you'd go feral. It's not fair."

There was a long, loaded silence, then he cleared his throat. "What puzzle pieces did you fit together?"

Men. So loath to share, like being emotionally vulnerable would drain their testosterone.

"Here's my hypothesis." I put my phone on speaker so that I could type notes as we spoke. "The two men run into each other as adults and Topher gets Raj to rob Krish. He knows the code, and thanks to the resemblance, plans to send his lookalike in his place to Los Angeles, presumably to pawn the ring. They probably agreed to meet up there when Topher was sent back to school because Topher didn't know that his dad was on to the scheme and they'd be busted at the plane."

"That tracks so far," Laurent said.

I fought with autocorrect for a second until it accepted my intended word choice. "If Raj was also in it for the money, could they get enough to set them both up off that one ring?"

"In the hands of the right collector they could. People like the arcane and the supernatural."

"Does Ghost Minder actually work as advertised?"

"No, that's not possible, but people think it does and stories have power. That's what makes the ring dangerous." His voice hardened. "I want it found and destroyed. Idiots with delusions of power believing they can control dybbuks."

"Adding that to the to-do list. I think at first this was about money, but somewhere along the line it changed, giving us a couple possibilities." I typed my notes as quickly as I could, keeping the phone on silent so it didn't make the irritating typing sounds. "First one is that Topher decided that Raj was going to betray him and ratted him out to Celeste in exchange for either cash or taking Raj's place as a blood donor."

"His parents would love that," Laurent said dryly.

"Right? Or, Topher stuck to the original plan and Celeste went after Raj on her own."

"She found out her blood bank was skipping town and wasn't happy," Laurent said with a yawn.

"You're very laissez-faire about donors."

"No, I think it's a disgusting exploitation masquerading as a business transaction." Jazz turned on softly on his end, disappearing as Laurent skipped through snippets of songs to land on a piano concerto. "But what am I to do? I have no energy to save everyone from the clutches of the supernatural." He sighed. "Maybe for some, it's a better way to make money than their other options. I won't judge Raj for needing cash or a couple for simply wanting a glass of champagne"—he said it as the French would—"on their anniversary. But it's tiring. I am, I confess, very, very tired."

I pressed my hand to my heart, taken aback by how much he was letting me in, but cherishing it for its rarity.

"I'm sure," I said lamely. Laurent gave everything to his fight against dybbuks. The physical toll alone had to be enormous, but combined with the emotional cost? There was nothing I could say to take that burden from him, but I could ease his worries with the Lonestars. "The Sharmas will have Topher on super lockdown, so I'll call Krish tomorrow after he's had a chance to calm down and arrange a meeting with his son."

"Bien."

"And I've asked Harry to talk to Zev about allowing me to speak with Celeste." I saved my list and closed the app.

"You said you'd stop that meeting."

"I stopped Harry from arranging the meeting directly with Celeste. I called him back tonight and asked him to set one up with Zev."

"What?" Laurent launched into a flurry of annoyed French, sounding wide awake. "Of all the harescattered schemes—"

"It's harebrained or scatterbrained," I said.

"Fuck the grammar."

"If you tell me that extends to the use of the Oxford comma, this partnership is over," I joked.

He growled at me.

Punching off the speakerphone function, I pressed the cell to my ear. "Take it down a notch, Huff 'n' Puff, you'll strain something. And hear me out."

Tense silence.

"Tell me yes or no," I said. "Topher will deny any involvement in Raj's death, and whether or not Celeste was the killer, the vamps'll issue a 'not guilty' statement."

"Yes," he said begrudgingly.

"Yes or no? Even if you and I retrieve Ghost Minder from whomever has it and destroy it before the Lonestars learn of the ring's existence, Ryann and Oliver are going to double down on one or both of us being the murderer. They'll want to close the case one way or the other."

"That doesn't mean—"

"Yes," I said slowly, "or no."

There was a long pause and I tucked the duvet cover around me like a security blanket. It would do us no good to avoid talking about this. Lonestars were dangerous to the people they protected, let alone a rogue wolf shifter and a Banim Shovavim. Still, even as Laurent sighed and took in a breath, I wished he would have said something, anything besides what he did.

"Fine," he growled. Then, a beleaguered "Fuck. Yes."

"We have to produce the killer and the only way to do that is to speak with Topher *and* Celeste, compare stories and catch the guilty party or parties in their lie."

Dead silence.

"I'm right and you know it. Look, this is the smartest way to go about it. I'm not blindsiding Zev, I'm respecting his power and asking permission to speak with his descendant on neutral ground. Basic *Godfather* etiquette. If he says no—"

"Horse head in his bed." There was the sound of Laurent punching his fist into his palm.

"Please. More subtle. A sturgeon wrapped in a bulletproof vest."

"Yes," Laurent said excitedly, like a kid delighted to find a friend who shared their interests. "Like Luca Brasi sleeping with the fishes."

I grinned. "All right, Sonny."

Laurent gasped. "I am Michael."

I made a gagging noise. "Every man thinks they're Michael and not every man is."

"That's correct, but I am."

"Okay, Corleone Junior."

"And if the vampire says yes, then you do not go see Celeste without me," Laurent said sternly. "I've got a lead on the dybbuk-possessed man and I've got to leave town."

"I won't."

"Because you're already on BatKian's shit list."

I shivered. "Trust me, I remember, but at the moment, Celeste and Topher are our only leads, and if the Lonestars find out about the ring, both our asses are toast. Toasted more than they are already. Charred to a crispy husk."

"Mitzi..." Laurent sighed. "Most people don't care about what's fair. Even if you hand the killer over to the Lonestars with Raj's blood dripping off their hands, they may still come after us."

"Huh?" I had conversational whiplash until I clued in that he was picking up the thread from earlier about people willing to believe he'd go feral. "I have to believe otherwise."

"The Banim Shovavim with convictions as sharp as her scythe." His disdain had teeth as pointed as his wolf canines.

Most people would back off to nurse the sting, not under-standing the difference between a bite that broke the skin and a half-hearted nip because that's what was expected of you. This was no different from my years of smiling and playing nice.

What had Laurent experienced to be so wary of optimism and basic decency? I was hardly Little Miss Sunshine, but the only way to break through his walls was throwing him off-guard with chutzpah. Call it gall, nerve, or arrogance, chutzpah involved a total commitment of belief, a ferocity of action. It was vital since Laurent had wrapped himself in barbed wire and turned earning his trust into a blood sport.

"Don't forget my left hook," I said.

He snorted a laugh and I smiled.

The world had slotted both of us into certain roles, though lately I'd wondered if hiding—first from my parents' killers and then societal expectations—had been a convenient excuse because I was scared of my real nature. The side that saw both Laurent and magic as dangerous thrills, and that quit a respectable job to work for a magic fixer instead of neutralizing any threat to me and my loved ones by simply burying my powers again.

What did that mean for me in terms of the Kefitzat Haderech?

"Call me when you hear from Harry." He hung up.

I contemplated the ceiling. For years my cousin Goldie had this Siamese cat called Clementine. An unholy terror who was all claws and teeth, Clementine only ever permitted Goldie to pet her. My injuries from her were legion, but all was worth it the day she finally allowed me to scratch her ears. I'd won over a cat —how hard could a wolf be to tame?

I fell asleep with a smile.

19

SADIE AND I ENJOYED SUNDAY BREAKFAST WITH homemade waffles, heavy on the maple syrup and whipped cream. I was shoving that one final piece beyond what I should eat into my mouth when Harry texted to say that Zev refused to speak with me but Harry was nailing down a time to meet today with the person who could set the ward.

One win was better than none. Now, how could I get Topher to crack without playing him against Celeste?

"Problem?" Sadie said.

"Work stuff." I drummed my fingers on the table. Going behind Zev's back on this was a bad idea, so I texted Laurent that Celeste was a no-go.

He replied that I should follow up with Topher, so I left a voice message asking Krish for a meeting.

Meantime, Sadie and I headed down to Granville Island to put together a gift basket for Juliette. My daughter had decided to spend the day with me since she was going to her dad's that night, but I suspected the real reason was that Caleb was busy. That's okay. Between her summer job, a boyfriend, and her friends, I wouldn't see much of her, so I'd take being her consolation prize today.

Since Juliette was staying with Tatiana, Sadie opted to dress up in case she met my artist boss. She'd selected a pink tank top worn under a light beige cardigan, a pink A-line skirt paired with a pink and white polka dot scarf, and pink cat's eyeglasses with no lenses. She finished the outfit off with white knee-high socks that reminded me a bit too uncomfortably of the Kefitzat Haderech and black ballet flats.

She breezed through the public market, enjoying the stares— both admiring and scornful— that she received. We'd already picked up fancy dry pasta, balsamic, and some delicate maca-roons, and were debating what else to add to the wine I'd already purchased when Sadie ran over to the specialty tea shop. She bumped into a basket held by a white woman with pinched features, but before my daughter could apologize, the woman shook her head, muttering about all the Japanese tourists.

I could have stepped in at this point but it was so much more fun not to.

Sadie's jaw clenched for a second before she widened her eyes, her hand covering her mouth. Bobbing in a half bow, she said, "Sorry, no English," in a super affected Japanese accent.

"Watch where you're going." The woman spoke slowly and loudly, under the misapprehension that all foreigners were, apparently, hard of hearing.

"I'll do that," Sadie said in her regular voice. "If next time you watch how you're blocking the narrow aisle with your basket, and oh, I don't know, stop making racist assumptions? I'm Chinese-Canadian and born here."

I looped my arm through Sadie's and the woman frowned at me.

"Teach your daughter some manners."

"Like your mother taught you?" I said politely.

Huffing, she dropped the basket and stalked off.

"Sorry," Sadie said to the young woman working there.

"Nah. That was aces. Let me know if you need anything."

We picked out some teas for the gift basket. These kinds of

encounters weren't new for Sadie, and for years she would have run away, embarrassed. Her confidence in calling people out now was thanks to Eli, who, cop or not, faced a lot of discrimination and didn't put up with that shit. However, I also knew my daughter well enough not to push her to talk about it. Most likely, she'd confide her feelings to her cousin Nessa, or maybe Caleb now. All I cared about was that she had a good support system.

We arranged everything in the basket, adding a bright bow that we'd bought at a stationery store, and Sadie held the gift while I drove us to Tatiana's house. I let the kid DJ, listening to an odd playlist of musicals, K-Pop, and the occasional disco classic.

I'd gone back and forth on having Sadie and Tatiana meet, but had ultimately decided that if my employer met my daughter and was familiar with her as a real person and not just a concept, then should push come to shove, Tatiana would be more inclined to keep her word and protect Sadie.

After one other errand, we pulled up to the mansion and Sadie whistled, rubbing her thumb and index finger together. "Cha-ching. Hope you're getting a good piece of this, Mom."

"I'm being paid pretty well. Now please pretend you have manners."

Grinning, she opened the car door. "I'm a good actress."

Tatiana's assistant Marjorie let us in, calling for Juliette before scurrying away into the back recesses of the house.

I led Sadie into the airy living room, and she put the gift basket on the coffee table.

"Whoa." She stopped in front of the *Dollhouse Collection* painting of Jackie O. "Did she paint that?"

"She did."

"She's really good."

"Don't tell her," Juliette said in her lilting French accent, stepping into the room. "Her ego is big enough." She was dressed in navy tights, navy shorts, and a navy and white striped shirt, accessorized with a red scarf tied artfully around her neck.

The two young women stared at each other for a moment before bursting out with "I love your outfit!" in twin squeals.

My kid preened under the admiration of this cool older French chick.

"This is for you," I said, sliding the gift basket toward Juliette. "For all your help recently."

"Merci à vous, but this really wasn't necessary." She lifted out the items, Sadie giving her opinion on what made each one great. Juliette read the label on the bottle of ice wine and shot me a sly smile. "I see you consulted with my uncle."

Sadie looked blankly between her and me for a moment. "Oh. Old kinda hot guy is your uncle?"

"Sadie," I hissed.

Juliette laughed. "Oui. And that is my new favorite name for him."

While the two chatted, my phone rang. "Excuse me, I need to take this."

I went into the hallway. "Hi, Krish, thanks for getting back to me so quickly."

"Topher's gone," he said tersely.

"What do you mean?"

"He snuck out his window on the second floor. Hang on." He covered the speaker, but was still audible, telling Ellis to calm down, they'd find him. "I'm back."

"When was this?"

"I don't know. Ellis went to ask him if he was hungry a few minutes ago and he wasn't there. We've called the Lonestars."

I punched the wall lightly. "What did you tell them?"

"That he's taken off and we're concerned that whoever killed Raj Jalota is after our son."

I paced the hallway. Krish and Ellis weren't about to admit Topher's role in this, but Laurent was out of town so, if anything happened to the kid, at least my partner had an alibi.

However, I didn't. Damn that kid—and his parents, since they obviously hadn't discussed the situation with him.

Topher might have taken off because he was fed up, but if he'd gone to Celeste? If they were working together, they hadn't yet had the chance to sync their stories because she was still asleep. I had to wring answers out of him before he had the vamp's protection. I checked the time. There were six hours until Celeste woke up at sunset.

"Call me the second you hear from him," I said.

"I will."

I rested against the wall, my head back. If I couldn't find Topher in time, then could I get the jump on him at Celeste's before he made contact? But where would the vampire be? I couldn't go poking around Blood Alley without Zev's permission, and even if he let me in, I doubted I'd be allowed to walk away again. I jammed the phone in my pocket, and walked into the living room, scrubbing all my worries off my face. "Hey Sades—"

"A party in my own house and I wasn't invited?" Tatiana said.

Sadie's mouth fell open. Hard to say if it was because the artist pronounced "party" as "pawtee" or it was seeing an eighty-year-old in an oversized old-timey painter's smock that was splattered in colors and worn over electric blue Lycra leggings. She'd switched her usual red glasses for a pair of sedate black frames with a smear of green paint on the corner of one lens.

Just the woman I wanted to speak to. "Tatiana," I said, "come meet my daughter Sadie."

"Hi," Sadie said, her hand outstretched.

Tatiana strode into the room and motioned for Sadie to stand up. "Let's get a look at you, mammele."

My daughter dropped her hand and did as instructed, looking vaguely apprehensive as Tatiana circled her, making "hmmm" sounds.

"Nice lines, pleasing palette, the girl has a good eye," Tatiana pronounced.

"High praise," Juliette said.

Sadie smoothed her cardigan down. "Thank you."

Tatiana snorted. "So how come you didn't pass that on to your mother? Sit. You look like you're giving a book report."

Wide-eyed, Sadie dropped onto the sofa.

I glanced down at my olive green capris and cream knit sleeveless top. "There's nothing wrong with my clothes."

"Olive should only be used with gin and vermouth," Tatiana said. "Life isn't a law firm. Liven it up a bit."

"You don't pay me enough to insult my fashion sense."

She shot me an affronted frown. "How is objective truth an insult?"

I shook my head. "Clothes aren't exactly a priority these days."

Sadie shrugged at Tatiana. "See? You try doing something with that attitude of hers."

I pushed my shoulders back, trying not to hunch defensively. "Wait here. I need to speak to Tatiana for a sec."

Juliette asked Sadie about good vintage clothing stores in town while Tatiana and I went in the hallway for privacy. When I told her about Krish and the ring and Topher possibly working with Celeste, Tatiana got this amused smile that didn't so much convey "good one" as "I am a cobra and this has just ensured a death strike. How fun." I swear I heard a rattle and I was super glad not to be on the receiving end of that venom.

"We have to do something or the Lonestars will pin this on Laurent and me," I insisted.

She removed her glasses and flecked the paint off with her thumbnail. "Krish should have taken my insistence of full disclosure at face value and told me about the theft and the bodyguard." She jabbed the glasses at me. "And you should have kept your word when you returned Don's notebook to me about staying out of this fakakta mess."

"If the Lonestars go after us, you think they'll believe that you aren't involved? When it was your SUV, your employee, and your nephew? Your reputation is hardly spotless."

A muscle twitched in Tatiana's jaw. Got her. She glared at me and stalked off.

Uncertain whether she was coming back, I returned to Sadie and Juliette, anxiously awaiting some verdict.

"I have a client, so I must dash. Bisous." Juliette kissed Sadie and me on both cheeks and left with her gift basket.

"Are we going, too?" Sadie said.

"Not quite yet."

She shrugged and pulled out her phone.

I gave my boss five minutes and then we'd go.

Tatiana returned four minutes and thirty seconds later.

"Well?"

"Undetermined," she said grimly. "I left Zev a message."

We chatted half-heartedly about her memoirs and whether she planned to write about her entire life or a particular period. She was undecided but wanted me to catalog everything.

Harry texted that he'd sent his guy to my place to set the ward.

Tatiana peered over my shoulder at the screen with absolutely no sense of boundaries, reading the message. "What is he talking about?"

"McMurtry. Long story."

Something flickered in the artist's eyes, there and gone too fast for me to parse out, and she looked away.

"Mom? We going?"

Frowning, I glanced at Tatiana, but she still stared off in the distance.

This sucked. Not only was this ward business cutting into my mother-daughter time, Sadie couldn't be at home while this was set up, because she'd have questions and wouldn't believe the answers. Or if she did, they might scare her. Much as I wanted her to know about magic, I didn't want her anxious about her house being vulnerable.

"Something's come up," I said. "Do you have anyone you can hang out with today?"

"No. Everyone's busy." She crossed her arms. "Aren't you and I spending the day together?"

"This can't be put off. I'm sorry."

"Your mom has business to attend to, so you stay with me," Tatiana said to Sadie. "You can learn how to pack canvases."

"Oh, no, I don't want to impose." It was one thing for Sadie and Tatiana to meet and quite another to leave my daughter here.

"How much do you pay?" Sadie cut right over me, her hands folded primly in her lap and her spine made of steel.

Tatiana arched an eyebrow. "You've got chutzpah, kid. I'll give you ten bucks an hour. Take it or leave it."

Sadie pursed her lips, thinking it over. "I'll take it. Okay, Mom?"

"Who's the boss here? I said it's happening, so it's happening." Tatiana put her arm around me, steering me to the front door. "This isn't just about you," she said quietly, tilting her head back toward Sadie.

"Sadie's a great kid, but you're going an extra mile here and I don't understand why."

Tatiana opened the front door, a troubled look flitting over her face. Her shoulders stooped, her normally spritely body betraying its age. "We have to protect the children. I failed to do so once. I won't now. Sadie is safe with me."

Who was she talking about? Tatiana didn't have kids. Unless she'd lost a child? I shook my head. I had to stop jumping to that conclusion. Regardless, there was a weight to her promise that I believed.

"Well, thanks again," I said. "I'll be back soon."

There was that flicker of immense emotion again, in the way she rubbed her fingers over her knuckles, her eyes at her feet, her shoulders soft. Then it was gone and she barked out a laugh. "You better. I don't pay overtime, to you or your kid."

Sadie was safe.

Our house would be safe. But sometimes these things cost much more than anticipated.

20

TWO MEN WAITED FOR ME ON MY FRONT STOOP IN THE afternoon sun. One looked like a kindly country doctor, complete with an old-fashioned leather physician's bag. The other was a towering wall of muscle in an undertaker's suit who didn't blink as often as he should, his eyes a glacial blue.

Doctor Dude jumped to his feet with a nervous glance at his companion. "Miriam?"

"Yes." I stopped short of the stairs, in case I had to make a run for it.

He picked up his bag. "I'm Phil. Harry sent me."

"Okay. And you are?"

The Undertaker sized me up like he was measuring the water content in my body and how fast he could squeeze it out of me.

I took a step back.

"Mr. BatKian requests your presence." His voice had the dulcet tones of steel wool on glass.

The head vampire here in Vancouver had already refused to speak with me so why the change of heart now?

I anxiously blinked away the image of that lumpy organ on the passenger seat, and as casually as possible, given I couldn't draw in a full breath, I eased my cell out of my purse, intending to text Tatiana. "Let me check my availability."

The Undertaker flicked his fingers and my phone flew from my hand to his before I'd typed the "p" in help.

Do not antagonize the man who could squash me like a bug. "Can I at least get my house warded up?"

Phil nodded, freezing mid-motion when the Undertaker cracked his knuckles. "I'm afraid I have another job to get to," Phil said, and swallowed audibly. "Now."

Ducking his head, he scurried across my neighbor's lawn, breaking into a sprint down the rest of the block.

I opened my mouth.

The Undertaker crossed his arms, his flexed biceps pushing against his surprisingly sturdy suit jacket.

"Your car or mine?" I said, with a weak smile.

The last time I'd been "escorted" to Blood Alley, a human had died. That was before I'd been explicitly warned off going there ever again by the same vampire who now had sent for me. I could barely start the engine; my hands were shaking so hard. Laurent was out of town, Tatiana was unaware of my location, and oh shit, Sadie.

My passenger shut off the radio, riding in stony silence, but after the third time I hit the brakes sharp enough to fling the Undertaker forward, he grabbed the wheel and wrenched it sideways into an open parking spot.

Car horns blared; I screamed.

After my life had stopped flashing in front of my face, which took a lot less time than I would have liked, I pried my fingers off the wheel. "Does Zev teach that move to all his minions, because for a vampire who doesn't like people touching his stuff, he certainly gives all of you free rein to put your fat fingers all over everything."

"Get out. I'm driving."

I crossed my arms. "Over my de—"

He gave a thin smile.

"My decided wishes otherwise." My icy panic had melted into a burning rage. My house was still unwarded and I'd been bullied into a meeting I might not survive. "You don't like how I drive, there's the sidewalk. Have a pleasant stroll."

While he let me drive, we hit every green light and found a parking spot across the street from Blood Alley in record time. I couldn't tell if that meant the universe was on my side or not.

The Undertaker hauled me into the hidden magic territory under the large metal sign reading "Blood Alley" that spanned the spiky gates, so I didn't have to spend energy cloaking to reveal it. Gargoyle statues crouched on each corner of the sign, their black eyes boring into me.

It was eerily deserted in the daytime, a hush enveloping the streets as if the very land slept along with its undead denizens. We headed up one of the narrow roads leading to the nightclub Rome, passing black lacquered doors shut tight, the red light-bulbs above each one dark.

When we got to the top of the hill, I paused. Rather, I tried, but the Undertaker had a firm hold on my elbow and he dragged me with him.

The sunshine didn't make the expanse of unkempt lawn between me and the club's front doors any prettier. If anything, the patchy spots and weeds gave it a forlorn air, made worse by the melancholy expressions of the gargoyles perched unevenly on the grass. They were only statues, but I swore they tracked my movements and my shoulders rose up to my ears.

I was ushered down a back hallway instead of through the main space, but there was a flurry of activity, with human staff in their "Rome" T-shirts hurrying past with crates of clean glasses, or wheeling kegs of beer, readying the club for this evening.

We stopped in front of the red door leading to Zev's office and I wiped my hands off on my pants. The last time I'd been here, not only had the head vampire destroyed an irreplaceable statue because it was chipped, he'd also compelled Laurent to kill Emmett and me. Then, when I'd tried to grab Zev's shadow to maybe turn the tables, it had turned to fog. I had no cards up my sleeve here, and that left me at a serious disadvantage.

The vamp enjoyed his head games. This sudden agreement and then forced participation was his first move, but I wasn't totally helpless, nor had I committed any breach of his precious etiquette. I had my magic and he was unable to compel me.

I pushed the employee aside and rapped on the door. "I'll take it from here," I said, when Zev called out for me to enter.

The Undertaker trained a bland expression on me before pivoting off without another word, but I'd like to believe that I'd amused him.

"One second there, mister!" I snapped my fingers. "Phone, please."

Once I had it back in my possession, I took a deep breath and stepped inside.

Zev's office was much as I remembered it, with custom-made furniture in sleek lines softened by the presence of an enormous Persian rug in deep reds and blues. The workspace was set up at one end, sharing the massive room with an art gallery filled with priceless original paintings and statues, all of them flawless creations.

Zev BatKian didn't stand for imperfections.

The master vamp sat behind his desk, opening mail with a pearl-handled letter opener, which he sorted into neat piles. Not one of his mahogany-colored strands of hair was out of place, his goatee was impeccably trimmed, and his fitted gunmetal suit showcased the strong line of his shoulders and flat stomach. Even if he'd really been as he appeared in his mid-forties, he'd be exceptionally attractive, so for someone who was at least several hundred years old, he was remarkably well-preserved. "Good afternoon, Ms. Feldman."

"Good afternoon."

At his elbow was one of Jude's oversized ceramic coffee mugs. I had its twin at home, although the handle was red, whereas on Zev's black cup it was purple. There was a tiny red heart painted at the bottom of mine. I leaned forward slightly to see his design, but at the sight of dark odorless liquid inside, decided I wasn't that curious.

"I'm surprised you're awake this early," I said.

He motioned to a chair, sapphire cufflinks winking. "The older you are, the less you sleep. It's sadly true of humans and vampires."

I perched on the edge of the seat. "Did you summon me to discuss my request to speak with your granddaughter?"

He laid the letter opener down and steepled his fingers together, regarding me with his shrewd gaze that seemed to categorize all my sins in a blink. "What came through your house that you're so concerned about?"

I blinked. "How did you know about that?" I made a grumpy-faced strong man pose. "Did the Undertaker tell you?"

Zev's brows furrowed together, then he laughed. "No. Rodrigo didn't mention it."

I wet my lips. There was no way to tell him about McMurtry without also handing him the details of my parents' murder. I wracked my brain for any way that this could come back to bite me in the ass, but failing to come up with something, launched into the tale from the beginning. After all, I still needed a ward and I'd learned from my dealings with Zev that sometimes it was better to be truthful because he appreciated that kind of radical honesty.

He listened intently, occasionally sipping from his mug, but his frown grew deeper when I got to the part about the shadow piloting the Lonestar. "You're positive that's what you saw?"

"Kind of hard to miss."

He leaned back in his chair with a troubled expression. This was why he'd brought me here.

"What's with that look?" Anything that disturbed a vampire's peace of mind was bad news. What horrible fate lay in store for me if I didn't find a way to ward against this thing?

"I didn't think what you described was possible. If any should learn of it—" Zev jammed the letter opener through the heart of his mail pile and I shrank back in my seat. "I don't know the name of the creature you described, if in fact it has one, but essentially, it's a demon parasite."

Whoa. I reached for the clasp of my purse to get my phone, before deciding that now was probably not the time to take notes, no matter how interesting a topic. "Is it killing the Lonestar?"

"On the contrary, but to clarify, I must back up. There are many different ecosystems in this world. Humans are acclimatized to whichever one they live in, but can have difficulty in a new system."

"Like with drinking water."

"Precisely. The entire earthly realm is like that for demons. It makes them sick." He chuckled at my surprised look. "Demons aren't invincible. They ingest these parasites before coming over to inoculate against all toxins."

"It's their travel vaccination." I gave an excited little bounce, knocking my purse to the ground. "Even so, how did it get in McMurtry?"

"He was in the demon realm."

My mouth fell open. "People can go to the demon realm?"

Zev spread his hands wide. "Apparently."

McMurtry's robotic response about fly fishing during his disappearance, the reason his cancer had gone away, it all made sense. "This is incredible. If it's not hurting him, then it's not like a dybbuk possessing a host. If Ohrist medical researchers got hold of this—"

He ran a thumb over the blade of the letter opener, his smile sending goosebumps over my skin. "The vampires would wage war, starting with you and everyone you love."

Message received, but why threaten me in the first place? This parasite inoculated demons against anything toxic to their system, but estries were demons and they created vampires so the parasites probably didn't hurt bloodsuckers. "I don't see why this is a problem."

"Come now, Ms. Feldman. I bet you were always top of your class." The knowledge-rich and benevolent vampire played teacher. His mocking tone set my teeth on edge, blowing away some of my fear. I almost liked him better when he threw off his trappings of humanity and let his monster out.

At least then neither of us had to pretend.

"I'm assuming that if this parasite has been feeding off McMurtry for the last thirty years that only Banim Shovavim can see it," I said, "because Ohrists aren't that open-minded."

"Correct."

I tapped my head. "Top of my class."

He gave me a snarky smile. "Correct, but irrelevant."

I threw up my hands. "Fine. I give up. Enlighten this poor limited human's understanding, please. Why would vamps care if this demon parasite cures cancer in us?"

"Perhaps we believe in the natural order of things."

I snorted. "That's rich coming from you."

His hand tightened on the blade of the letter opener, blood welling between his fingers, but he didn't wince, didn't even take his stormy brown eyes off mine.

The pulse fluttering in my throat was like a timpani beating against the thinnest layer of skin. "That was uncalled for," I said. "I apologize. May we continue?"

"We may."

Plop. Plop. A crimson pattern bloomed on his desk.

I couldn't grab his shadow to toast him, he saw through my cloaking, and he'd easily dodge any moves Delilah brought. If only I understood what my magic had been telling me about dealing with vampires. There had to be a way out of this, but under the weight of his ancient gaze, my mind went blank.

I focused on the puzzle I could solve. Okay, why would a vampire care about a demon parasite that inhabited humans? What would be the disadvantage to the undead?

"The parasite protects humans from vampires," I guessed.

"Specifically?" He pulled his hand from the blade, the wound sealing.

I ticked items off on my fingers. "Either the parasite wards vampires off somehow, making it impossible to feed off humans, or it keeps humans from being turned. You're a big proponent of synthetic blood, so I'm going to go with door number two. You can't make us into your kind." I sat back and crossed my legs. "What did I win?"

"How about a kiss?" Zev murmured into my ear.

I hadn't even seen him move. My brain screamed run, but my body pushed closer to his, craving the sensation of him sinking his fangs into me. "How are you compelling me? I'm immune."

"I unmuted my natural allure, but I assure you, it's not compulsion. I have no need to force anyone." His low chuckle wrapped around me like silk. "This is all you."

My lips parted on a breathy sigh but I dug my nails into my palms to keep from thrusting them into his hair and closing any gap between us. "Impossible. The only thing I feel for vampires is disgust."

"And yet, look at you. I see your desire." His hands slid up my arms, pinning my shoulders against the chair. "I smell it." His fangs scraped against my throat. "You disparage our humanity, think my kind an abomination, and yet you want me the same as any other man you desire. Tell me, Ms. Feldman, of the two of us, who is the delusionist?"

My nipples were hard and my underwear wet. I licked my lips, shivering when his eyes darted to my mouth, because that hadn't been an invitation. Desperate to regain a measure of control, I shoved him off me. "Enough with the game playing. It's getting old. Now, I'm expected at Tatiana's and I have a house to ward up, so I'd like to leave."

"Phil can't protect you against the parasite. I can." He shook his head. "By all means, phone Harry, describe the exact nature of your problem, and see what he says."

"What's it going to cost me?"

Outwardly, I remained calm, but my stomach was a hard lump. I'd have given him blood, but he wouldn't be interested. What if he meant to prove another point? What kind of madness was my life where donating blood to a vampire was the easy answer?

"I can ward your house up against anything demonic that tries to enter, but you'd have to invite me inside."

"I'm not giving you free access to my daughter. You already threatened her once."

He shrugged. "My understanding of the situation is different now. I won't hurt your child."

Because of Tatiana's protection? That didn't stop him harassing me. "I don't believe you. I'll find another way to—"

Zev stood up and, placing his laptop under his arm like he was about to go off for a stroll, kicked his desk into the wall hard enough to make it splinter.

A couple shards of desk shrapnel grazed my calf and I jumped out of my chair, holding it in front of me like a shield. Except the longer the two of us stood there, me shaking and Zev staring dispassionately at me, the more it felt like a red cape being waved in front of a bull.

Every violent outburst of Zev's was conducted with a methodical coldness. Nothing cracked his glacial shell. Had he forgotten how to feel or was it a self-protective measure in the face of immortality?

Neither idea was much comfort.

"Come." He motioned for me to walk with him through his art gallery.

I pried my grip off the chair, forcing down my nausea and schooling my features as best I could to match his expression of polite indifference. For the record, he was way better at it.

We stopped in front of a fresco, the paint cracked with age. An enormous horned demon was two-fisting humans, someone's bloody legs hanging out of its mouth.

"Should this demon appear in the streets," he said, "people would scream and flee. I would laugh."

My nerves were raw and I was hanging on to any pretense of civility by a thread. I didn't have the energy, nor frankly the time for one of his philosophical bents on the morality of the undead. "Because our suffering is irrelevant to you."

"Your hypothesis is patently untrue. However, this is a discussion of perspective." He gestured at the fresco. "To humans, this demon is terrifying. To me, he is nothing. That tiny parasite, on the other hand, is a nightmare because it would upset our ability to continue."

I planted my hands on my hips. "This relates to my daughter, how?"

"Perspective. Her father is a human police officer, a fact I was unaware of previously. Dead children get a lot of coverage, and I am nothing if not practical."

"But middle-aged ex-wives aren't as headline-grabbing."

He smiled, the corners of his eyes crinkling. "You're very suspicious. Perhaps I want somewhere to hang out. Let my hair down with someone who doesn't kowtow to my position."

Sure, he could join Sades and me for our *Buffy* re-watch. Zev wouldn't feed off Sadie, but since she was Sapien, he could turn her should he be inclined to break his word. Then again, there was no love lost between BatKian and myself. If he wanted me dead, I'd be dead. He didn't need to get into my house for that, so why did he want this deal? I came up empty-handed.

His threats were exhausting, but I understood those. That almost-kiss—I squirmed, not wanting to revisit it in too much detail—it hadn't meant anything on his part. It was just a means to an end, proving a point. But coming into my home? Did he want some hideaway where no one would think to find him?

Did this have to do with Tatiana's protection?

Or was all of this less about me and more that Zev would go to ridiculous lengths to torment Laurent?

I was a pawn and I couldn't even see the gameboard, but what choice did I have? Better the devil I knew…

"Agreed. On the condition that you get me to Celeste." I unclenched my fists. "Please."

He picked a piece of lint off his suit jacket. "Celeste will speak to you or not of her own volition."

"The Sharmas called the Lonestars. Right now, they have no idea that Celeste may be involved in this murder. If she is and I get to her first, I'll hand her over to you to deal with and not them."

"That's a bluff, Ms. Feldman. The Lonestars will do the same thing."

"Usually, I'd agree, but if Celeste murdered Jalota, then she left the corpse out where it was found by Sapien police. Prime directive violation. Are you certain they won't deal with her themselves?"

The vampire picked up a soft cloth from a nearby small table and polished an ornate silver frame. Slowly and thoroughly.

I ground my teeth together, clasping my hands in a tight grip behind my back.

"On the north side of Mountain View Cemetery," he said at last, "there's a crypt whose angel is missing a wing. Make sure you locate the correct one."

"Missing wing. Celeste is inside?"

"No. The grave directly behind it. Take three handfuls of dirt, face the moon and say her name."

"You're messing with me," I said uncertainly.

The vamp's lips quirked up. Barely. "Is that a statement or a question?"

"A statement."

"But you weren't sure."

I shot him the finger. Behind my back. "Where is she really?"

"Take the left-most lane up from the entrance of Blood Alley tonight at 11PM and go to the third door on your left. You'll find her there."

In the heart of vampire central. Well, if trouble started, at least there would be human witnesses. "What about the ward?"

Zev tossed the cloth back on the table. "I'll come by your house around 3AM tonight."

"Then I look forward to inviting you in at that time."

"Mmm, I'm sure. And Ms. Feldman?"

I raised my eyebrows in question.

He leveled a grim stare at me, his lips pressed into a thin line, and I tensed, convinced he was going to rescind the offer because he doubted my sincerity. "Don't make me regret this."

21

Much as I was itching to wrap this case up, I had no desire to run all over town trying to find Topher. Celeste was still asleep, so I'd catch him at Blood Alley tonight, assuming that's where he was going.

I texted Sadie when I got outside Tatiana's place, not up to conversation. I was reasonably sure I hadn't made a huge mistake agreeing to let Zev into my home, but myth, legend, and hardwiring left me with a seed of malignant doubt.

Tatiana escorted my daughter to the car, but she didn't grill me. "All sorted?"

"Yup."

She patted Sadie on the shoulder. "If I ever need child labor again, you'll be the first one I call."

My daughter pressed her hands to her cheek and fluttered her lashes. "I'm honored."

Tatiana laughed and trundled back to the house.

"She's cool." Sadie clicked in her seatbelt. "What are we doing for dinner?"

"Is that all I am to you? A feeding machine?" I adjusted my rearview mirror and put the car in gear, driving slowly through the residential neighborhood.

"No. You're also a valuable laundry drone."

"Just for that, you make dinner."

"Tacos it is." She slipped on her headphones, leaving me free to listen to my own music.

True to her word, Sadie cooked. I'd been conscripted as sous chef when there was a knock at the door.

Ryann Esposito waved at me through the peephole, and oh joy, she'd brought Oliver Anderson with her. There was a time when a knock during dinner meant a kid selling chocolates for their baseball team or an enthusiastic adult asking if I had a moment to discuss the plight of the hungry in my community. I folded the cuffs of the cardigan I'd thrown on over my hands. Tonight I'd invite a vampire into my home to stop a demon, but I didn't even have that modicum of choice when it came to the Lonestars.

I threw open the door. "To what do I owe the pleasure of your company?"

The head Lonestar wore a white, long-sleeved ruffled dress that hit mid-thigh paired with black Doc Martens. Her hair was still shaved, but she had a sparkly blue flower barrette on one side. Kicking butt, *Little House on the Prairie*–style.

Oliver's silver fox vibe was dimmer today. His rumpled shirt was misbuttoned, he hadn't shaved, and he rocked the slightly stunned, wide eyes of the over-caffeinated.

"We got a call from a former Lonestar, name of Fred McMurtry," Ryann said.

I kept my face carefully blank. "Who's that?"

"The man you were harassing," Oliver said.

Ryann placed a hand on his sleeve. "The man you spoke with."

"If he presses charges…" Oliver smiled thinly.

"I didn't harass him. I merely asked him a question."

Oliver crossed his arms. "About what?"

A lifetime of habit screamed at me to lie, but a little truth might work in my favor. "About the night my parents died. The house fire. It's all a blur and I hoped to learn more to get some closure. That night has haunted me my entire life."

Ryann's shrewd gaze locked onto mine and I blushed, having given away more than I intended, but all she said was, "I verified what you said about your magic. It wouldn't have ripped out the heart."

"Told you."

"Where's Amar?" Oliver jabbed a finger at me, his gold star tattoo winking in the sunlight. "Because the Sharma boy is missing."

I stepped onto the porch, forcing them back a couple of steps. "Laurent's out of town."

"Then why is his motorcycle parked outside Hotel Terminus?" Oliver said.

"He bought a truck."

"Fucking unbelievable." Oliver hooked his thumbs through his belt loops. "Does he have you totally conned or do you dybbuk-killers stick together?"

"Have you even been investigating or are you sitting around waiting for me to lie so you can convict an innocent man for nothing more than your prejudices?" I said in a low voice. The stress of choking down my anger so I didn't upset Sadie caused my temples to throb like I'd been concussed again. "Is there a single Lonestar who isn't corrupt? One who actually cares about law and order and justice? You're not law enforcement," I said, thickly, "you're thugs."

Ryann sighed. "That's unnecessarily hurtful."

"Watch your mouth," Oliver said.

"Or what?" I slammed my hand against the door. "You'll throw me on Deadman's Island for the horrible crime of being different?"

Ryann's phone rang and she excused herself, going down the front path to the sidewalk to answer it.

Oliver leaned in. "You know what hunters used to do to your kind?"

"Do tell."

"There was a sarcophagus called the Way Finder. Its insides were studded with nails so that when two hunters blazed white hot light inside of it to cleanse BS like you, the more you thrashed around in it, the more effectively we could bleed the darkness from your soul." He slowly crumpled his hand into a fist, his eyes gleaming. "The purified ones would come out from this contemplation chamber reborn."

The color drained from my face and I clutched the doorframe. There was no dictionary in which contemplation was a synonym for torture. Equally as terrifying as this device was the fact that Ohrist hunters knew about the Kefitzat Haderech and had devised their own take on the conditions put in place by the angels.

"That's not rebirth," I said. "It's an execution."

"Not the hunters' fault if you people failed to be purified. Now, if I had my way?" He glanced at Ryann, slowly pacing up and down the sidewalk, still absorbed in her call, then spat on the ground at my feet. "You'd never make it to Deadman's Island."

The air crackled between us, Delilah itching at me to be let loose.

If Sadie hadn't dropped a glass in the kitchen at that moment, I would have done something I regretted.

Ryann rejoined us. "Sorry about that." She wagged a finger at me. "You said you'd have that satchel for us today."

"Uh, yeah. That didn't work out."

She dropped her peppy manner with a sigh that seemed to shiver up from the very marrow of her bones. "Give me something to work with, Miriam. I'm trying to help you, but you keep stonewalling me. I know that you have more information than you've let on."

"This was a waste of my time," Oliver said. "Do what you came here to do already."

Ryann pulled something out of her pocket. She clutched it in her fist for a moment, then slowly opened her fingers to reveal a thumb drive. "Cooperate with us or I give the footage of you in the car with Jalota to the VPD."

She glanced meaningfully at Eli's mailbox.

"And by 'cooperate' you mean say Laurent did it?" I held up one finger like I'd had a brilliant idea. "How about this? You shove your blackmail up your ass or I'll go nuclear and make magic so public the Men in Black will need more cages in Area 51 to house all of us."

"I want you to be honest," Ryann said, her eyebrows raised, giving me little nods of encouragement.

"Hey." Eli stood on the front walk in his suit, looking confused.

I scrambled for some way to explain these two, wrestling my anger under control.

Ryann spun around on her tip toes. "Sultan of Swing Chu." She curtsied.

My heart dropped into my stomach. How did she know about Eli's police baseball team nickname?

He grinned widely at the younger woman. "Junior, you brat."

She flew off the stairs and the two of them hugged.

My jaw hit the ground at about the same time as Oliver's. "How do you two know each other?" I said.

Eli slung an arm over Ryann's shoulders. "You know Deputy Chief Constable Esposito? This is his daughter, Ryann. He used to bring her to the station all the time, made us rookies babysit her."

That's how she'd known about Eli getting pressure to solve the case. Her dad was his boss, and judging from the double takes that Oliver kept doing between them, he did not appreciate one bit being kept in the dark about that. Interesting. Did Ryann have her own reasons for wanting magic to be known by certain officers? I filed it away for later.

Ryann jerked a thumb at Eli. "He always made me do my homework."

"I also kept a hidden stash of Oreos for you." He let her go, shaking his head. "Man, your dad hoped you'd go to the Academy so badly. Still, being a life coach sounds like a good gig. Helping lots of people?"

I snorted and Eli shot me a curious glance.

Ryann twirled her hair. "Oh, you know, I had to walk my own path. Use my gifts to change the world through positivity."

"Cool." He said it with forced enthusiasm. "So, what did you want to see me about?"

I could have kissed Eli for assuming this was about him, and then smirked because Ryann stammered uh and um, with no lie handy.

"They're here to see me." Three pairs of eyes whipped my way.

If Eli and I were to have a reckoning over this, so be it, but if I gave in to blackmail now, it wouldn't stop. Not with these people.

"You're working with a life coach?" Eli said.

Because I didn't have things figured out after all the upheaval in my life? I exhaled, ready for battle, but then inspiration struck.

"I'm working on being honest." I snatched the thumb drive out of Ryann's hands and handed it to my ex. "You need to see this. Then we need to talk."

Even if I couldn't find a way to allow Eli to see magic, I could come clean about this.

"Okay." He tucked it in his pocket.

Ryann looked at me thoughtfully, then motioned for Oliver that it was time to go.

He shot me a look filled with hate and stalked off without another word.

She squeezed Eli's shoulder. "Until next time, Sultan."

"You bring the Oreos, Junior."

She snapped off a smart salute and left.

I watched them drive off in Oliver's BMW, wondering how

soon they'd be back. Their visit showed how crucial it was for Laurent and me to reveal the truth so that the wrong person didn't go down for the murder. "Want to come in for tacos?"

"Nah. You guys have *Buffy* tonight. Just send the kid over after." He rubbed his head. "That boy is going to be here this week, isn't he?" He made a face. "Caleb. He has a name. Sadie had a stern talk with me."

Good for her. "And you'll be nice to Caleb because your daughter really likes him," I said, "and because Goldie was nice to you."

"I'm totally lovable. He's a horny octopus."

"Eli!"

"I won't say anything bad in front of either of them, but you gotta give me this outlet."

"Fair enough."

"And if Caleb pulls one wrong move?" Eli jiggled his handcuffs.

"Okay, well, that's not creepy or an abuse of power or anything." I shooed a fly away from my face. Oh wait, Eli had probably been joking. I grasped his forearm. "Seriously, though. Watch what's on that thumb drive and then we'll talk."

He laughed nervously. "You're freaking me out a little, Mir."

"I know, but we'll deal."

"It's what we do."

Hoping that would still be true once he saw the footage, but relieved that I'd taken control of the situation for better or for worse, I returned to the kitchen to find that dinner was ready, but at the expense of an enormous mess. "Why is there a pickle on the floor? You weren't making up new flavors, were you?"

"I got hungry and that one slipped off the fork." She picked it up and tossed it in the composter. "Let's eat."

After dinner we watched *Buffy*. We were on "Forever," where the Scoobies attend Joyce's funeral, and Anya, the vengeance demon, was telling her human boyfriend Xander how meaningful it was to be able to create life.

233

I hugged a pillow to my chest. Perspective. Did Zev have human children that he'd outlived? Was creating vampires his way of achieving that? How close was Zev to Celeste? Had he changed her simply because she was his progeny, albeit far removed, or was there an actual bond there?

I'd kill anyone who hurt my daughter.

"Ow. You're crushing my toes." Sadie pulled her feet out of my lap.

"Sorry." I mostly stayed focused on the rest of the episode, and afterwards, when my daughter went to grab last-minute items for the week, I called Jude and told her where I was going.

"Should you mount an attack without the French foreign aid there for backup?" she said.

"I'll take Emmett with me. Tell him to get ready and dress menacingly."

"He won't be a liability?"

"He's strong and it evens the numbers. Topher and Celeste, Emmett and me. Besides, it's good to bring muscle. Celeste isn't as old as Zev, so she won't be able to find me if I'm cloaked, and even Zev can't compel me."

Sadie poked her head in the kitchen, her backpack slung over her shoulder. "Later, Mom."

Be safe. Be smart. I love you so much. I blew her a kiss. "See ya, kid."

She went out the back door, throwing me a wave as she jogged down the stairs.

Should things go poorly with Zev, at least she'd be safe from him at Eli's, since he'd have to be invited over Eli's threshold to get in to that side of the duplex. I'd see if Zev could ward up the entire property against anything else.

"If I haven't checked in with you by morning, call Laurent," I said to Jude.

"Why? So he can find your body?"

"Yes. And don't renege on your promise. Pluck my chin hairs or I'll haunt you and make sure you never get laid again."

"Empty threat, doll. Emmett's presence is doing that just fine. Wear good underwear if you plan to die," she said. "You don't want Laurent to find you in your granny panties."

I hung up on her throaty chuckle. There was nothing wrong with cotton underwear. Other than the fact that mine were beige. And boring. And there was this pair of peach lace ones that I'd never had the opportunity to wear yet and I was totally doing this for me to feel confident from the inside out. Not because I was going to die and certainly not because Laurent might ever see them.

Cursing, I went to change my underwear.

When I got to Jude's condo, I texted her to send Emmett out.

He showed up wearing leather pants that were too short, a leather jacket unzipped to show off his hairless clay chest, and a black leather cap. At least he hadn't brought the cane. He got into the car, settling himself with a grunt.

"The rest of the Village People couldn't make it?" I said. "Put on your seatbelt."

He clicked it in. "Don't give me grief, lady. The menswear selection at Jude's is limited. It was this or a kilt and I go regimental." He leered and cupped his crotch.

I rolled my eyes. Emmett was the lewd equivalent of a seven-year-old boy doing his best to gross people out. "Stand down, Ken Doll. You don't have genitals." I merged with traffic on West Fourth Avenue and headed for Blood Alley.

Emmett gasped. "Malicious lies."

"Jude told me."

He pressed his thighs together, the leather squeaking. "You women discuss those things? Is nothing sacred?"

I patted his shoulder. "A cock does not a man make. You're perfect as is, so quit trying to shock people."

"Really?" He shot me a sideways glance.

"Yes. Really."

He adjusted his cap to a jaunty angle. "I'm gender-fluid anyway. So, what trouble are we getting into now?"

"Visiting with a vamp."

"Another one?" he whined, kicking at my floor mat. "Haven't we learned our lesson with vamps?"

"We're not killing Celeste, just getting answers from her and an Ohrist. Menace appropriately and I'll find something else for you to do next time."

"Can I at least punch the human?"

Might as well keep my partner happy. "Once, but not in the head."

Emmett cracked his knuckles. "Don't worry. I'll hide the bruises."

With reassurance like that, what could possibly go wrong?

22

Try as I might to see the hidden Blood Alley on my own and stroll in like a badass, I had to use my cloaking, dropping it once I was inside like a little kid popping out from under a blanket, and startling two Ohrists looking for the night's entertainment.

The black lacquered door that Zev had directed me to looked identical to the other ones, other than a small sign reading "auditions" taped to it. There were two red lightbulbs, currently off, mounted above it. The lightbulbs were a rating system of danger from one to three, but of course, this was according to vampires, not humans.

"Are they looking for actors? For a blockbuster?" Emmett mimed shooting a gun, then spun around to shoot again. "Look at these chops. I totally want to audition."

"I've got no clue, but you have a job already." I rapped on the door, but no one answered. "We've got half an hour to kill so let's wait over here and see who shows."

We settled ourselves a few doors down, using the crowd milling about for cover. Lightbulbs went on and off around us, doors opening to reveal glimpses of a huge room with an MMA cage in it (three red lightbulbs), a room where everyone sat on mats watching a vampire contortionist (one bulb), and a pool hall with vamps dressed like James Dean lining up shots. I didn't understand why that last one was also a three-bulb room until the door opened at the same time that an Ohrist lost a game and they had to pay up. In blood.

The oddest line-up formed outside the audition door, with adult Ohrists of all ages, ethnicities, and fashion choices. A man with beads threaded into his beard and a vintage Rolling Stones T-shirt stood behind two women in skinny stilettos and short dresses, while a bald-headed man who was ninety if he was a day beamed serenely, his thumbs hooked into his suspenders.

Topher showed up at five minutes to eleven, took in the line-up with wide eyes, and came to a dead stop. Steeling himself, he walked to the front and pounded on the door.

When people yelled at Topher to get in line, Emmett and I flanked him.

"We'll handle this," I said.

Topher jumped. "What are you doing here?" He gaped at the leatherman—leathergolem—punching his fist into his palm.

"My associate and I want to chat. Kind sir?" I nodded my chin at Emmett and he muscled Topher up the lane toward Gargoyle Gardens.

Most people were still enjoying the attractions behind the doors, so few patrons were making their way to Rome and the delights on offer inside the club.

The golem slammed Topher up against the marble base of the largest gargoyle statue, pinning our target in place with a heavy clay hand.

"This is harassment," Topher sputtered. "I'm telling the Lonestars."

I held out my phone. "Please do. Then we can all chat about how you and Celeste killed Raj."

"I didn't do shit," Topher spat. "And I don't know who this Celeste chick is. I'm here to see a friend."

"You didn't deny knowing Raj."

"Uh... I don't know him."

I tsked him. "My sixteen-year-old lies better than you."

"You might want to rethink your parenting, toots," Emmett said.

"Shut it." I mimed zipping my lips, then turned to Topher. "We know you had Raj steal Ghost Minder and that he was Celeste's blood donor. I was in the car with Raj and I saw your flashbang."

I saw nothing of the sort. It had been a physical cannister, not magic, but among my chief weapons were fear, intimidation, and the channeling of the most boss TV cop ever.

Pulling an orange lollipop out of the pocket of my red jean jacket, I tore off the wrapper and jammed it in the corner of my mouth. "Raj will never get his physics degree or run another D&D campaign, and for what? Did you think the help was expendable and you wanted all proceeds from the ring, so you didn't have to go to your fully funded university education at a top school, flying there on Daddy's plane? I can't tell what's worse. Your laziness or your greed."

Topher struggled against Emmett but didn't free himself. He really did have low level magic or he'd have attacked by now. "You have no idea what they expect of me."

"Then you grow the fuck up and use your words. Raj. Is. Dead. I'll give you a moment to think carefully about what you say next." I sucked on the lollipop.

"Is your sugar low?" Emmett said. "We're in the middle of an interrogation and you need a candy break?"

I sighed and shook my head. "All those hours of watching re-runs and you can't recognize I'm channeling Kojak?"

"Who's Kojak?"

"The ultimate cop."

"Eh. I'm more of a Columbo—dicknuts!" Emmett shook out his hand which now had a perfect imprint of Topher's upper teeth.

"Nice. We could get you a mouthguard with that," I said.

"For what?" Topher said.

Emmett leaned in close. "When I break all your teeth."

The golem was working out very well. I was so clever.

I smiled at Topher. "Ready to answer?"

He turned stricken eyes to mine. "Does Dad know about the ring?"

"Yes."

His shoulders slumped and a heavy sigh shuddered out of him, then he tensed up, his lips flattened. "Good. I'm glad he knows. Yeah. I hired Raj to steal it, but I wasn't after the money and I wasn't there when he was killed."

Extrapolating from that, he was after something. What did he want and had he ordered the hit?

"Let's see if Celeste can clear things up," I said.

Emmett manhandled Topher back to the door. The light bulbs now glowed red and the line-up was gone.

Three large round tables had been set up inside. All the humans had taken seats, leaving a larger, more-stately chair at each table empty. A hum of nervous chatter pervaded the room.

"Are they speed dating the vampires?" I crunched my lollipop, savoring the over-saccharine orange flavor.

"Idiot," Topher scoffed.

Emmett boffed him upside the head.

A bell rang and the room fell silent, all the Ohrists craning their heads expectantly at a door in the back. Three vampires entered—a black male in this incredible purple bejeweled tunic and skinny pants, a white goth female in a short skirt and torn fishnets, and a white androgynous bloodsucker in a yellow suit with a matching yellow hat who glided over the floor like royalty.

They circled the room, pausing in unison to look directly at us. Two pairs of eyes flashed red and I pushed back behind Emmett, but the female vampire said something in a low voice and then each one took their seat.

The bell rang again and the humans went around the table saying their name and a short description of their favorite foods.

They each had thirty seconds to speak before the bell would ding and it became the next person's turn.

I choked on a piece of candy. The humans were auditioning to become blood donors.

The vampires each had a clipboard on which they made notes, and occasionally they would ask for clarification of spices or side dishes. Once everyone had spoken, there were a few moments of tense silence, and then several new vampires entered the room, going around and touching certain people's shoulders.

Most of the individuals who'd been rejected rose with a defeated air and left quietly, but one man burst into tears, falling to his knees and begging, while another woman swung at a vamp. Both had their necks broken.

My lollipop fell out of my mouth and hit the floor.

The androgynous vampire flicked their eyes my way, their fangs descending. Trembling, I bowed my head, biting the inside of my cheek to prevent any noise from escaping, while I picked up the candy and shoved it in my pocket.

Topher's jaw was clenched, his chin jutted up, but his breathing was shallow. Only Emmett seemed unconcerned by the entire thing.

The bodies were cleared away by the lower ranking vampires with bows to the three who were still seated.

The few humans who remained stood in a line.

Each of the vamps stood up, grabbed the head of the closest person from their table, and sank their fangs into them. There was no warning, no compulsion, no easing them into it, just a naked violence. The Ohrists cried out, their bodies bucking, and I pressed my fist against my mouth to stifle my cry.

They repeated the procedure on each of the remaining individuals. Finally, the androgynous vampire pointed at a chubby woman with thinning hair in bright sweats, who jumped up and down like she'd won the lottery. The vampire escorted her through the back door, the unsuccessful candidates from that table leaving without protest.

The male vamp also made his selection—twin brothers in their mid-thirties—but the female vamp dismissed everyone and walked over to us, her two inches of gold bangles jangling. She tossed her straight red hair off her shoulders, and farted loudly. "Want to sign up?"

Undead colon gas ranked somewhere between dry brimstone and juicy dog farts. It had a spiciness requiring a certain aridness, yet a richness of aroma traditionally attributed to a wetter passage.

Emmett gagged, creaking cheap leather, and Topher threw an arm over his nose and mouth.

I tried not to breathe as I spoke. "Your grandfather sent me."

Celeste narrowed her green eyes, her heavy liner cracking with the motion. "Whatever." She pressed a button on the wall, and a panel at the front of the room slid open, revealing a massive television.

Onscreen, the show was partway through a 1980s cheesy vampire B-movie. Celeste cackled when the vamp with the shellacked slick of black hair moved in on the hapless woman's neck in slo-mo.

"The ones that go all deer in the headlights are no fun." Celeste gave a couple of jabs in mid-air, rattling her bracelets. "I like them feisty."

Emmett shoved Topher in a chair, then with two fingers, he stabbed from his eyes to Topher's in warning.

"Why'd you kill Raj Jalota?" I said, blocking Celeste's view of the screen.

She stared at me blankly.

"Mid-twenties, resembled this guy?" I motioned at Topher.

The vampire laughed. "I get who you mean, but why would I kill him?"

I nudged Topher, who'd gone pale. "Care to field this one?"

His brow furrowed, like he was working through calculus

242

problems or struggling to plot a new way to evade his parents. "But," he said, then stopped, then began again, "you—you killed him." Very unhelpful. Thanks.

"No. You thought I would when you ratted Raj out for leaving." Celeste farted again, sniffed, and pursed her lips. "Do you know how hard it is to find a human who doesn't make me play bass? Raj was a dream."

"He was leaving you," I said.

"Get real. He was so addicted to my bite, he would have come back any day now if he hadn't been killed." Instantly, things clicked into place. Raj's excessive perspiration and twitchiness had been a result of withdrawal. I just had the wrong drug.

Celeste licked her lips and leaned in to Topher, who shrank back. "You seem to know a lot about what went down. Did you kill my favorite snack?"

Topher eeped. "N-no."

Emmett slapped his leather cap against his thigh. "Come on. Look how much blood this dude is wasting. It's pouring out of his mouth."

Celeste glanced at the television and chuckled. "Right? He's worse than some frat boy doing a kegger. Good luck getting that white shirt clean, dipshit," she heckled.

Topher stood up, his hands clenched into fists at his side, and his gaze darting jerkily around the room. "N-no," he whispered. "That can't be it."

Celeste nudged Emmett. "Watch this next part. It's hilarious."

"You had to have killed Raj," Topher said plaintively. "You did it."

Celeste shrugged, not even making eye contact. "Buddy, I don't know what to tell you. I got nothing, nada. Now zip it, you're interrupting a good scene."

Topher's features slackened and something in him broke. It was a small thing, like there had been a string tied between his spine and an invisible balloon over his head. In that instant, the balloon popped and he collapsed inward, eyes hollow, mouth open. "No. There's no way."

Celeste wasn't paying attention, too busy hamming it up with Emmett at the bad vampire film. But I'd lived on the fringes of my own life long enough to detect the importance of what you could notice about people when they were being quiet.

Topher looked like someone had told him all his worst nightmares were real.

And then he snapped.

"Answer me!" He threw a chair at her.

It hit her in the shoulder and Topher stepped back, his Adam's apple bobbing.

Celeste blurred over to him, grabbed him by the shirtfront and threw him against a wall. It didn't even crack, but Topher went down like a ton of bricks.

Emmett and I exchanged wary glances and I tensed for more violence but Celeste was already watching the movie again, laughing, and commenting to Emmett about it.

The golem chuckled weakly.

I knelt by Topher, checking his pulse. Still alive, though he'd gone cross-eyed. "Solid structure on these walls."

"Zev reinforced the shit out of these rooms," Celeste said. "Soundproofed them, too." She smiled, her fangs in full view. "Got any other questions?"

Sweat trickled down my spine. There was a clear path between me and the door, and if this went sideways, I'd grab Emmett, cloak us, and bolt, but I couldn't help glancing down at Topher, still out cold. "If you didn't kill Raj, who did?"

Celeste shrugged.

"You don't want the ring?"

"Nah. What the hell do I want to control dybbuks for? Do I look interested in being middle management?" She went back to her program.

"Fucking hell!" I snapped. "Someone killed that kid."

"And believe me," Celeste said, "I want to know who as much

as you do. But I don't. So I might as well enjoy this cinematic classic before I get back to replacing him." Her eyes flicked back to the screen.

Emmett was still fake laughing at the movie, and sending nervous glances at the vampire.

I massaged my temples. All the Sharmas had an alibi. Don Egerts only wanted the notebook back. Celeste didn't kill Raj, and since Topher betrayed Raj to Celeste, figuring she'd take his partner out of the picture, he didn't kill the other man either.

I lightly slapped Topher's face to dispel the grogginess.

He fluttered his lashes open, groaning.

Slapping his cap on his shiny clay pate, Emmett grabbed Topher under the arms and hauled him back into the chair.

I crouched down beside Sharma-the-Younger. "What was your deal with Celeste? Speak up. We're so close."

He shook his head violently from side to side. This visceral reaction didn't make sense. Topher wanted Celeste to kill Raj, but since she hadn't, then he wasn't guilty of anything prosecutable beyond burglary and I doubted Krish would have him charged.

"Topher," I said gently. "Talk to me."

"Did Dad kill Raj?" he said in a dull voice. "Did he mean to kill me?"

"What? No." I forced him to look at me, infusing my voice with every ounce of sincerity. "He thought you'd be in the car and was going to sic a babysitter on you at the plane to make you behave. He didn't know Raj was taking your place."

Krish, you idiot. I told you that you should have talked to your son and sorted all this out. The love between parents and children was a heavily braided rope frayed badly with resentment and regret, and with Krish and Topher it was a hairsbreadth from giving way.

Topher bit the inside of his cheek, then nodded as though confirming something to himself. "In exchange for letting

Celeste deal with Raj's betrayal," he paused, glancing up, "she'd turn me."

I opened my mouth, shut it, then opened it again. Though it made perfect sense. For a kid chafing under his parents' expectations, this was a hell of a middle finger. It also put his comments at our first meeting about having years to figure out what he wanted out of life into a new context.

"You'd turn an Ohrist?" I said.

"Why not?" Celeste shrugged. "If it was good enough for dear old granddad, it's good enough for me." She farted again, a series of short, sharp blasts, followed by one long deep toot. She pressed on her stomach and two quick farts rumbled out. "Oh yeah," she sighed. "That's got it."

"For the love of everything unholy, open the door," Emmett groused.

Topher jumped up. "Then turn me. Now."

"Eh," she said. "I think not."

"So much for honor among thieves," I said. "Choose a better partner next time."

Topher whirled on me. "I don't even have Ghost Minder because you fucked it up and took the satchel."

I did a double take. "What are you talking about? I don't have it."

He rolled his eyes. "I heard Dad talking to Mom. He said he had to tell the Lonestars that the BS and the wolf had it. I didn't understand what he meant, but it was Ghost Minder, wasn't it?"

Krish was selling us out? Why now? Had the Lonestars learned about the ring? My skin dotted with goosebumps, the icy sensation digging deep into my chest and burrowing into my brain.

Oliver. He was committed to the "dybbuk killers" taking the fall. I'd foiled the Lonestars' attempt to blackmail me with the footage, and now Oliver had made his next move, by pressuring Krish to turn us in.

I wormed my hand into my pocket to find my phone and warn Laurent.

Celeste snapped off the television with a chilling suddenness. "You're a BS?"

Emmett moved to stand shoulder-to-shoulder with me.

My magic rose hot and fast, but I kept it tightly coiled under my skin. "What of it?"

"I've never tasted one before." She pushed Topher out of the way and circled Emmett and me. "I'd be quite the superstar if I added you to the tasting menu."

"Try it," I said, proud of the menace in my voice. What was it with Zev and his relations having it out for me?

Emmett slid a sideways glance at me, then his eyes morphed into cosmic swirls and starlight, his voice a dreamy croon. "Twinkle, twinkle, little star."

Celeste jerked her head to him. "What did you say?"

I shook Emmett's arm. "Snap out of it."

We had to get out of here before she forced me into a life of addiction and subservience, and if Emmett spouted more mazel destiny nonsense at me like he had at our first meeting, I wouldn't be able to think clearly.

"Little star," he repeated.

Celeste looked at me. "Is it true? The golem has necromancy magic?" I nodded and she hesitantly touched Emmett's face. "Mom? Is that you? Your little star is here."

I frowned. The golem stared at a distant point between the two of us. Was his pronouncement directed at the vampire and not me?

Topher ran at Celeste again, but Delilah leapt up, grabbing his arms and twisting them behind his back.

"The hunter picked the wrong prey," Emmett said, an entire galaxy growing and exploding in his eyes. "And another star is snuffed out." He pretended to blow out a candle.

Celeste looked at me, her brows knit.

247

"Exactly," I said. For once the golem's divination magic was working in my favor. "Prey on me and you'll be sorry."

"Take me," Topher begged. "Turn me."

Celeste sighed. "Eh. What the hell."

"No!" I yelled.

Delilah shoved Topher at Emmett, who blinked back to awareness and grabbed him, kicking Celeste away.

"Emmett, get him out of here!"

In a blur, the vampire grabbed me, yanking my head to the side. "I don't have to feed on you to kill you," she said. "Now tell your friend to let go of the boy."

Emmett froze, Topher's sleeve gripped in his fist.

Delilah head-butted the vamp in her back and I stumbled forward, free.

The bloodsucker grabbed my shadow's head and smashed her knee into Delilah's nose.

I swayed, blood spurting out from my own nose, and my magic pulsed insistently.

"Yeah, yeah," I slurred, wiping blood away with my sleeve. "Have at her."

Magic surged up Delilah's arm into a shadow scythe. She jumped up and spun, the scythe cutting through the air with a whistle.

The world ground down into slow motion. "Noooooo!" I cried, reigning in my magic as hard as I could.

Delilah stopped so suddenly that I was knocked back a few steps. The weapon hovered against Celeste's neck, a single bead of blood dotting her skin.

Of all the moments to figure out what my magic had been trying to tell me. I bent over, my hands braced on my thighs, and my heart going a mile a minute at how narrowly I'd avoided signing my own death warrant.

Celeste touched her finger to the blood and licked it off. "You should have followed through." She snapped her fingers and the lights went out, my magic disappearing.

I ran forward, crashing into a chair. From Emmett's cursing, he'd done the same thing, but he shouldered the door open, hauling Topher outside. I'd almost followed when two vampires hauled me back.

"Chain her up," Celeste said. "And find the others."

The door slammed, leaving me in the dark in more ways than one.

23

THE VAMPIRES DRAGGED ME DOWN SOME underground passage to a damp concrete room where I was handcuffed on a short chain to a heavy ring attached to the wall. The bloodsuckers exited through a thick wooden door, one of them encouraging me to scream all I want because no one would hear me.

A carefully conducted scientific study—i.e. hysteria—proved that to be true.

I slid down the wall, my throat sore from yelling, and clasped my nose, gingerly prodding the cartilage. It wasn't broken, but I hissed at the tender spots along my cheekbones.

My phone had no service in here, nor could I escape via the Kefitzat Haderech because of the handcuffs.

Jude knew I'd come to Blood Alley to interrogate Celeste and she'd find Laurent when I didn't check in, but the vamps wouldn't admit to keeping me prisoner. I'd have to pick the lock and break myself out. There were Wiki tutorials on it, how hard could it be?

Problem number one was that the tutorials assumed you had something to pick the lock with. There was nothing in my pocket other than my car keys; I didn't even have a bobby pin. I felt around for anything that would free me, but the cell was bare. I'd had some crazy self-destructive negative thinking in the days following my parents' murder, but the thoughts that flooded my mind now were worse because they were about Sadie.

As horrible as it had been, I'd seen my parents die. They hadn't left me on purpose, whereas Sadie would be left questioning how I could walk out on her, wondering why I hadn't loved her enough to stay. I mentally shoved all negativity behind a closet door and threw myself against it to seal it up, drowning it in a loud rendition of "I Will Survive."

Emmett had made it out with Topher and he'd tell Jude I was in trouble. I had to believe that. If she couldn't help, well, I had magic and intelligence and I'd get out of here. Fuck everything trying to take me from my daughter.

I turned my left wrist over, palm up, grateful that I only had one hand to free, and inserted a thin dark sliver to suss out the shape of the lock mechanism.

Attempts to uncuff myself left my arms wracked with such bad tremors that steadying them against the wall didn't help. A hot sharp pain rolled outwards from my shoulders and I slumped down in exhaustion, conceding defeat. My powers didn't include fine motor skills.

New plan: expand my magic inside the lock and break it open.

With every successive attempt, hope ping-ponged through my chest, only to be rapidly crushed by hollow defeat. I bit down on my parched lips and dug into the lock with renewed enthusiasm.

The cell door opened, but I barely glanced up.

Zev strode through, his features arranged in bland inquisition. "Is my time a joke to you?"

"N-no." I pressed back against the wall, the cold seeping through my light jacket.

He crouched down with a tutting sound. "We had a deal and you stood me up."

Zev didn't show anger. He could be about to snap my neck or wag a finger and either one would be done with that same polite smile that chilled me to the bone.

"I was in here," I whispered.

"For attempting to kill my granddaughter."

"It was a mistake. She was going to turn an Ohrist."

"You have an answer for everything, don't you, Ms. Feldman?" He struck me across the face.

A needle-sharp agony spiked from my injured nose up through my skull and I almost passed out. Woozy, I focused on breathing, his words almost inaudible over the sound of blood rushing in my ears. "What are you going to do to me?"

His nostrils flared almost imperceptibly as if testing that my fear was at an acceptable level, then he stood up. "I'm not going to do anything. You've already had an eventful night, what with the break-in at your house and all."

A cold chill skittered up my spine. No. This was another mind game. I wouldn't give him the satisfaction of playing along. Except... he had been at my home.

I pushed unsteadily to my feet. "What did you do?"

He clasped his lapels, rocking back on his heels. "Absolutely nothing. Detective Chu got a bit banged up by that old Lonestar when he went to investigate the noise, however."

I thrashed against the cuffs. "You bastard. You let him face McMurtry and that parasite on his own?"

"I made sure to check in on him after the fight, as the concerned neighbor I claimed to be. He'll live. Can't say the same about that bookshelf upstairs." Zev arranged his expression into exaggerated concern. "Your visitor was not happy to find you'd gone out."

I pressed a shaking hand to my stomach. "How did you see upstairs? I didn't invite you in and Eli doesn't own my half of the house."

"Your daughter invited me. Lovely girl."

My mouth filled with a sour saliva, the surge of adrenaline

sending my heart thudding against my ribcage like it was trying to escape. I lunged for Zev and was jerked back against the wall, bashing my shoulder against the cement. "Stay away from her. We had…"

"A deal?" He laughed and unlocked my cuff. "Have a pleasant day, Ms. Feldman." The vampire strode off.

I rubbed feeling back into my arms, my entire reality upended. Eli had been attacked, I still had no way of keeping demons out, and now a powerful vampire had an all-access pass to my home.

Scrubbing my hand over my face, I forced myself to look at the positive side. I was free… and Krish might already have sold us out to the Lonestars.

Nobody stopped me on my sprint out of Blood Alley and back to my car. I plugged my dead phone in to charge and raced home, both fast and furious. I would have gone straight to Laurent's place but I had to check on my family first.

Eli and Sadie sat on the front porch, oblivious to the late afternoon heat. Still in her pajamas, my daughter rested against her dad, her leg jittering at top speed. She straightened up when my car pulled up to the curb and bounded toward me, speaking before I'd even gotten out of the car.

"Mom! Where were you? Your alarm went off last night and Dad went to check but you weren't…" She stopped mid-sentence, her eyes wide. "Wha-what happened to you?"

I touched my bruised face with a laugh. "It's stupid. I worked through the night with Tatiana and I was so tired that I tripped into a—"

"Door?" Eli said coldly.

I nervously bobbed my head. "Yeah, and my phone is dead. I'm so sorry you were worried." I hugged my daughter, glancing over at Eli who sat there, stone-faced.

He'd watched the footage.

"I just…" Sadie took a deep breath. "Dad heard a weird noise,

253

so we went over, and someone had broken in. You were gone. I didn't know where you were and I hated it."

I kissed the top of her head. "I'm so sorry, sweetheart. That must have been really scary, but even if anything was stolen, the important thing is that neither of us were home. We'll upgrade the motion sensors so it doesn't happen again."

She searched my face for a moment, then with a sad expression, her shoulders slumped. Did I need to expand on my lie and make her feel better?

"Sades, honey, go inside," her dad said. "I want to talk to your mom."

She ran into his half of the duplex.

I walked up our front sidewalk with a tight chest, fiddling with my keys.

Eli stood up on the stoop, in his suit pants and a crumpled tank top. "Who hit you?" He folded his arms, his biceps flexing.

I touched my face, thankful that I'd cleaned the dried blood that was crusted around my nostrils off with some wet wipes on the drive home, and that the pain had receded to a dull throb under my panic. "I got into an accident."

"Yeah?" Eli raised an eyebrow. "The same accident that broke into your place? Who the hell was that guy, and what was he looking for?"

Me.

"Beats me." I brushed my fingers against the bruise on his jaw. "Are you okay?" I said softly.

He pushed my hand aside. "How the fuck did you end up driving some other car with my murder victim in it? And why didn't you say anything? This is a massive fucking conflict of interest on my part. How am I supposed to explain this?"

I twisted my engagement ring around my finger. "I didn't want to make things worse for you."

"How much worse could it get?" he said incredulously.

When I didn't answer, he went dangerously red.

"It was a work thing. I was giving someone a ride to the

airport, but I'd never met the person and I didn't realize that Jalota was impersonating my passenger."

"Topher Sharma," he said. I blinked and he laughed without any trace of humor. "I'm capable of tracking that much down."

I clutched his sleeve. "Did you speak to the family?"

"And say what? I don't even know what's going on!" He took a breath, his fists clenched. "Was this the day of the murder?"

"Yes. And I was in the car, but we crashed and I blacked out. I didn't see who killed him. Believe me, I wish I had."

Eli paced in a tight circle. "Give me something I can understand, Mir, because I'm lost. You quit your job, start working for some woman who gets you tangled up in a murder case, and now you're staying out all night and coming home battered? This isn't like you."

That was the hell of it. It was, because I'd chosen this. Well, I'd chosen my magic but now was not the time to split hairs. I curled my fingers into my palm, his lost expression begging me to say something logical to make sense of this.

"That break-in wasn't random, was it?" He grasped my hands. "Tell me. I can help you."

Oh, babe. You couldn't even solve the murder case that your own ex was caught up in.

I animated my shadow to dance around him, even touch his face, and while he shivered, his eyes never left mine, his brows furrowed. I sighed, briefly considering punching him in the face to break the perception filter, but his living room curtain twitched, and I couldn't dump this knowledge on Sadie.

Not right now.

"Magic is real," I said. "If you don't believe that, you won't believe anything."

"This isn't a joke!" He yanked his hands away.

"I know," I said, softly.

"What do you want me to tell my daughter?"

I closed my eyes briefly against his deliberate choice of possessive pronoun. My chest tightened into a knot, rage

255

burning its way through me like poison, but this fight would have to wait until the Lonestars had been dealt with.

"There's nothing to tell." I was proud of how steady my voice sounded.

"Do you think our daughter's an idiot? Sadie knows you're hiding something from her. She told me."

I took a step back, shaking my head. "You're lying. She'd have said something." I was the parent she could always talk to.

Wasn't I?

"Ask her." When I hesitated, glancing back at my car, because it was urgent that I find Laurent, Eli threw up his hands. "Or don't. You'll do whatever you want anyways."

My vision slipped into Delilah's green overview, each beat of my heart a war drum's call to violence. I hung in that state, time suspended for a second until it stretched, then snapped.

"Fuck you."

Eli blinked at my ferocity. "Huh?"

"You say that like I've always behaved however I wanted, but I wanted our marriage, not going to sleep night after night by myself because the only men interested want me as much for a nanny as a partner." I slashed at the air, punctuating my points. "I wanted to see kids' eyes light up when I introduced them to magical new worlds, not drown in the minutiae of construction law. I have played by every rule expected of me." My expression turned to granite. "And yeah, some shit happened that I'm doing my best to handle, so spare me your judgment, Eli."

My ex gave me a wary look, like he'd responded to a call at some shady warehouse and was sussing out how much of a threat this situation was. "Give me a reason to," he finally said.

"I don't have time for this," I muttered.

Eli caught my arm as I turned to leave. "You aren't going inside to assess the damage?"

"Later. I have to get back to my busy schedule of alienating my family by doing whatever I want." I tugged free and marched back to my car, driving over to Hotel Terminus with shaking hands.

Eli wouldn't let this go until he had answers, and I didn't blame him. I'd have freaked out if I was in his position, especially knowing that Sadie could easily have been there during the break-in. I should have stuck with my attempts to show him magic, whacked him over the head if that's what it had taken, but at this point, it was what it was.

Sadie was another matter. Eli had felt like the more pressing Sapien to convince of magic, and truth be told, I hadn't been all that keen to rip that blinder from Sadie's eyes.

Or to have her think that her mom was seriously deluded.

It was time to talk to her, but for the life of me, I had no idea how to begin this conversation.

My phone finally charged enough to turn on. The bing of missed calls and texts didn't stop for a full minute, most from Eli. At least I didn't have to call him back. I phoned Jude on Bluetooth instead.

My best friend answered, frantic, but after assuring her I was okayish, she in turn calmed me down reporting that Emmett had made Topher phone her and she'd taken Sharma home. Both were fine, though the kid was furious that I wouldn't let him die horribly and become a vampire.

Yeah, well, he could get in line.

She also said she'd left a message for Laurent. At this point I wasn't sure if it was better or worse if he didn't know about last night.

I slowed down when I hit Railtown. Historically, this tiny neighborhood had been the heart of Japanese-Canadian culture in Vancouver before that community was forced into internment camps during World War II. Now, like every other square inch of my city, it was being gentrified, the old warehouses and factories converted into microbreweries and office spaces for graphic designers and architects.

When I cut the engine, my turbulent emotions around Eli

and Sadie were a heavy ball pulsing at the back of my skull, but I forced myself to put it aside and keep a clear head for what I next faced. Slamming the car door closed, I marched across the street to Laurent's place. Over top of the boarded-up front entrance was a sign with flaked-off letters reading "Hotel Terminus."

The old three-story building had sleek, sharp edges tempered by rusted wrought-iron balcony railings and a faded chevron pattern in black running horizontally between each floor. Dirt streaked the stone exterior and there were bars over the frosted windows on the ground floor, but its ramshackle exterior hid a lovingly restored interior.

Laurent roared up on his motorcycle. Swinging his leg off with a coiled fury, he ripped off his helmet as he stalked closer, raking a critical eye over me. For a moment his gaze lingered on my bruised face.

I hid my injuries behind my hair. "Laurent, listen. Krish sold us out and told the Lonestars we have the satchel. I'm positive Oliver blackmailed Krish and this is his next move in cornering us."

When he stopped in front of me, his eyes had regained their usual acerbic distance, but he brushed my hair out of my face with surprising gentleness, tilting my chin up to examine the damage, just as he'd done the day of my car accident, and my breath caught. "You agreed not to see Celeste without me, *partner*."

I pulled away, regretting it instantly, and grinding my teeth together against the bolt of pain that spiked down the front of my face. "I went where Topher was."

"Always ready with an answer, huh?"

Amazing how males kept lobbing that fact at me with such contempt. Imagine that. I had answers and agency, and I wasn't going to apologize for either.

"Right now, we need a battle plan." I headed to the side door —the only usable entrance—each breath draining my small and precious puddle of energy. I turned back, motioning for him to unlock the door. "Get pissy later."

A wounded expression flashed over his face so fast I wasn't sure I'd seen it, his thick lashes a dark sweep against his olive skin.

I shifted my weight onto one foot, rewinding the conversation to see where I'd misstepped. The problem wasn't the conversation. I'd pushed him to be partners, made a promise not to see Celeste without him, and then done the opposite. Whether or not the circumstances demanded I hie off on my own, I could have at least left him a message, explaining what had changed. Instead, I'd phoned Jude, conveniently sidestepping any argument Laurent would have rightly made. Hell, I hadn't even asked Jude to phone him unless I hadn't checked in by morning.

I forced myself to approach him, but only managed a couple of steps. Perhaps this talk was better at a distance. "Laurent—"

He kicked gravel out of his path, steadily stalking closer. "Who killed Raj?" He shoved his helmet at me and pulled out his keys, opening the door in terse silence.

"I don't know."

He froze for a second, then snatched the helmet away. "Are you fucking kidding me?"

"Trust me, I'm as pissed as you are, but every single suspect on our list has been crossed off." Following him inside across the polished expanse of checkerboard parquet, I updated him on my adventures at Blood Alley. Well, most of my adventures. My encounter with Zev today wasn't relevant to our current predicament.

Laurent had turned the original lobby into a huge living room, its walls a deep red. Under the warm lights, they'd glow, almost like being inside a rose petal, but only filtered sunlight made it through the front windows today, the atmosphere muted.

He tossed his helmet and leather jacket on the bench next to an old upright piano between a couple of black floor lamps fashioned to resemble classic London streetlights, and I sat down on the other side of the room on the massive sofa in the seating area by the log fireplace, finishing up my tale.

Laurent listened in silence, his eyes on the gently arched ceiling painted a pale yellow, and when I was finished, he crossed to the 1940s radio on the mahogany dining room hutch and snapped it on, lowering the volume so that the jazz tune was barely audible.

I curled into one corner of the couch, letting the charm of this room work its magic and calm me down.

Boo, his gray kitten, scampered into the room. She danced around Laurent's legs, almost tripping him as he made his way to me, then snagged a claw into the hem of his jeans.

"Boo!" he snapped. "Fous le camp!"

She sat heavily down on her rump with a mewl, so I picked her up and scratched her behind the ears until she purred and snuggled against me.

"We need to get Krish to recant," I said.

"Then why didn't you go over there as soon as you learned what he was up to?" Laurent snapped his fingers. "Right. You couldn't. See, I got back to town to find a dozen panicked messages from Jude and went straight to Blood Alley to find you."

He may not have arrived within my desired timeframe, but he'd come to help me, just as I'd known he would, just as I'd come to warn him. Ever since we'd worked together to find Jude, a thread had bound us. It was black and tied in complicated knots, but it kept holding firm. To me, it was an anchor. What was it to Laurent? My guess was a noose.

I added Laurent to my ever-growing list of people to have a heart-to-heart with. He was in no place to hear me out, though, so it would have to wait. "Did you kill the dybbuk you were after?"

"I'm extremely good at my job." He scratched the stubble on

his jaw, his eyes heavy with a weariness born from years of this toil. "Alors, where were we? Yes. A helpful Ohrist informed me that you'd only left Blood Alley about an hour ago. Did you go dancing at Rome? Take in a fight?"

I petted the kitten, refusing to be drawn into an argument, and trying to keep us on track. "Something like that. Do you think Krish is doing this to get a deal for Topher? Remember, he was worried his son had killed Raj and they still haven't spoken about the matter."

Boo jumped off me to pounce on a shoelace laying on the floor.

Laurent gave a tight shrug and rather than sit there with him glowering at me, I went over to one of the framed prints of vintage alcohol ads lining the piano wall and straightened it.

Someone knocked on the door and I jumped, but Laurent went to answer it with a loose-limbed stride.

"Cloak if you need to," Laurent said, and opened the door.

"You." Eli laughed bitterly. "Did you hit her?"

"Watch yourself," Laurent growled.

I couldn't see my ex from my angle, but there was a moment of silence before Eli spoke.

"Let me talk to Miriam."

Seriously? I clenched my fists and moved into view. "Did you track me, asshole?"

"I called Jude, asking where you might be."

"You mean you browbeat her."

Eli shrugged, his tie knotted tightly, and his police badge in view.

Laurent spread his hands wide. "In or out, Mitzi?"

Now was the worst time to continue this argument, but part of me craved this fight. "Let him in."

24

LAURENT RAISED AN EYEBROW, BUT STEPPED ASIDE.

Eli stormed toward me, a white paper crumpled in his fist that he held aloft. His loud strides halted, his gaze flicking from the bookshelves packed with neatly organized titles that ran the length of the wall, to the piano, to the curved staircase polished to a high gleam that led up to a boarded-off second floor.

He frowned, but his anger shone out of him bright and clear when he thrust the paper at me. "Care to explain this?"

Laurent's cribbed handwriting was written in stark black ink, from when he'd played around with the codes in Don Egerts's book.

"Why is my murder victim's name all over this napkin?" Eli shook it in my face.

I snatched it away. "You went through my things?" I said, coldly.

Boo bolted for the hallway at the back of the building.

"Damn right I did, because I was looking for answers that you wouldn't give me." Eli's bellow echoed off the hotel walls.

"Take a breath, man," Laurent said.

Eli whirled on him. "If you dragged her into this murder, then so help me, I will bury you."

Laurent puffed his chest out and stepped closer, his wolfish smile in place. "Go ahead."

"Stop it!" I muscled between them, jabbing a finger at Eli. "You are so out of line. How dare you go through my things and harass Jude, you stalker? Where the fuck are our years of trust?"

Eli looked abashed for a half a second. "You have the balls to ask me that? I'm working a murder case that has no weapon and no suspects, but my kid's mother is neck deep in this thing? You want to talk about trust? Start showing some." He jammed his hands in his pockets, the fight draining out of him. "Be smart for Sadie's sake."

I rubbed the back of my neck, trying to put our therapy practice of seeing things from the other's perspective into place. Eli was frustrated, probably getting pressure to solve this murder, and after the break-in, scared for both me and Sadie.

"Your job is dangerous, too. Criminals come after cops. Don't be a hypocrite." I crossed my arms. Maybe not quite the most empathetic sentiment, but it was all I had.

"Occasionally, they do," Eli said. "But I've never come home to a B&E with my face beaten to a pulp. Are you enabling him?"

The fury rolling off Laurent was a hurricane beating at my back.

"Don't be a dipshit," I said. "If he hit me, I'd rip his balls off."

Laurent chuckled, most of his anger dissipating. "True."

"I think it would be best for Sadie to live with me for a while," Eli said quietly, but firmly.

I stuffed my clenched fists into my armpits, restraining Delilah from hurting Eli through sheer willpower. "Over my dead body."

Laurent glanced at my animated shadow and then moved closer to me, touching the small of my back. "Why don't you get your head out of your ass and see what's right in front of you," he snapped at Eli. "You have no idea what Miriam has gone through to keep her daughter safe. She'd die for her kid."

I leaned against his steadying hand, soaking in his warmth

and strength, but mostly amazed that he put himself into this conflict for no other reason than to defend me. Especially when he had every reason to still be angry at me for being such a lousy partner.

The shifter looked off toward the windows, his even white teeth worrying at his bottom lip before he blinked it off. "Not just Sadie either." He waved the hand that had been on my back at my ex, and I mourned the loss of contact. "She made sure you were safe too, because that's what she does with the people she cares about, though for the life of me, I can't see how you're worth it."

Laurent wasn't my knight in shining armor, he was far too tarnished for that. And there was a difference between being saved and having someone in your corner. I felt like a boxer in the seventh round, already bleeding from jabs and uppercuts, with neither the odds nor the crowd in my favor. Then came this lone voice cutting through everything else to cheer me on, and his encouragement and belief in me was exactly the thing that could turn the tide, because I was no longer alone and adrift.

Sadly, before I could set Eli straight, every trace of my former husband and the father of my child fell away, leaving me with cold, stern Detective Chu. "I'd like you two to come down to the station for a chat."

He grasped Laurent's elbow to escort him outside.

Laurent growled, his hands shifting to claws, and he swiped at Eli, slashing through his jacket deep enough to expose glistening muscle.

Eli's mouth fell open, and he stared at blood welling up through the torn skin with wide eyes.

I made a high note of panic in the back of my throat. Laurent had attacked Eli. What was even happening? I had to do something, fast.

But before I could, Eli dropped into shooter stance, facing the shifter square on with his feet firmly planted hip-width apart, and a steady grip on his gun. "Step away from her."

Laurent flexed his claws, his death wish gleam in his eyes. "Shoot me and it'll be the last thing you do."

Eli's trigger finger twitched and my heart slammed into my throat.

"Enough!" I waved my arms up and down.

"Step aside, Mir," Eli said.

For all Laurent's bluster, he made no move to harm Eli further. Then it hit me: he'd done that to show Eli what he was. To break the Sapien perception filter through pain and something that couldn't be explained away by shadows and illusion. He'd put himself in danger to show Eli. And he'd done that for me.

Something fuzzy curled in my chest despite the chill of panic. I took a breath. "You want answers, Eli?" I said. "Here they are. This is what I've been trying to tell you."

Delilah closed in on Eli.

His eyes darted from my animated shadow to me and his gun hand shook, blood from his injury staining his sleeve. "You drugged me."

"You're not crazy and you're not high. Magic is real."

"Stop it! You don't think I'd have noticed... that..." He trained his gun on Delilah who stood with her hands up.

"I hid my powers after my parents were murdered."

"No," he said in a tone brooking no argument, "it was a house fire."

"To cover up a targeted hit."

Delilah inched closer and Eli dropped his guard. Just for a second, but it was enough.

His claws now back to fingers, Laurent leapt the space between them and grabbed Eli's gun hand, aiming it upward until he disarmed him. The Ohrist tossed the gun on the ground.

Eli's legs buckled and Laurent caught him under the arms, leading him to the sofa.

"I'll get you a drink," I said, and hurried over to a decanter on the dining table. If I'd scripted the worst possible way for all this to go down, I couldn't have imagined this level of totally fucked.

"That's what you were hiding," Eli said bitterly, sitting down hard.

"You didn't see it! I wasn't trying to hide anything!"

He twirled a finger around the hotel. "I'd say otherwise."

"Watch it," Laurent said.

"Do you know how many times I tried to show you? Your natural perception filter was too strong. I even told you flat out that magic was real."

"So this is my fault?" Eli pulled off his jacket, fashioning it into a tourniquet for his injured arm.

"I didn't say that."

I handed the drink to Eli but before he could take it, Laurent gently tipped the bottom up towards my mouth. "Have a sip. You don't need this stress right now."

Eli glared at him. "She's fine."

"Is she? Or is it just easier for you to assume that?" Laurent countered.

"You've known her for what? Five minutes?"

"Yes, and even I can tell that she tries to do everything herself."

"Takes one to know one," I said. The scotch was smooth and mellow, warming a path to my fingers and toes.

Laurent made a snarky face.

"Is this how it is now, Mir? The hell with seeing my side of things?" Eli demanded.

"I do see it—all too clearly. Do you?" I handed the rest of the drink to him. "Admit it. You worked through your sexual identity issues and worked your way up to your dream job because I was always there for you."

"You could have said no at any point." A muscle ticked in his jaw.

"Or you could have seen what was happening and not asked

it of me in the first place." I spread my hands wide. "Now you know everything. What are you going to do?"

He shot back the finger's worth of scotch and put the empty glass on the ottoman.

Someone pounded on the door.

Laurent raised an eyebrow. "Another husband?"

"Why have one when you can collect a whole set?" I said, drolly.

Eli flinched, as if this too was now within the realm of possibility and I rolled my eyes.

"Open up! It's the Lonestars," Oliver yelled.

"Lonestars?" Eli reached for his empty holster.

"Magic cops." Laurent retrieved the gun and handed it back to Eli. "Stay in the elevator. You'll be out of the way but still hear everything."

"I'm not letting you face them by yourself," I said.

Eli busied himself with some cop check of his gun. That was the last thing we needed in this equation.

"You have Sadie to think of," Laurent said, "and there's no point in them getting both of us." He paused. "Look after Boo for me."

I pressed my hand to my chest, my eyes wide. "Are you asking for help? 'O frabjous day! Callooh! Callay!'"

"Incorrigible." Laurent tucked a lock of hair behind my ears, his fingers lingering on the curve of my jaw, and I leaned into his palm.

"I'll take care of her." I looked into his eyes, wanting to say something reassuring, or about how grateful I was for his help with Eli. "Try the shortbread. It's really good."

His lips quirked up, then with a quick squeeze of my shoulder, he released me.

"Laurent."

He turned back.

"I'll get you out," I said.

Eli holstered his weapon and stood up.

Laurent glanced at him briefly. "Still believing in what's fair, huh, Mitzi?"

"You said it yourself, I do that with the people I care about."

Laurent's eyes softened from brilliant emeralds to a lush grassy color that I imagined Narnia had turned once it was freed from endless winter. He paused like he was going to say something, but there were more loud knocks, so he gave me an enigmatic smile and went to answer the door.

I let myself absorb his absence for two seconds before I ran to Eli, my black mesh cloaking swimming up over both of us.

"What are you doing?"

I slapped my hand over his mouth, listening to Oliver demand entrance. "If you want to get out of this alive, keep your mouth shut," I whispered, my lips up against his ear. "There might be people with shifter hearing and the Lonestars' prime directive is to keep magic hidden. Nod, if you agree."

He did, reluctantly, and I steered him past the two other male Lonestars who'd been brought as backup.

"You saw the satchel on the surveillance footage," Ryann said. "Fan out and find it."

"Hang on." Laurent held up a hand. "How do I know you're not going to plant it?"

Good point. He'd have smelled anyone who'd previously come into his space to plant evidence.

"You want to frisk them?" Ryann said. "Gentlemen, if you will."

Laurent patted them down, then stepped back, his expression hard.

Eli opened his mouth to say something, but I shook my head at him, and pushed him past the stairs to the large elevator situated to the right of the staircase. The copper doors carved with diamonds and swirls were open enough for us to slide through both them and the cage gate.

"They didn't see us." Eli whispered. He spun around slowly, taking in the bunker-like room lined in iron with the cuffs attached to the wall by thick chains. Did Zev and Laurent use the same dungeon architect? "Ryann's one of them?"

I peered out through the doors. The Lonestars were making plenty of noise opening drawers and tossing cushions. We were probably okay to whisper in here.

A glass crashed against the floor.

Laurent growled. "A break for a break. I'll start with your femur."

"Threatening Lonestars?" Oliver said. "That alone can get you locked up."

I tugged Eli more neatly under the cloaking. "Ryann is head of the whole bunch."

He rubbed his temples. Yeah, given her tie-dyed leggings and T-shirt with the word "groovy" written in wavy psychedelic letters, I'd struggle with that, too.

"They don't have a warrant." Eli looked pained, though he remembered to whisper against my ear.

"Lonestars. Wild west justice."

One of the backup magic cops walked past the elevator, peering inside. His eyes slid over us. "Clear," he called, and kept going.

Eli let out a soft gasp.

Out in the living room, Laurent planted his hands on his hips. "So I've gone feral, beyond reasoning, and am slaughtering people, but I'm also stupid enough to tell Krish I have Jalota's satchel? To what end?"

"You blackmailed him," Ryann said.

"Because I need the money?" Laurent scoffed. "First off, I'd get a higher price from another collector than the original owner, and second, I kill dybbuks. If I got my hands on that ring, I'd destroy it."

"Would you? Because according to Mr. Sharma, the blackmail wasn't about cash," Oliver said. "It was about his silence. You planned to keep Ghost Minder and control dybbuks. That led you to Sharma's ring, and you got Topher involved, but he panicked, scared of what you'd do to him, and pulled Raj into it. Topher's devastated over what happened."

"All wrapped up with a bow on it. Except for the fact that Ghost Minder is a myth. Clever marketing made up to swindle idiots." Laurent poured himself a shot and tossed it back. His back was to Ryann and Oliver, but his distress flashed across his face when he didn't have to present a mask of confidence to them.

"We only have your word for that," Oliver said.

Laurent turned around sharply, his glass clutched in his hand. "Let me explain it then in a way that even you can understand. You don't need a ring to control dybbuks because any sin you can think of, they willingly undertake. They are made of rage and hunger, in control of a human body with speech and intellect. No coercion necessary."

The Lonestars were backing him into a corner. I silently willed him to tell them about Celeste.

Eli elbowed me hard in the ribs and pointed.

Delilah was on her way out of the elevator. I glanced down, but we were still cloaked by the mesh.

Wow. I'd never deployed both kinds of magic at once before. I reeled my animated shadow in, narrowly missing one of the Lonestars passing by.

Laurent refilled his glass and held it up in cheers. "Your funeral, man."

Oliver threw him a contemptuous look, but Ryann's brows furrowed.

"Nothing in the kitchen or bedroom," one of the backup Lonestars said. "Axel's just doing one last look around."

"Check the toilet tank," Laurent said. "I put it there with the gun to take out Sollozo."

I stifled a snort.

"Who?" Oliver looked at his partner, confused.

Ryann shook her head. "It's a *Godfather* reference." She

turned to Laurent. "How'd you convince Miriam to go along with the plan?"

"She's a BS," Oliver said. "They're evil. End of story."

Eli took a step back from me and I glared at him. Eight years of marriage and knowing me better than anyone else and now you believe some rando telling you I'm evil? Thanks a lot, dumbass.

"You think I'd team up with a BS?" Laurent sneered. "Give my allegedly criminal intentions some credit. The only reason I worked with her before was she paid me enough to overlook my contempt for her kind and she led me to a dybbuk I'd been tracking. You remember Mei Lin? The one you forced me to let go, who then slaughtered her entire crew?"

Even now that idiot had my back, and I was supposed to stand here and do nothing? My cloaking flickered.

"Don't you dare expose us," Eli hissed.

"You'd do more than team up with a BS, though wouldn't you?" Oliver said.

I frowned. What did he mean? Was he talking about me or someone in Laurent's past?

The claws on Laurent's right hand sank into the wooden table like it was butter. He locked eyes with the Lonestar, a hint of fang in his grim smile. "I'd be very careful with what you say next."

Ryann's confused stare matched my own, but before I could puzzle out the subtext, there was a shout.

"We got it!" Axel came running into the living room with the satchel. "It was under his tub."

Laurent briefly closed his eyes.

"Guilty." Eli looked smug about his pronouncement.

No, someone had planted it in the one place Laurent wouldn't sniff out their presence. The tub was outside under a covered area and the breeze would have blown all traces of an intruder away.

My ex jabbed me. "Are you sleeping with him?"

Unable to ream him out with the absolute hypocrisy of this statement given his revolving door of boyfriends, hookups, and one-night-stands post-divorce, I shot him the finger instead. Then I yanked him back into the main room, still invisible to the others.

Ryann dumped the contents on the table. Among Raj's passport, phone, and a sweater was a velvet jewelry box. She snapped the box open, and while I couldn't see the ring from where we stood, Oliver laughed softly.

"Got you," he said.

Laurent smashed the shot glass against the wall. "Someone's framing me. Topher paid Raj Jalota to steal Ghost Minder from his father's private collection," he said. "And then double-crossed his partner, selling him out to a vampire in exchange for being turned."

"Celeste BatSila," Oliver said. "Krish mentioned you'd bring her up, so we checked with Celeste. Topher has been harassing her to turn him, despite the prohibition. Needless to say, she sent him away."

"Because vamps are so trustworthy," Laurent said. "She's an Ohrist and Zev had her turned."

"Regardless, that's not relevant to this investigation," Ryann said, and pulled out a set of silver handcuffs. "You have the ring."

The backup Lonestars grabbed Laurent, but he threw them off, his eyes wild.

"I'm not going to Deadman's Island." His spine bowed and his face bulged and contorted, his muzzle popping out with a crunch.

Eli shuddered at the sound of breaking bones and turned away, but I forced myself to bear witness to all of this, because I *would* save him, and anyone in on this frame job would pay.

The magic cops jumped the shifter, Oliver included, but Laurent snarled and managed to get free, raking Axel across the face with his claws.

Sighing, Ryann jabbed Laurent in three different places. "No one's going there yet."

He shuddered, morphing back to human, and collapsed on the ground, his clothes partially torn.

She snapped the cuffs on him and grabbed the satchel. "Take him away."

They hauled his prone body off, the side door slamming behind them.

The black mesh of my cloaking fell away. "You see?" I said. "Neither of us did it. Laurent is being framed for a murder he didn't commit."

"Did someone plant evidence at your place as well? Is that what the break-in was about?" Eli tightened his makeshift tourniquet.

"No," I said.

He gave a curt nod, then headed for the door.

"Eli." I tried to remember that I loved him, seeking a precious memory to hang on to, but all I felt was fury.

He waited for me to expand on my answer, but when I didn't, he shot me a single, cold look. "Stay away from Sadie."

25

I STAYED UP SETTING MY HOUSE TO RIGHTS AFTER THE break-in, staying busy so I didn't dwell on Laurent bound by silver cuffs and thrown in some cell. The upstairs bookshelf was indeed toast, as Zev had said, but the dented hallway wall, torn carpet, and chipped off paint could all be fixed. If only my sense of security was as easy to salvage. McMurtry had taken my parents; he wasn't going to take my home, my sanctuary.

Boo and I crashed, and I dreamed that I was in a forest searching for Sadie, but every time I glimpsed her, a wolf howled in distress. I ran faster, but was trapped by the thick leaves. I woke up Tuesday twisted in my blankets with the kitten curled into a fuzzy ball on my pillow.

I rolled onto my back, blinking at the noon sun streaming through my partially opened curtain, bone-tired and calculating the minimum number of hours before I could go back to bed.

Boo mewled and pawed at me. Scooping her up, I took her outside in the yard to pee, since all I'd grabbed was her food before leaving Laurent's. Aside from bowls, I hadn't found any other cat supplies there, so I'd wrapped her in a soft towel to bring her home in my car.

Yawning, I rocked my pelvis back and forth to loosen up my back. Everything hurt. Tatiana better pony up for regular healing sessions because another couple months of getting battered on the regular and I'd lie down one day and never get up. I'd waste away in bed, slowly going mad until I became a horror story, with local kids daring each other to breach my bedroom and come out alive.

Well, if Sadie played her cards right, she could charge enough to cover university tuition. I grimaced. I had to check in with her, but for the first time since Eli and I had broken the news of our divorce, I dreaded seeing my daughter.

After showing Boo the food and water bowls that I'd set out in the kitchen, I sat on the back porch nursing a coffee I barely tasted and staring wistfully next door at Eli's for any flicker of movement, but his curtains were drawn tight.

Knocking her father down and punching him in his stupid head until he got over himself would distress my child, thus I would take a time-out until we were both able to use our words. If that didn't work, then his stupid head was fair game.

Eli's back door swung open and Sadie stepped out carrying a full garbage bag. She pulled up short at the sight of me.

"Morning." I waved, tentatively.

Sadie bit her lip, her eyes darting from me to her dad's kitchen. "Is your face better?"

Apparently my concealer's "super coverage" didn't live up to its advertising. I gently prodded my nose. "Not broken. All good."

She nodded and jogged down the stairs to the garbage cans by the garage. When the lid clanged shut, I called out, asking her to come over.

Sadie came through the door in the fence between our yards that Eli had installed years ago. "You got a kitten?"

I scratched Boo's ear. "I'm keeping her temporarily for a friend. Do you have some questions for me? About what's been going on?"

"What's the cat's name?" She stood next to the stairs, her hand out for the cat to sniff.

"Boo."

She made kissy noises at it. "Is your friend away for a long time? Because this little precious seems to like it here."

I spun my coffee mug in my hand, staring into the dregs like they had divination powers. "I don't know. Sit down, honey."

She sat stiffly on the bottom step, looking up at me, instead of beside me like she usually did, and crossed her arms.

"There are some things about my new job that I can't talk about. Yet. I promise you that I will, but the important thing is that this was a good change for me."

My daughter stared at me stonily, looking so much like her father that I winced. "Great talk."

"That tone is uncalled for."

"No, it's totally called for because you're doing it again."

"Doing what?"

Boo hopped down the stairs to Sadie and my daughter put the kitten in her lap, stroking her fur. "I don't care that you quit your boring librarian job at the law firm, but something happened with Jude a few weeks ago," Sadie said. "You both acted like it didn't, but I'm not dumb. You didn't trip into a door. You talk about me being old enough to act like a grown-up and have the hard conversations but you're still treating me like a little kid."

I set down my coffee mug with a thunk. I'd prided myself on projecting a strong confident front for her. Truth be told, I didn't want her to know what I was dealing with now. I doubted Eli would either. Her inability to see magic meant we could protect her innocence. But still, she wasn't a kid anymore. She wasn't an adult either, but she was old enough and savvy enough to know when I wasn't being straight with her.

"You're right. I can't tell you everything that happened because some things are confidential when I work with Tatiana as part of the job. What happened with Jude is also her own story to share or not. As for the bruise…"

I animated Delilah to crouch on the railing, but Sadie didn't see her. There was no way to explain any of this without breaking through Sadie's perception filter, but there was also no way I would physically hurt her to make that happen.

"I accompanied Tatiana to a party the other night. Some of her acquaintances are not the best and there was a lot of free booze. I pissed someone off and got punched." Substitute Blood Alley for party and vampire for someone and it was kind of true.

"Jeez, Mom! What kind of rowdy crowd are you hanging out with?"

Boo nipped at Sadie's hand and jumped onto the stairs.

"Trust me, I know better now."

"Maybe you should quit. Your old job was boring but it was safe."

I ran my finger around the rim of my mug. Sadie had always been the most supportive person of me following my dreams, and hearing her suggestion hurt. "I'm trying to reconcile who I am and what I want for maybe the first time in my life and working for Tatiana is the best place for me to be. Are you okay with that?"

"I dunno. I guess. Dad's job is dangerous, too." Nuzzling the kitten one more time, she brushed cat hair off her top. "I gotta go. Caleb and I are going for a bike ride."

"Wait. Your bike didn't shrivel up and die from neglect?"

"No, that was your exercise bike." Sadie winked at me.

"Touché."

She petted Boo one more time. "Later, Mom."

"Sades? I'll be more honest, okay?"

"Okay. And don't look so worried. I don't hate you or anything." Throwing a wave over her shoulder, she disappeared back through the connecting fence door into Eli's yard.

The kitten brushed against my bare foot.

After that totally draining conversation, I fortified my body with buttered carbs and my emotional state with Retribution Red Lipstick. Needing armor, albeit cute armor, I threw on a long, dark-purple ruched skirt that looked woven from the night sky and a black off-the-shoulder shirt.

After a quick stop to get some kitty supplies, Boo and I went to Tatiana's. My employer had been noticeably silent since I'd seen her last, but one way or the other, she was aware of Laurent's plight. We'd comb through the current suspects one more time and if none of them could possibly be the murderer, we'd unearth whomever was and get Laurent released.

Nobody answered my knock. Not Juliette and not Marjorie or Raymond, Tatiana's assistants. I tried the knob, and finding it unlocked, stepped into the hallway with a loud hello.

"In here," Tatiana called out.

I entered the living room where Tatiana was having a tea party, looking sleek and elegant in a black Chanel pantsuit with white bouclé trim. She poured piping hot liquid into exquisite china cups with gold bands around their rims. A sumptuous array of tiny sandwiches and delicate jewel-tone petit fours were stacked on a three-tiered platter.

Ellis and Krish, the guests of honor, were sitting oddly stiff on a loveseat. Shifting Boo's cat carrier to my other hand, I was about to ask what had crawled up their asses and died, until I noticed the plants. Tatiana's home had always had a greenhouse air to it, but now it was jungle-overgrown. Tendrils of leaves wrapped around the Sharmas' legs, pinning them to the couch, with a thick vine like a seat belt across their hips.

"Aha," I said. "Botanical prison, I presume."

The couple shot me looks of surprise. Right, they'd sold me out as well and only Laurent's vehement denial that he'd never work with a BS had kept the Lonestars from coming after me.

For now.

"Help us," Ellis wheezed pathetically.

A frond vibrated menacingly at me. I shot Ellis a "so sorry" smile that didn't reach my eyes.

The curtains, which were drawn tightly, imbued the usually light and airy room with a dark gloom, but a small table lamp threw enough light for me to animate Delilah to stand behind me.

Setting down the carrier, I sat next to Tatiana, and helped myself to a petit four topped with a strawberry.

Ellis rattled her cup against her saucer and Krish coughed on a mouthful of tea.

Tatiana let Boo out and the kitten hopped into the artist's lap. My boss looked closely at my bruised face and a cactus plant on the windowsill imploded. "Love the nose reconstruction, bubeleh. Very Picasso." She held the tea pot out. "Darjeeling?"

"I'll pass. We need to chat about medical benefits sometime. How's Laurent?" I crossed my legs, swinging my foot, and nibbling on my creamy tangy pastry with its crunch of filo dough.

I'd picked up the phone multiple times to contact Ryann and ask about my team member but I'd chickened out. They'd left me alone for the time being and I could do more good out here. The justification of the cowardly, resting on a foundation of self-disgust that I didn't examine too carefully.

"He's... furious, but unharmed." Tatiana's mouth pinched tight. "They dared to cage him."

I unbunched my fist from my skirt and patted her hand. He was alive. Anything else could be dealt with. "So... what are we chatting about?"

"That very topic." Tatiana placed a napkin in my lap, gesturing at the crumbs falling off my pastry. "The Sharmas were about to express their deep concern over my nephew's arrest."

"It's unfortunate that he chose to blackmail my husband," Ellis said, cool as a cucumber. "Now he faces the repercussions of his actions."

"We're both intelligent women," Tatiana said. "Lies don't become us."

I coughed to hide my snort.

My employer shot me a sideways glance before refocusing on her other guests. "Recant your statement and all will be forgiven."

Ellis shook her head. "I'm afraid that's impossible."

An overinflated purple spiky flower slammed down like a mace next to Ellis's foot, scattering razor sharp petals and she splashed tea onto the floor.

I wiped my mouth off delicately with the napkin, forsaking another treat—a noble sacrifice. "Neither Topher nor Celeste killed Raj, so your son isn't guilty of any prosecutable offense beyond stealing Ghost Minder. You're not going to press charges so why give Laurent to the Lonestars? Did Oliver force you into it?"

"Why would he do that, when, as you said yourself, Topher isn't guilty? No, I spoke to the Lonestars because actions have consequences. Despite your insistence otherwise, I know Laurent has—" Krish struggled to free himself but was slapped back into submission by an elongated snake plant leaf.

"Sit. Eat," Tatiana said.

Kudos to the Sharmas, they each managed to muscle down a tiny sandwich under Tatiana's vulture-like stare and hostile plant life. I'd never be able to swallow food with that level of stress. Well, not a frou-frou sandwich at any rate.

I'd been extremely clear with Krish during Operation Fake Satchel that Laurent and I didn't have the bag, so why lie? I narrowed my eyes at him and he nervously looked away. Had someone forced his hand? But who was left?

I bolted up. "Whoa! You know who murdered Raj, don't you? If this killer is coercing you into blaming Laurent, tell us. We can protect you."

"Not so long as my nephew is imprisoned," Tatiana said.

"After that," I said pointedly.

She sniffed, but didn't contradict me.

There was a sharp rap on the door and Tatiana brightened. "My other guest is here."

"How come everyone else got an invite?" I said. "If I hadn't shown up, I'd have missed this delightful party."

Tatiana patted my hand. "Worry not, your presence has made this even more interesting. Come in," she yelled.

Her front door opened and closed and even footsteps rang out across her polished floor.

Boo hissed, all her fur standing on end, and I glanced over my shoulder into the foyer.

A familiar man in a dark suit held a huge golf umbrella over an equally familiar, similarly dressed individual. Zev BatKian took off his sunglasses and smiled. "Good afternoon, Miriam."

The head vampire was not just awake during the day, he'd gone outdoors. Oh, fuck.

26

ZEV STOOD ON THE THRESHOLD OF THE LIVING ROOM, surveying it like a general on the battlefield. Even though his shadow could dematerialize, the vampire himself couldn't, otherwise he wouldn't have had to brave the outdoors to get here, but his ability to be awake, let alone in the sunshine—even under cover of the umbrella—spoke to his incredible power. A hush drifted over us.

In the silence, the Undertaker—Rodrigo—collapsed the umbrella, balancing on his feet like a boxer and assessing everyone in the room for potential threats. Under his spiffy chauffeur's cap, it had the effect of being a strange marriage of unnerving and silly.

"Rodrigo, my man. What's new and exciting?" I said.

He ignored me. Progress.

Tatiana stood up, her hands outstretched. "Zev, glad you could make it."

The vampire clasped her fingers, and they kissed each other's cheeks.

Delilah, who'd been standing like a sentinel this entire time, fell apart into inky splotches and I pressed back against my seat.

"Your invitation was so enticingly worded." The bloodsucker

who wanted me dead said this to my boss. Wonderful. "I simply couldn't miss this gathering." He flashed his fangs and the Sharmas gripped each other's hands.

Tatiana willingly let him into her home? How was she so confident that he wouldn't show up and kill her?

Seeing him again made my face throb, though through the hazy pain came an interesting thought: I no longer had to grab a vampire's shadow to kill it. It was true of Celeste, was it the same with her great-great-whatever-grandfather?

"Make yourself comfortable," our hostess said. She sat down next to me, and under cover of reaching for a cucumber sandwich, pinched my thigh hard. "Don't," she murmured in a tone infused with steel.

What was it with old Jewish women and the pinching? My bubbe had done the same thing.

I shoved another petit four in my mouth and smiled tightly.

Zev strolled slowly along the row of planters, nudging some dirt off the rim and back into the pot on one, separating some tangled flower heads on another. "Your family has caused me no end of trouble." He spoke so softly that normally, we would have had to lean in closer to hear him, but the silence was so absolute that his words carried perfectly. The Sharmas appeared to be doing their part to further reduce sound by not breathing.

The *Godfather* theme played in my head.

"Your son assaulted my granddaughter." Zev could have been commenting on the weather for how indifferent he sounded, but Ellis stifled a cry. "And I had to field annoying questions from the Lonestars, including Celeste's innocence in the murder of an Ohrist. What a disappointing breach of protocol from respected businesspeople such as yourselves."

"We don't know anything about that." Ellis turned as pale as her hair and Krish gripped the arm of the loveseat.

The plants winding around the Sharmas snapped back into their regular sizes with such immediacy that the couple pitched forward before they caught themselves.

Tatiana's slight shake of her shoulders, as if releasing a bit of tension, was the only indication that she'd used her magic. Every time I thought I'd figured out how powerful she was, I got the sense of depths I couldn't begin to fathom.

Boo jumped off the sofa to investigate the planters, batting her paw at one droopy leaf.

Krish found his composure first. He pulled himself up to his full height and met Zev's eyes. "We did our civic duty regarding the satchel. If the Lonestars are investigating Celeste, take that up with them, and as for our son, he would never harm anyone, unless he'd been threatened first."

Boo crept up on the vampire but he nudged her away with a highly polished black shoe.

"Your son is a petulant brat who didn't get his way into being turned." Zev broke off a dead bloom with a sharp snap.

The Sharmas jerked back like they'd been shot.

"He would never…" Ellis whispered.

Zev's eyes lit up and he turned to them with his hands on his hips. "Go on."

"Never want something so reprehensible," Krish asserted, putting his arm over his wife's shoulder.

I crammed another tiny pastry in my mouth, in awe of his chutzpah. Shame Zev was going to kill him.

"There's the good old Ohrist spirit." Zev slapped his thigh. "What exactly do you find so abhorrent? Immortality? A longevity allowing for unbridled creation and passion? Is your imagination so limited it cannot appreciate anything beyond the scope of your experience?"

I opened my mouth to add a couple of refuting points to his PR spiel, but Zev held up a finger.

"I wasn't speaking to you."

I sighed and the couple looked to Tatiana, like students waiting for the teacher to answer.

"It's our very demise that sweetens life," Tatiana said to the vampire. "Is your imagination so limited that you can no longer remember the joys of being a regular human?"

"Never give me your regular human bullshit again!" Zev tore a bulb of wildflowers out of a hanging basket, scattering dirt. His eyes blazed red and his fangs descended out from his bared lips.

Shrinking back, I threw my hands over my head because this was the first flash of anger that I'd ever seen him display. The room went tense, overwhelmed by the sound of Zev's harsh breathing. I peeked through my fingers.

Even Tatiana looked frightened, which scared me more than anything because she'd always been so confident in her ability to handle Zev. I shivered, pulling my light cardigan closer around me, eying my chances of fleeing out the front door to safety.

The vampire made no further outbursts, instead wrestling his display of temper under control: unclenching his fists, retracting his fangs, slowing his breathing. His eyes, finally, returned to their normal shrewd brown and he dropped lightly into a chair between myself and the Sharmas.

It took all the humans, including Rodrigo, a moment to unfreeze.

"Apologies, Tanechka." Zev pulled a linen handkerchief from his pocket and dabbed at his brow. "Old memories, yes?"

Tatiana flushed and looked away.

I, on the other hand, was rapt. Tanechka? What the hell was the deal between these two that she'd cracked his perfect composure?

Ellis gathered up her purse. "Your granddaughter must have believed that the imposter was actually Taroosh and gone after him when my son refused her offer."

"Exactly." Krish nodded at his wife. "Now, if you're finished harassing us, we'll take our leave." He took Ellis's hand and I braced myself for a slaughter.

I mean, I probably would have interfered, at some point, because while Krish was a rat and they were both liars, they didn't deserve to die, but the vampire let them get up.

"Do remember," Zev said with that smile that made me shiver, "that I gave you a chance."

He nodded to Rodrigo, who pulled out his phone.

"Wait!" I jumped to my feet.

Everyone stared at me but I didn't have a plan beyond stopping the Undertaker from carrying out whatever destructive order he'd been given. It's not like Zev had been about to send the Sharmas an edible arrangement. The last time I'd seen him order someone to take care of something it was to kill Kirk, a new vampire who'd betrayed him.

Boo paused her cleaning for a second, but I wasn't interesting enough to hold her attention, and she returned to her task with soft licking sounds.

"The real murderer is out there," I said. "They're the one whose caused all these problems and are forcing you two to go along with their plan, right?"

Krish and Ellis remained silent.

Eli had said on more than one occasion that there came a time in every case when you had to go back to the basics. I'd ruled out everyone I'd suspected wanted Raj dead, and yet he'd still been killed and the satchel taken.

"Who'd want to control dybbuks?" I said, sitting back down.

"Laurent," Krish said. He met my eyes. "Possibly you. We know you're Banim Shovavim."

Ellis nodded, a disapproving frown on her face.

Tatiana made a *pshaw* noise. "Either of those two wanting to control dybbuks is utter garbage and you both know it."

Especially since Laurent didn't believe the ring worked.

I looked down at my feet, unable to accuse Tatiana after she'd defended me. Whoever controlled dybbuks would be powerful and she did enjoy power. It might also explain why she was so opposed to Laurent killing them. It fit, but it didn't feel right.

"If I had any interest in Ghost Minder," Krish said, "I'd have already used it for my own gains."

Ellis got a suspicious look on her face and turned to Zev, but

I spoke up before she landed herself on the vampire's bad side. Correction: worse side than she was already on.

"Celeste had no interest in it," I said, "and Mr. BatKian has no need of such an artifact, given his position as head of the vampire community."

Zev had been running a finger over the velvet armrest, a bored look on his face, but at my words, he stilled, his eyebrows shooting up for a second.

Truthfully, it could have been Zev, if his hatred toward Laurent stemmed from the fact that he wanted to build a dybbuk army and the shifter kept getting in his way, but Laurent would have known if that were the case.

And I was right back at square one.

"Help me out," I implored the Sharmas. "There's no way that this person is more dangerous than Mr. BatKian."

"The first intelligent thing you've said." Zev crossed his arms.

"We'd like to leave," Krish said.

I looked at Tatiana for help, but she shook her head. "If the Sharmas are unwilling to cooperate, then there's little we can do."

Ellis and Krish got halfway across the room when the vampire spoke.

"I dislike imperfections," Zev said mildly. "They are like weeds in a garden, and I have dedicated my very long life to rooting them out. Therefore, in service of bettering your lives, I shall remove your greatest mistake. That is to say, your son."

Ellis stumbled, softly crying out Topher's name, but Krish kept a firm hand on her elbow.

"This is madness! No one else has to die," I said. "Can't you see how scared they must be to walk away after that threat?"

"Then they should convince me otherwise," Zev said. "'It is not in the stars to hold our destiny but in ourselves.' Shakespeare," he added at my frown.

The stars, twinkling, a hunter who had picked the wrong prey...

At once, the entire case rearranged itself. Emmett's prophecy wasn't about Celeste. There were many other stars out there, but only some of them hunted.

A Lonestar.

Specifically, Oliver.

The man with an affinity for torture and execution methods done to Banim Shovavim by hunters. The man who'd planted the satchel at Laurent's house, because he couldn't stand people who were different.

A dark turbulence swirled up from deep inside me like the current of a stormy sea and I stabbed the serving fork into the heart of a petit four, its raspberry center bleeding onto the china display platter.

"They need to be put down like dogs." My words were a savage growl.

Delilah spun around me like a whirlwind, scattering napkins to the ground.

"Enough!" Tatiana snapped.

A broad plant leaf boffed me across the head, and I dropped my magic, but not my snarl.

Zev jerked his chin at Rodrigo, and the man disappeared for a moment, returning with Krish and Ellis in his grip.

"Share your epiphany, Ms. Feldman," Zev said.

"It was the fucking Lonestars."

"Language," the vampire chided, "but continue."

I struggled to moderate my tone. "I couldn't understand why Oliver was so focused on Laurent. A lot of people despise him for killing dybbuks, but the Lonestar latched on to him immediately and that was it. Laurent was positive that he was being framed and he was correct."

"Lonestars killed Raj?" Tatiana said.

"My guess is Oliver Anderson specifically. He saw an opportunity and he took it."

My boss leveled a shrewd gaze at Krish. "You told him about the theft when it happened, didn't you?"

He opened his mouth, a look of protest on his face but Zev raised an eyebrow and the man froze.

Ellis closed her eyes. "Tell them," she said in a broken whisper.

Krish sighed heavily. "Oliver knew."

"Did he plan to kill Topher or did he know Raj would be in the car?" I said.

Ellis groped for her husband's hand.

Tatiana shrugged. "Does it matter? Either way, he was willing to commit murder."

There was no way Oliver had pulled this off without Ryann's permission. She was too smart to fool. I twisted my napkin into a pretzel. I admired that Lonestar, in the way that one did with an adorable tiger cub—well out of claw reach. She was a woman, on the young side to be in charge of all Lonestars, with a strong sense of self, and she packed a hell of a magic punch. She even cared about Eli.

I bit my lip. *Had* Ryann been trying to get me to share the truth of this case with my ex? Was the thumb drive not blackmail, but a covert way to get past Eli's perception filter? But if she suspected Oliver, why not shut him down? "Who else was involved? Did Laurent kill a person connected to Oliver?"

"I doubt it. Lonestars keep a record of all the dybbuk-possessed who Laurent dispatches," Tatiana said. "It would be too easy to make that connection, and besides my nephew would have remembered if that was true."

At our first meeting, when Laurent had killed Alex, he'd spent a moment with the man memorizing his features. I was positive he could recall every life he'd taken.

"Not that, then." I tapped my foot. "Oliver despises Banim Shovavim," I said. "And here's Laurent, an Ohrist, behaving like one by killing dybbuks."

The kitten brushed against my leg and I picked her up,

scratching her at the base of her tail to loud purrs. Lonestars may not have pulled the trigger on my parents, but they were complicit nonetheless, and now at least one of them had committed murder.

My mouth fell open. "They violated the prime directive by leaving Raj's corpse for the cops to find." A cruel smile flitted over my lips. "I'm going to destroy them."

Boo protested my momentary lapse in loving her by batting at me with her paw.

"These are Lonestars," Tatiana said. "You have to prove it beyond a shadow of a doubt, otherwise there won't be anywhere you can hide."

"We will," I said, petting the cat again and piecing together my strategy. "Here's the plan. Krish is going to Lonestar HQ and tell Ryann and Oliver he lied. The story is Mr. BatKian killed Raj because the deceased went after Celeste. Moreover, Zev planted the satchel and then bullied Krish into lying about Laurent having it."

The shocked silence was so profound that I stuck my finger in my ear and rubbed it to make sure I hadn't suddenly gone deaf.

"You intend to use me as a scapegoat?" the vampire said in a low voice.

I licked my lips, intending to explain that it was more using him as bait since he was the only one who couldn't be touched, but before I could croak out a word, he broke into belly laughs.

He wiped his eyes with a manicured finger. "For the life of me, I can't decide if you are the bravest or stupidest person I've ever encountered."

"Technically, you're not ali—" Tatiana elbowed me and I moved on. "Krish can't say it was Oliver because the Lonestar will deny it and Laurent won't be freed. His release is the trigger to get Oliver to act. You're outside their reach and there are plausible reasons for you protecting Celeste and having history with Laurent. I've seen his scar."

"A delightful memory," the vampire said.

I grimaced. Psycho.

"We can't," Ellis said. "It's impossible."

"What did the Lonestar possibly threaten you with to make him a greater threat than me?" Zev said.

I turned away so the vampire didn't see my eye roll.

"Oliver would kill *both* our children if we didn't comply," Ellis said.

Zev snapped his fingers. "Why didn't I think of that?"

The Sharmas looked like they might puke.

Tatiana tapped a spoon against her cup. "With this new information, they'd have to release Laurent."

"I vow not to harm your daughter," Zev said. "What's it to be?"

"Please." Krish folded his hands together in a begging motion. "Kill me instead."

"I think not." Zev smoothed out his pants and stood up.

"Turn Topher," I blurted out. At the Sharmas' horrified looks I added, "This is what your son wants."

"Last year he wanted a Porsche. He got drunk and forgot where he left it," Krish said.

Ellis shook her head. "He wants to take over the family business."

"No, he doesn't," I said. "I'm hardly a fan of humans being turned, but he went to a lot of trouble to arrange this. Misguided and homicidal though it was. At some point, you have to respect his wishes. Give him the freedom to explore what he wants out of life, even if it's scary or hard to understand. I hear that you're sad, and as a parent I can only imagine how upset you are right now. But things are the way they are. He should have done a better job of talking to you and you should have done a better job of listening."

"Take her advice." Rodrigo's grip on the couple tightened and the Sharmas winced. "It's better than the alternative, if you don't mind me saying so, sir."

Zev waved a hand that his words were fine.

"Turn him." Ellis nodded. "Topher's smart. He can help your business."

"Are you insane?!" Krish's eyes practically bugged out of his head.

"He'll be alive, Krish. Take the deal."

This family was doomed to a life of heartbreak and perhaps worse if Topher ever came after them, but for now, he'd get his wish, and his parents would have a son who was, if not alive, then around.

"I'm not convinced." Zev tapped a finger against his lip.

"Topher's death gains you nothing except a momentary satisfaction at erasing a petty annoyance," I said. "You don't get a lot of Ohrists. He could be an asset and the Lonestars can't raise a hand against you with their involvement. How often do you get a chance like this?"

"She has a point," Tatiana said. "Plus, this way you have a hold on the whole family."

"Yes, thank you for that." I glared at her.

I didn't care what happened to the Lonestars involved. Twinkle, twinkle, little star... they'd hunted the wrong prey and now they'd be snuffed out, like Emmett had prophesized. If my next sock in the Kefitzat Haderech was ankle-length, I'd live with that. Well, I'd argue like hell, but since the Lonestars lived by the prime directive, they could damn well die by it.

"Turn Topher," I said firmly, "and you get to do whatever you want with the guilty Lonestars."

"You've barely seen a hint of what I can do, Ms. Feldman." Zev straightened a cufflink. "And yet you send people to me to do with as I please so easily."

"I'll sleep at night just fine."

"We're agreed? Krish talks to the Lonestars and once all this is settled, the Lonestars and Topher are Zev's," Tatiana said.

Ellis nodded, but Krish still looked doubtful.

"My people will protect you," Zev said. He chuckled at our stunned expressions. "I told you, I dislike imperfections."

Krish and Ellis exchanged glances, then he nodded shakily.

"I'll go with you to HQ, cloaked of course," I said. "If Oliver and Ryann aren't working together, he'll go off on his own after Laurent is released and I'll stay on him. Someone else can watch Ryann.

"Once you are successful, you will turn the guilty party over to me," Zev said.

"Yes, provided I get my shot at them first. Laurent wasn't the only one on the line here. The Lonestars came for me as well and they'll pay for that."

"Beyond what Zev dishes out?" Tatiana said.

"We'll call that the grand finale." I explained my hastily thought-out plan. Tatiana made a few improvements, then signed off on it.

"It's a bold move." Zev stroked his goatee. "You're sure you can achieve this?"

I nodded. "I'll bring the guilty down if it's the last thing I do."

"Then I agree," Zev said.

"As do we," Ellis said.

"You have twenty-four hours," Tatiana told me. "I won't have Laurent rotting away for any longer if they don't release him immediately. Silver is terrible for his skin."

The hourglass had been turned over, precious grains of sand slipping through. Get proof, humiliate the guilty, and free the wolf. I nodded, my desire for vengeance worn like a cloak of invincibility. "Done."

27

THE VAMPIRE TOLD US TO WAIT UNTIL SUNDOWN, SO Krish and I agreed to rendezvous at Lonestar HQ at 9:30PM. He'd set up a meeting with Ryann and Oliver for that time.

Tatiana ordered me to leave Boo with her. I protested that she didn't have cat supplies, but she sent one of her assistants to the pet store, so I was on my own now.

Maybe Sadie and I should get a kitten.

I phoned Eli, but unsurprisingly he didn't answer. Knowing him, he'd still listen to the voicemail, so I said that if he wanted to capture Raj Jalota's murderer to meet me at home later.

A large part of my plan depended on Eli's thirst for justice, his willingness to play by an Ohrist set of rules, and his acceptance that magic was real. The only sure thing in my favor was his deep belief in law and order.

He'd either show or he wouldn't.

There was nothing else on my end to prepare for the meeting later, so I used this window of free time to deal with McMurtry. I slipped into the shadows in my hallway and stepped out in the cave. "Do you ever leave?"

Pyotr raised his head from the table and yawned. The TV was off. "You bring pet?"

"Emmett? No. Not this time."

"Pet not allowed anymore. I kill pet if he comes back." He glowered off into the space over my shoulder, as if suspecting Emmett was hovering there in the darkness. Pyotr still wore the same uniform he had the last few times and I wondered if all his clothes were like that or this was also part of the job description.

"About that." I handed him a box I'd wrapped up nicely. "I wanted to apologize for him last time and thought you might like something like this. You know, to help pass the time between travelers." It was a cheap 7-inch tablet that I'd bought on Sunday on the way from Granville Island to Tatiana's place.

The gargoyle tore the wrapping off the gift and lifted out the tablet hesitantly. He sniffed it, but when he bit it, I pulled the device away and opened the lid.

"It's for watching movies. I preloaded a bunch." Showing him how to boot it up, I opened the folder on the desktop.

"Is *Fast and Furious*." His voice caught in a sob and he clutched the tablet to his chest.

I grinned. "That's right."

He fluttered his wings. "Now I see car fight shark and big monkey and sidekick Shrek."

I rubbed the back of my neck. "Oh, uh, well, those are the director's cuts. These are the regular versions so they're a little different."

He grandly waved a hand at the socks. "Choose."

There were a whopping two of them: a frilly green ankle sock, and a loosely knit multicolored trouser sock, its weave filled with holes and mistakes. Neither inspired confidence.

Morally, I was on shaky ground. Since the last time I'd been here, I'd killed a vampire (good, probably) but also agreed to hand over at least one Lonestar to certain death (kind of bad, but I felt more good, overall) and saved Topher (mixed feelings, but mostly good). My relationships with Eli and Sadie were strained (bad) and Laurent was still imprisoned.

"Got anything else?" I said. "How about a pair of stockings?

Double your legs, double your fun!" My eager smile didn't make that any less creepy.

The neon sign winked on. Its wonky letter was fixed but it made that same buzzing sound. *Why was the baby Banim Shovavim born with sunglasses on?*

"I don't know, okay? Just tell me your stupid punchline already." Given my sock choices, if I was already screwed, then I was under no compunction to play nicely. I took the trouser sock, my nerves frayed.

The sign changed to an emoji face with a deadpan expression and the door opened for me to proceed.

Fixing McMurtry's address in northern British Columbia in my head, I went on my way. The sign didn't show up again or drop rocks or potholes in my path, but the lack of game playing wound my agitation higher and higher, and by the time I stepped out on McMurtry's driveway, I felt wild and tight, like electricity danced over my skin.

I inhaled a lungful of crisp, clean air, my eyes automatically orienting toward the glacier-topped Hudson Bay Mountain. Feathery high grasses stretched out as far as the eye could see. How many hours had I passed as a child, tramping similar fields flat and staring up at the same white clouds drifting lazily through the same purple-blue sky? Beyond the low fence and McMurtry's wood cabin were a cluster of aspens, their leaves a silvery hue. Two poplars flanked the driveway, bees buzzing around the sticky buds.

My childhood stomping grounds were beautiful. I'd forgotten that, my memories tainted by blood. I shook off my edginess and knocked on the door.

The retired Lonestar didn't look surprised to see me. He sucked on the cigar clamped in the corner of his mouth and blew out a clove-scented plume of smoke.

"I heard you dropped by," I said.

"Nice of you to return the favor." McMurtry moved aside to allow me entry, but as I did, I stayed as far away as possible from the dark puppet master working Fred's strings.

He showed me into a living room that had never seen a woman's touch. Stuffed bear, deer, and moose heads were mounted on three walls of dark wood paneling, while the fourth wall boasted a faded wallpaper mural of a beach in Hawaii. That was so retro, it was almost cool.

The smell of stale smoke, not so much.

Fred tapped his cigar in an ashtray overflowing with butts and ash that was wedged onto an outdated coffee table between a bunch of batteries, some remote controls for the large-screen television, and an open hunting rifle next to a spray bottle of gun lubricant. He sat down on a sturdy dining room chair that had been dragged in, rubbing his knee.

I perched on the arm of the leather sofa, the bright sunlight streaming in through the open windows illuminating the fine layer of dust over everything. "If my parents really died in a house fire, then why did you come after me? Twice?"

He closed the rifle with a click. "You gave me quite the knock to my skull when we met. I don't take insults like that lightly."

"Tell me the truth about the night of my parents' murder and I'll apologize. Did you kill them?"

"I already told you, there was a house fire. I don't know anything about a murder." McMurtry aimed the gun at me, then chuckled and put it down.

"Remember, I gave you a chance."

Delilah jumped up tall and proud, wielding the scythe. Excellent—my hypothesis that it worked on demons was correct, otherwise I couldn't have manifested the weapon.

Fred coughed on his smoke, thumping his chest. "What in the holy hell?"

This time I spoke to his shadow. "You have some sentience or you wouldn't have reacted so badly when I questioned you last time. Drop whatever's keeping McMurtry from remembering or we do this the hard way. My scythe is a handy vampire-killing gizmo and vampires were made by estries. I'd love to see if it also works on things like you."

For a moment, all went still, then a surge of black rushed from the shadow, through the strings and up the man's body into his head.

Fred screamed, his hands in his hair, and he turned black eyes on me. "I remember," he whispered. Blood trickled out of his left nostril. "Fishing... lies." He yanked on his hair with a sob. "Burning." He fell to the ground, writhing.

I crouched down next to him. "Did you kill them?"

He shook his head.

"Who did? Who gave the order?"

His body spasmed.

I grasped his shoulders. "Tell me!"

His thrashing, the darkness in his pupils, all of it vanished. McMurtry sat up braced on his elbows. "Do you really want to know?" he said in a voice tinged with madness. His lips curled into a Cheshire Cat smile. "Really truly?" He cackled, the laugh sending shivers down my spine.

The shadow now hung suspended on the wall, the connecting strings bunched tight in its fists.

What were my parents caught up in? They were dead and this man was demonically infested—what would be my fate? I just wanted a name, a reason that my childhood and my innocent happiness had been ground to dust.

"Tell me," I said in an even voice.

The Lonestar's lips parted with a tiny expulsion of air at the same time a sharp snap jolted his head. Limp, he fell against the floor, his neck at an awkward angle. His shadow glowed an impenetrable black for a second, then the glow winked out, leaving a normal shadow and no more strings.

Had the parasite killed him to keep him from answering? Could it do the same to me if I pursued this?

The alarm on my phone beeped. If I didn't leave, I'd have no time to get ready before meeting Eli. I glanced at Fred. Should I call someone? And say what? I coughed, the sweet smell of a campfire tickling my throat.

The seam of the outside wall burst into flame and I froze until the deer head caught fire and fell to the shag carpet. Swallowing a scream, I shielded myself.

A parasite couldn't set a fire, which meant... the murderer who had killed my parents was back.

I sprinted out the kitchen door into the field, "Come Fly With Me" in my head drowning out my racing heart, and huddled under a tree. I should have kept running but I couldn't. I hadn't seen my own home destroyed and there was a perverse desire to watch McMurtry's place burn down to nothing.

Flames licked and hissed through the cabin, sending a black plume into the sky. All was still out in the field, and if someone had killed Fred through the open window, they were gone now.

I was no closer to understanding anything than when I'd first contacted Fred. Was a demon involved in my parents' deaths? Maybe, maybe not. Any Ohrist with that magic ability could have snapped Fred's neck through the open window, just as someone had with my mom and dad, and if one old vampire like Zev had intel on the parasites, they could be common knowledge among all the ancient ones.

Sirens grew closer, a far-off red truck tearing down the rural road. Only the front half of the home was engulfed: the area where Fred's body lay. The firefighters would be here before the fire spread to the field or woods out back, before any neighbors' houses were in danger. The universe's most considerate murderer had struck again.

The heat shimmered against my skin but was no match for the inferno blazing within me. Fred's involvement in my parents' murder had cured his cancer and bought him decades of life, but in the end, it had killed him. It wasn't justice, it was pointless. Just like my whole quest for answers. I crouched down, letting dirt fall through my fingers. Ashes to ashes.

I'd tried and failed. I murmured an apology to my parents.

Brushing off my hands, I stepped through the shadows under the fir tree into the Kefitzat Haderech, landing awkwardly and rolling onto my back.

"Wait for movie to end," Pyotr said. He must have actually looked at me because he swore in Russian and hit a key, shutting down the sound of revving motors.

He prodded my cheek, his fingers coming away streaked with soot, then plucked an unopened bottle of water out of thin air and handed it to me. "Drink."

I gulped the lukewarm liquid down, trying not to sob because it felt like glass against my throat. I'd inhaled more smoke than I realized. The last third of the bottle I poured over my head, raking my fingers through my hair and over my face.

The neon sign had appeared again. *Why was the baby Banim Shovavim born with sunglasses on?*

If I'd had the strength, I'd have chucked the water bottle at it.

"I don't know the answer and I have no idea what you want from me, okay? I don't always make the best choices. You got me. Surprise: no one does. I'm trying my best, but those fucking angels who started all this only see in black and white, and nothing is that simple." I crumpled the bottle in my hand. "I keep lying to my kid, but I don't know how to make her see magic and part of me doesn't even want her to have to face that. You can't reduce those decisions to purely bad or purely good. Some things are unjudgeable."

Pyotr took the bottle away from me. I hadn't even noticed that I'd cracked it. "She brought me present," he said to the sign.

It wore its impassive face once more, but it gave a tiny nod.

"Answer riddle," Pyotr said.

I was sooty, exhausted, aching, and sad. But the gargoyle hadn't illuminated the sock pile yet for me to choose one, so I'd do some word association to solve the riddle and make the KH happy: sunshine, bright, shades… shadows. Light. Dark. It was simplistic and moreover, wrong, to reduce these terms to good and evil.

I stilled. Terms and conditions.

"When the angels set the conditions on Banim Shovavim magic," I said, teasing my thoughts out, "they said we'd be damned *if* we lost our way. Not when. They abhorred Lilith enough to brand her a demon and had already killed her non-magic children. So why *if* and not *when*?"

The sign gave nothing away but Pyotr nodded at me to keep going.

I walked in a slow circle, trailing a finger over the rock face. "It comes down to Lilith, doesn't it? She saved us somehow. Or her magic did. The angels couldn't force damnation on us."

The sign stuttered again, showing the same jerky images of the angels on the hilltop set to the same narration as the first time I'd seen it.

"The angels couldn't find them to kill them," the male narrator said, "but fearing their magic, they convened to set conditions on these powers."

A woman joined the angels in an image I'd not been shown before. Straight of spine and with a defiant ferocity in her expression, her black hair streamed in the wind. "Lilith laughed at Senoi, Sansenoi, and Sammaneglof," the voice said. "Her new children were not the helpless infants she'd birthed before. Her magic ran through their veins and they could not be directly harmed by the angels."

The sign faded to black again, but I bounced on my toes, my fatigue banished. "That's the key!"

It was like a legal contract where one word could suddenly shift the balance of power from one party to the other.

"The angels couldn't hurt us directly," I said. "So they created this story you tell us. Well, only part of the story, but stories have power and the angels knew that. They'd created an entire one to fit Lilith that lives to this day, the one of a demonic monstrous woman unfit for the first man and thus, discarded. They planted the idea Banim Shovavim were evil and let our own judgments and perceptions about who we are destroy us."

I'd spent my life behaving according to other people's expectations, being the good girl, being responsible. Taking on others' burdens and doing more than my share of emotional labor. So many women did. If I hadn't reclaimed my magic, the growing weight would have crushed me. Just like the angels' story would have.

How diabolical and brilliant to use our human desire for validation against us. I clenched my fists thinking about that poor woman doomed to roam the Kefitzat Haderech, asking me to kill her. She'd believed the angels' version and damned herself and yet, she could have been her own salvation.

"How many times have you shown the whole story?" I said.

The sign shook its head, its eyes downcast.

"But the Kefitzat Haderech is tied to our magic, isn't it?" I said. "It's just that the darkness is neither inherently bad nor good. Is that why you give us the riddle? It's your way of giving us a hint?"

Why was the baby Banim Shovavim born with sunglasses on?

Banim Shovavim magic was within us, while Ohrists' abilities came from tapping into ohr, a supernatural life force. Their magic was rooted in the ability to manipulate light and life energy, and ours with death and darkness. However, neither our darkness nor our magic was evil, while ohr and Ohrist powers weren't necessarily good. The angels were wrong about everything.

They were definitely wrong about me.

I smiled. "Because she was made in the shade."

A bell rang, the neon sign lighting up in a happy face.

The gargoyle patted my head and pushed heavily to his feet. "You have defeated the angels."

"Achievement unlocked!" I clapped.

A small toy treasure chest appeared on the table, like the one Sadie's dentist presented brave kids with after their check-ups to reward them.

Pyotr opened it. "Pick a prize."

I chuckled at the offerings, rummaging past the toy soldiers with parachutes you could fling in the air and watch sail down, past the bottles of bubbles and the scented erasers, the racing cars and the tiny animal figurines.

"All that business about choosing a sock was simply part of the test to mess with us?" I said.

"Yes."

"I knew they couldn't be the means by which we travel."

The gargoyle made a *pfft* noise. "They are socks. Is ridiculous idea."

"So you cart them here as psychological mindfucks?"

"No. They come here on their own. We've never understood why. Test is good way to get rid of them."

"Well played." Chuckling, I was about to choose a ring with a huge gaudy pink "diamond" on it, when a flash of white caught my eye.

I dug through the chest and pulled the domino out with trembling fingers. The face of it was empty save for the black line delineating the two sides.

A blank. A wild card.

As many times as I turned it over, it didn't morph into something harmless, free from prophecies and card games.

"Did you put this here?" I shook the tile at the neon sign.

It disappeared and I hurled the domino at the wall.

The gargoyle picked it up and placed it back in my hand, folding my fingers over it. "This is your prize."

I was letting myself be defined by external forces again, and by my personal history that pretending to be blank and hide my magic had kept me safe. But there was power in being a wild card, in being a blank that, as in dominoes, could be played against any tile. It was unpredictable.

I clutched the domino tightly. Wild card. I liked the sound of that.

Whomever had killed Fred intended to scare me, but I wasn't backing off that easily.

I shoved the tile in my skirt pocket. "Until we meet again, my good stone man."

"You keep making it weird." Tutting, the gargoyle returned to his movie.

I cut through the KH and into my living room, a huge grin on my face. I used the time until the meeting to shower quickly and eat, stepping onto the front porch five minutes before I'd told Eli to meet me.

He was already there. I relaxed, because the biggest hurdle had been overcome.

"Now what?" He stood angled away from me, a wary look on his face.

I tossed him my car keys. "Now we end this."

28

Eli drove to Stanley Park, riding the bumpers of the cars ahead and braking too sharply. He questioned me on a couple of points while I explained the plan, then told me that Sadie now believed the police had caught the man who'd broken into my place.

"You weren't lying," I said. "He won't be a problem anymore."

Eli lapsed into silence for the rest of the journey.

I was calm, the domino was in my pocket, and the warm breeze through the rolled-down window ruffled my hair. Streetlights winked on, the city coming alive with the buzz of nightfall in the summer.

Traffic crawled into Vancouver from the North Shore over the Lion's Gate Bridge, but the lane into Stanley Park was clear, families having gone home for the night or already parked to see the musical at the outdoor theater.

We hit the small roundabout and I pointed to the stone bridge. "That way."

I drew my cloaking over me and while Eli flinched, he didn't comment. I tuned him out, focused on getting us into the Park, since this was my first time accessing a hidden space in a moving vehicle.

On the whole it was pretty successful. There was a moment when my view split double: the real Stanley Park overlaid with the magic version, and the car froze as if suspended in mud.

Eli hit the gas a couple times, swearing, then with a loud grinding rev, the vehicle jerked forward, the lights and concrete replaced by towering trees and the rich scents of earth, pine needles, and seawater.

He slammed on the brakes, his hand dropping to the gun on his hip. "Where are we?"

I shoulder-checked that there were no other cars behind us. "I told you we were going into one of the hidden spaces. Pull over if you're going to freak out."

"I'm not—" A muscle twitched in his jaw and he pulled over, getting out to crane his neck up at the treetops against the dusky sky.

There was a loud hiss and the sky over Deadman's Island beyond the treeline belched a corrosive orange cloud.

"We need to keep moving," I said.

Eli put the car in gear and slowly drove down the dirt road. "Did you always know this was here?"

"Specifically? No. I stayed far away from the magic community after my parents were killed, but did I know that hidden magic spaces existed? Yes. Turn here." I pointed at the narrow dirt road.

He didn't say anything else as we pulled into the parking lot and his expression didn't give anything away.

Krish paced back and forth in front of a Range Rover.

I got out of the car. "You showed. Thank you."

Sharma stopped. "Like I had a choice? Zev ordered one of his goons to drive here with me. Said he was protecting his interests."

"Isn't he a vampire?" Eli said.

"Yes." Krish moved next to my ex, thinking he'd found an ally, and jerked a thumb at me. "She made a deal for him to turn my son. Are you a parent? Can you understand what this is like?"

Given Eli's flinty stare, he could imagine all too well.

I jabbed a finger into Krish's chest. "I'm keeping your entire family alive."

"I had it under control," he said.

"And you only had to implicate an innocent man to do it. It would have brought me down as well."

Eli moved closer to me. I'm not sure he even realized it, because he was frowning at Krish.

"Your son robbed you and then tried to have his partner-in-crime killed so he could become a vampire," I said. "He's getting exactly what he desired. And if you'd been honest that you'd told Oliver about the theft in the first place, things could have worked out differently. So don't you dare put this on me."

"Mir," Eli said mildly.

Delilah was choking Krish. We'd been through a lot recently and I didn't blame her, even though it wasn't as professional as I'd have liked to have been.

"You've got one job." I reluctantly recalled my magic. "Don't mess it up and disappoint BatKian."

Krish straightened his shirt, shot me a look filled with hate, and headed for the hollow tree entrance.

Cloaking, I followed, but Eli hadn't moved, standing there with his brows drawn together. "If there's something you want to say," I said, "spit it out quickly, because we're losing him."

He shook his head. It wasn't like Eli to keep his opinions to himself, and his silence was killing me. I wanted to force him to speak, but I focused on the fact that he was still here, and the rest could wait.

Not for long, mind you, because I had a few things to say to him.

Our whole party ended up inside Room C again, with Eli and

me squashed into the corner so no one would bump into us and reveal our presence.

Krish sounded credible when he told Ryann and Oliver that Zev killed Raj for something he'd done to Celeste and then framed Laurent because of the bad blood between them.

"Does the shifter have something on you?" Oliver demanded. He'd gotten some sleep and a shave. Good. He'd look spiffy for his spectacular take-down. "Your original statement was that Amar had done it, now you come in here with some tale about the vampire? Is he blackmailing you? Bribing you?"

"No," Krish said. "I was too scared to speak up before."

Ryann was crocheting some rainbow-colored thing that looked like a sleeve, the hook and yarn flying between her fingers. Her legs were outstretched, her toenails painted a pretty cool metallic blue in her flip flops. "Why aren't you scared now?" she said.

"Tatiana said she'd protect me if I told the truth."

Eli started at that. I raised my eyebrows at him, but he shook his head.

"Bribery." Oliver smacked the table. "Just like I said."

"Ask BatKian," Krish said, his hands balled into fists on top of the table.

Ryann lay her crocheting down and pulled out her phone.

"Come on, Esposito," Oliver said, two red spots hitting his cheeks. "Even if the vamp confirms it, it means nothing. If he says it was internal business, we can't touch him."

Ryann stood up. "He won't implicate himself if it isn't true. I'll be back."

She left the room, shutting the door behind her.

Oliver leaned back in his chair, dancing a pen over his knuckles. "You sure you want to go through with this?"

"You don't scare me," Krish said.

Oliver jabbed the pen tip in the wood and Krish jumped. "If she comes back with confirmation, I won't stop until I've discovered how you got his cooperation, and then?" He pulled the pen out, dancing it over his knuckles again. "It's not good to lie to the Lonestars."

Krish buried his face in his hands.

I wished I could squeeze his shoulder or offer some words of comfort.

Eli absently stroked his chin.

Ryann returned shortly. "He confirmed it. I've ordered Laurent's release."

"This is bullshit," Oliver muttered.

Krish closed his eyes for a long moment. "So I can go?"

"For now," she said. "There may be follow-up on your original statement. You really shouldn't lie to Lonestars."

He bolted.

I grabbed Eli's arm to keep him from following.

"Sharma lied," Oliver said.

"BatKian backed him up. It's out of our hands." Ryann wound up her crocheting.

"How convenient," her partner said. "Amar gets away with murder."

"And Miriam can't be charged with violating the prime directive because we have no proof she had any knowledge a crime had been committed," Ryann said. "It is what it is. Tatiana's protection extends far enough that we can't go after Miriam based on a hunch."

Next to me, Eli tensed.

I couldn't read Ryann's tone of voice, and I didn't care. My neck had been taken off the chopping block—on this matter at least. However, I still had to determine how guilty she was in Raj's murder.

Oliver white-knuckled a chair. "Anything else you need me for, *partner?*"

"You want to help me deal with the angry—" Ryann watched him leave with a sigh. "So much for that."

I nudged Eli and we hurried down the corridor after Oliver.

The Lonestar left the building and got into his BMW. Krish was already gone.

Eli drove again so I could call Tatiana and let her know Laurent was free and that Oliver was on the move. My boss was at the Sharma house with the family and the vampires, waiting for the Lonestar to show up there.

"When this is over," I said to her, "I want to discuss my job description. Expand it to include saving enthralleds, and possibly sub-contract other tasks out." I no longer feared the judgment of the Kefitzat Haderech, and this wasn't about karma points, it was about who I wanted to be. I could make a difference. I was about to bring down a corrupt Lonestar, and one day, I'd be strong enough to stand on my own and not work for Tatiana. Use my magic purely on my own terms.

I'd be unstoppable.

"We'll talk," Tatiana said and disconnected.

Oliver zipped into traffic on West Georgia Street, Eli keeping a couple of car lengths behind him.

Office building lights dulled the stars overhead to faint dots. After being in the Park, the amount of light pollution here in the city was really noticeable.

"Don't let Oliver see you," I said.

"Oh, is that how it works? Thanks." Eli flipped on the A/C. "What deal did you make to protect Sadie and me?"

"Huh?"

"That's why you're working for that woman, isn't it?"

I rested my cheek wearily against the glass. "Does it matter?"

"Yeah, it matters, Mir. You're doing fuck-knows-what, tangling with vampires, wolves, and magic cops to protect us. Why?"

I did a double take. "You're asking why I would protect you and Sadie? Are you kidding me right now?"

"Why did you get into a position of needing to protect us after all these years? Everything was fine."

"It wasn't fine," I snapped. "I hid my magic so my parents'

killers wouldn't come after me. I shut part of myself down, and when that was no longer an option, I had to form some alliances." I didn't bother telling Eli about Alex attacking me because I didn't want him to accept my magic out of guilt. We had history; we loved each other. I'd accepted the full story of who he was, now it was time for him to accept mine.

"You couldn't go back into hiding?" he said.

After a week that had felt like a never-ending nightmare, I was trying to secure a victory based on a plan held together with spit, luck, and none of the reluctant allies killing each other. Diplomacy required energy I didn't have. "You mean go back in the closet?"

"It's hardly the same—" He caught my contemptuous look, and switched lanes, dropping back another car length.

I rubbed my hand over my eyes. "I loved and supported you to have the freedom to go for the life you wanted. Even if sometimes, as a cop's wife and then as a single mom, that was hard and scary. Now I'm asking for the same respect."

"Accepting that magic exists is hardly comparable."

"I get that it's a way huger thing to wrap your head around, but it's also who I am. It took me a long time to accept that part of me, but now that I have, I'm not relinquishing it." I fiddled with my engagement ring. Most of the time, I barely noticed it. Even with its symbolism removed, it was comfortable and familiar and I didn't want to take it off.

"That said..." I took a breath. Eli deserved to know the truth, not just be blamed. "There's something else I've accepted. The choices I made over the years were exactly that, mine. It's not on you that I didn't speak up sooner about a lot of things. You had no way to listen if I kept silent."

Now would be a good time for him to acknowledge my words and promise to stand by me.

"Does Sadie have your magic?" he said. "Or would she have been born with it?"

"Ohrists are born with it but Banim Shovavim powers hit in

311

puberty. The magic would have shown up by now." I shrugged lightly. "It can skip generations. She's a Sapien like you."

An apology from him wasn't forthcoming. I held out my hand, the sapphire on my engagement ring glinting from a streetlight, then I took it off and shoved it in my pocket next to the domino. "You can't keep Sadie from me, not physically and not by poisoning her opinion."

We were halfway across downtown before he answered me. "I won't."

It was a hollow truce.

I kept my focus on Oliver's car, but he didn't turn onto any of the streets that would take him over the bridges out of downtown.

"Why is he still heading east instead of to the university? Shit. He's going to Laurent's place." I called up Tatiana's contact, but Eli grabbed the phone away, ending the call before it went through. "What are you doing?" I reached for the cell but he tucked it under his leg.

"The fewer people or creatures or whatever showing up to tip him off to our presence, the better."

"But..." I wanted to fight him, then I cut myself off. Eli was right. He had years of experience as a cop with this stuff to know how to handle it. I had to trust in his expertise. "Okay."

Eli stopped at a red light.

I banged on the dashboard. "He's getting away!"

"We know where he's going. We'll catch up." Eli paused. "Why does he hate the wolf?"

"His name is Laurent and a lot of Ohrists do." I explained the difference between Sapiens, Ohrists, and Banim Shovavim.

"And no other Ohrist can scent dybbuks?" Eli swung the car onto Main Street, cutting through Chinatown. Neon signs beckoned customers into Asian restaurants running the gamut from hole-in-the-wall noodle houses to expensive fusion places.

"Only if one trained like Laurent did. But no. No others can."

"Trained how?" Eli parked the car a couple of blocks away from Hotel Terminus.

"I don't know." I unbuckled my seat belt and took my cell back.

We couldn't continue the conversation beyond that point because I had to cloak us both.

Neither Oliver nor his BMW were anywhere in sight, but I was positive he was here.

We snuck up to the side door, which was locked.

"Oliver either locked it behind him or got in through the back," I whispered.

Eli tugged me with him to the back alley, eyeing the wall. "Wait out front. Stay hidden," he whispered. "Give your friend the heads-up when he gets here. I'll go in this way."

"We don't split up."

"Let me do my job, Miriam." Even whispering, he was stone-cold Detective Chu.

Stung, I nodded tightly, then I caught myself and dropped the sulk. I hadn't trusted him to keep out of sight when we tailed Oliver even though he must have followed people a zillion times and now I was doing it again. I was totally backseat driving the expert. "Good luck."

He caught my fingers as I turned to walk away and wrapped me in a hug. "Do anything stupid and I'll find a reason to arrest you."

I relaxed in his embrace. "Your apology sucks."

"No, that's a threat. You took it as an apology? Wow. Awkward." He grinned when I punched him. "Go." He broke away from the cloaking and with a running jump pulled himself up to the top of the wall.

His upper body strength was frankly ridiculous.

Laurent pulled up in a taxi soon after. He had blood on his rumpled shirt, bags under his eyes, and a hard set to his features that would send most people fleeing.

I curled my hands into fists so I didn't hug him.

He inserted his key into his door and I made a *psst* sound.

I whispered into his ear. "We think Oliver's in the hotel. Eli's there as well but he's on our side."

Laurent jangled his keys, his mouth quirking in a half smile. "Where's my kitten, Mitzi?"

"Tatiana took her from me." My lips were pressed against his ear, one hand flexing on his strong shoulder. I longed to rasp my teeth against the cartilage, suck his lobe into my mouth, and make him shudder. Instead, I stepped back. "Be careful."

He still couldn't see me so the wolfish grin he threw my way was aimed slightly over my shoulder, but he was close enough for me to see the deranged glint under half-closed dusky lashes.

"We both know that isn't going to happen," he murmured, and went inside.

29

Totally tense and listening for every little sound, I crept in behind Laurent, who yawned and flung himself onto the sofa to pull off his shoes.

"You know I can smell you, right?" he said. "It's summer, man. Take that extra shower."

Oliver stepped out of the elevator on the far side of the former hotel lobby from Laurent. "How'd you get the vamp onboard?" the Lonestar said.

"Hands in pockets." Laurent waited until the Lonestar did as commanded and couldn't use his magic, since he needed his hands to do so. "I didn't do shit. I was locked up, remember?" Laurent kicked his shoes out of the way. "Guess BatKian suffered a crisis of conscience and decided to do the right thing."

Still cloaked, I tiptoed to the opposite side of the curved staircase from where Oliver stood and ducked down, watching him intently, my hands wrapped around the railing posts like I was choking the life out of that bastard.

"How did you know about my magic?" Laurent stretched his arms out along the couch.

"After darkness comes the light."

Laurent rolled his eyes. "Oh please. I'm not putting up with your unannounced and unwanted presence to be quoted those stupid hunter mottos in my own home."

Oliver had used a quote about killing my kind on his dating profile to look deep? That psychopath.

"Don't insult my calling," Oliver said.

He was an actual hunter? Black shadows swam over my skin, churning faster and faster. Had he killed Banim Shovavim? This was no longer merely about justice for Raj, it was now to avenge any of my kind that this piece of shit had ever harmed.

"Didn't the gene pool breed your kind of stupid out?" Laurent scoffed.

"Generations of my family put our lives on the line to eradicate the scourge of the Banim Shovavim," Oliver said, "and you willingly took that dirty magic inside you. You're worse than a BS."

I slammed my hand over my mouth to cover my gasp. Laurent had a touch of Banim Shovavim magic? How? Ohrists couldn't take on new abilities… could they? Jude had infused Emmett with power he wouldn't normally have had with his divination, but he was a golem.

Laurent's training that seemed to haunt him, his ability to survive blindspots… it came from having Banim Shovavim magic.

A slow smile broke over my face, and the shadows shifting over my skin slowed and disappeared. I wasn't alone. Our final act had to finish playing out, but all I wanted was to drop my magic and ask Laurent a thousand questions, like whether he felt the same way knowing we shared magic? I wanted to forget about murder and vampires and demons and bask in our connection, listening to jazz on his radio and having a glass of wine. Two friends who understood something about the other that no one else could.

Laurent's lip curled, his eyes flat. "That's why you murdered an innocent kid?"

"Innocent?" Oliver snorted. "He freely gave his Ohrist blood to feed the undead, whereas I gave his miserable life purpose."

"To frame me. How noble."

"To ensure that no other Ohrist ever got the same idea as you. I let the BS live to do the only thing she's good for. Killing dybbuks and keeping Ohrists safe from those atrocities."

My hands clenched into fists. Let one atrocity deal with another?

"And if you wouldn't respect your blood," Oliver continued, ignoring the dangerous charge of energy rolling off Laurent, "then you didn't deserve to..." He looked at Laurent and swallowed.

"Live?" Laurent prompted in a cold voice. When Oliver nodded, the wolf shifter strode toward him. "You're not noble, Anderson. You're nothing more than a garden variety racist." His French accent was more pronounced, his disdain fairly dripping off him. "You're also a coward. A real man would have come after me directly."

Oliver whipped out a hand and flicked his fingers.

Laurent's shirt tore open like he'd been raked across the chest by large claws.

I covered my mouth with my hand—was this how Raj had died? Had he processed what was happening? I hoped it had all been over too fast for any fear or suffering on Raj's part.

Had Laurent looked the slightest bit perturbed, I'd have jumped in to help, but he didn't stop prowling forward. He even swiped a finger across one of the bloody gashes and licked it off, his face lighting up with his slightly unhinged smile. "Did you really think you'd get away with this?" he said.

"With upholding our bloodlines?" Oliver said. "Yes."

Blood streamed out of Laurent's nose and ears. He roared in pain, but didn't stop moving forward.

Dropping my mesh, I sent Delilah jumping across the railing to crack Oliver across the jaw.

He staggered back, rubbing his jaw and blinking at my

appearance. That was mildly satisfying, but kicking him in the balls while he begged for mercy would be better.

"Laurent went easy on you," I said. "I won't."

Oliver flicked his hand.

An uncomfortable heat speared through me and I stuck out my tongue, panting to cool it, the fine layer of saliva feeling like it was boiling.

"We hunters should have killed you all."

I couldn't speak due to my tongue feeling like it had been thrust into a witch's cauldron, but Delilah launched a flurry of attacks to break his concentration.

Oliver raised his hands like a conductor...

... and fell to the ground convulsing.

The heat and swelling immediately disappeared, but my tongue was lightly scalded. I ran around the staircase in time to catch Eli pull the Taser probes off of Oliver.

"That's two counts of attempted murder." Detective Chu was in the house.

I put a foot on Oliver's prone body. "Make him confess to killing Raj."

"That's not how this works, Mir."

Oliver stopped spasming and curled into a pathetic ball.

"Did you hear what he said?" I glared at my ex. "He hunted Banim Shovavim."

"I heard." He kneeled on the Lonestar's back, handcuffing him.

"At least rough him up a bit," I said.

Eli shot me a look of exasperation.

Laurent jerked his chin at Eli. "Nice silver cuffs, but he's not a werewolf."

Eli grinned. "Eh, I'm sure I'll get a chance to use them on one."

Jeez.

"You Saps can't do shit to me," Oliver spat, uselessly trying to avail himself of his magic, which was somehow contained.

"Even if there was something to prove, it's magic. Saps can't take that to court."

"That's true about the way the vic was killed. But funny thing," Eli said. "I got an anonymous tip today about the primary murder site and sent the forensics team in to examine the SUV in question. They found a hair that I bet will be a match. That same call put me on to you and I just witnessed you attack two people. That's enough to bring you in."

Laurent laughed.

"That vehicle was detailed. You planted it," Oliver said.

Eli wrenched Oliver's arms up behind his back. "Watch what you accuse me of. I'm not crooked."

"No one planted it," I said. "It really was found. Tatiana held off from detailing the car until she learned who the murderer was."

"My dear aunt." Laurent tapped his head. "Always thinking of an angle."

A police siren drew closer and then cut off outside the hotel, the red flashing light strobing through the dirty front windows.

Eli yanked Oliver to his feet. "That's Detective Tanaka and our ride."

The side door opened, but it wasn't Eli's partner.

"How could you, Oliver?" Ryann had entered, her upbeat energy muted.

"Ryann, I'm innocent."

"You have no idea how badly I wanted to believe that." Ryann grasped Oliver's wrist and pushed up his sleeve, revealing that familiar gold star tattoo.

Oliver struggled, but between Ryann and Eli, he was held fast.

Laurent leaned in, watching the proceedings with the same anticipatory gleam I expect I displayed.

We'd done it. One corrupt Lonestar had been brought down and despite all odds, this Banim Shovavim had gotten the justice she'd sought. I sent Raj the thought that he could rest in peace now.

Oliver stopped struggling, his face going pale. "No, come on."

Ryann pressed her thumb to his tattoo and Oliver screamed. The gold star flickered brightly, then blew away, leaving unblemished skin. Twinkle, twinkle, little star... the hunter becomes the prey... another star is snuffed out.

I shivered in delight. "Ooh, that was good."

Laurent huffed a laugh.

Oliver glared at his boss. "Lonestars stick together."

"We're supposed to," she said in a quiet voice. "But you taught me that I have to do what's right, not what's easy."

He looked at her, stricken. "Ry."

"It's over," she said.

Eli pulled me aside.

"I don't want to miss this," I protested.

Laurent was speaking quietly to Ryann, while Oliver hung his head in the face of her disappointment.

"I'm a shit," Eli said.

"Oh. Okay. Go on."

"Your friend saw what I'd been overlooking for years because it did make my life easier. Through our marriage, our divorce, raising Sadie, you, Miriam Feldman, have been remarkable. Even if I didn't know about the magic, I let you sacrifice your dreams to be there for our family. And I am so, so sorry." He crossed his heart. "This may take me time, but I'll support this new chapter of your life."

I hugged him. "Jude knows a good Ohrist therapist we can see. We did pretty well in therapy when we broke up. We'll ace this, too."

He looked at me anxiously. "Are we good?"

"We are."

Ryann finished speaking with Laurent and waved Eli over. "Take him away, Detective Chu."

"Yes, ma'am." Eli winked at her, then touched my arm. "My apology is complete."

I notched my chin up. "There will still be recompense in dessert form."

"We'll see." He led Oliver away, but right before he walked out the door he called back, "I'll get these nulling cuffs back to you soon, Junior. Thanks for coming through with them."

My mouth fell open. Eli had planned this? Even when he was angry with me? Wait... that meant...

"Did you know the whole time?" Laurent asked before I could. His composure reminded me of Zev's, and I moved next to him, not to chide him, because his anger was justified, but to let him know I had his back. He didn't take his eyes off the Lonestar, but his shoulders lost some of their stiffness.

"I wasn't completely certain." Ryann gestured at me. "Why do you think I pressed you for the satchel? If you had it and Oliver didn't, then he wasn't guilty."

"Right, the BS must be a killer," I sneered.

Ryann's eyes sparked dangerously. "I wanted my partner to *not* have done it. The man who took me under his wing when I was a rookie, who mentored me and supported my bid to become head Lonestar. Beyond that, I didn't care who the guilty party was."

I'd been angry for the five minutes that I believed Laurent had done it. If a mentor and close friend had used their position for their own twisted beliefs, I'd do anything to find proof they were innocent.

"You used me and you let Laurent be arrested, knowing he wasn't guilty."

Laurent crossed his arms, regarding Ryann with a stony stare.

"I was going to give Eli the thumb drive, not as blackmail, but because it's hard to overcome that perception filter." She ran a finger absently over her own star tattoo, her tone wistful. "I know because when my Ohrist mom died, my dad didn't see my magic for a long time." She shook off thoughts of the past. "You have every reason not to trust me or any Lonestar," she said, "but I'm on your side. One day, I hope you see that."

I hoped so too, since it might be nice to have a Lonestar in my corner, though I doubted Laurent would forgive her anytime soon. "Maybe don't do your magic chakra hurting thing anymore," I said sullenly. "That would be a good start."

Ryann laughed.

"Anderson will never get to trial." Laurent collapsed on his sofa. The bleeding had stopped, but he looked haggard. "Not if Mitzi cut a deal with BatKian."

"Doesn't matter," I said. "Eli wraps up this case and you and I are free. I didn't violate the prime directive."

"I know." Ryann smiled evilly. "I did."

Laurent whistled.

"Huh." I sat down on the bottom stair. "I wondered why Oliver let the body be found by Sapien police. Despite his other actions, he seemed like the kind of guy who took the prime directive seriously."

"He did arrange for an Ohrist to find it. The call was kicked up to me the second it came in," Ryann said. "But it bothered me. With the ratio of Sapiens to Ohrists, one of our people happened to find a body in the middle of the forest? A body that had been killed recently enough it was still fresh and was likely a magic crime? What were the odds? So I called Dad."

"That buys you some points, Lonestar," Laurent said. His eyes were closed and he rested his head back against the sofa cushions.

The Deputy Chief Constable at the Vancouver police department who put Eli on the case. "Will your father be in trouble for this prime directive thing?"

"No, since I enlisted his help. I have leeway on the prime directive if I act for a greater good. Since this all seemed fishy, I intended to panic the killer by having it exposed to Sapiens. But with the way things turned out, magic will stay hidden. Oliver will be given an Ohrist lawyer who'll go for an insanity plea deal."

"BatKian will take him before he serves his sentence," I said.

Oliver's end would be painful and bloody, and I felt nothing except satisfaction that he'd been caught. He'd been willing to pervert justice because of his disgusting prejudices around bloodlines, so dying at Zev's hands, whom he'd perceive as another atrocity, was fitting.

"The best outcome for all concerned." Her perky smile flickered, and despite my lingering anger, I gave her a sympathetic smile, which she returned with a nod. "Until next time, Miriam."

"May it be a long time from now."

"Hey," Laurent said, not lifting his head off the couch cushion. "You owe me."

"I'll pay up. Promise." Humming, Ryann left.

"Pay up how?" I said.

"Destroy Ghost Minder." Yawning, he opened his eyes. "I'm glad that's finally over."

I pasted on a bright smile. "Yeah. Me too." I paused, thinking of Fred and the demon parasite and all the directions that danger came from in the magic world. "Do you not have wards?"

Not that it would surprise me if he didn't, but he assured me he did.

"Then how did Oliver break into your house? What's the point of them if they don't keep danger out?"

Laurent stretched out his shoulders. "If you invite someone in who you know intends to harm you, then you need to reset against that person again before their next visit. I let the Lonestars in when they came to arrest me, knowing the visit wouldn't turn out well." He dug his thumb into a spot on his neck with a sigh. "I didn't get a chance to reset before Oliver came back today."

I frowned. "Is it a big deal to reset?"

"Not at all. You say a couple of words and it does a kind of factory reboot." Laurent yawned.

"Awesome. Well, I'll let you get some rest."

Wincing, Laurent got up. "I'll walk you out."

"That's not necessary."

He ignored me. "I've never told anyone that I have Banim Shovavim magic."

We stopped next to the side door.

"Are you ashamed?" I said.

"Yeah. I care so desperately for other people's approval."

I nodded sagely, relief coursing through me that my magic didn't disgust him. "If you could only believe in yourself. You'd shine like the special snowflake you are."

He snorted. "I just..." He flicked a finger between us, his expression serious. "I like having this in common."

"Me too," I said softly.

"My champion of all that's fair." His whiskey-soaked voice intoxicated me.

I swayed toward him like a flower to the sun, my fingers barely twitching away from pressing against him. "Yeah, I think I'm supposed to get a token for all my hard work."

"Vraiment?" His lazy grin set butterflies loose in my chest. "None of that 'good deeds are their own rewards'?"

Was I reading this wrong? I blushed. "No, of course, I was happy to do it. So, I should be going." Immediately. I gave a laugh that sounded forced. "I could sleep for about a year."

"Same." He rubbed a hand over his stubbled jaw. "Though I should shower first."

I was a simple woman and simple visuals worked well for me, like Laurent wet, naked, and steamy. I swallowed, thinking bland olfactory thoughts because a jolt of heat had shot up through my core. "Definitely you should. Okay, then."

Laurent's gaze sharpened.

My heartbeat picked up and I sucked my bottom lip into my mouth, my eyes locked on his.

He tilted his head, his lips parting and—

The door crashed open.

324

"Helllooooo roomie!" Emmett strutted in, waving his cane like a baton. "Dude, take a shower. You look like shit."

Laurent's hand shot out and he slammed Emmett against the wall. "Go. Away."

"Nope. He's all yours." A pile of boxes with Jude's legs entered behind the golem. She dropped them on the ground, brushing off her hands and quirking an eyebrow. "Tatiana didn't phone you?"

"No," Laurent said. He menaced really well, but Emmett was already dragging his stuff in, and Jude would do anything to be rid of the golem, and the shifter's intimidation just slid right off the other two.

Jude patted his shoulder. "Take it up with your aunt. Emmett has joined her Scooby gang and he'll be living with you."

"Not ever," Laurent said.

"She said it was Miri's idea."

They both looked at me.

"Not exactly." Way to get everything I wanted but with the world's worst timing. I rubbed my hand over the back of my neck. "I mentioned saving enthralleds as part of my job description, but—"

"You did?" Laurent's eyes lit up like sunshine on the best summer's day ever, their warmth for me and me alone.

The air swirled around us, subtly electric. The thumping of my heart was a drumbeat urging me to reach for him and abandon myself to the coming storm.

Jude cleared her throat. "In exchange for a hotline that Tatiana is going to set up for people to report dybbuk enthrallment, Emmett is going to help Mir out and live here because it's easier for him to come and go undetected."

Laurent looked from me to the golem and punched the wall. "Merde!" He stormed out of the room.

"Yeah, I could use a drink," Emmett called out, rummaging through a box. "Thanks!"

"So…" Jude clasped her hands in front of her. "Did we interrupt something?"

"I'm going home," I growled.

Emmett held a pair of dangly earrings up to his head. "See you tomorrow, partner."

"Hey," Jude protested. "Those are mine."

Being a fixer in the magical community was more fun than I'd given it credit for with secret knowledge, magic enemies to outwit, and Laurent. One of these days, I'd even discharge my babysitting duties.

But that day wasn't today.

"See you tomorrow," I sighed.

Thank you for reading MADE IN THE SHADE!

Things heat up in A SHADE TOO FAR (MAGIC AFTER MIDLIFE #3)

Miriam's hot flashes leave her shvitzing, and 10PM is the new midnight, but she still craves an adventure, sexytimes (and maybe a nap.)

When I stole a demon artifact for a client, I never expected it to result in a magic curse. Failure to reverse it will result in the death of someone close to me, the end of my uneasy alliance with the head vampire, and open season on my family.

As if that didn't suck enough, my screw-up on a dangerous fact-finding mission may have kicked my sexual tension with the wolf shifter in the balls. At least I'm not obsessing over it, since fighting through a maze of mind games, tested loyalties, and secrets is consuming all my energy.

So, glass half-full.

Now armed with my trusty to-do list, I'm determined to multitask my way to victory like a magic badass.

Yaas, Queen.

Get it now.

Every time a reader leaves a review, an author gets ... a glass of wine. (You thought I was going to say "wings," didn't you? We're authors, not angels, but *you'll* get heavenly karma for your good deed.) Please leave yours on your favorite book site, especially Amazon to help other readers discover my stories.

Turn the page for an excerpt from *A Shade Too Far* ...

EXCERPT FROM A SHADE TOO FAR

In just over half an hour, I'd either have pulled off an impossible heist during an illicit underground magic fight, or I'd be dead. Oh, and to make things interesting, I had to accomplish this feat on a private tropical island filled with shady Ohrist guests swanning around sipping champagne while openly flexing their magic in front of each other.

Then there was my employer, Tatiana Cassin, who moved through the crowd like an eighty-year-old shark in a sea of guppies acting like they had teeth.

My boss chatted briefly with everyone, who paid their respects *Godfather*-style. The few who snubbed her received a serene smile with a hint of menace, which made most of them scurry over to correct their misstep. She didn't give a damn what anyone believed of her, actively encouraging all the rumors about her presence today.

I had much to learn from Obi-Wan Corleone.

An Indian woman in an orange saree, who was literally as insubstantial as the smoke from her cigarillo, waited impatiently for her turn with Tatiana next to a man in a kilt with skin as hard and bizarrely defined as an alien exoskeleton.

Tatiana's bloodred silk couture gown weighed more than she

did, but her blue eyes were as sharp as the bone spikes magically fanning out from the neck of a Black woman in a fitted tuxedo, who bent to kiss Tatiana's wrinkled hand.

They both looked majestic, whereas I was shvitzing worse than an old Jewish man in a sauna due to my overly starched formal housekeeper's uniform worn by all the servers employed by Santiago Torres. I swear, the combination of sweat and polyester had terraformed a microbiome in my armpits.

Note to self: next time I secretly crashed an event, wear breathable fabrics.

My golem partner nudged my hip, both of us hidden under my magic cloaking. "How much longer?" he whined in a whisper.

Sighing quietly, I showed Emmett the old windup watch on my wrist—exactly like I had the other dozen times in the last half hour. Five minutes to showtime.

He rocked back and forth from his heels to his toes but was distracted by a woman sashaying by in a flowy caftan made of living bees. With his hands, he measured his hips in comparison to hers.

"I could rock that," he mused, looking sadly at his sweatpants and runners.

I tapped my index finger against my lips, directing him to keep quiet. While no one could scent us or detect my heartbeat under the black invisibility mesh created by my shadow magic, they could hear us speaking.

Everyone was taking their seats for the outdoor fight, except for Emmett, me, and the security team, who made no attempt to be subtle. They patrolled through gardens where short bulbous cacti nestled in beds of red rocks, between rows of gently swaying palm trees, along the beach with the aquamarine Sea of Cortez beyond, and around the perimeter of the ring.

Taking calming breaths of warm, salt-tanged air, I pulled out the domino that I'd won in the Kefitzat Haderech and ran my thumb over the single black line carved into the tile face. Neither

Tatiana, nor our client, Vancouver's head vampire Zev BatKian, had been able to learn much about what we faced en route to our target: the Torquemada Gloves. The vault containing them was in the basement of Torres's opulent mansion and had a heart-beat-monitored door.

That was it. A whopping two facts: basement and special door. I was literally operating on nothing.

And if my manipulative employer and the most paranoid vampire in Canada couldn't sniff out any more details than that, no one else could.

Did working for Zev leave an oily feeling deep in my soul? Why, yes. Did I have a choice? Also, yes. Though with my family's safety and my continued breathing at stake, it wasn't a difficult one to make.

I wouldn't betray Zev, yet he'd still taken a few dozen opportunities to press upon me the importance of loyalty. Not being a total moron, I'd understood his feelings on that subject at our first encounter. At this point, he was just beating a dead horse about how scary he was. It had taken all my willpower not to affect a terrible Dracula accent during our last meeting and say, "I vant to suck your blood. Blah. Blah. Blah."

Another reason I wasn't all that worried about the vampire if I failed? He'd be late to the party. Torres's people would have already killed me, being trained to suss out threats using both magic and high-tech means. However, if I didn't present the Torquemada Gloves to Zev, I could kiss the ward to keep out demons and other dangerous supernatural baddies goodbye. I'd blown my first shot at the vampire's assistance and this gig was the rare gift of a second chance.

Thankfully, he couldn't accompany us to the island. Even if he'd dissolved into smoke and snuck through the lowered wards alongside Tatiana, as Emmett and I had under my cloaking, the fights were held in broad daylight, precisely so no unwanted bloodsuckers showed up. Zev might be able to go outside under an umbrella on a sunny day in Vancouver, but the tropical sun here would incinerate him.

I curled my nails into my palms to keep from scratching my itchy armpits. Had the makers of these uniforms never heard of natural fibers?

Two minutes left.

Positive thoughts, Feldman. I wasn't coming into this totally unprepared. In fact, my entire life had trained me for dealing with the unknown. Forty-two years of experience, my honor roll chops, ex-librarian meticulousness, resilience from navigating a divorce, and some pretty sweet magic talent made me a force to be reckoned with. I bounced on my toes, as alert as an Olympic sprinter braced for the starting gun.

With a smile as suave as his bespoke linen suit, Santiago escorted Tatiana to her ringside seat, which was in my direct line of sight. He'd been hosting these championship fights for over forty years, and Tatiana had attended every one with Samuel, her aficionado husband.

Though this was the first time since his death seven years ago that she'd made an appearance.

Santiago's wife, Sherisse, a frosted blonde with a distracted air and leathery skin, joined them. Tatiana leaned over Santiago to speak to the woman, who shook her head with quick nervous movements. When Tatiana sat back in her seat with her chin propped on her fist, Santiago turned a hard look on his wife, but was all smiles again when he resumed chatting with my employer.

There was no way to contact Tatiana to learn if there was an unanticipated and unwelcome wrinkle in our mission, because I couldn't carry a phone for fear of it being tracked. Once the fight was over, Emmett and I were to meet back at the private plane she'd chartered, but until then, we were on our own.

A bell rang out and a loud cheer went up.

Showtime.

BECOME A WILDE ONE

If you enjoyed this book and want to be first in the know about bonus content, reveals, and exclusive giveaways, become a Wilde One by joining my newsletter: http://www.deborahwilde.com/subscribe

You'll immediately receive short stories set in my different worlds and available only to my newsletter subscribers. There are mild spoilers so they're best enjoyed in the recommended reading order.

If you just want to know about my new releases, please follow me on:

Amazon: https://www.amazon.com/Deborah-Wilde/e/B01MSA01NW

or

BookBub: https://www.bookbub.com/authors/deborah-wilde

ACKNOWLEDGMENTS

Thank you to my editor Alex Yuschik for ensuring that all the crazy twists and turns in this book were clear. And for always pushing me to dig deeper and make my story a thousand percent better.

Sending my deep gratitude to all you readers who stuck with me through these strange times. Pandemic fatigue is a thing, but you kept buying my books and cheering me on. At a time when I couldn't see friends in person or travel to replenish, your love kept me going. <3

ABOUT THE AUTHOR

A global wanderer, former screenwriter, and total cynic with a broken edit button, Deborah (pronounced deb-O-rah) writes funny urban fantasy and paranormal women's fiction.

Her stories feature sassy women who kick butt, strong female friendships, and swoony, sexy romance. She's all about the happily ever after, with a huge dose of hilarity along the way.

Deborah lives in Vancouver with her husband, daughter, and asshole cat, Abra.

"Magic, sparks, and snark! Go Wilde."

www.deborahwilde.com

Made in the USA
Monee, IL
10 May 2022

96188297R00198